W9-BFA-200

Catch Me If You Can

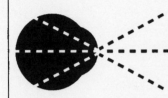

This Large Print Book carries the
Seal of Approval of N.A.V.H.

Catch Me
If You Can

Jillian Karr

G.K. Hall & Co.
Thorndike, Maine

Copyright © 1996 by Jillian Karr

All rights reserved.

This work is a novel. Any similarity to actual persons or events is purely coincidental.

Published in 1997 by arrangement with Avon Books, a division of The Hearst Corporation.

G.K. Hall Large Print Romance Collection.

The text of this Large Print edition is unabridged.
Other aspects of the book may vary from the original edition.

Set in 16 pt. Plantin by Juanita Macdonald.

Printed in the United States on permanent paper.

Library of Congress Cataloging in Publication Data

Karr, Jillian.
    Catch me if you can / Jillian Karr.
      p.   cm.
    ISBN 0-7838-8230-0 (lg. print : hc : alk. paper)
    1. Large type books.   I. Title.
  [PS3561.A69278C38   1997]
  813'.54—dc21   97-21612

With love —

For both of our Larrys and for our children, Mitchel, Rachel, and Steven.

And for Marianne and Ky, dear friends, two of the strongest, finest people we know.

Prologue

Arizona, 1990

As the three young women galloped beneath a topaz sun toward the high rocks of Sedona, the mountains loomed above them like a solid curtain of fire. This was an ancient place, a place steeped in Native American lore and legend, a place where many believed powerful vortices came together, resonating with mystic vibrations that could conjure up the past and the future.

At this moment, however, Catriana Hansen had no thought for the future — her only concern was for the present. She reached the grassy, flower-strewn clearing first and gave a whoop of delight that echoed back through the canyon to the other girls.

"Here's the perfect spot," she called out, and swung from the saddle with the ease of a young woman who'd been riding all her life. "There's even some leftover wood from a campfire."

Her younger sister, Meg, and their friend Jordan Davis caught up with her as Cat was spreading the Hopi blanket across the stubby grass. In no time at all the horses were tethered to a cypress alongside the stream that gurgled past ancient red rocks carved by wind, water, and the quiet passage of time.

"I may be a born and bred Arizonan, but if I had to eat barbecued steak and beans one more night without a break, I think I'd barf." Meg grinned as she inhaled the scents of garlic and ginger and then began eagerly unwrapping the cartons of Mongolian chicken, moo shu vegetables, and clumpy white rice. They'd begged one of the wranglers to smuggle the Chinese food in with the week's worth of food and supplies he'd brought to the ranch from Phoenix that afternoon.

"Oh, look, there's even fortune cookies and chopsticks," Jordan enthused. She flipped open a thermal pouch and extracted two cans of Coors and a Coca-Cola. Her sigh was heartfelt as she blew her dark bangs out of her eyes and popped the Coors' tab. "This is the life."

"And just think, Tex," Cat grinned, "you gave up a summer of sailing and tennis and lobster every night in the Hamptons so you could work your tail off brushing down horses and escorting dozens of greenhorns through rattlesnake country."

"Not to mention sneaking out with you two desperadoes for a sunset picnic in the mountains when we're supposed to be mucking out Stable B."

"I got news for you, Tex. Stable B will still be there when we get back." Cat grimaced, reaching for a beer.

"I know, I know. Lucky thing no one told me when I signed on for the summer that I'd have to wallow in manure — or pick cactus spines out of Mrs. Dennison's butt." Jordan took a long, cool swig from the can as Cat and Meg doubled over with laughter. "That's only one of the stories I've spared my mother in my letters." A devilish smile played at the corners of her mouth. "I'm saving it to tell her over dinner at the country club."

"Nasty girl," Meg said, but there was bubbling affection in her voice, and for the next few moments the three young women chattered with the easy camaraderie of close friends as they lit the fire and heated their food in the tin pie plates they'd snuck out of the ranch kitchen beneath their shirts.

By the time the sun dipped behind Coffeepot Rock, bruising the apricot sky with streaks of lavender and purple, they were languid and content, their stomachs full of spicy food chased down by beer — except for Meg, who skipped the Coors since she was in training for the next Summer Olympics in Barcelona. Tall and lithe, with the toned limbs that came from swimming countless laps across the dude ranch's Olympic-size pool before and after work every day, she contentedly sipped her Coke as she leaned against a smooth rock.

It had been a splendid summer and it was only half over. And for the Hansen sisters, between semesters at Arizona State, the Spinning Circle Dude Ranch just outside of Sedona was a much more pleasant place to spend a summer than cooped up serving burgers in a fast-food restaurant or shuffling papers in the filing room of an office. The fresh air, sunshine, scenery, and the good-natured flirting of lanky, suntanned ranch hands beat air-conditioning, traffic, and time clocks hands down.

Of the three young women, Jordan Davis was the oldest at twenty-one. She'd be entering her senior year at Bryn Mawr in the fall, and this summer was her first real stab at independence. Her parents had been stunned when she'd told them she wouldn't be summering in the Hamptons with them this year — she'd landed a job, all on her own, at the Spinning Circle Ranch from June to August.

That was the best decision I ever made, Jordan reflected, her hazel eyes resting first upon Meg's pretty tanned face and her striking aquamarine eyes, and then upon Cat, a honey-haired imp who'd managed to break the hearts of nearly every ranch hand on the place.

What would I do if I'd never met these two? Jordan mused, her heart swelling with affection as she reached for the bag of fortune cookies. She'd never had friends quite like them before. There'd been an instant connection, a quick sure bond. Cat kept insisting they all must have been sisters in another life, and Jordan, despite her practical nature, was inclined to believe her.

Jordan's stint at the Spinning Circle Ranch had begun disastrously the very first night when Travis Ward, one of the hands, had tricked her into believing she'd been assigned wake-up duty and had to get up at 5 A.M. to rouse the ranch by clanging on the iron triangle that hung outside the mess hall. The next morning she'd innocently done just that, rising in the dark and stumbling outside in her Patagonias and unbrushed hair — only to be called a dang fool by the irate foreman and shouted at by the owners and half the guests, who weren't expected to rise before eight.

The Hansen sisters had dragged her into their cabin and dried her tears. Within five minutes they had had her gasping with laughter over their plot for revenge.

That night, Cat had kept Travis busy necking in the barn while Meg and Jordan had sneaked into his bunk and sewn shut the fly of every single pair of jockey shorts he owned.

From that moment on, the three of them were inseparable. A mere glimpse of Travis, or the mention of his name, sent them into whoops of laughter.

When Jordan and Meg had tried to commiserate with Cat over her distasteful role in the scheme, she'd flashed them a quick sideways glance of pure mischief and drawled, "Don't give it another thought. He may be a royal turd, but old Travis happens to be one hell of a kisser."

11

Now, as dusk fell over the clearing and Jordan passed out the fortune cookies, she wished for a moment that she could stop time, that she could make this incredible night, this whole incredible summer go on and on.

But that's stupid, she told herself. The future awaited her. With any luck, by next summer she'd have a job at a Madison Avenue ad agency, an apartment of her own in New York, and a life away from her parents.

"You first, Tex, before it's too dark to read," Meg instructed, her face eager in the glow of the campfire.

Jordan glanced down at the slip of paper she'd pried from her fortune cookie and frowned. "It's a rhyming one," she said slowly. "Kind of strange."

"So what does it say?" Cat prompted.

"The message of this fortune should be loud and clear. Cherish all your loved ones by keeping them very near." She wrinkled her nose. "What's that supposed to mean?" she demanded. "It gives me the creeps. Your turn, Cat."

Cat pulled the slip from between the crispy wafers and read aloud. *"You are domestically inclined and will be happily married."*

"Not to Travis Ward, I hope," Meg muttered cheerfully.

"Not on your life. He's a good kisser, but he's got buffalo chips for brains." Cat drained the last of her beer. "Now you, Margaret Elizabeth. Last, but not least . . ."

"Okay, here goes." Meg began to read in a singsong. *"Cowards die a thousand deaths . . ."* Her voice trailed off. She finished quietly. *"But brave men only once."*

The three girls stared at each other across the wavering amber flames.

"That's the dumbest fortune I ever heard," Cat said quickly.

"It's stupid, all right," Jordan added. "Doesn't mean a damn thing."

All at once they noticed that the clearing had grown darker, as if someone had abruptly snuffed out the daylight. Shadows crawled up the walls of the rocks, and even the flames of the dying campfire seemed to dwindle. One of the horses whinnied, sending Meg jumping to her feet.

Cat saw that her sister's fingers had flown automatically to her throat, to touch the dreamcatcher necklace she always wore.

"Time to head back," Cat declared. She scrambled up and began gathering the empty cartons and cans while Jordan packed away the utensils and shook out the blanket.

"Meg. It's only a silly fortune cookie." Cat touched her sister's shoulders as Meg continued to stand in silence, staring out at the mountains. "Jordan's was weird, too. Some loony must have written them."

"I know, but . . ."

"It's this place, too," Jordan said softly. "I don't know if it's the vortices out here or all the mysticism associated with Sedona, but suddenly I think we should get the hell out of here."

"Me, too." Meg shivered. She tossed her fortune into the campfire, and the other girls quickly followed suit.

As Meg began kicking dirt into the fire, she noticed the air had grown sharply cool. "Right now, mucking out Stable B sounds downright appealing," she said with a forced laugh.

They gathered up the horses and extinguished the campfire without another word spoken among them. As the first stars popped into the deep purple sky, they strapped on their gear, mounted, and rode. Fast and furious, they headed toward the ranch.

But no matter how swiftly they rode, or in what direction, the future loomed, waiting.

And together, the three of them were galloping straight toward it.

1

"Stop being such a slugabed, young lady. Time to rise and shine."

Burnsie's voice scraped at Meg like sandpaper across glass. Meg groaned and burrowed her head under the pillow. "Ten more minutes."

"No can do." Alice Burns yanked the pillow away and tossed it on the floor. "If you want to get your swim in before the hotel pool is full of more screaming kids than a roller coaster, you'd best hustle your tushie out of that bed."

"It can't be six-thirty already." Meg struggled to a sitting position and blinked fuzzily at the hotel bedside clock. "Oh, God, I've only had five hours of sleep — and the first four don't count."

She threw herself back down on the bed and rolled over, pulling the blankets up over her head, but the older woman reached out a hand and yanked them away.

"Meg! You'll be miserable if you don't get your

15

swim in. You made me promise I'd get you up in time to hit the pool. . . ."

"Okay, okay," Meg muttered groggily. "I don't need sleep anyway. I'm an automaton. Wind me up and I smile, I eat chicken, I kiss babies, I cut ribbons, I . . ."

"You knew what you were getting into, young lady," Alice Burns admonished, but her baggy brown eyes twinkled as she watched Meg stumble blearily from the bed. "I've been through this with seven Miss Americas, and you all start to sound alike by August. Hurry, now, the car will be here at nine."

"Give me two minutes to pee."

"Take three."

Three minutes. Then the rush is on, Meg thought wearily as she closed the bathroom door and leaned against the white tiled sink. But at least the swim would relax and energize her for the grueling day ahead.

Meg stared at herself in the cloudy hotel mirror and shut her eyes against the sight. Ghastly was the word that came to mind, she thought — a face that would sink a thousand ships. Her toffee-colored hair hung in overteased clumps around her face. The mascara she'd been too tired to remove last night was streaked down her cheeks, and she knew that even once she cleaned it off, the dark lilac circles would still be there.

Three more weeks of this mind-boggling torture, she thought. Three more weeks of flying from city to city; of fourteen-hour days; of speaking, signing autographs, and hosting fashion shows. *Then I can relinquish the limelight to some other unsuspecting fool who will spend the next year of her life logging more miles than Amtrak, picking at more chicken dinners than the Colonel himself, and smiling, smiling, smiling, until she thinks her impeccably made-up face will crack.*

"Burnsie, just tell me three things," Meg implored over the flush of the toilet as she yanked open the bathroom door. "Where am I, who am I, and what am I doing today?"

"Take it from me, honey, you don't want to know," Burnsie replied cheerfully as she tossed her pink flannel nightgown into a plastic laundry bag and began repacking her suitcase. In all these months, Meg had never seen Burnsie sleep in anything other than rosebud flannel. The woman was always complaining of the air-conditioning and carried a jet-buttoned gray wool sweater everywhere she went, but underneath the bulky sweat suits and cardigans, she enveloped her doughy form in plunging red lace bras and panties. Meg got a kick out of her idiosyncracies: Alice Burns was a sharp old bird with a kooky sense of humor, a fondness for Zane Grey westerns, and a talent for tracking down cookie-dough macadamia nut ice cream, which Meg found truly amazing. The other chaperon, who alternated months with Burnsie in the never-ending rounds of Miss America as she zigzagged across the country, was a humorless stick of a woman whose poof of platinum hair, ubiquitous pearls encircling a

17

reedy neck, and clawlike pastel fingernails made her look like a freshly groomed standard show poodle, an image augmented by her mincing gait and high-pitched voice.

"The sun's coming up and I'm not getting any younger," Burnsie commented as Meg pulled on her coral Speedo swimsuit and slipped her feet into her thongs.

Feeling more awake now that she'd splashed cold water on her face and brushed her teeth, Meg spared a moment to glance out the window at the pale amber sunshine just beginning to seep across the horizon. Pretty. Peaceful. And the pool would be peaceful too, if she made it down there before those kids Burnsie had reminded her about came cannonballing off the diving board.

She grabbed her tote bag and goggles and sailed out the door. "Always slowing me down, Burnsie," she called over her shoulder, but her uptilted blue-green eyes were sparkling as Burnsie scooted to keep up.

Hazy sun warmed Meg's shoulders as she drew in a breath of magnolia-laden Atlanta air tinged with a hint of chlorine. She tossed her towel down on the chaise lounge as Burnsie picked up the hospitality phone to order breakfast. It looked like it was going to be a beautiful day. Too bad she'd be in and out of limos and air-conditioned buildings for most of it. Now that she'd shaken away the sleep cobwebs, she remembered that she was scheduled to speak at Franklin Roosevelt Junior High, then dash to an American Association of

University Women luncheon, followed by a rib-bon-cutting ceremony at some new multiplex cinema and a swing by the studio for a live interview on the 5:30 P.M. news before she and Burnsie headed out to the airport for their 8 P.M. flight to New Orleans.

Don't think about it or you'll want to crawl right back into bed, she warned herself, twisting her long, wavy hair into a topknot. For just a moment she breathed deep, soaking in the fragrant stillness of the morning, letting the sunshine caress her upturned face.

The rooftop pool was deserted except for Burnsie propped in a chair, a dog-eared copy of *Riders of the Purple Sage* on her lap.

It was hard to believe that in a few short weeks her "reign" would be over. *I'm going to miss you, Burnsie,* Meg thought as she wriggled her ginger-painted toenails from her thongs.

It was time to move on, she thought, climbing nimbly up the rungs of the diving board, her bare feet making only a whisper of sound against the metal. Time to think about law school, about registering, buying books, and settling into campus life after the past year's frantically nomadic existence. Time, maybe, even to think about having a date. A real date, with a real man — without Burnsie or Old Poodle Puss tagging along.

If anyone had told Margaret Elizabeth Hansen when she was growing up in Tempe, Arizona, that she would someday be Miss America, she would have hooted them right out of her grandmother's tidy little suburban backyard. Margaret Elizabeth Hansen at age ten had been a pigtailed pipsqueak, with perennially skinned knees, braces, and a penchant for practical jokes. She could talk a lizard off a rock, and told everyone in Tempe who would listen that she was going to be a policewoman when she grew up. She was going to arrest bad people, like the ones who'd robbed and killed her parents in their drugstore, and she was going to lock them up in jail so they couldn't hurt anyone else ever again.

Unlike her sister, Catriana, three years older and into makeup, parties, boys, and malls, Meg had never even watched the pageant or entertained a single fantasy about parading across the stage in a beaded evening gown and glittering crown. She smelled faintly of chlorine instead of Charlie and spent every minute of her spare time in the YMCA pool. Her swim coach had told her grandmother that if Meg worked hard she'd have a good shot at the Olympic team.

And so for eight years she competed in swim meet after swim meet, shooting through the water like a darting minnow. Moving up through the rankings, she pictured herself winning the gold medal, standing proudly on the victor's platform as they played "The Star-Spangled Banner" and draped the medal around her neck.

The Olympic gold medal was her dream. But as the years passed and the skinny, headstrong young girl grew into a slender, determined young woman, another dream fixed itself in her mind as well. She no longer wanted to be a policewoman, to capture and punish bad people like the ones who had killed her parents when she was six. She wanted to become a lawyer — a prosecuting attorney. And to earn her degree from Harvard Law School because it was the best.

Waking and sleeping, Meg trained and studied and dreamed and swam. As the years passed, the dreams became more vivid and more tangible, and they were almost within her grasp. Winning the gold would bring its own glory, but after that would come the money to pay for college and law school. Harvard would cost a small fortune, but commercial endorsement contracts would take care of all that.

Then everything slipped through her fingers. Just shy of her nineteenth birthday, she came down with mono, blew a series of meets, and by the blast of a whistle missed placing on the U.S. team.

Meg was devastated. All her dreams died. She'd never get to Harvard. She had some scholarship money and some she had saved from her summers working at the Spinning Circle Dude Ranch, but it would be nowhere near enough. Heartbroken, she'd hunched in the beanbag chair in her room and cried for five straight days. Then she'd tossed out her broken dreams like chlorine-rotted Speedos and convinced herself that Arizona State was plenty good enough for a home-grown girl from Tempe.

Then just before Meg's senior year, Jordan had

come up with a brilliant idea. Cat had taken those pictures of her, and miraculously, everything had fallen into place.

Whenever God closes a door, He opens a window. Gram's favorite saying. Well, he'd sure opened a picture window this time — one as wide as America.

It had been an unbelievable year.

Feeling that she could almost touch the cloudless blue sky, Meg bounced lightly at the edge of the diving board, lifted her arms over her head, and with a little jump, soared into a graceful, perfectly executed arc.

Only the chatter of mockingbirds disturbed the perfect stillness of the new day as she melted into the tepid water and glided into the first of her standard fifty laps. She brushed against the turquoise tiled wall and pushed off with her toes, letting her mind float ahead to the life waiting for her when this crazy year was over. The teensy apartment she'd rented in Cambridge, the day-in, day-out sameness of campus living that would engulf her like the comfy flannel jacket she'd worn through her winters at Arizona State. Just what the doctor ordered.

I'm going to blend into that campus like one of a zillion autumn leaves — like any other student weaving her way through those halls of ivy. Meg could almost smell the crispness of those autumn leaves, the newness of the textbooks, the mustiness of the old classrooms filled with ghosts of scholars past. She couldn't wait to mothball her tailored suits and pumps, to slip on her fleece sweat suit and her old Nikes, to amble past ivy-covered brick buildings with a group of new friends, to linger over chili fries, conversation, and cold beer — maybe with a *guy. A guy who doesn't know a thing about my having been Miss America, who only knows me as one damned sharp first-year law student.*

I'll spend half a day just browsing through the bookstore, Meg promised herself, hoisting her lanky frame, dripping, from the pool. Sparkling droplets splayed across the tile as she reached for her crocheted cover-up.

And, she swore to herself, *I won't wear a drop of makeup for the whole first semester.*

Three more weeks.

"Last one to the shower springs for Juicy Fruit at the airport," she called to Burnsie with a grin, and broke for the elevators.

"Cheater!" Burnsie bellowed, lurching up from her chair and nearly colliding with a family of four claiming the lounge chairs next to hers. "You got the jump on me." She darted with surprising agility past the newcomers and scurried after Meg toward the bank of elevators.

Neither Meg nor Burnsie noticed the two men wheeling the laundry cart into the service elevator.

The red-haired man called Frank, a beefy Mick Jagger with sideburns, punched the number seven on the elevator panel and futilely tugged his maroon jacket sleeves closer to his fleshy wrists. *Shit,*

23

why didn't I swipe a bigger jacket? This thing was designed for some twerp twenty pounds lighter — someone not packing a .45. But screw it, he thought. In a quarter of an hour, this part of the job would be done and he'd be free of this getup.

His taller companion, sporting a blond crew cut, Nordic cheekbones, and narrow sky-blue eyes, waited until the elevator doors had closed before speaking into the microphone hidden inside his shirt collar. "J.D. — time to serve up the worms." Bramson's voice was icy smooth. Frank wished he had a voice like that, a voice that broads creamed for, that curled around women like a wet, slippery tongue. "Early bird is circling back to the nest."

As the expected reply crackled into Bramson's ear, he nodded tersely to Frank. "It's a go."

"You bought our grandmother *what?*" Meg gasped, setting down her empty coffee cup on the room service tray. She plopped onto the dinette chair, which was upholstered in the same muted blue-greens as the rest of the suite, and reached for a cranberry-orange muffin. The connection to London was so clear she could hear the low chuckle Cat tried to smother.

"A sequined vest," Cat repeated, and Meg could just picture the impish smile on her sister's lovely heart-shaped face.

"Where in the world is Gram going to wear a sequined vest? Church? Bingo? Mrs. Wheeler's Christmas party?"

24

"All of the above. She loved that rhinestone hatband with all the feathers I brought her from Nice last year. You know, Gram is much hipper than you give her credit for, Meg."

Oh, Cat, if you only knew, Meg groaned inwardly. Gram wouldn't hurt Cat's feelings for the world, but she'd confided privately to Meg that if she was forced to wear any more of her eldest grandaughter's outlandish presents around town, she'd soon be the laughingstock of Tempe. Her friends already teased her mercilessly about the studded purple suede cowboy boots and the rhinestone hatband Cat was so proud of — the ones Gram wore whenever Cat came to town, then stashed at the back of her closet the minute Cat flew off for her next photo assignment. Jeanne Hansen, a French war bride who had settled in America nearly fifty years ago with the ease of butter melting into freshly baked croissants, shared Meg's down-to-earth taste — while Cat adored everything funky, bright, and brazen. No matter where her assignments landed her, Cat with uncanny radar zeroed in on every offbeat boutique and gallery from Seoul to Santa Fe.

A rebellion of sorts, Meg supposed, after her divorce. A freeing of the vibrant soul that had been squelched by that uptight, corporate bastard Cat had been married to.

Now it seemed Cat was finally putting all the pieces back together. She'd really found her niche with her photography — in the past two years she'd gone from freelancing to a plum job with *Celebrity* magazine. There was no question about it. She was good. Many of her best shots captured the tongue-in-cheek lunacy paraded down designer runways or celebrated the unique cachet of Hollywood's hottest. Movie stars whose style bent to the unusual knew photographs by Cat Hansen would always capture their distinctive personalities and imbue them with drama.

And best of all, with success after success, Meg saw her sister's self-confidence coming back. Cat had had a rough time of it, but now she had a great job, a new boyfriend, and an optimism Meg hadn't seen in her in a long time.

"I thought we agreed on a Wedgwood vase," Meg reminded her sister as she speared the last strawberry from the fruit plate. Her stomach cramped as she popped it into her mouth — nerves, probably. "This is Gram's seventy-fifth birthday, remember. And she's been talking for years about replacing the Wedgwood planter we broke that Halloweeen night."

"Picky, picky. For your information, the vase is already bubble-wrapped and cushioned inside my carry-on — right on top of the vest," Cat informed her smugly.

Meg poured a third cup of coffee for Burnsie, who by her estimation should be finished in the shower within the next thirty seconds. Burnsie's pattern was so familiar that Meg could predict what her chaperon would order for dinner two seconds after they'd glanced at the menu. As she set the coffeepot down, her stomach twinged again.

Shit. She hoped she wasn't getting the flu. She had to keep rolling on this schedule from hell. Three more weeks . . .

"Meg — are you there? What's going on?"

"Nothing, I'm . . . feeling kind of weird. Light-headed. Maybe I overdid my laps."

"Maybe you're just plain exhausted. Only one day off a month, a different city every night — your own family doesn't know where you are half the time. Thank God Jordan is a damned efficient publicist, or we'd never catch up with you. A year like you've had could wear out the Energizer bunny." Cat's voice grew quiet and Meg could hear her unspoken concern. She could just picture Cat worrying her teeth along her lower lip the way she always did when she was anxious about something. "I don't know about you, baby sis, but I'll be glad when you're out of the lime-light. Any more problems?"

"From ORBA? Not since Cavenaugh was sentenced."

"Well, at least that son of a bitch will be out of commission for the next few years. But I hope they haven't cut back on your security. ORBA still has plenty of other kooks in its ranks. Still got those extra guys?"

"Nope. They were canceled after Cavenaugh went to prison."

Before Meg was a week into her reign, Jared Cavenaugh, president of the radical Organization for the Right to Bear Arms, had spearheaded a hate campaign against Meg and her gun control platform — an escalating campaign of threats that had landed Cavenaugh a felony conviction.

Meg rubbed her lips. They felt tingly. "Don't worry so much, Cat. Really, we're fine, Burnsie and me. Anyway, I've got to run. Give Gram a kiss for me, and tell her that the minute the pageant's over I'm hopping the next plane home for the biggest birthday bash she's ever seen."

Meg slid the receiver into its cradle and checked her watch. Half an hour until the limo came. She hurried to the mirror over the bureau and fastened big silver hoops in her earlobes. They matched the silver conch trim on her fringed white leather jumper. She studied her reflection. Not bad, but the bright teal silk tee needed a little something, she decided, and rummaged in her jewelry pouch for her dreamcatcher necklace. The small loosely woven circle dangled from a thin leather thong. It looked like a shiny spiderweb studded with a little pearl and a tiny turquoise nugget. A delicate trail of beads swinging at the bottom was accented by a single white feather.

Meg tied the Indian-made thong around her neck. Perfect.

Too bad I don't feel as good as I look, she thought with a small grimace as she centered the Miss America tiara on her head. At that moment she heard a heavy thud from the bathroom.

"Burnsie?" She turned quickly, then clutched

the bureau for support as a wave of dizziness made her wobble. What the hell? "Burnsie," she muttered through oddly numbed lips, and stumbled unsteadily toward the bathroom. It seemed a thousand miles away.

There was no answer. Only the running of water and a faint tinny ringing in her ears.

"Burnsie, are you . . . all right?" she called, leaning against the closed bathroom door. The knob felt cold and slippery in her hand. She fumbled to get a grip on it and the door gave way.

"My . . . God . . ." Through the steam Meg could make out Burnsie slumped across the rim of the tub, her arms splayed on the floor. Blood dribbled from her mouth, trickling down the outside of the tub.

Suddenly the room began to spin. Meg grabbed on to the sink for support. What had happened to Burnsie? What was happening to her? She tried to kneel down beside Burnsie, but her legs buckled and then she was falling, falling. . . .

Meg grasped at the towel rack, desperately clutching the thick terry towel in her fingers. And then she heard the crash as her jaw hit the wall and the towel rack clattered against the tile floor. Then there was only a hazy throbbing pain, the taste of blood soaking her tongue, and a jackknifing cramp in her stomach.

She heard the men talking as if from the far end of a black tunnel. Deep, disjointed voices. They made her feel cold inside.

"Looks like Early Bird got her worm," one said, laughing. "Coffee's nearly gone, and nothing left of the muffins but a few crumbs."

Help us. Why don't they help us?

She felt herself being lifted, bundled into something warm. *Thank God.* But it was dark, and she was so cold.

Don't forget Burnsie, she wanted to tell them, but her lips wouldn't form the words and then the dizziness came back.

The hospital. They're taking us to the hospital.

But the ambulance felt like a roller coaster, and it was pitch-dark, stifling. Why was it so dark? *I can't breathe,* she screamed. *It hurts.*

But no sound came out.

"Hey, you. The laundry's in the basement. Where are you going with that cart?"

A new voice . . . What did he mean, laundry cart? This is an ambulance.

"I said stop. You can't . . ."

An explosion roared in Meg's ears. *A . . . gun . . . ?*

No!

"No, honey, Mommy and Daddy aren't coming home anymore." Gram looked so tired, and her usually pink face was the color of oatmeal. "Mommy and Daddy are in heaven now."

"No! They can't be. I want them. Cat — Gram. Make them come back!"

Cat hugged her close, and Meg could feel her sister's warm tears seeping into her Minnie Mouse T-shirt. Then Gram, with her familiar vanilla smell, was hugging them both and crying.

Bad men killed them. They're dead. I'll never see them again.

But at the funeral home, she did. Daddy in his navy blue Easter suit. Mommy in her favorite lace dress. They looked so strange, like big stiff dolls.

"Mommy, Daddy — come back."

The darkness clamped down on her.

Come back. . . .

Come back. . . .

2

Costa Rica

The Jeep bounced along the snaking mountain path, spraying stones and dust in its wake. Apart from the grinding of the gears and the occasional harsh caw of a chachalaca, it was quiet. The driver and passenger did not speak until they reached the edge of a forest.

"Señor, from here we must walk," said the smaller man, the guide, in heavily accented English. He slung his carbine over his shoulder and started up the rock-strewn path.

It was darker and cooler in the forest, the almost impenetrable columns of evergreens blocking out the late August sun.

Corey Preston removed his sunglasses and dropped them into the pocket of his khaki shirt. His heavy-lidded tawny eyes narrowed on the balding spot on the back of the guide's head. He'd seen Méndez's lackey eyeing his emerald ring — what would the little fool think if he knew that beneath this shirt was a vest with half a million dollars sewn into the lining?

His sensual, predator's lips curled into a sneer. He was as exhilarated as he'd been on his very first safari. Only this time, he wouldn't be close enough to witness the kill.

With his bronze tanned skin and thick curly black hair, Corey Preston had the dark, seductive beauty of a young underworld Adonis. In this environment, he could have passed for a native. He moved like a native, too, following the guide with long, energetic strides, his holstered Glock pistol slapping against his muscled thigh as he maneuvered the twisting inclines. His respect for Méndez grew as they made their way through what appeared to be virgin woodland. It was true what he had been told — without a map and a guide, no one could possibly find Méndez's head-quarters.

It was a difficult ascent, and when they at last reached level ground and approached the walls of the compound, the little guide's dark-skinned forehead glistened with sweat. Corey Preston wasn't even breathing hard.

He was proud of his endurance. He trained four hours every day, rigorously disciplining body and mind. The machines gave him lean, sculpted muscles. His thirty-hour fasts toned his spirit. He was a soldier, a general, and he'd come to inspect the last battalion before sending them into battle.

A guard with three gold teeth threw down his cigarette and swung open the spiked steel gate, then slammed it shut immediately after they'd passed through. *Christ, the man smelled like he'd bathed in urine and garlic.*

The guide led him past low wooden buildings thick with dust. There was no one in sight except two men with rifles slung across their backs. They were loading boxes onto a camouflaged truck parked just outside the windowless headquarters where Jorge Méndez waited for him.

"I remember what you drink, El Director." With leisurely steps, the hulking Méndez crossed the tiny barren room to hand his visitor a glass of Tanqueray. *"Salud."*

Corey felt a surge of pleasure at the deference with which Méndez greeted him. Here was the foremost bomb expert in the Third World, a genius of death and destruction, ushering him into his private headquarters like visiting royalty. And why not? Méndez would be paid three million dollars by the time this operation was over. No small change, not by anyone's standards.

Corey sipped at the liquor, the heat of it matching the anticipation that sizzled through his veins. He felt Méndez's gaze on him, relaxed and confident, as Corey surveyed the detailed map of the United States that blanketed the chipped gray wall.

"Your men are all in place?"

"Sí, señor. The devices are already in your country as well — we are ahead of schedule. B-Sector will reassemble them, and C-Sector will handle distribution."

34

Pulling colored pushpins from a corkboard, Corey began stabbing them meticulously into place, as single-minded as a cannibal at dinnertime. "Now let us be clear on the order in which your men destroy the targets."

Méndez nodded. "Then you have decided — the Empire State Building is first. I assume you want the explosion at night when there are no visitors."

"At noon."

A smile of admiration touched Méndez's lips. "As you wish, El Director. It will be done."

Corey Preston studied the map again while beside him Méndez waited, his raptor eyes as shiny as razor blades.

The crowning moment will be the Capitol, Corey thought, adrenaline coursing through him like liquid fire. *It will serve those slimeballs right, trying to legislate the Second Amendment out of existence.*

They'd said he couldn't run a company, a lousy *Fortune* 500 company. But he was going to run a war that would bring back democracy to America and would ensure his family's fortune for generations to come.

America would wake up, all right. He'd set off an alarm clock they'd never forget.

After he'd reviewed the timetable with Méndez and they'd finished the rest of their business, Corey removed his shirt and tossed the money vest to Méndez. "You'll get the other two and a half million dollars when the job is done."

Méndez nodded. Then he flicked on the inter-

35

com beside the fax machine and spoke a single word. "Ready."

He led Corey across the dusty courtyard to the compound gates. "El Director," he said, pointing a ragged fingernail toward the tree-covered mountain range to their left. "I have taken the liberty of arranging a small demonstration."

Before the words were out of his mouth, a deafening roar rocked the mountains. The ground trembled.

And in the distance, a charred hole gaped where before there had been a mountain of trees.

Corey fixed his gaze on Méndez with a look of ice-cold admiration. "It's a pleasure doing business with you."

3

London

"Unbelievable! *Now* the rain stops," Cat muttered, poking her head outside the second-floor window of Vince's rented house and scowling at the freshly washed morning sky. With only two hours left before she was meeting Vince for lunch and then leaving for the airport, the clouds had lifted and in their wake an amber sun glowed fuzzily through the mist. She'd been on assignment in London for four and a half days, and this was her first glimpse of sunshine. Not that that was unusual, but she'd been hoping to take some pictures in Hyde Park and Kensington Gardens once she'd finished shooting Brad Pitt for the next issue of *Celebrity*. And until now, the weather hadn't cooperated.

Well, she'd better make the most of the next few hours. Cat hooked her camera bag over her shoulder and let herself out the front door, hoping that if she hurried, she'd still have time to jump in the shower and wash her hair before meeting

Vince at Logan's Brasserie at one. *Our last afternoon together for a while,* she thought with a slight pang as she ran down the stairs and out into the damp narrow street.

Her mouth curved upward in a smile as she strode beneath a china blue sky, her Reeboks squishing on the still wet pavement. In baggy turquoise jeans and a flowing white poet's shirt, with dozens of slender golden neck chains jangling with each step, she looked younger than her twenty-six years. Almost like a college student — a free-spirited artist or drama major. Her gamine face shone bright and alive, her eyebrows slimly arched over astonishing lime green eyes. Chin-length honey-brown hair swung buoyantly forward with each step.

Maybe I'll wear the red leather mini with the safety pin suspenders, Cat thought as she hurried along Curzon Street toward Hyde Park. *Vince goes crazy every time I wear red. If that outfit doesn't wake him up after half a day in the editing room reviewing dailies, nothing will.*

Cat was still on a high from the exhilaration of seeing her color photo of Winona Ryder beaming from last week's issue of *Celebrity* — her first cover. It jumped out at her from every newsstand. And the Brad Pitt shoot had been fantastic. She couldn't wait to see the contact sheets.

Things were definitely on a roll, clicking into place faster than the shutter on her camera. Since she'd joined the staff of *Celebrity,* the checks had been flowing in regularly. More important, she was gaining respect and making a name for herself.

Who'd have thought that Cat Hansen, who'd switched college majors more often than Paris changed hemlines, who'd dabbled in jewelry making, sociology, and folk-art history before discovering her talent with a camera, would end up with the perfect job, blissfully happy and getting paid for it?

Growing up, she'd always secretly wished she could have been more like Meg, who was so focused, who'd worked single-mindedly toward her Olympic dream and then Harvard. Meg had always known who she was and what she'd wanted. But even by her senior year in high school, Cat wasn't sure. Whenever she'd sat in her room, nibbling on a pencil, surrounded by college course catalogs and wrestling with decisions about her future, she had been filled with a frustrated envy of Meg's driving self-assurance.

Now we're both on course. I have my first cover, and Meg's only a few weeks away from Harvard.

Thank God Meg's year as Miss America was almost over.

Cat cut along Shepherd Market and headed for Hyde Park's main entrance. She'd been worried, more worried than she'd admitted to either Meg or Gram. She couldn't wait for Meg to be back in college, out of the spotlight, and a less visible target for those gun-worshiping lunatics in ORBA.

Leave it to Meg to choose gun control as her

Miss America platform and to stir up every crazed right-winger in the country. Over and over, Cat had tried to persuade Meg to choose a less inflammatory platform. But it had been no use. When it came to gun control Meg was as hard-boiled as a deviled egg. Strange how the two of them had reacted so differently to their parents' murders — Meg becoming adamantly committed to gun control, believing it would decrease the violence escalating in society, while Cat had made up her mind when she was fourteen that if there were dangerous people out in the world, she was going to arm herself against them. And she had, buying her own gun the day she was of age, the same way some teenagers ran right out to get their driver's licenses, and practicing at the gun range on weekends and over summer vacations. She'd often lain in bed at night, wondering if her parents would be alive today if only Dad had reached the gun at the store.

But she'd never been able to bring Meg around to her point of view. Meg would sooner touch a scorpion than a gun, and as Miss America, her vocal support for Senator Farrell's heavy-duty gun control bill had stirred up a hornet's nest in her own home state, where guns and cowboy boots were almost standard issue. It had *really* riled those creeps in ORBA, Cat reflected, stepping over a deep puddle. Yet Meg never let up. Even the torrent of death threats hadn't fazed her.

As far as Cat was concerned, Cavenaugh could

stay in jail until Congress found a way to pay off the national debt.

A few more weeks, Cat told herself, and Meg's fifteen minutes of fame would be up. *She'll be just another anonymous law student up to her elbows in torts and Gram and I will sleep better at night.*

As Cat passed through the park's stately entrance and dashed along the Serpentine — the crescent-shaped lake that linked the parks — the trill of laughing children sent her reaching for her camera. The midmorning light danced off raindrops still pooled on the pathways and clinging to the shrubbery and flower beds like the sequins on Gram's new vest.

"Hey, Mum. That lady's snapping our picture." The freckle-faced boy in the light green rugby shirt pointed a grimy finger at Cat. She glanced up from the viewfinder with a smile.

"Do you mind?" she asked the thirtyish-looking woman who was crouched next to a stroller, dangling a ring of multicolored plastic keys in front of a pink-cheeked little girl in a Winnie-the-Pooh sundress. "I'm a photographer. . . . These are just for fun."

The woman, who looked like she could use a cup of tea and an hour's nap, shrugged her thin shoulders. "I don't mind. But now he's bound to show off for you. Just watch."

Sure enough, the boy began doing cartwheels in the wet grass around the statue of Peter Pan, slipping and falling with such a silly, giggly laugh that his baby sister shrieked with glee and threw

41

the keys into the mud. Cat found herself laughing, too, and snapping picture after picture.

She stared longingly at the pudgy little girl with ice cream stains down the front of her dress. *My baby would have been three in October,* she thought with a sharp twist of pain. Strange, how every now and then the hurt came back, as fresh as ever, even after all this time. She wondered if Paul, ensconced in Seattle with his new Martha Stewart clone of a wife and their infant twins, ever thought about the baby they'd lost together — if he ever got this choking lump in his throat. Or was he too happy with his new family to remember?

If, if, if. You can't keep looking back and wondering. It's a waste of energy, and besides, what the hell good does it do? Paul's moved on and so have you. What more could you want, anyway? You're crazy about your work and about Vince.

But lately, with Vince in London while she'd been at home in New York, she'd found herself wondering if he truly missed her as much as she missed him, wondering if Vince felt there was more to their relationship than just affection and great sex.

Don't rush things, she told herself. Give it time. Yet her mood had inexplicably changed. Cat snapped the cover over her lens and slipped the camera back into its snug leather bag as the mother waved good-bye and maneuvered the stroller down the pathway.

The lightheartedness with which Cat had photographed the children had fled, replaced by a vague empty feeling. Maybe she'd been in the London fog too long. She shivered as the sun was swallowed once more by a dismal mist and raindrops sprinkled across the lake. Too many days without sunshine could shadow the soul.

Well, she'd be home tomorrow. After an overnight stop in New York to drop off her film at the magazine and touch base with Simon about her next assignment, she'd be back in Arizona with Gram, sitting on the porch, drinking lemonade and unwinding. She needed the break. These last few months had been solid work, one shoot after another.

The rain began to sheet down from a leaden sky just as she reached Vince's house. Cat ducked inside the low-ceilinged front hall and piled her camera case atop the overnight bag in the corner. The rented house smelled like Vince — Joop and the tang of citrus from the basket of oranges he always kept on the living room table. Whether he was editing a movie in London, New York, or L.A., Vince's basket of oranges always made him feel at home.

Cat inhaled deeply and gazed about the comfortable old-fashioned house that suited him so well. The editing of *All Work, No Play* would be finished soon, and Vince would be following her back to New York. But first they'd have one last matinee in this snug little house. She anticipated the expression on Vince's face when she sashayed into the restaurant in that red leather mini. She checked the fridge on her way to the shower. On the top shelf, alongside a jar of capers and a dried out wedge of cheese, she saw what she was looking for. A new canister of whipped cream.

Yum. A slow, naughty grin lit her piquant face. *Guess that'll take care of dessert.*

The waitress hooked her pen inside the black leather order book and winked at Cat. "Save room for some dessert, luv. Chef made a lovely apple rum tart laced with caramel sauce."

"Thanks, but I whipped up something special at home," Cat demurred.

"When did you have time to bake?" Vince's brows lifted in surprise. Then he winced as she kicked him under the table. "Oh, *that* dessert," he blurted, and then grinned. "The quickie. I mean, the quiche — the fruit quiche." He was now as red as Cat's skirt, and the waitress was laughing.

"So you prefer the quiche to the quickie?" Cat drawled as the waitress zoomed off for the kitchen.

Vince grabbed her hand. Tall, gaunt, and handsome in a rumpled kind of way, with his short dark beard and intense olive eyes that analyzed the world with a fierce intellectual curiosity, he had a way of stroking her fingers that made Cat tingle. "Not on your life, sister."

"Oh, so you think of me as a sister?"

"No nun I ever met would be caught dead in that getup," Vince told her in a deep, growling voice, eyeing her black scoop-necked T-shirt, which accentuated the fullness of her breasts straining against the leather suspenders. Cat felt a warm glow inside her — in so many ways, Vince was good for her, especially after the debacle that Paul had made of her self-esteem.

"I want you to promise me something," Cat said, leaning closer. She stroked the fine hairs on the back of his hand.

"Yes, I'll use up the entire canister of whipped cream — if there's time. So eat fast."

"Vince, get serious. I want you to promise you'll *try* your best to make it to my grandmother's birthday party. It's important to me. You told me you don't have to be in L.A. to start cutting that next movie until October. If you keep your assistants working overtime, couldn't you wrap in time for the party? It's not until the middle of September."

The waitress set a plate of spinach soufflé smothered in anchovy sauce in front of Cat and ground fresh pepper on Vince's beef fillet.

Vince reached for his fork. "I'll do my best, but I can't make any promises, Cat. I'll let you know in a week or two."

"But you're still planning to go rafting in Colorado with Barry and Jim before you go to L.A."

"That's got nothing to do with this. We've had to postpone that trip twice already. Trying to nail down a weekend when the three of us were free was a bitch."

Cat took a sip of wine, trying to hide her hurt.

Don't push. Maybe he doesn't want any strings at-tached right now, but you know he cares for you.

At least she thought he did.

Vince flicked the beaded strands of Cat's ear-rings with his finger. "Hey, where'd that smile go? Come on, you know I'll give it my best shot. God knows, I want to meet the famous Gram. From all the stories you've told me, she has to be one incredible lady."

"Absolutely the most incredible," Cat said with a forced smile. *Okay, calm down,* she told herself. *It's not as if he rejected you. It's not as if we're joined at the hip.* Yet she couldn't contain the stab of disappointment. From the way he'd answered her, it was apparent that Gram's party wasn't high on his list of priorities. *Maybe I'm not either,* Cat reflected with a small tug of anger as she watched him refill their wineglasses. Have I just been kid-ding myself all this time?

"You'd get a kick out of her," Cat continued with an effort, though her throat was dry. "She's one dynamite lady."

"Sounds like she's had more adventure in her lifetime than Schwarzenegger and Stallone com-bined."

"I know there are things in her past that she's never even told us," Cat said quietly. "It's painful for her to talk about the war, even after all these years. Sometimes I wonder if I'd have been as brave as she was when she joined the Resistance."

Born in Paris, her grandmother had been barely out of her teens when she'd met Skip Hansen and

Jack Galt, two young American intelligence officers in wartime France. Often acting as a courier between them and the Resistance fighters, Gram had risked capture, torture, and death to fight the German enemy.

"Any of her old war buddies coming to this shindig?" Vince shifted his chair closer to the table. All around them the clamor of the other diners rang through the room, and snatches of desultory chatter burst in and out of their conversation.

Cat took another long sip of wine, trying to let the full-bodied fruitiness wash away the sour taste of Vince's indifference. "My grandparents' old friend Jack Galt is coming in from West Virginia," she answered, keeping her voice light and cheerful. "He's now an antiterrorism advisor to the government — spends a lot of time in the Mideast. We haven't seen him since my grandfather's funeral, but he and Gram call one another fairly often. It will be so wonderful for her to see him."

"Speaking of wonderful" — Vince grinned — "that whipped cream dessert should make our last afternoon together pretty memorable. What time is your flight?"

"Six-thirty."

Vince glanced at his watch. "Eat faster."

They heard the phone ringing as Vince turned the key in the lock.

"Catriana. Thank God you're there. Have you heard?"

"Heard what? Gram, slow down, I can barely understand you."

"Oh God, Catriana. It's Meg."

Cat closed her eyes, wincing as much from Gram's splintered voice as from what she was saying.

No. No! Meg's fine. I talked to her just a few hours ago.

As the words spilled from Gram like sharp pebbles, Cat gripped the phone, her brain whirling in confusion.

Burnsie drugged . . . intensive care . . . a bellman dead . . . Meg abducted . . .

This can't be true. It's a mistake.

From a long way off she seemed to hear Vince asking what was wrong. The cloying smell of oranges engulfed her, a sour taste filling her mouth.

Then she heard her own voice whispering. "I'll be on the next plane."

4

"She still sleeping?"

"What do you think? You gave her enough stuff to down an elephant."

Frank glanced over at the still figure sprawled across the blanket in the back of the van. Her face was turned away, but he could see the purpling bruise swelling across her chin. She had a damn good body underneath all those ladylike clothes. Long and lean and sexy, just the way he liked them. His eyes swept downward. Her pretty little fringed outfit was twisted up beneath her hips, exposing a tempting length of sheer stockinged thigh and peach bikini panties. A slow heat started in his groin, building, making his palms start to sweat. He dragged a hand through his scraggly red hair.

"Cut it out, Frank," J.D. grumbled, never even looking up from his crossword puzzle. "Director won't like it."

How the hell can he hear my eyeballs move? Frank wondered, his beefy frame tensing. *The asshole probably knows exactly how many rats are crawling through the corners of this fucking warehouse.*

The van was parked in a warehouse on the outskirts of Savannah, in a low, red-brick building adjoining the Samson Brothers Oyster Cannery, a cannery that looked exactly like every other warehouse in the twelve-block vicinity. It was a good place to lie low until nightfall. So far, except for that bellman, there'd been zero problems. Frank didn't anticipate any complications from this point on.

The Director, whoever the hell he was, would be pleased.

Frank had worked with Bramson and Ty before, but never J.D. J.D. was top dog on this operation — a cold-dicked bastard if Frank ever saw one and just the type to whisper reports of any little error into the Director's ear. Frank didn't like him. Didn't like his long, pock-marked face, his squeaky clean black hair tied in that ponytail, or his fucking polished fingernails. But Frank was a professional — he took orders from whoever paid him, and he did what he was told.

Bramson lifted the headphones straddling his blond crew cut and stretched. "Same stuff on Early Bird as before. Missing — no leads. Ty, that guy you shot? He croaked an hour ago."

Ty Mather reached into his pocket for a stick of gum, his hand brushing the .38 strapped at his waist. At twenty-three he was the youngest of the group but also the largest, heftier than Frank by a good thirty pounds. Six three and two hundred and twenty pounds of sheer muscle. "Remind me to send flowers."

The girl moaned.

"Pass me one of those pastrami sandwiches," Bramson ordered, as he stepped over her and reached into the cooler for a Snapple.

"You're out of luck, pal." Frank jerked his head toward J.D. "Guess who had the last one. Looks like you'll have to settle for ham and cheese."

"I've had worse," Bramson commented calmly, his blue eyes unreadable as he opened the Snapple and took a swig. He motioned toward the unconscious woman on the floor. "What about her?"

"She won't even know she's hungry until we're halfway to the Caribbean," Frank said. He glanced at her again, remembering how silky her hair had felt when he'd lifted her into the U-Haul, how the light floral scent of her perfume had mingled with the coppery smell of her blood. He'd copped a feel when no one was looking, and remembering, he swallowed, wondering what their orders would be once they had her safe on the boat. Miss America. Shit. He'd give his first-born for ten minutes with her. Ten lousy minutes. He didn't even care if the others watched.

His balls itched. He restrained the urge to scratch them. Instead he stuck his hands into the pockets of his jeans. They'd all ditched their ill-fitting, borrowed hotel uniforms for comfortable jeans and windbreakers. It would get cold out on the water at night.

Dressed casually in dark colors, they'd had no problem driving out of Atlanta once they'd dumped the other car and transferred their cargo. In another hour they'd pack the U-Haul with crates, put the woman into one of them, and head for the coast.

"Keep right on sleeping, babe, if you know what's good for you," Ty muttered, and Frank saw Ty appraising her too, his thin mouth curling downward beneath his sandy mustache. Ty moved closer, standing over her, his big hands splayed on his hips. He snapped his gum loud and steady. A strange light glinted in his eyes.

"At least for the next few hours," Frank added, and Bramson grinned over his sandwich, sucking mustard off his thumb.

The boat was coming in after midnight. By then Early Bird should be just about ready to wake up. And when she did, this little job would get real interesting.

5

ORBA LEADERS QUESTIONED
IN MISS AMERICA KIDNAPPING

Jordan Davis tossed the folded newspaper down on the gleaming surface of her granite desk, leaned back in the swivel chair, and stared at the ceiling. She knew that the reception area outside was a whirlwind of frenetic activity — phones ringing off the hook, reporters clamoring for statements — but after the nightmare of the past twenty-four hours, she needed just five minutes to regroup.

The comfortable creak of the peach leather beneath her aching shoulders was the only sound in her meticulous, sage-carpeted office on the top floor of the M. Dixon and Associates P.R. firm. She had turned off the ringer on her telephone, desperate for a brief reprieve from the chaos before gearing herself up for CNN.

Oh God, Meg, where are you? What have they done to you?

Meg Hansen was without a doubt the most outspoken, dynamic, and influential Miss America anyone had seen in a long time, and that had made Jordan nervous all along. Meg's vehement gun-control platform had garnered her some really nasty enemies. But even in her darkest imaginings, Jordan had never dreamed they'd go this far. Just thinking about Meg in the hands of those bastards was enough to tighten the knots in her stomach and send threads of tension twisting along her shoulder blades.

She rolled her head, her dark bangs feathering across her forehead as she stretched the aching muscles in her neck. She couldn't stop thinking about the sickening diatribe of threats those ORBA scumbags had sent to Meg last winter. A chill prickled her skin beneath her rose silk blouse, and Jordan leaned forward, shivering involuntarily as she gazed once again at the newspaper photo of Jared Cavenaugh's handsomely smarmy face.

Son of a bitch, she thought, glaring at the picture. *You and all your fanatical ORBA friends make the NRA look like a pack of Webelo Scouts. If you've hurt Meg . . .*

Jordan rubbed her temples and tried to blot out the frightening images in her mind. She had to focus on getting Sheila through this interview with CNN, on doing her job. The press was going wild with the story, and if she started thinking too much about what was happening to Meg, she would break down — right on the evening news. Every nerve in Jordan's body was taut as she reached for the stack of telephone messages that had accumulated during the press briefing this morning.

Alana Thornton's curly blond head poked around the oak door, her thickly lashed dark eyes peering in like an inquisitive raccoon's. "Good, you're back. Lori's on line one, Alex Woods is on line two, Tom Brokaw's on line three — *and* the CNN camera crew just arrived for the two o'clock interview with Sheila Tomkins. And also" — Alana frowned — "as if you don't have enough on your mind, a sort of strange call came in earlier. Some guy said Lori won first prize in a coloring contest and wanted to know her school's address."

"What?" Jordan's brow furrowed.

"He said they wanted to deliver the computer art gizmo she won in time for the first day of school. Obviously, we didn't give out any information. I wouldn't even bother you about this, except that when I asked him to leave a number he hung up. I thought it was kind of weird."

"It is." A slight uneasiness sped through Jordan. "Let me know if he calls back."

"You got it." Alana glanced down at her notepad. "I better get back to the camera crew. Still doing this in the conference room?"

"That's the plan. Sheila's already down there. Tell Brokaw I can make Sheila available to him at three-thirty."

Sheila Tomkins, the media relations executive from the Miss America Organization, had flown in from Atlantic City within hours of Meg's disappearance to consult with Jordan. As the account executive from M. Dixon responsible for the Miss America account, Jordan had been working with Sheila ever since the ORBA threats first surfaced. But the media circus surrounding Cavenaugh's arrest and trial had been nothing compared to the frenzy unleashed by Meg's disappearance in Atlanta yesterday.

Since Sheila's arrival in New York yesterday afternoon, Jordan and her staff had spent the night grilling her before a video camera, role-playing, and rehearsing answers to a hundred different questions. Jordan had thrown her every curve ball, and then replayed and critiqued the videos of their mock interviews, subsisting on adrenaline, caffeine, and prayers until daybreak.

Sheila had fared well in this "dress rehearsal," and Jordan felt fairly confident that she could handle being in the hot seat. But with the press, anything could happen. Too little sleep on top of all the tension and pressure could spell disaster. The FBI had warned them to say as little as possible to the press, but Jordan knew you had to give them something. The trick was to keep the advantage over the media. Yet, one unexpected question, one fumbled answer, and all hell would break loose.

Jordan would never forgive herself if some inadvertent comment put Meg in further danger. After all, it was her fault that Meg had started on the pageant circuit in the first place.

"Get the CNN crew some coffee, will you, Alana? And tell Alex I'll be with him in a sec." Jordan shot one graceful hand toward the phone. She stabbed the first flashing button, praying Mike didn't want her to pick Lori up early.

"Hi, sweetie pie." Jordan forced herself to relax, all the way from the crick in her neck down to the peony-painted toenails squished inside her low-heeled pumps. She tried to block out everything else and focus on Lori for just a few moments. "Did you have fun at the zoo?"

"YEAH!" The child could barely contain her four-year-old enthusiasm, and as always, Jordan's heart lifted at the sound of her daughter's voice. "I sawed the elephants, and Daddy bought me a manilla ice cream and my own cotton candy."

Great. Jordan rolled her eyes. *Thank you, Mike. Cavities on top of divorce. Just what we need.* "I'm glad you had fun, honey. You guys were very lucky the weather cleared up. Listen, did you color a picture for some kind of contest? At school, or with Daddy or Mrs. Chalmers?"

"No . . . oo. But I sent for pencils from the Lucky Charms box. Did they come?"

"Not yet, sweetie." *No coloring contest. Probably nothing. But when I pick up Lori tonight, I'll go in and mention this to Mike.* "Lori, I can't wait to hear all about the zoo, but right now Mommy has to go back to work. I'll pick you up at Daddy's after dinner."

"Daddy says we're eating dinner at ten o'clock."

"Nice try, kiddo. You and your daddy both know your bedtime is eight o'clock. You can tell me all about the elephants on our way home. Mommy's got to go now. Love you."

"I know. Bye."

Jordan's smile vanished as she switched over to line two. "Alex, there's no way I can keep our dinner date tonight. CNN is setting up in the conference room even as we speak."

"Easy, Jordan. I can imagine what you're going through. Any word?"

"Not a damned thing."

"Our newsroom is going nuts. This is the story of the year. I can't wait to see the ratings."

Electricity tinged Alex's usually smooth voice, and she could picture him pacing the length of his plush corner office at Rockefeller Plaza: tall and rangy, his gold cuff links sparkling against the crisp whiteness of his shirt, his sandy hair curling softly at his collar as he surveyed the New York skyline from his NBC office suite.

"My meeting with our West Coast affiliates will run the rest of the day — the usual dog and pony show — but I should be able to get out of here by eight — eight-thirty, tops. I'll bring the Chinese carryout if you'll fill me in on all the lurid details."

Jordan's hazel eyes clouded over with weariness. "It sounds great, Alex, but I'll have to pass. We worked through the night, and I'm dead on my feet. Lori's expecting me to pick her up at Mike's at seven, and then I'm going home to crash. Beverly's taking over for me here until morning in case something develops during the night."

Alana reappeared in the doorway, signaling frantically, and Jordan sprang to her feet. "Sorry, Alex, gotta run. They need me in the conference room."

"I need you, too, Jordan. And I miss you. Call me if there's anything I can do."

Jordan hung up and grabbed for her makeup bag, praying she didn't look as exhausted as she felt. *Too bad I didn't meet that man years ago — before Mike Bannister careened into my life,* she thought, hurriedly dusting blush across her wan cheeks. The face her father had always proudly proclaimed as "elegantly patrician" gazed back at her from her compact mirror, but Jordan felt no pride in her small upturned nose or perfectly oval face; they struck her as blandly ordinary. Her large, wide-set eyes had always seemed her best feature. Framed by spider-black, curly lashes, they could invite someone in or shut them out with a flicker. Since Jordan was fifteen, she'd subtly intensified their expressiveness with muted earth shades of liner and shadow. Her mouth she'd long since dismissed as too wide and too long, though Mike had told her she had the sexiest lips he'd ever seen.

Mike. Frowning, Jordan dabbed on fresh lipstick and some undereye cream to conceal the dark circles, then stuffed the tube back into her bag.

An hour from now this wretched interview would be over. All Sheila had to do was concentrate, think on her feet, and try to keep one step ahead of the reporter's line of questioning.

You've been through worse, Jordan reminded herself, squaring her shoulders. You've survived boarding school, debutante balls, three years of marriage to the most bull-headed vice cop in New York, and fifteen hours of childbirth.

You can survive your client facing CNN.

Mario Minelli chucked his cigarette butt onto the littered curb and scowled across Madison Avenue at the ladder of windows climbing into the cobalt sky. The eighteenth floor had been lit like a Christmas tree all through the night, and now the street below was crawling with camera crews.

Some reporter types walking by had said something about Miss America. Must be what all the commotion was about. Mario scratched his day's stubble and dug another cigarette out of the torn pocket of his jeans.

He didn't give a shit about Miss America. The only broad he cared about was one Jordan Davis. But Mario was beginning to think she lived in this fucking office building.

There were so many people going in and out of the goddamn place, she'd probably slipped out without his realizing it. He bit a hangnail from one grimy finger. He wanted to go in and check but couldn't risk it.

Sweat poured down his face, turning the neck of his Harley T-shirt dark gray. He shifted back and forth from one foot to the other, his torn, taped-together Sporto boots splitting further with each movement. If he didn't take a leak soon, he'd explode.

Stay or go? Stay or go? Shit, man, if I don't get the lowdown on this bitch today, I'll just have to come back and sweat my ass off out here again tomorrow. But if I don't connect with that high-school punk pretty soon, he'll score from somebody else.

Mario squinted up at the windows again, flexing his balls and grimacing at the awful throbbing in his bladder. Right now he hated Jordan Davis almost as much as he hated the boss.

But he'd stay. Mario would rather piss his pants than piss off Mr. Sima. Even from prison the boss was the boss and orders were orders. So if the boss wanted the lowdown on Jordan Davis — where she lived, where she worked, where she went for lunch; shit, even when she took a dump — then, hell, he'd get it.

Screw that punk kid. There's a hundred more out there like him waiting to buy weed. I'll wait on Jordan Davis for as long as it takes.

61

6

"Get away from me."

Meg slithered up the bed, twisting as far away from Ty Mather as the wrist chain shackling her to the headboard would allow.

"Take it easy, baby. Ty brought you a little present." His eyes flashed with a hint of mockery.

"Unless it's the key to these handcuffs, I don't want it."

"Oh, you'll want this all right, baby." He advanced toward her, holding out his hand. "You'll want it real bad." In the big, calloused palm was a bar of Dove. "You're starting to stink. We're going to let you take a shower."

He reached toward her with his other hand and Meg flinched as his sausagelike fingers stroked through her matted hair.

"I told you to get away from me!" Despite the strength in her voice, icy crystals of fear crackled through her.

Ty grinned. He ran the tip of his tongue along his sandy-colored mustache. "Frank said he's real sorry we don't have any bubble bath stuff for you.

He's even sorrier that he lost out when we drew straws. See, I get to supervise your little shower."

"Go to hell." Meg glared at him, struggling to hide her fear. If he touched her in the shower, she'd fight him with every ounce of strength she could muster. True, she felt as smelly and rank as a week-old dead fish, but she'd rather let her skin turn green with mold spores than allow this bastard to put his hands on her.

How many days had she been on this boat now? Three, four? She hadn't once been allowed out of this tiny, dim inside cabin with its maple walls and sparse furnishings. She had no idea where she was, or who they were. She wasn't even sure if it was day or night — the fluorescent light over the bed was always on. They'd unlocked her handcuffs only long enough to lead her to the small adjoining bathroom several times and had refused to let her wash, not even her hands. Fear had racked at her every single moment since she'd first regained consciousness and found herself shackled and alone, wearing only her bra and torn panties. Why were they doing this to her?

She wanted to go home.

On the untouched tray beside her bed, a fly explored the brown, dried-out cut apple and the slab of grease-congealed frozen pizza they'd left her for dinner. She'd been too seasick even to look at any of the junk food they'd brought her before this — cans of greasy cold chili, nachos, Spam sandwiches lathered in mayonnaise. She knew she'd have to eat something soon, or she'd grow too weak to function, but right now her biggest worry was the man standing over her, studying her with those eerie gray eyes. Eyes as small and deadly as a rattlesnake's. Strange that such a big man should have such tiny eyes. He looked as if he could break her in two with one flick of his wrist and then eat a steak dinner.

Meg shrank as far back into the corner as she could, meeting his eyes with a defiant glare. "I don't want to take a shower. I'd rather stink."

"Nobody asked you, baby." Ty laughed and grabbed the front of her T-shirt, yanking her forward. "Haven't you figured out yet that you're not calling the shots?"

He stuffed the bar of soap into his shirt pocket and unhooked a key ring from his belt loop. One smooth click freed her numb, aching wrist from the manacle. "Move it."

Ty dragged her into the bathroom and shoved her toward the shower cubicle beside the tiny enamel sink. "We can do this the easy way or the hard way." He gestured toward her T-shirt, the one the red-haired man, Frank, had tossed her when he brought the food tray. "Take it off or I'll do it for you."

This can't be happening. Meg stared into those cold rattlesnake eyes, searching for a shred of human decency. "Can't you just give me a moment of privacy?" she heard herself ask. "It's not as if I can escape. Where am I going to go?"

"This ain't the *QE II* and I'm not your goddamn cabin steward," Ty told her, and suddenly his hand slid down to the pocket knife dangling on his key ring. "Think of me as Captain Hook," he sneered, grabbing her arm. With a swift motion he swept the knife up to her face and flicked out the blade. Before Meg could do more than whimper in fear, he had slit through the front of her T-shirt and yanked it away.

"Okay, okay," Meg gasped. She fumbled behind her back with the clasp of her bra, willing her numb fingers to hurry as she saw impatience flash in his eyes.

"Panties, baby," he snapped, and this time she obeyed without question.

Humiliated and terrified, Meg shrank beneath the intensity of his appraising gaze. *Please, God, don't let him touch me,* she prayed, her heart slamming into her rib cage. She curled her fingers as he reached forward, ready to claw his eyes out, but all he did was turn on the shower and push her into the fiberglass cubicle.

Meg tried to pull the door closed. He kicked it wide, bracing it open with his boot, and tossed her the bar of soap. "Make it snappy. It's getting steamy in here."

Meg turned away, trying as best she could to shield her nakedness without turning her back on him. She wanted to die. She wanted to disappear down the drain with the water and the soap scum.

Instead she forced herself to wash, scrubbing her gritty skin and dank hair, letting the droplets stream like hot tears down her face. She blotted out the crawling despair she felt as she lathered her skin under the blond hulk's scrutiny. The pelting water pummeled against bruises she didn't know she had. *Where did all these bruises come from? What did they do to me while I was unconscious?*

To her frustration, everything since that morning in the hotel room was a fuzzy blur.

Burnsie. What happened to Burnsie? Do they have her here, too? So far, there'd been no way to tell. Meg only knew that she was on some kind of a boat, maybe a yacht, but with no porthole in her cabin she couldn't tell much beyond that.

She'd seen only two men, this bastard and Frank, but she knew there were others on board. She'd heard different male voices, muffled through the walls of the cabin, drifting in and out like the lolling rhythm of the waves. Frank was the one who always brought her food. And he was the one who had taken her picture, forcing her to sit in that chair clad only in her bra and torn panties — and her dreamcatcher necklace. With trembling wet fingers, Meg touched the tiny pearl at the center of the necklace. It seemed like her only link with the world these men had dragged her from.

Why had they done this to her?

One answer kept battering through her brain: ORBA.

They're finally making good on all their threats, she thought as she watched the dirty gray water swirling at her feet. Then, out of nowhere, a camera flash replayed itself in her mind's eye, bringing with it a sudden realization. *That's why they took that picture. . . .*

Oh God. Meg threw her head back and let the water rain down against her shoulders. *They're sending someone that picture. Is it Gram . . . Cat?*

A sob broke from her throat as she envisioned the pain, the terror that photo would wreak.

Arizona, home, safety, felt as if they were a galaxy away.

"Okay, kiddies, time to put your rubber duckies to bed."

Frank loomed up behind Ty so quickly that Meg gasped. He peered at her with rapt interest, his gaze fixed on her body as he tapped Ty's shoulder. "The Director wants you on the phone ASAP. I'll tuck our little princess into bed — maybe if she's real lucky I'll even tell her a bedtime story."

Ty turned off the water. "Fun's over for now, baby. You be a good girl and I might let you take another shower tomorrow."

Then he was gone, leaving her alone in the cubicle with Frank.

Without the hot water running over her body, the air was startlingly cold. Meg shivered, crossing her arms desperately in front of her in a feeble attempt to cover herself.

"I need a towel," she managed between chattering teeth. "Please."

"I like the way you say please." Frank leaned back against the door frame.

She could see the struggle going on inside him,

67

lust warring against restraint.

Do they have orders not to rape me? Meg wondered with a faint dawning of hope. *If so, whose?*

"I'm freezing to death," she murmured. "A dead hostage won't be worth a damn to you or whoever the hell you're working for."

"Think you have things all figured out, don'tcha?" His beefy face twisted with irritation. "That big mouth of yours is what got you into trouble in the first place, princess. Maybe we oughta find something else for you to do with it."

He laughed a moment as Meg gazed at him in frozen fear. Then he reached into the cupboard behind him and grabbed a towel, dangling it just out of reach. "Say pretty please."

I hate you. If you were lying in a pool of your own slimy blood right now, I'd step on your fat ugly face.

But she forced out the words. "Pretty . . . please."

He laughed again and tossed the towel at her. "Since you asked so nicely . . ."

Bastard. Meg hid herself in the towel, welcoming the shred of modesty and the warmth it provided her.

He tugged her out of the shower stall, barely stepping aside so that their bodies touched as she passed. Without another word he dragged her back into the cabin and pushed her toward the bed.

Meg huddled on the edge of the mattress, feeling sick and weak and pitifully vulnerable as she clutched the towel to her. From the built-in chest of drawers, Frank pulled a purple-and-aqua nylon jogging outfit. "Ain't exactly Bloomingdale's, but it beats loafing around in your birthday suit. Not that I'd mind, but we've got orders to treat you nice."

"Whose orders?"

Frank fixed her with a stare as cold as death as she squirmed into the jogging suit beneath the cover of her towel. "You don't really want to know, do you, princess? They said you were smart. A Miss America with some brains as well as looks. Well, use your head."

Meg zipped up the neck of the jogging suit and lifted out the dreamcatcher charm, her fingers unconsciously circling the fetish. Her Hopi friend Cheveyo had given it to her when she was eight and having all those nightmares about her parents' deaths. Whether by magic or by psychology, it had banished the bad dreams and brought her comfort over the years. "I just want to know what's going on. I don't understand why you're doing this. Are you part of ORBA?"

He yanked her wrist back into the manacle clamped to the bed. "If you want to get out of this in one piece, babe, don't ask any questions. Don't make any waves. Do what you're told. If you keep your mouth shut, we just might let you go back to your nice little life when all this is over."

He stared into her widened eyes and let his breath out in a long whoosh. "You're really something, princess, you know that? If things were different . . ." He lifted the dreamcatcher from her neck and tugged, pulling her closer, reeling her in like a fish on a taut line. "Oh yeah, baby."

"Please. Don't break it."

He pulled it tighter.

Cold rage knotted her stomach. "Please," she grated out. "I've had this necklace since I was a little girl."

"What'll you give me if I let you keep it?"

"My autograph." Meg's teeth clenched, the muscles in her neck stiffening. "Now let *go.*"

He lowered the necklace with slow precision, deliberately letting the back of his hand stroke her breast as he set the fetish back in place.

"Keep your hands to yourself, you bastard." It burst from her before she could contain it. Her eyes flashed with a raw hatred that shook the air between them. "Or else I swear I'll kill you."

"With what, a squirt gun? Or you gonna try one of these on for size?" He opened his blue linen jacket and pulled a MAC-10 from his shoulder holster, leveling it at her forehead. "Still think these babies ought to be outlawed? Bet you'd trade your pretty little necklace for the chance to use this on me. Yeah, you holier-than-thou gun control freaks really slay me."

Meg's heart pounded in her ears as she stared down the barrel of the boxy assault pistol. *Stay calm. He's toying with you, trying to bait you. Don't let him. Don't look at the gun. Look at his face.*

"Let me guess," she heard herself say. "You want to be a policeman when you grow up. I'm sure you'll make your mother very proud."

The veins in his neck twitched. "You got a real attitude problem, you know that, princess?" He jammed the pistol back into the holster. "Well, somebody oughta teach you . . ."

"What's going on in here?" A man she'd never seen before filled the doorway. A humid breeze suddenly wafted into the room, carrying the faint tang of salt and seagulls. The man wore a short-sleeved navy shirt and pressed khaki trousers. His long black hair was slicked back into a ponytail, exaggerating the rough boniness of his long pock-marked face. From the way Frank froze at the sound of the man's voice and the beads of per-spiration that sprouted above his red eyebrows, she guessed this was the guy calling the shots.

"J.D., uh, I . . ."

A flicker of venom sparked in the other man's eyes, stopping Frank cold.

So his name is J.D. Meg gulped in this particle of information, studying every plane of his face, committing it all to memory. She prayed she'd live long enough to describe every one of these bastards to a police artist.

"Just trying to teach the lady some manners," Frank blurted. Trying to seem casual, he pulled a pack of cigarettes from his pants and shook one out.

J.D.'s voice cut like a whip. "We're having a meeting on the aft deck. *Now.*" He jerked his head toward the hallway, gave Meg one cold, dispassionate glance, and turned on his sandaled heel. He was gone with only a faint whiff of spicy cologne.

Frank threw her one last malevolent glance. "You heard the man. Later, princess." The door slammed shut behind him.

Meg huddled on the bed, staring in despair at each of the four brown paneled walls. Futilely she tugged at the manacle binding her wrist. *Think — you have to get yourself out of here. These boys are playing for keeps. They're up there right now, having a meeting, probably deciding what they're going to do with you.* A shudder spasmed through her. If things didn't go their way, she sensed they wouldn't hesitate to kill her.

Who the hell are they and what do they want? If only I knew.

The shower had revived her will to survive. She had so many dreams — law school, a career, meeting the right man, finally falling in love. There had to be some way out of this. *Think.*

Frank was right — she *was* smart. If there was a way to get out of this alive, she'd find it. Or die trying.

As Meg hoisted herself to a sitting position, she forced her brain to ignore the bruises tingling all over her body. She eyed the tray of cold, nauseating food. Reaching out her free hand, she swished away the fly.

"There isn't enough here for both of us, buddy. And much as I'd like to leave this muck for you, something tells me I'd better keep my strength up. So, *bon appétit.*"

Somehow, she forced down pizza that tasted like grilled cardboard and all of the rotting apple, refusing to think about the fly that had been squatting on it a few moments ago. She needed to stay strong and alert. She needed to rest, to eat, to prepare. She might have only one opportunity to escape, and she damned well better be ready for it. If she tried to get away and they caught her . . . Meg shivered. She didn't want to think about that.

She wanted to think about Cat and Gram and going to Harvard, about the whole beautiful life waiting for her back in the normal world where things like this didn't happen. Where the biggest challenge she would face was making the *Law Review* — not surviving a bunch of thugs with guns for brains, animals who'd just as soon kill her as look at her.

From this point on, she told herself, digging her nails into her palms, it's sink or swim. Think, wait, act.

Sounds like a plan to me.

7

"Christ, Jordan, you look like hell." Mike Bannister leaned his shoulder against the door frame and studied her in the dim hallway light outside his Brooklyn apartment. "I've seen corpses who look more alive."

"Terrific line, Mike. Get many dates with that one?"

"Don't get touchy on me, angel," he said, straightening. "I only meant the strain is showing. No word on Meg?"

"Nothing. And I've asked you not to call me that anymore."

That unreadable expression entered his eyes — the "cop" look, the one she had never been able to decipher. "So you did."

Jordan pushed past him into the apartment, flinching as her shoulder brushed against his biceps. *Idiot,* she chided herself, as she forged ahead into the cramped living room. *You've been divorced from the man for nearly two years — and still you sizzle at the merest touch of him. Grow up.*

Behind her, Mike closed the door and followed her into the room. If he felt any of the same heat she had, he gave no sign of it. "Have you spoken to Cat or Mrs. Hansen?"

"Briefly."

"Look, I know you must be worried sick about Meg, but you have to know none of this is your fault."

"I don't want to discuss it." Her voice was tired, curt. "Back off, Mike."

"What's eating you?" he asked mildly.

"You've got frosting on your chin."

"Book me. Guilty as charged." Mike swiped at his deeply tanned face and licked the frosting off his thumb. "But I'm not the only culprit. Lori's in the kitchen up to her elbows in chocolate. We made cupcakes — my grandmother's recipe. Want one?"

"Ice cream, cotton candy — *and* cupcakes all in one day, Mike? Terrific. Very smart. The poor kid will be on a sugar high for a month."

"Does that mean you *don't* want a cupcake, Jordan?"

His crinkly eyes laughed at her, daring her to laugh back. Instead, Jordan's already frayed temper began to snap.

Damn him. She wasn't up to coping with Mike tonight. She felt as if she'd just crawled out of a swamp, and he looked fit, calm, and irritatingly handsome in his worn Levi's and the open-necked navy shirt Lori had given him for Father's Day. When Lori had spotted it at Macy's, Jordan had at first resisted. Then she'd bought it anyway (blowing her budget in the bargain), knowing it would complement his swarthy good looks. And it did. Mike's silky dark hair shone nearly blue-black against the deep navy fabric and his steel blue eyes seemed to flash with an even darker intensity than usual.

At five feet eleven, Mike was a good four inches shorter than Alex Woods, but he had the sinewy physique of a dockworker, all iron toughness and bare-knuckled strength. Fine dark hairs curled along his taut forearms and chest. *Don't look at his chest,* Jordan warned herself and fixed her gaze resolutely on Mike's raised eyebrows.

"Dammit, Mike, I'm beat. I don't have time for these games, or to make inane chitchat with you — or to eat dessert." She stomped toward the kitchen, her pumps clacking on the linoleum as she swerved around his mountain bike which, typically, Mike had left parked against the scuffed living room wall. Grimacing, she sidestepped his dirt-encrusted Nikes and the ancient gym bag he'd managed to retrieve year after year from their Salvation Army donation. "I'd appreciate it if just one time, Lori was packed up and ready to go when I got here. *Just one time,*" she stormed, tripping over a paper bag bulging with empty soda bottles. "I still have a million things to do, and all I can think about right now is crawling into bed."

I could help you out with that, angel.

He didn't say it, but he might as well have.

Jordan stopped dead and looked back at him. There it was, in that slow, lazy, lopsided grin that had always made her heart turn over. She heard him think the words as clearly as if he'd spoken them aloud.

"Done that, been there," she said crisply, and plunged through the swinging kitchen door. Then she froze in her tracks.

The tiny room looked as if an earthquake had shaken loose every bowl and utensil from the chipped wood cabinet and had splatter-painted batter across every surface. Jordan didn't know whether to laugh or groan as she spotted Lori, speckled in chocolate, nibbling a smushed, half-eaten cupcake at the round Formica table. But it wasn't the knowledge that Lori's striped T-shirt would never come clean or that her yellow shorts looked like they'd been finger-painted with fudge that made Jordan stiffen, her body going as rigid as the wooden spoon propped in the mixing bowl.

It was the woman. The woman with the wide blue eyes and shiny auburn hair wisping free of her French braid. The woman with the tangerine tank dress skimming her slim figure and the silver hoop earrings dangling from her ears. The woman whose tanned, braceleted arm was wrapped around Lori's little shoulders.

"Hi, you must be Jordan. I'm Clancy Boynton." She grinned, wiping frosting from her hand before extending it to Jordan.

"Clancy works with Daddy at the police station, Mommy. She's funny. She can talk just like Donald Duck."

"My claim to fame. Wows 'em every time." Clancy laughed.

Jordan forced herself to smile as she shook Clancy Boynton's hand. "Looks like you've had quite a party."

"We sure did." Mike spoke behind her, so close she could feel his breath on her neck. "These ladies tried to teach me the fine points of cupcake decorating, but I'm an eater, not a froster."

Feeling stuffily overdressed in her tailored ivory business suit, and as awkward as she had at her first piano recital under the scrutiny of her mother's bridge club, Jordan walked toward Lori and tipped her chin up. "Somewhere under all that frosting I think I recognize my little girl," she said lightly.

Lori giggled. "Do we *have* to go now, Mommy?"

" 'Fraid so, sweetie. By the time we get home and find a parking spot it will be past this little cupcake's bedtime, and I still have lots of work to do tonight. Why don't we go into the bathroom and get you cleaned up?"

Clancy carried Lori's plate and empty milk glass to the sink and reached for the sponge. "I'll take care of KP duty," she volunteered. Her smile was easy and natural. "Bye, Lori. We'll try our luck at peanut butter cookies next time."

Jordan noticed how Clancy reached into the

cabinet under the sink for the dishpan and the Joy without missing a beat. *She sure knows her way around Mike's kitchen — and probably his bedroom, too,* Jordan thought, fighting against the ridiculous twinge of jealousy that sprouted like an unexpected weed in her carefully tilled garden. As she shepherded Lori through the hall toward the bathroom, she kept her face carefully schooled in a neutral expression, aware of Mike leaning against the wall, watching them. *What does he expect?* she asked herself in annoyance as she began to gently sponge Lori's face and hands and to blot up the T-shirt as best she could. *That I'm going to break down and cry because he's dating someone? What an ego.*

Suddenly Jordan just wanted to get home, away from Mike, from Clancy, from any thoughts of what they might do together in this apartment after she and Lori had gone. Intent on getting away as quickly as possible, she sent Lori scooting back into the living room to gather up her toys, but when she started to follow, Mike blocked her path.

"What's wrong, Jordan?"

"Not a thing."

He narrowed his eyes, scrutinizing her. "I know you better than that. Your eyebrows are steaming."

"Skip the third degree, Detective Bannister. I think you've been a cop too long."

"If it's Clancy, I just want you to know —"

She held up her hand. "Mike, I don't want to

know," she said quickly. "I don't want to know a single thing about you and Clancy. But there is something else you can tell me."

"What's that?"

She could hear Lori humming the *Sesame Street* theme song as she ran around the living room stuffing coloring books, crayons, and her Barbie doll into her Barbie tote bag. She also heard the clatter of dishes in the kitchen as Clancy Boynton cleaned up. "Did you enter Lori in a coloring contest?"

Mike frowned. "No. Why?"

Jordan's heart began to thump oddly beneath her linen suit jacket as she stared at him in dismay. "A man called my office today and told Alana that Lori won a coloring contest. He wanted her school address so he could deliver her prize — an art computer. I thought that maybe you . . ."

"No way." Mike's brows drew together, and the worry lines around his eyes seemed to deepen. "Did Alana get this guy's name or phone number?" he asked sharply.

"That's the weird part — when she asked, he hung up."

It was obvious Mike didn't like the sound of this. But she could tell by the tone of his voice that he was doing his best not to scare her.

"It's probably nothing, but I'll swing by in the morning and talk to Alana myself." He spoke casually. Too casually, Jordan realized, her stomach somersaulting with sudden apprehension.

"Could be some kind of a scam or some slick encyclopedia salesman with a backdoor pitch. I'll check it out."

She nodded, her throat dry. Their eyes met and held. Jordan knew they were both thinking the same thing. All the time Mike had worked undercover he'd lived with the fear that someone he had busted would try to exact revenge, revenge on his family. Time and again he'd coached her on safety precautions, warned her to be alert for anything unusual or off-key.

Mike reached out to take her hand, engulfing it for a moment in his own warm, strong one. For an instant Jordan's fingers curled instinctively around his. Then she caught herself and pulled away, fighting this absurd urge to lean against him, to rest her head on his chest and draw on some of his toughness, some of his strength.

"Don't sweat it, Jordan," Mike said quietly. "I'll check it out tomorrow."

She nodded wordlessly, studying his face. Suddenly Mike looked so tired, but a different kind of tired than he'd appeared in all those months toward the end of their marriage when he'd been drinking and working with manic zeal.

"How are things going for you?" she asked tautly, and with the words came a red-hot unbidden pang. *Listen to us,* she thought, a knot tightening in her chest. *We were so impossibly in love, and now we talk to each other like a couple of strangers. Even about Lori.*

But there's no going back, Jordan reminded herself sternly for the umpteenth time as Mike raked his knuckles through his hair and gave a slow sigh. Those last bleak months during the disintegration of their marriage had left permanent shadows darkening the spaces between them — deep, aching gulfs that could never be breached.

"I take it one day at a time, angel." The old endearment hung between them like a shattered wind chime before he went on. "One long, hard, sober day at a time."

She managed to smile. "I'm glad for you, Mike. You've got a life back." She heard Clancy warbling out "Sitting on the Dock of the Bay" over the clatter of dishes. Jordan turned away.

"Did I tell you my transfer came through?" Mike started after her along the corridor to the living room, where Lori sprawled in front of the TV watching *Full House.* "As of last week, I'm working bomb squad. No more undercover. Period."

"Congratulations. I hope it works out for you." For a brief moment, Jordan wondered how he would weather the change. His undercover work had consumed his life for the final years of their marriage. She'd never seen anyone as ferociously dedicated to a job as Mike Bannister had been. If he'd been half as dedicated to their life together as he'd been to infiltrating that seedy world of pushers and gun peddlers and pimps, they might still be sharing a bed, a home, and a future. But there was no point in dwelling on what had gone wrong. Jordan had learned a long time ago that when something wasn't working, you either fixed it or cut your losses, moved on, and never looked back.

"Time to hit the road, Lori. Give Daddy a kiss good-bye."

Fifteen minutes later, she and Lori were in her blue Honda heading toward Soho. A car in New York was a four-wheeled albatross, Jordan had discovered after reluctantly dipping into the trust fund her grandmother had left her to buy this secondhand heap. She'd hoped that having a set of wheels would make things easier and allow her to spend more time with Lori after the divorce, but most of the extra time was squandered hunting down parking spots. Struggling just to keep Lori in Keds and dance class, she couldn't justify spending five hundred dollars a month for a garage space, so every night she jockeyed back and forth outside her building looking for a well-lighted spot out of the path of the garbage trucks.

Jordan threaded through traffic on autopilot, so bone-tired that at first she didn't notice the dented green Escort trailing several cars behind them. Sometime while Lori was chattering on about the zebras and monkeys she'd seen at the zoo, Jordan became aware that every time she changed lanes, the Escort followed. Turning left, she peered in her mirror. He was still there.

You're being paranoid, she told herself, her palms damp on the steering wheel. *Meg's kidnapping is affecting your reason. Why would anyone be following you?*

Why would anyone say that Lori had won a coloring contest?

As she approached the next intersection, Jordan checked the side mirror and made a sudden lane change, slipping between a mail truck and a bus. Quickly she yanked the steering wheel into a right turn, her heart pounding. The Escort sped on.

Ciao, baby, she thought on a thin note of triumph.

She knew she was letting nerves, exhaustion, and a stupid phone call play havoc with her common sense, but she couldn't help glancing over her shoulder as she locked the car and hurried toward the front stoop with Lori. The smell of cooked cabbage and cumin greeted them, drifting from Mrs. Patel's open window. It was a comforting smell, a familiar smell. They were home.

She was halfway up the stone steps when she spotted the Escort.

It eased down the cross street, the driver a nondescript blur. As Jordan held her breath, it slowed down for a split second, then accelerated out of view.

She called Mike the second they walked in the door.

"A green Escort? Slow down, Jordan — run through this again. Did you get the license number?" Mike demanded.

Her eyes followed Lori as she threw her Barbie tote bag on the sofa and skipped off to her room. "I couldn't read it. I wasn't even positive he was following me until he circled by the apartment."

Mike spoke calmly. "Keep all your doors and windows locked, and I'll see if a patrol car can cruise by periodically and keep a lookout. Do you want me to come over?"

"No. No. I'm fine. We're fine. Mike, do you think this is someone who's after you?"

She could picture him grimacing, narrowing his eyes. "I'm damned well going to find out."

Jordan curled into the wicker chair facing the window and drew her knees up beneath her white silk robe. She took another sip of Chablis. Before her, moonlight flickered across the small terrace with its potted ferns and begonias, dappling the old bricks with random patches of brightness.

What's wrong with me? It's four A.M. If I don't get some sleep I'll never make it through the day. And none of this is helping Meg.

But neither the wine nor the humid summer breeze ruffling through her hair, carrying with it the scent of rain, could help lull her toward sleep.

It was on a night like this that I met Mike.

Twenty-two, fresh out of Bryn Mawr, and on her own in the city for only three months, working as a junior copywriter for J. Walter Thompson, Jordan had made dinner plans with her college friend, Leigh Bryant. Arriving first at Delaney's, Jordan had edged her way through the noisy throng of young uptown executives and managed to claim a seat at the gleaming brass-and-mahogany bar. She positioned herself with a view of the door, ordered Chardonnay, and tried to ignore the hunger pangs growling in her stomach.

Fifteen minutes later, with no sign of Leigh, the slick joker who'd propped himself on the stool next to hers began making a damned nuisance of himself.

First he tried to buy her a drink, and when she refused, he dragged his stool closer so that his knees bumped hers. He leaned in so close she nearly choked on his Christian Dior cologne as he nudged her arm and informed her conspiratorily that he liked women who played hard to get.

"I'm meeting someone," Jordan answered, shooting him the look she'd seen her mother give cloying boutique salesclerks.

"Lucky for me," he said with a wink, " 'someone' must be late."

The man had blond hair, parted on the side and blow-dried to perfection. Jordan could picture him spending hours before the mirror, adjusting the perfect knot in his Hugo Boss tie, repeatedly practicing that smirk.

She ignored him and took another sip of wine. As she sensed that he was continuing to stare at her, a tightness knotted in her neck. *Leave me alone,* she thought, unconsciously drumming her fingers on the bar. *I've had my fill of creeps who don't understand what "no" means.*

Where was Leigh? They were going to lose their reservation if she didn't get here soon.

"I'm Sean Hamilton." He downed his second

Manhattan and leaned over. "Much as I hate to state the obvious, it seems you've been stood up."

Jordan pretended not to hear, glancing deliberately past him toward the door.

"Bartender," he called, flipping a ten-dollar bill onto the bar. "I'll have another Manhattan and the lady will have . . . whatever she wants."

"The lady *wants* you to leave her alone," Jordan retorted.

Sean Hamilton's close-set brown eyes twinkled with confidence as he reached across the bowl of salted peanuts and covered her hand with his long fingers.

"Come on, babe. Relax. I don't bite."

Jordan jerked her hand away. "Look, pal," she said furiously, jumping off the stool. "You're not getting the message." Her voice shook. "I'm not interested in having a drink with you, and I'm not in the market to be picked up. So just leave me alone."

"Hey, whoa. You got the wrong idea, babe. I'm not some pencil pusher trying to get you in the sack. I'm your brass ring. I happen to be one of the top financial analysts on Wall Street. When I talk, people listen, you know what I mean?"

"Well, listen to this. Leave — me — alone."

"You heard the lady."

They both turned toward the voice that was as low and rough as fine-grained sandpaper. Sean's glossy image faded into dim soft focus as Jordan stared into the gunmetal-blue eyes of the brawny man standing behind them.

"I thought you'd never get here. What tied you up?" Some devil prompted the words from her mouth, allying her instantly with this black-haired stranger, whose features were more sexily rugged than polished, whose five o'clock shadow accented his strong jaw and the slender cleft in his chin. He answered without missing a beat.

"It's a long story. I'll explain over dinner." An edge rippled beneath the glance he shot Sean Hamilton's way, a cool, hard edge that made Jordan's spine tingle. And made Sean Hamilton hastily slide off his stool.

"Uh, no offense meant, pal. Just keeping the lady company," he muttered. Without a backward glance he slithered past a group of Asian businessmen and out the door.

Meeting the stranger's eyes, Jordan burst out laughing. "Thank you for coming to my rescue."

"All in a day's work." He flipped a black leather case from his sport coat's breast pocket, and Jordan's eyes widened at the sight of the NYPD badge and ID card.

"Officer Mike Bannister," she read aloud, and then smiled. "My knight in shining armor."

"Off duty. Can I buy you a drink?"

"No." She shook her head slowly, finding herself lost in the electric intensity of those magnetic blue eyes. "I'm buying you one. It's the least I can do."

And somehow, when the page came a few minutes later and Leigh apologized on the phone that her business meeting had gone terribly awry and she wouldn't be able to get away for dinner after all, Jordan wasn't the least bit disappointed to leave Delaney's with Mike Bannister. It was a soft, lovely night and they walked easily together as the hazy darkness drifted down around them, stopping at a flower vendor where Mike bought her a single peony, and then continuing to a little French restaurant on West 55th called La Bonne Soupe. There, over fresh salad, tomato bisque, and crusty baguettes, they talked for the next three hours in the little dining room upstairs. By the time Mike took her home, she was more than halfway in love with him. She knew all about his married sister in the Bronx and his parents in West Orange. She knew he'd bypassed law school to become a cop after his kid brother died of a drug overdose.

Something about Mike Bannister made her feel safe, and it wasn't just because he was a cop. His candid no-bullshit attitude and the surprising gentleness she saw in his eyes drew her to him, making her feel closer to him than she'd felt to any man. And later that night when Mike kissed her as they stood on the crumbling cement stoop of her dingy little walk-up, she felt a pure, radiating heat that lingered long after she'd gone to bed.

He'd called her at seven-thirty the next morning to make a breakfast date.

With a sigh, Jordan drained the last of her wine. Who would have thought that two people once so connected would end up in separate apartments, with separate lives, held together only by the tiny daughter they both loved?

Wearily she padded across the living room, straightening the afghan heaped across the back of the apricot wicker sofa, then stooping to retrieve a stray crayon that had rolled under the heavy-leafed dieffenbachia. For a moment in the dimness she paused, staring around the little two-bedroom apartment she and Lori had moved into after the divorce. How far she had come since that first cockroach infested walk-up she and Mike had filled with her sparse apartment furnishings, the heirloom Hepplewhite bedroom set that had been a reluctant wedding gift from her parents, assorted plants and books, and Mike's prized movie poster collection.

And how much she had lost.

Lori cried out as Jordan passed her room, and Jordan froze, then pushed open the partially closed door. The night-light cast a pale ivory glow on the eyelet-trimmed comforter. Jordan frowned as she saw that Lori was so twisted up in the sheet that her head was sticking out of one end while a tiny foot poked out of the other.

She's warm, Jordan thought in dismay as she pressed her cheek to Lori's burning forehead. Carefully she unwrapped the sleeping child from her cocoon of blankets and straightened her sweat-damp pink nightie.

How could anyone be so little, so fragile, so sweetly beautiful it made your heart ache just to look at her? Jordan wanted to catch the little girl up in her arms and keep her close and safe forever. Instead she rinsed a washcloth in cool water and gently stroked it across Lori's forehead and cheeks. Lori whimpered in her sleep and opened her eyes.

"Mommy."

"Yes, sweetie, I'm right here."

"My tummy hurts."

"Try to sleep. I'll sit with you until it feels better."

Lori snuffled once and then squirmed onto her side.

Baby, don't be sick, Jordan prayed silently, holding the hot, moist little hand in her own cool one. *Please, not now.*

8

"One Rolex watch, silver-and-gold stretch band. One diamond-and-onyx ring. Black Christian Dior sunglasses. Set of five keys, brass lion's head key ring with a pair of emerald eyes. Gray eelskin billfold, five hundred and fifty dollars in large bills, Visa gold card . . ."

The exit warden's voice droned on as he emptied the manila envelope and, item by item, checked off the contents against his list.

Clearly bored, the prisoner stood with his hands behind his back, rocking on his heels.

"Sign on the dotted line and you're out of here, tough guy."

Russell Sima snatched away the pen, scrawled his name across the yellow prison form, and tossed the Paper Mate back at the warden, forcing him to fling up an arm to catch it.

Screw this bullshit Mickey Mouse routine. All he wanted was a bottle of Chianti, a pepperoni pizza, and an hour to get laid by a beautiful woman, in that order.

"You miss one appointment with your parole

officer, Sima, and we'll be only too glad to haul your ass back in here," the warden barked after him as he sauntered toward the glass doors.

Sima slipped on his sunglasses and kept walking, ignoring the warden and the husky black guard beside him. When he reached the automatic doors, the slender mustachioed man paused only long enough for the guard to activate the control switch; then he strode through alone, squinting out at the bright August sunlight.

The black BMW was waiting in the visitors' parking lot. Leonard leaned across the front seat and opened the passenger door.

"Welcome home, Mr. Sima. You're looking good, real good."

"Let's get the fuck outta here."

Half an hour later, Russell Sima was escorted by a smiling maître d' to his old table at Ernesto's. While Leonard poured Chianti into two tall wineglasses, Sima took his first bite in five years of Mama Ernesto's garlic bread.

"Ah, I've dreamed about this bread. Five fucking years I dreamed about this bread. You got the picture of the kid, Leonard?"

"Yeah, Mario got it. And he got the whole lowdown on Bannister's ex-wife, just like you wanted. No sweat. But, Mr. Sima — and forgive me for second-guessing you — can I say something here?"

"Certainly, Leonard. Speak." Sima was in a benevolent mood. Even Leonard's gutteral rasp sounded like Pavarotti compared to the relentless whine of his cellmate. Chianti slid down Sima's throat like nectar.

Leonard leaned forward across the checkered tablecloth and lowered his voice. "Are you sure this is the way you want to go with this thing? I mean, revenge and all. Sure it feels good for the moment, but it can lead to all kinds of unnecessary trouble. Who needs it?"

"I need it." Sima ripped another chunk of bread from the loaf and contemplated it. "That shit Bannister did something no one's ever done. He sent me away. Stole five years of my life. You think I'm gonna let him get away with it? Eat something, Leonard, I don't like dining alone."

"Sure, Mr. Sima, sure." Leonard swiped his bread stick through the scoop of butter. He crunched his teeth into it, spraying sesame seeds as he spoke. "But — and you'll pardon me for saying this — you just got out. You're about to diversify. And I'm certain your new associates would prefer you keep your nose clean for a while. . . ."

"Leonard." The menace in the soft voice hung over the table like a cloud of poison gas. "Don't talk with your mouth full."

"Sorry . . ."

"And another thing I want you to remember. I pay my lawyer to think for me. You — I pay to act. *Capisce?*"

"Absolutely. Only a suggestion. Forget it, forget it. . . . More wine, Mr. Sima? Waiter, can't

94

you see Mr. Sima wants another bottle of Chianti? Pronto!"

As the waiter uncorked another raffia-wrapped bottle, Sima rattled off the order — minestrone, Mama Rosa's lasagna, beef *braciole,* a large pepperoni pizza, and two cannoli.

"Leonard," Sima said, when the waiter had scurried into the kitchen, "let me see the picture."

A good-looking kid, he thought, as he studied the dark-haired little girl sailing down a park slide to her mother's arms. *You can definitely see she takes after the broad.* The child's pigtails streamed behind her, and she was wearing a pink-and-yellow bathing suit that showed her little round tummy. She was laughing, her mouth wide open.

That schmuck Mike Bannister doesn't deserve such a sweet-looking little bambina. And he won't have her for long, Sima thought with malicious satisfaction.

Carefully tucking the photograph into his eelskin billfold, he inhaled the delectable aroma of tomato sauce and garlic as the steaming bowl of minestrone was set before him. He was good, that Bannister, very, very good. He'd fooled Russell Sima, no small feat. Sima'd had no inkling that the tough young street thug he knew as Bruno, the guy he'd planned to put in charge of the warehouse district, was a fucking undercover cop. Not until Bannister practically had the cuffs on him. Even then, he almost couldn't believe it. He'd have bet a kilo of his best stuff it was some kind of practical joke.

Ah, Bruno, you were slick. But Sima's better. And Sima always has the last word.

Bella vita. Life was good, he thought as he spooned parmesan over his soup. And when he brought Mike Bannister, that son of a bitch, to his knees, it would be even better.

"*Mangia,* Leonard. Eat." He smiled expansively, gesturing with his spoon. "Don't let your soup get cold."

Mike forked the lukewarm Szechuan chicken straight from the cardboard take-out box into his mouth, his gaze fixed on the computer printout before him. The list contained the names of every drug dealer and sex offender he'd busted undercover. Mike scanned the pages, heedless of the din in the station house.

"Hey, got another fork?" Clancy Boynton perched herself on the edge of his desk and leaned over the carton, helping herself to a chunk of spicy chicken. "Never mind, we'll pretend it's finger food." She laughed, craning her neck to peer at the printout before him. "Whose ass are you after now?"

"Just running down a list of creeps."

"Need any help?"

"Only with the almond cookies. Have one."

Clancy took them both, ignoring Mike's raised eyebrows. "Can I help it if I have a sweet tooth?" She grinned, then jumped off the desk, backing just out of his reach. "I'll pay you back tomorrow night after the movie. Only my dessert won't have any calories." She was gone with her flashing smile before he could swallow his mouthful of fried rice.

One thing about Clancy Boynton — Mike never knew what she was going to say next. He liked that, and he liked Clancy. She was a good cop, and a good friend. And she wasn't too bad in bed, either.

But she wasn't Jordan.

Mike picked up a yellow highlighter and tossed the half-empty food carton in the metal trash can beside his desk. He wished he could stop thinking about that damned phone call. But ever since Jordan had told him about the phony coloring contest, he'd had a strange feeling in his gut.

Who made that call? And what the hell was behind it? And did he really think he might find the answers somewhere in this printout?

He reached inside the desk drawer and pulled out the bronze-framed photo of Lori and Jordan that he kept next to the procedures manual. All of the other guys in the station house who were divorced kept only pictures of their kids around. But Mike had never seemed able to get rid of this picture — it was of Jordan and Lori at Lori's second birthday party, their heads tilted together, party hats slanted across their foreheads.

No one had better try to hurt them — either one of them.

He picked up the printout again, just as the chief bellowed out his name.

"Bannister, we got a bomb threat over at Union

Station. A white male handcuffed to his briefcase has locked himself to the turnstiles. SWAT Team's on its way. You and McDougal get your butts over there."

Mike let the printout drop back amid the pile of papers, folders, and files. Shit. Tonight he'd planned to start checking out which of these assholes had been recently paroled. He ran this check several times a year — it made him sleep better at night knowing who was in and who was out. But especially now, after that phone call about Lori, he needed to know. . . .

It would have to wait. Everything would have to wait.

As he passed Clancy's desk, he snatched the last almond cookie from her fingers while she was talking on the phone. He was already out the door, McDougal at his heels, before she could say a word.

But as Mike slid behind the wheel of the police car, the grin faded from his face. It was one thing stealing a cookie from right under Clancy Boynton's pretty little nose. It was another trying to get the bite on the bad guys.

Especially when they wanted to bite first.

9

Cat let the sheer white curtain fall back into place and turned away from the pandemonium outside Gram's living room window. The throng of reporters had burgeoned in the past few hours, milling on the parched lawn, trampling the cactus beds, clamoring for a statement. The fervor was fueled by the same grim news that Gram had imparted to Cat when she arrived yesterday morning.

A van that may have been used to smuggle Meg out of Atlanta had been found abandoned outside of Savannah.

"The FBI has impounded it and they're running the usual tests," Gram had told her in the kitchen, squeezing Cat's clammy hand between both of her thin, blue-veined ones. "There was blood on the floor."

Meg's blood? Cat had blinked hard to erase the crimson stain spreading through her mind's eye.

Even now, hours later, shock still numbed her. As Cat moved like a sleepwalker through the living room, she found little comfort in the familiar beloved furnishings of the home where she'd grown up. Still less in the fact that it had been three hours and Vince hadn't yet returned her transatlantic call.

"If you don't stop looking so morbid, I'm going to get Reverend Beck over here to give you a sermon on faith." Gram's familiar vanilla scent accompanied her into the rose-papered living room. She carried two steaming mugs of strong creamed coffee.

"That would be one way to get some sleep," Cat shot back as Gram set the mugs on the square, walnut-veneered coffee table. "I can't help it, Gram. I'd give anything if Meg would waltz through that door, plop down on the sofa, and ask what we've whipped up for dinner."

"And that's exactly what she'll do soon enough. We *will* have her back."

Jeanne Hansen stared determinedly at her granddaughter through the wisps of thick iron gray hair that had escaped from her ponytail to trail around her weary face. At nearly seventy-five, she was still a beautiful, active woman. Though the blush she usually wore had faded from her high cheekbones and the fine crow's feet around her eyes dug deeper than usual, she still possessed a timeless elegance, with her piercing ice blue eyes and fine-boned features. The body encased in baggy blue jeans and a thin white cotton sweater was as trim and graceful as a dancer's, toned by daily walks with Mrs. Ingersoll down the street.

Her students at Arizona State, where she had taught French lit as an adjunct professor for the past fifteen years, called her *le petit Napoléon* behind her back because of her exacting standards and four-page reading list. But every one of them lived for the hope that she would invite them to help her whip up one of her famous French dinners, where she was known to delegate tasks around her kitchen like a ship's captain, directing the chosen few as they whisked egg whites, chopped scallions, and sautéed mushrooms in wine sauce. In symphony, those students would serve up a five-star feast and then Jeanne Hansen would challenge them, as they lingered over brandy and brie, to her own Francophile version of Trivial Pursuit, all while her Elvis Presley records played on the stereo.

Cat sank alongside her on the blue-and-gold flowered chintz sofa, her hair swinging forward across her cheeks. "Why don't they at least call?"

Gram's mouth thinned. "They will."

Above them, in Meg's old bedroom, they could hear FBI Special Agent Philip Evans fiddling with the electronic monitoring equipment he and Agent Varga had ordered. Special Agent in Charge Joseph Varga, who in just a day had become like part of the furniture, was on a conference call in the den with Jordan Davis and the pageant officials.

"Vince hasn't even called," Cat muttered, running a hand through her hair.

Jeanne, who'd glimpsed her eldest granddaughter's tears yesterday after she'd hung up with Vince, said nothing.

Staring at her coffee mug, Cat tried to ignore the queasiness rolling through her. She and Vince had spoken for less than ten minutes. She'd begged him to let his assistants put the finishing touches on the movie, to fly overnight to the States and lend her some desperately needed moral support. It wasn't his refusal that cut her to the quick so much as the way he'd refused. His reaction was annoyed, abrupt, as if her request was totally off the wall, unthinkable, out of bounds.

She looked up to find Gram staring at her. "You'd never say it in a million years, but I know you're thinking the same thing I am, Gram. I seem to have an uncanny knack for picking men who aren't there for me in a crunch."

"Maybe it's just that you haven't met the man who's quite as strong as you are, Catriana, as steadfast, sweet, and loving as you deserve."

"So you think Vince isn't right for me?"

"It's not what I think, Catriana. It's what you think."

A silence fell between them like the settling of a thick snow over a gnarled road, a silence broken only by the intermittent sound of Varga's now familiar voice. Gram reached into the pocket of her baggy jeans and pulled out her antique tortoiseshell cigarette case.

She's started smoking again. Cat groaned inwardly as Jeanne fished out a cigarette and lit it.

So that whiff of cigarette smoke I've been picking up on hasn't come from the FBI agents after all.

After trying to quit a dozen times in half as many years, Jeanne had flushed all of her cigarettes down the toilet on Valentine's Day, betting Meg one hundred dollars that she'd never light up again. That she'd come this far was a record — she'd never lasted more than two weeks before.

"Gram, I wish you wouldn't," Cat murmured in soft dismay as Jeanne took a deep drag.

"When Meg comes home I'll fork over my hundred dollars and start over. I promise, Catriana."

As Gram finished her cigarette, Varga strode into the room.

"Nothing new, ladies. Sorry. While we're waiting, I have a few more questions. . . ."

Varga was a soft-spoken bulldog of a man whose craggy face generally showed less emotion than Mount Rushmore. He'd already conducted a two-hour interview with them yesterday. Now, directing his penetrating black squint at them, he grilled them further and in detail about Meg's friends, enemies, her boyfriends, competitors, swimming coaches, neighbors, classmates, professors. Was there someone who had a grudge against Meg, someone who was jealous or who stood to gain by her abduction? What had been her recent mental state, had she hinted at anything that might have been off-kilter, was she concerned for her safety?

"Concerned for her safety?" Cat exploded,

thumping her mug down on the coffee table. "Of course she's been concerned for her safety! The Organization for the Right to Bear Arms sent her death threats for the better part of a year, its president went to jail because of them, and fifteen thousand of its members are up in arms — no pun intended — and you ask if she was concerned for her safety?"

"Mr. Varga," interjected Jeanne, ever the diplomat, with forced calm, "I assume you're questioning Jared Cavenaugh."

"Yes."

"And whoever's running the show at ORBA while he's in prison?"

"That would be Charles Latham." Varga paused, flipping his notebook back several pages. "Seems Mr. Latham's vacationing in Mexico. We're in contact with the authorities down there and are in the process of locating him."

Cat leaned forward. "Do you think that this whole thing is a plan to trade Meg for Cavenaugh — to try to get him released from prison?"

A shutter clamped down over the agent's face. "Let's not get ahead of ourselves, Miss Hansen," he said. "We don't know for certain yet that ORBA is responsible for the kidnapping. Right now they're certainly at the top of our list, but we need to explore every possible suspect."

Cat started as the doorbell chimed. Looking toward the window, she saw the postman outlined through the curtains. "I'll get it," Evans said quickly, bounding down the stairs.

They all clustered in the entry hall, staring at the familiar white Tyvek envelope with the red-and-blue markings, labeled PRIORITY MAIL, UNITED STATES POSTAL SERVICE.

It wasn't a bomb, but it might as well have been. Nothing could have prepared them for the photograph that Evans's cotton-gloved fingers pulled out.

"Oh, my God. *No.*" Gram swayed and Varga grabbed her by the elbows. Scowling, he eased her into the bentwood rocking chair beside the fireplace.

"Easy, Mrs. Hansen. Let's have a look at it."

Though Gram's cheeks were as white as bleached rock, Cat couldn't even move toward her. She was rooted to the spot, staring transfixed at the picture Evans held by its lower edges.

It was Meg. But Meg as they'd never seen her before — as they never could have imagined. Cold horror froze Cat's bones as the FBI agent angled the photo to deflect the glare of daylight flooding through the windows.

Meg was shackled to a chair, wearing only her bra and panties — and her dreamcatcher neck-lace. A purple bruise marred the left side of her face from her eye to her chin, and her usually lustrous hair hung limp and stringy across her sunken cheeks.

It was her eyes, glazed and brimming with ter-ror, that filled Cat with unspeakable horror.

"What have they done to her . . . ?" Gram whispered brokenly. She covered her face with her hands. "Why would they hurt my sweet little Meg . . . ?"

"Try not to overreact, Mrs. Hansen." Evans carefully set the photograph on the dining room table. "Remember, their intent is to frighten you."

But as Cat moved toward her, she saw the agents exchange glances.

"I'll call Washington," Varga said.

Cat sank to her knees beside the rocker, wordlessly hugging her grandmother's bony shoulders as Varga picked up the phone.

Take that, you bastards. And that.

The jarring report of the gun roared in her ears, despite the wax earplugs meant to shield them. A painful jolt thrummed through her shoulder, energizing her and sending adrenaline ricocheting through her veins with the icy thrill of a speeding luge.

Cat shoved in a new cartridge, narrowed her eyes, and fired again.

And again.

Her arm ached, her hands were numb, but she didn't care. As each bullet found its mark, raw energy coursed through her fingers, willing them to pull the trigger until yet another clip was emptied.

When it was, Cat stared at the cardboard target, sucking slow, ragged breaths into her lungs. Dark holes gaped from where the chest had been. Her barrage of bullets had repeatedly ripped right through the heart.

"Those sons of bitches who've got your sister better pray the cops frisk your ass before their trial. Unless Meg's already kicked their asses clear up their throats." With a mournful, but half-admiring smile, Lee Wister stuck a pack of Marlboros into his shirt pocket. Cat lowered the gun.

She turned to the stocky, denim-garbed attendant, sweat filming her upper lip. "Damn straight, Lee." Cat handed him the SIG Sauer. "That felt good. This little baby is almost as comfortable as my own."

"You've got a real steady hand there, Cat. Know what? If you ever get sick of taking pictures of all them fancy movie stars, you could get a job training other women how to handle these babies."

Cat slid off her safety glasses and with the sleeve of her khaki T-shirt wiped the sweat from her eyelids. She felt drained and exhausted but strangely calm. Funny how a few hours of target practice could make her feel in control again. But as she scanned the nearly empty shooting range, where only one other person tested his skill, her sense of empowerment began to dissipate. The real, cold, cruel world was still here, and Meg was still missing, her fate unknown. A sense of her own helplessness flooded back.

Driving home, Cat punched the radio buttons in rotation, seeking news. There was nothing she hadn't heard dozens of times before. Frustration

ticked inside her. With a lemon sun blazing overhead, she pulled onto Gram's dusty street, its
lawns studded with clumps of saguaro cacti. She
passed sun-bleached adobe homes, kids playing
soccer, and a bumper-to-bumper chain of TV
news vans lining the curb.

The hairs on her neck prickled like the tiny
spines of the saguaro. Something had happened.
She knew it.

Her tires spewed gravel as they squealed up the
drive. *Get out of my way, you damned vultures,* she
silently screamed as she bolted through the
crowd. When she burst through the kitchen door,
Gram, Varga, and Evans were huddled around
the table.

"Cat, they called the pageant," Gram blurted
out. "They said Meg's alive. . . ."

"Is she all right?"

"As far as we know." Varga's tone was mad-
deningly unemotional. "They wouldn't let anyone speak with her."

Cat glanced frantically from his stoic face to
her grandmother's stricken one, then studied
Evans's thoughtful expression as he toyed with a
pencil.

"Okay, give me the bad news," she said quickly.
"What do they want?"

"Want? Oh, not much." Evans cleared his
throat. "Only the repeal of the Brady and Ungar
Gun Control Laws, an hour's worth of airtime
on the Miss America Pageant to refute your sister's gun-control platform, and Jared Cave-

108

naugh's immediate release from prison."

Cat took a step backward, her brain reeling in shock. Everything in the room seemed to pull away, then rush back toward her. It took a moment for the impact of Evans's words to register, for the momentous repercussions to sink in — for the white-hot anger to ignite inside her. "So it *is* ORBA," she said in a flat, hard tone.

"Maybe. They're calling themselves Operation Wake Up America. Could be a militia group. Or someone else with a similar agenda — we can't make assumptions yet, Miss Hansen. The caller's voice was electronically disguised. He referred to himself as the Director." Evans's lip curled and he tossed the pencil on the table, then met her gaze squarely. "But if I were a betting man, I'd put my money on Charlie Latham."

"What happens now?" Gram asked, struggling to speak with her usual self-control. Cat noticed the pile of cigarette butts in the ceramic cactus ashtray she'd last seen buried under the extra pillows in the linen closet.

Varga answered her. "At this point, Mrs. Hansen, Washington takes over. The White House and Attorney General Kendrick will be calling the shots."

The White House. Cat was having trouble taking it all in. She concentrated on the one thing that seemed most important. "Did they trace the call?"

"Not enough time. The Director circumvented the caller ID system and got off the line in twenty-eight seconds, long before the tracer could pinpoint him," Evans explained.

Cat threw her purse on the counter, trying to think clearly. She met Gram's overbright blue eyes. "Are you okay?"

"Yes. I suppose. At least we've finally heard something."

As Cat slipped into the chair beside her, a sudden thought struck. "How do we know the call was for real?"

Varga cleared his throat. "That's something we need your help with. It might be a bit upsetting, but we need you to verify something. They asked the caller for some kind of proof, something no one else would likely know, in order to ascertain that they were actually dealing with the kidnappers." His dark eyes were as opaquely blank as a cleanly washed blackboard. "They said . . . Well, there's no delicate way to put this. Does Meg have a scar on her right breast?"

Jeanne Hansen clenched her eyes tightly shut. Cat felt a sickening lurch of fear.

"Yes, a small one." Jeanne's voice was barely audible. "She had a cyst — it was nothing — oh my God."

Cat's scalp tightened with rage. Damn them, damn them to hell. She picked up Evans's pencil and stared at the sharpened point. "So what happens next?"

"We stall them while we keep searching for her. And we wait for the Director to call back." Varga pulled a single cigarette from his pocket and stuck it, unlit, between his full lips.

Cat's muscles went slack. All of the energy that had infused her after target practice seeped out of her like the last drops of water from a canteen. She stared hopelessly at the phone.

Ring, damn you, ring.

Two more days of deafening silence crawled by with no word from the kidnappers. Cat and Gram paced the varnished floors, picked at their food, tossed in their beds, and waited and prayed. Jordan called twice each day, as anxious and tense as they were. She kept blaming herself, wishing she'd never started consulting with the Miss America Organization, wishing she hadn't then urged Meg to go the pageant route for scholarship money. No matter how many times they assured her it wasn't her fault, she was inconsolable.

A steady stream of friends brought meals, hugs, and words of hope, battling their way through the media encampment settled on the trampled lawn like a horde of prospectors all panning the same creek bed for gold.

The tension in the house was as thick as rawhide.

At eleven o'clock Thursday morning while Gram was picking up her mail at the university, Vince called.

"Sorry it took me so long to get back to you, Cat, but things have been crazy around here. I bet they are around there, too."

"You could say that."

111

"Any news other than what's on TV?"

Sitting in the bentwood rocker, Cat stared at two bronze framed photographs of Meg set between Gram's collection of Native American kachina dolls on the middle shelf of the bookcase. "Vince, let's dispense with the sudden concern," she said carefully. "If you really gave a damn, you'd have called me back before now."

There was a strained silence. "Look, Cat, I only have a few minutes. Do you really want to waste it arguing?"

"What's the big hurry? Where are you off to?"

Again that strange hesitation. "Glasgow. Cerise has a renovated castle there complete with a fifty-seat screening room, and since the final cut's ready to show to the studio brass, she wants to take the weekend to screen it for them and talk about the marketing plans."

Cat's throat tightened. She blinked back the sting of hot tears. Cerise Hutton, the hot female director of the moment, was an intense redhead whose earthy vocabulary and voracious sexual appetite were well known. How convenient of her to have her own castle.

"Sounds charming."

"Cat, don't be this way. My career is riding on the success of this film, and it's not as if I could do one damned thing to help your sister even if I *did* fly over."

Her voice emerged in a fragile quiver. "I'm the one who needs help."

His exasperated sigh seemed to hiss through

the phone lines. "Hell, what do you want me to do?"

He might as well have slapped her. Cat forced herself to speak in a low, flat tone that hid the pain twisting through her. "Nothing, Vince," she said coolly. "Absolutely nothing."

Cat punched the volume button on the CD remote and leaned against the headboard of her bed. She hugged her eyelet lace pillow, stretching her neck from side to side, willing the lilting strains of Kenny G's saxophone to relax the corded muscles along her shoulders.

"Catriana, are you sleeping? May I come in?" Gram opened the door a crack and Cat jolted upright. The music had masked the sounds of Gram's Jeep pulling into the driveway. "You'll never guess what I found waiting in my E-mail." Jeanne's thin cheeks were flushed with excitement as she stepped into the small, sunny yellow bedroom and closed the door. "A message from Jack Galt."

"From Washington? Does he have news about Meg?" Cat clicked the volume down on the CD player as her grandmother sat beside her on the bed.

Gram kept her voice low. "Jack has two close contacts inside the agency and he was able to learn some interesting things. He wrote the whole message in our old code," she added. "Lucky for him I haven't gone senile and forgotten it." Her lips compressed with satisfaction. "But you hit it exactly right, Catriana — ORBA *is* the prime suspect."

"I knew it! Who else . . ."

"As a matter of fact, there's a short list of perhaps five other groups or individuals who can't yet be ruled out."

"Why hasn't the FBI told us anything about all this?" Cat leaped off the bed and began stalking back and forth on the braided rug. "They know we're starving for news — why are they keeping us in the dark?"

"They'll only tell us what they want us to know, and when they want us to know it."

"Gram, I'm sick of being so helpless. I feel like a goddamn marionette."

"Calm down, Catriana. There's not a thing we can do. Except be patient and let the professionals find Meg."

"I'm fresh out of patience. I have to do something or I'm going to lose my mind!"

Jeanne gave her an appraising glance, her eyes narrowing. "Maybe it's time we cut those marionette strings," she said thoughtfully.

Cat went still, recognizing the signs of a plan jelling in her grandmother's shrewd brain.

"There's no doubt in my mind that Jack has more information than he was willing to divulge to me, code or no code. Why don't you fly to Washington and see what you can find out from him?"

Cat caught her breath. "Do you think he'll talk to me?"

"*Make* him talk to you." Gram stared fiercely into her eyes. "Jack might even have an inkling who this 'Director' is. Believe me, his people will have answers to questions Varga, Evans, and the rest of them haven't even thought of yet. Go get those answers."

Fifteen minutes later, Cat was packed and on her way out the door to a waiting taxi. She paused in front of the living room bookcase and stared at the two photographs of Meg, one showing her in front of the YMCA pool as a young girl of seven, the other taken on the steps of the library at Arizona State the day before Meg's college graduation.

"Don't worry," Cat whispered as the cab driver leaned on his horn. "You're going to be okay, even if I have to find you and bring you back myself."

10

Washington, D.C.

Cat hadn't seen a picture of Jack Galt since the last photo his wife had sent of the two of them the Christmas before she died, but Cat would have recognized him even in a crowd. He had arrived first at the Lincoln Memorial and was waiting for her on the steps just as they had arranged. With his shock of dark hair, randomly shot through with coarse silvery strands, and his trim wiry build, Jack Galt didn't look anywhere close to his seventy-five years. His brown eyes were deep-set and piercing, and he moved with the athletic grace of a man who still played racquetball every morning.

So this was Grandpa Skip's buddy, the man who'd worked with him in military intelligence during the war, the man who'd always claimed that if he'd met Jeanne Hansen first, he'd have married the daring young Frenchwoman whose exploits in the underground rivaled any bravery on the battlefield. Cat tried to imagine him as her grandfather, but she could summon up only a mental picture of Jack Galt as a thin young lieutenant on whose shoulders rested the fates of forty-six French Resistance fighters. She could see him now in the fuzzy picture Gram kept on her nightstand, arm in arm with Grandpa Skip — Gram in long dark braids beside them hoisting a bottle of wine to celebrate the end of the war.

When Jack kissed her cheek, she felt as if she were greeting an old friend. He smelled of lime aftershave and was comfortably dressed in beige twill slacks and a crisp navy blazer. He asked after Gram and thankfully skirted over all the other niceties to get right down to business.

"I know you want everything I've got about your sister's kidnapping," he told her as they trudged up the wide stairs toward the towering statue of Lincoln. A feeble breeze wisped Cat's bangs back from her forehead. Even at nine A.M. the humid Washington heat was a killer. "So here's what I can tell you so far. The White House has people working around the clock on this case, and Kendricks has made sure it remains top priority. You have to understand that everything that can be done is being done."

Cat dodged a noisy procession of grade-schoolers trooping down the staircase with their teachers. "What about Latham? Have they found him yet?"

"Yes. The FBI has had legal attachés questioning him at our embassy in Mexico, but he's got a solid gold alibi. He's been down in Ixtapa for the past two weeks. . . ."

"Which doesn't mean he didn't hire someone," Cat interrupted.

Jack Galt nodded and stopped to face her. "That hasn't been ruled out. Neither has it been established."

"What are you telling me, Mr. Galt?" She met his gaze square on, trying to control the stinging frustration that always seemed to bob close to the surface these days. "I know there's a theory floating around. Be straight with me. Who else would have a motive?"

"Any number of factions. In addition to ORBA there's the Citizens for a Free Society, the Patriots of the Second Amendment, munitions manufacturers and importers, neo-Nazis, and survivalist groups — you name it, the list goes on and on."

Cat's voice was low. "But you told Gram they have a short list."

Galt thrust his hands deep into his pants pockets and stared out toward the reflecting pool. "They do. And they're following up on it. But you have to leave this to the professionals, Cat," he added, turning back to her. His brown eyes were somber. "We're dealing with some very dangerous people. Big-time people. So, it's absolutely imperative to let the big guns handle it. No pun intended."

Cat said nothing until they reached the top of the memorial and stood in the shadow of the huge marble statue. "I promised Gram I'd get some solid information. No offense, Mr. Galt, but right now I don't know anything we didn't know before. You can't expect me to go home to her empty-handed."

A hint of a smile tugged at Galt's thin mouth. "You look so much like Jeanne right now, it's uncanny. In fact, if memory serves me, the first time I met her was in Paris on a hot cloudy day just like this. She was crouched in the back of a stolen ambulance, disguised as a nurse." His eyes took on a faraway expression. "We were trying to evacuate a few key people and the odds against us were momentous. But your grandmother wouldn't give up. We made it through, due to her tenacity."

"She told me about that day. And about the time she saved your life," Cat said evenly, her green eyes flashing into his.

Galt stared back, unflinching, and Cat realized that if she'd expected to throw this professional intelligence officer off balance, she'd misjudged. He'd undoubtedly faced down much tougher opponents than she would ever be. But she had to play all her cards, every single one that would help her get the information she needed.

"Yes, your grandmother saved my life, at the risk of her own. And now I'm doing all I can to assist those trying to save your sister."

"Not good enough, Mr. Galt." Somehow, Cat found the courage to challenge him. "Gram sent me here for answers, and if you don't give them to me, you're letting her down, not just me. For starters, there must be some speculation as to the identity of this 'Director.' "

He gave her a rueful smile. "You don't pull any punches, do you? Young lady, that's the Skip Hansen in you coming out. I never met anyone as plainspoken as him, nor as loyal. Look, Cat." He put a hand on her shoulder. "Do you think I want to see you in the same jeopardy as your sister? Even if I gave you this information . . . what good would it do you?"

"I'd know who we were up against. Maybe it would give me a better idea what to expect."

Jack Galt studied her long and hard, his mouth a grim line. "I shouldn't do this; it's against all my professional judgment, all my instincts. But you're right," he said quietly. "I do owe Jeanne, and I suppose it wouldn't hurt for you to know exactly who we're focusing on."

Cat's pulse quickened as he pulled a notepad and a black Mont Blanc pen from his breast pocket and began to scribble.

All around her tourists were milling, gazing up at Lincoln seated majestically on his marble pedestal or consulting tour books and wandering among the Greek columns. The sun glared down between thin clouds in a sky as blue as old Delft, but all Cat saw was Jack Galt's precise black writing crawling across the page. . . .

He handed her the paper in silence. Cat stared hungrily at the four entries:

Ryan Industries
Talon International
Christopher Hemmings (founder — Patriots of the
Second Amendment)
Ivan Guenther, (president, Desert Scorpions —
survivalists)

Cat looked up at him. "Thank you."

"It's too early to be certain that it's someone on that list, but along with ORBA, all of them have the means and the motive to pull off something of this magnitude. Trouble is, there are at least a dozen others who could be right up there with them, and any one of them could be the Director."

"How long will it take to zero in on one of them?" she asked.

"There are parallel investigations going on twenty-four hours a day. Every lead is run down until it's exhausted."

"Sounds to me like these people can use all the help they can get."

They had started walking toward the steps, but Jack reached out and took Cat's arm, forcing her to face him. His face was as stern as Lincoln's. "Don't get any ideas, Cat. Don't make me regret that I told you any of this."

She gave him her most reassuring smile. "There's nothing to worry about, Mr. Galt. I won't do anything stupid. I'm just going to make a few phone calls. You see, I have a few connections at the magazine who might . . ."

"*No*. Don't, Cat. Promise me."

"I can't." For a moment there was taut silence. Each stared the other down. And then Galt took the paper back from her hand. Cat thought he was going to tear it up, but instead he began to write once more and then capped his pen and thrust the paper back at her.

"Look," he said grimly. "Instead of sticking your nose into this, why don't you contact someone who's already done the legwork? This individual is one of the best operatives I've ever encountered. Call this number, leave your name, and use 'Scrabble' as your password."

"Scrabble? You've got to be kidding." It sounded unreal, like something out of a James Bond movie.

Jack Galt shook his head. "Scrabble. Don't forget."

"Is he with the CIA?" Cat asked, gripping the paper tightly between her fingers. "Or the FBI?"

Galt pursed his lips. "I can't tell you who he works for. I can't even tell you his real name. As it is, he's going to be mad as hell that I gave you his code name and this number, but . . ." The ghost of a smile flickered across Galt's face. "Let's just say, he owes *me* a favor."

Slowly, Cat nodded. She stared at the name Jack had written, then looked into his eyes. "Thank you. From me — and from Gram. I hope" — her voice faltered — "I hope you'll be coming to Gram's birthday party. To celebrate with me and with Gram — and with Meg."

"I hope so too, Cat," he said, taking her hand. "With all my heart." She heard the unspoken emotion warming his voice. "You're staying at the Mayflower? Fine. I'll reach you there if anything else comes up."

"So in the meantime I just sit and wait for this guy to return my call?"

"That's my advice, but I can't guarantee he'll get back to you at all. He may not even be in the country right now. But if he does contact you, ask him your questions and take whatever he'll give you. And then go home to Jeanne."

Gratitude welled up in her as they said their good-byes. She watched as he descended the staircase and disappppeared among the tourists and ice cream vendors milling along the Mall. Cat lingered, staring out at the glassy waters of the Potomac.

Sit tight, be a good girl, mind your manners, don't make waves.

Cat peered down at the scrap of paper again, pondering the last name Jack had written across the very bottom of the page.

Dagger.

She didn't know whether to laugh or cry. What the hell kind of name was that?

By the next evening Cat realized she was no good at waiting. Here she was in the shadow of every major agency involved in finding her sister, and she was no closer to learning a damn thing than when she'd been cooped up back in Arizona.

All of Washington beckoned to her in the lights outside her hotel window, and she was prisoner to a telephone that hadn't rung.

She'd spoken briefly to Gram and to Jordan and had picked at some fruit and tuna salad from room service. Her eyes were bleary from poring over the tiny print in the phone book, searching to match the prefix from Dagger's phone number with one of the government bureaus or intelligence agencies listed. No such luck. When her gaze fell across a heading for the Department of Commerce, something had clicked. *I'll bet with a phone call or two I can find out who's on the board of directors of Talon International and Ryan Industries.* Her fingers itched to make the call. *But on the other hand, if Dagger can't get through, he might never call back. . . .*

In the end, she decided to give him until the end of the day. Who knew what time zone he might be in? *By tomorrow morning, though,* Cat decided, pacing until she wore a track into the carpet, *I'm calling the Department of Commerce's Corporate Divison and finding out who sits on the boards of Ryan Industries and Talon International.*

After three more cups of coffee, Cat tossed the phone book off the bed and threw herself down on the paisley print comforter to practice her waiting technique. The television droned monotonously from its armoire, in sync with the vacuum cleaner whirring down the hall.

If I hear CNN's Headline News *echo one more time that authorities still have no lead on Meg's whereabouts, I'm going to throw this coffee carafe at the screen.* Cat drained the dregs from her cup and began pacing once more from window to door to closet with ever increasing tension. It would take only a phone call to request the adjoining suite she'd been offered at check-in — more room to pace. She wondered if it was still available. Maybe tomorrow, if it turned out she needed to stay in Washington for a few more days.

As if by mental power alone she could force Dagger to call, Cat stared at the telephone on the nightstand beside the king-size bed. She felt as if every muscle in her body were coiled as tightly as the phone's spiral cord. "Call, damn you."

By eleven o'clock, she couldn't stand waiting any longer. Cat grabbed up the receiver and punched in Dagger's number again. With frustration knotting inside her stomach, she listened to the same recording as before, a woman's cool, pleasant voice asking her to leave a message after the beep. "This is Catriana Hansen again." It was an effort to keep the impatience out of her voice. "I'm at the Mayflower Hotel. Please call me back as soon as possible. I'm in dire need of a Scrabble partner."

She felt like an idiot as she left her number once more and slammed down the receiver.

"Scrabble. Shmabble. Tomorrow morning I'm calling the magazine and asking Simon to check out what we've got on Christopher Hemmings and Ivan Guenther. *Celebrity* must have files on these jokers. And then I'll go down to the Department of Commerce and wade through every damn record they have."

By the time the quartz crystals on the little bedside clock flicked toward midnight, exhaustion was getting the better of her. She slipped out of her clothes and took a quick cool shower in an effort to stave off sleep, leaving the bathroom door ajar so she could listen for the phone. But even the shower didn't revive her.

Too tired to dry her hair, Cat made a quick check of the room, double locked the doors, and grabbed the canister of Mace she kept in her purse. Her eyes were already drifting closed as she shoved the canister under her pillows and pulled the cool cotton sheet up over her naked body.

She crashed into oblivion and knew nothing more until she sensed the shadow standing over her. She swam up from sleep, dragging her eyes open, and saw the dark male figure beside her bed. Adrenaline punched through her stomach, and without thinking, she grabbed the Mace and sprang up with it in one fluid movement. But the man seized her wrist in a manacle grip. With a motion even faster and more agile than her own — and far stronger — he pinned her down against the pillows and tossed the Mace aside.

His voice was as low and menacing as the wind that rises before a storm. "I don't think so."

11

Dan Rather's somber face stared out from the forty-foot TV screen in the entertainment room of the Preston family's Palm Beach estate.

"We've just received word that one half hour ago a bomb threat was issued by the group claiming responsibility for the kidnapping of Margaret Hansen, the reigning Miss America."

Corey toyed with the square cut emerald ring on his finger, leaning forward on the ivory damask sofa with a slight smile as the newscast continued.

"In a letter sent by facsimile to the *New York Times*, the self-proclaimed director of Operation Wake Up America issued a rambling pro-gun statement and demanded that the *Times* run that statement in its entirety on tomorrow's front page. If not, Operation Wake Up America has threatened to begin systematically blowing up American national monuments. . . ."

The girl wandered in from the sauna, naked except for the thick black towel wrapped around her hair.

"Corey," she cooed, "I'm getting bored. Let's play."

"Not now."

"But Corey . . ."

"I said *not now.*"

He punched up the volume on the remote, his cold tawny eyes never leaving the wide-screen TV suspended from the ceiling.

"The letter also reiterates the group's previous demands for the repeal of the Brady and Ungar Laws and the immediate release of ORBA president Jared Cavenaugh from prison. If these demands are not met, the kidnappers insist they will kill Margaret Hansen, who has campaigned vociferously in favor of gun control legislation. The FBI has determined that the facsimile originated in San Francisco. We now switch live to the White House, where Press Secretary Howard Donavan is releasing a statement. . . ."

The girl swept the towel from her hair and bent at the waist to fluff the mane of long black tendrils that had so intrigued him last night in the Coco Palms Bar and Grill. Her nubile breasts dangled and bobbed as she put on a show of drying her tresses, but his eyes never glanced her way.

She threw herself down beside him on the ivory damask sofa and gazed around the cavernous sunken family room of the Palm Beach house he had led her into sometime after four in the morning.

They'd swum under the waterfall, shared some joints in the lush garden whirlpool, surrounded by bougainvillea and rustling palm trees, and sometime around dawn they'd made love on the mahogany wet bar in the teak library.

They'd done it again in his massive mirrored bedroom, which was twice the size of her apartment in Fort Lauderdale — a bedroom dominated by the enormous plate glass display case housing his gun collection — a collection she'd told him reminded her of something belonging to a museum.

She reached for the tulip-shaped crystal bowl glistening with cocaine and fashioned two neat lines on the black marble coffee table. Noisily, she snorted one up each nostril. Beside her, Corey switched over to CNN.

"Turn that off, will ya? Who gives a shit about all this Miss America crap?" she exclaimed, laughing, reaching for his crotch. "Corey . . ."

He shoved her hand away. "Shut the fuck up!"

She sighed, and rubbed a long, sleek finger into the fine powdery residue. Slowly, a smile broke across her baby-doll face.

"Here, sweetie, have a taste," she invited, snuggling close to his bare dark-tanned chest and nestling her finger between his lips.

This time he stood up, reached down to grasp her by the arms, and hurled her across the room.

"Dolph!" He barked into the intercom on the coffee table.

The blond bodyguard appeared at once through the French doors that opened onto the pool terrace. He ignored the wails of the naked girl sprawled amid the scattered dirt, broken pottery, and uprooted philodendrons flanking the fireplace.

"Take the bitch home. She's overstayed her welcome."

Within moments Corey had quiet in the house again — quiet but for the CNN update live from the White House.

"Security has been beefed up at the Capitol and around other national monuments in response to this latest threat. . . ."

Half an hour later, Corey flicked off the television. He'd heard all he needed. As he passed through the state-of-the-art weight room and hurried up the stairs toward his private wing, his mind was a whir of schedules and decisions.

"They can beef up security all they want," he scoffed, his long bare feet padding across the thick moss green carpet in his bedroom. "They'll never find the little firecracker that Méndez cooked up for them."

He ignored the tangle of cinnamon-colored silk sheets he and the girl had left trailing off the king-size bed as he walked toward the fireplace. Warm sunlight bounced off the mirrored ceiling and glittered on the ancient Celtic warrior shield mounted over the green marble hearth, illuminating the ornate scrollwork carved into the metal.

Corey reached up and slid the heavy shield to one side, and instantly the fireplace wall swung silently away from him. As he stepped into the halogen-lighted office, he pressed a wall switch, and behind him the fireplace wall glided back into place.

With pride he stared around the low-ceilinged windowless room with its wraparound laminate bookcases, surveying the volumes on guerrilla warfare, hunting, and weaponry. The lower shelves were neatly crammed with frayed issues of *Soldier of Fortune* magazine, the upper with exotic potted plants, several of which were poisonous. A fourteenth-century Chinese painting of a feudal battlefield hung over the green marble desk where his computer was set up. Beside it was his trophy, glittering on a blue velvet pillow. He paid no attention to the paper spewing continuously from the fax machine as he pressed a button and the computer sprang to life.

A surge of almost sexual excitement coursed through him. He was in his element here, more so than anywhere else except perhaps the jungles of the Congo. This was his domain, his fortress, the core of his secret empire. From here he could spring like a lion, without bloodying his paws.

It had originally been a safe room, one of two built into the house to his father's specifications — insurance, his father had always said, against kidnappers who'd preyed on corporate moguls and their families during the seventies. Corey had ordered the whole thing redone six months after his father's fatal heart attack last year while his mother was consoling herself on the French Riviera with the emir of Kuwait's second cousin.

The guy had obviously done a good job drying her tears, since aside from a few postcards, a teary phone call at Christmas catching Corey at his villa in Corfu, and a flood of American Express bills Corey sent on to the accountant, he'd heard nary a word from her. She'd given no hint that she was ready to return to the States, not even for the upcoming season in Palm Beach.

Which was all well and good, Corey thought as the computer screen flashed his greeting of choice, an ancient Chinese military principle: THE SUPREME ART OF WAR IS TO SUBDUE THE ENEMY WITHOUT FIGHTING.

Scanning through the directory, he found and unlocked the Latham file. His fingers flicked deliberately across the keyboard.

Oh, Charlie. You poor dumbass bastard. The things you've been doing.

When he was finished, Corey spun the leather swivel chair toward the desk phone and punched in a series of buttons. As he expected, the line was still untapped. Clear sailing. He entered another series of numbers and smiled while he waited for the voice on the other end of the line.

"This is the Director." Corey spoke with the clipped, terse authority of a field commander. Or the CEO of a *Fortune* 500 company. *I can wield more power by crooking a finger than James and Uncle Kent can piece together with their whole fucking board of directors,* he thought with satisfaction. He picked up his trophy — the sparkling tiara belonging to Miss America.

"Good work, E-Sector. I'm pleased. Tell Méndez to put C-Sector on alert — they'll know what to do next."

12

The reverberations in the media following Meg Hansen's kidnapping were mind-boggling, even to a seasoned publicist like Jordan, who was at the epicenter of it all. When the kidnappers sent copies of their photo of Meg to the media, all hell broke loose.

On Thursday *Prime Time Live* aired a special on terrorism hitting home in America, *Hard Copy* was leading off with a different aspect of the story each night, and Meg's battered face on the cover of *Time* peered out from every newsstand in the country, while the *Globe* and the *National Enquirer* seemed to be vying with each other over which one could scream out more macabre Miss America speculation than the other.

It was the story of the moment. But the moment was becoming an eternity, an agonizing eternity of headlines and speculation, of waiting and uncertainty.

As Jordan conferred in her office with Sheila and Alana, a notepad before her, she wondered how long things could continue at this level of unrelenting tension, and if the terrorists would make good on any of their threats now that the *New York Times* had refused to capitulate to their demands.

Meg, what are they doing to you? I can't take much more of this.

She'd been devastated by the kidnap photo, trying to reconcile the buoyant athletic friend she'd met at the Spinning Circle Dude Ranch with this grim, frightened prisoner. She'd wept for an hour after seeing it for the first time.

And now, as if it wasn't difficult enough dealing with the life-and-death terror surrounding Meg's kidnapping and all its repercussions, there was another problem. By the time she'd left for work this morning, the fever Lori had started running last night had spiked and her stomachache had worsened.

She'd told Mrs. Chalmers to give Lori Children's Tylenol every four hours and see if she could squeeze in an appointment at the pediatrician's — and to call if the fever didn't go down by this afternoon.

"My head is splitting." Sheila moaned as she leaned back in her chair. "Anyone have some Motrin?"

Jordan reached into her top desk drawer and tossed her a half-empty bottle of pills. "Help yourself. I don't think a whole bottle could put a dent in mine." She scowled down at her notepad, none too happy with the latest situation confronting her. "Sponsor or no sponsor, Hy Berinhard is a royal pain in the ass." Frowning, she twisted a strand of shoulder-length dark hair between her fingers. "And I'm damned if I'm going to let him use this tragedy to his own ends."

"If that man had his way, we'd have Geraldo doing a live hookup with the kidnappers during the middle of the pageant," Sheila mumbled, popping three Motrin into her mouth and swallowing without any water.

Alana shook her head. "Does he really want to leak a statement to the press implying that the pageant might actually comply with the kidnapper's demands for airtime?"

"Unfortunately, yes." Jordan's scowl deepened. "Even though the government's made it clear that they want us to refuse any and all demands. He thinks the ratings will soar through the roof if the public thinks something might happen on air. More viewers, more shoe sales."

Hy Berinhard, owner and CEO of Hi-Way Athletic Shoes, had made billions in the footwear industry since 1981. As the pageant's leading sponsor, he'd monopolized the two-hour meeting this morning, making it clear he intended to milk the situation for all it was worth.

"The man sees everything as a business opportunity," Sheila muttered, rubbing her temples. "The question is, how are we going to handle this? He *is* our biggest sponsor."

Sitting at the massive burled wood conference table this morning with the other sponsors and pageant officials, Jordan had listened, appalled that any rational person would advocate playing with someone's life. Even when the pageant officials had made it clear that they would comply with the government's antiterrorism policy, Berinhard had continued to argue.

"There has to be a way to handle Berinhard," she muttered. "Let me think it through while you . . ."

Before Jordan could finish her sentence, Alex Woods rapped on the open office door.

"There's a rumor going around that you've been holed up here all day and haven't yet had lunch."

Jordan managed a smile and leaned back in her peach swivel chair. "What's lunch?"

"If you'll give me half an hour, I'll remind you."

Alex's handsome, bemused expression and the low growling in her empty stomach made the decision easy. "You've got a deal. We were just wrapping up here anyway — and I think right now I'd kill for a pastrami sandwich." She groaned, pushing to her feet.

Alex was pacing in front of the elevators and talking rapidly into his cellular phone by the time Jordan had grabbed her purse from the drawer and shot off a few last-minute directives to Alana. "Our half hour started five seconds ago," she told him apologetically as he folded and pocketed the phone. "I have a meeting at four."

"Anyone I know?"

"Special Agent Jeff Cooper of the FBI — ever met him?"

Alex hit the lobby button and backed her into the corner of the elevator, grinning as he bent to kiss her. "No. Should I be jealous?"

"Absolutely." Jordan closed her eyes as their lips met briefly. As always, Alex's lips felt cool and inviting. She leaned against him, the fresh spicy scent of his Drakkar Noir cologne filling her nostrils.

Then her eyes flew open as the elevator doors slid apart, and, chuckling, Alex led her into the hubbub of the lobby.

The pungent scents of corned beef, sour pickles, mustard, and fresh hot bialys assaulted them as they pushed open the door of Sol's Deli. The smell of food triggered such intense hunger pangs in Jordan that by the time the waitress brought her an enormous mound of shaved pastrami layered between two thick hand-cut slices of rye bread, she could only stare at Alex in gratitude.

"Thanks, you're a lifesaver." She took a long gulp of iced tea. "Do you know that I had lunch in that booth over there with Meg and Cat only a few months ago? I told you Cat's a photographer — she works for *Celebrity* and was here covering the Dustin Hoffman movie shoot in Central Park. That family's going through hell right now."

"So are you. Now that I've put food in front of you, what else can I do?"

"Find Meg. Arrest the kidnappers. Cancel the pageant. Cure Lori's stomachache, and ship Hy

Berinhard out on the next space shuttle."

"That's all?"

"And then you can take me and Lori to Tahiti for a month."

She took another sip of iced tea, then grinned at him as she set the glass down. "No, make that two months."

Alex leaned forward, his gold cuff links glinting in rich contrast to the chipped Formica tabletop. "Just as soon as this is over, I'll clear my calendar. We'll head for Tahiti, or Bora Bora or wherever you want to go. But . . ."

Jordan stopped with her sandwich in midair, fearing what was coming next. "But you won't want to take Lori out of school," Alex said. "So maybe you should put Mrs. Chalmers on standby."

Jordan set her sandwich back on her plate. "Forget it, Alex. It was just a fantasy. I won't have any vacation time until next spring, but . . ."

"But what?" Alex reached across the table and took her hand. "Why do you have that hurt look in your eyes?"

Because you never want to include Lori in anything, Jordan thought, caught between irritation, anger, and sadness. Alex was always sweet to Lori, but he kept his distance. He brought her little presents now and then, but he never once got down on the floor and played with her, never wanted to take her to the park on a Sunday afternoon or just go out, the three of them, for pizza. "I wish you wanted to get to know Lori

139

better," she said carefully, studying his face. "She won't bite. I promise."

"Don't be silly, Jordan." Alex signaled for the check, trying to appear nonchalant, but Jordan heard the defensiveness in his voice. "I think Lori's a great kid. But you have to understand — Susan and I never had any children. I'm not even an uncle." He gave a rueful laugh. "Somehow I just can't see myself hanging out at McDonald's on Saturday nights." He shook his head, as if the very idea were ridiculous. Then his eyes sobered, fixing her with the earnest expression that made him so accessible to executives and mail room clerks alike. "It's obviously something I need to work on. If it makes you happy, Jordan, I'll try."

"It would make me happy — happier than a trip to Tahiti or anything else." Her hazel eyes clouded as she leaned forward in the booth. Somehow, she needed to make him understand. "You know that my relationship with my parents hit rock bottom when I was in college, and we've never been able to heal the rift. My brother is much older and since he's been in Seattle, his life revolves around his family and his law firm. Really, Alex, Lori's all I've got."

"Wrong, Jordan." Alex reached across the table to cup her chin. "You've got me."

His smile was so engaging, so contrite that an answering smile tugged reluctantly at her stiff lips. "This has been the most sane, most normal moment I've had in days, and I thank you for it. But if I don't get back to the office, the chaos will be beyond belief and I won't get to see Lori again tonight before she goes to sleep. And she wasn't feeling well this morning, so . . . ."

"Hey, Pop, didja hear? They found Miss America!"

Jordan's head came up as the deli owner's son, Max, barged out of the kitchen with a tray of fresh potato salad. Sol looked up from the cash register, his hands frozen on the keys.

"They let her go?"

"No — the cops found a body. It's on all the stations. They think it's her, but they're checking dental records. . . ."

Oh God. They did it, they really did it. She never had a chance. Jordan's stomach lurched. She slid out of the booth in one motion and jumped to her feet. "Alex, they're insane." Her voice was a horrified whisper. She saw her own shock mirrored in the grimness of his face.

"That they are. Come on, we've got to get back. . . ."

He thrust a twenty-dollar bill at Sol as they ran out the door. "Our newsroom must be going crazy," he told her, and held her tightly for a moment as passersby dodged around them on the street. "I'll call you as soon as the rubble's cleared. Let's hope it's a mistake, but if you hear anything in the meantime, call me and make sure Helen puts you right through."

Jordan didn't stop running until she reached the tall mirrored elevators in her building. The eighteenth floor was in an uproar. She blinked as

141

people shouted the news to her, but she didn't stop for anyone as she dashed straight for the conference room. It was already packed with silent people huddled tightly around the wide-screen TV.

This is a nightmare, she thought, beyond tears as she watched reporters shout questions to a Coast Guard official in Miami.

"We have nothing further to release to you at this time," the blond, stiff-jawed official said. "All I can confirm is that the body of a young Caucasian woman fitting the description of Margaret Hansen was retrieved by the Coast Guard several miles off the southern tip of Florida this morning at 9:57 A.M. It appears the young woman had been in the water for several days. The coroner's office is now examining the body in an attempt to make a positive identification. . . ."

Jordan grasped the back of a conference room chair as the floor seemed to drop out from under her. *Oh, please, don't let it be her.*

She felt exactly as she had when her parents took her to Disneyland for her eighth birthday and she'd ridden a roller coaster for the first time. She'd hated it. Just when she'd thought she'd finished the worst plunge imaginable, another stomach-lurching one loomed right ahead.

Now she was too old to scream and too unnerved to close her eyes against the overwhelming terror. She had no choice but to hang on tight and ride this one out — and pray that the whole damn roller coaster didn't crash.

142

13

Washington, D.C.

Terror pounded through Cat as she stared through the dimness, straining to see the face of the man who held her completely powerless. She tried to scream, but the only sound that came out was a strangled sob, and before she could try again, strong fingers dug into her cheekbones and against her lips to silence her.

"If you make a sound, you'll regret it. I don't want to hurt you, but I damn well will if I have to."

There was no doubt he meant it. Even through the darkness, broken only by a wedge of light from the slightly cracked bathroom door, Cat could see the determination in his face. It was a dark, cynical face glaring out from beneath a shock of straight black hair that nearly brushed his shirt collar. Handsome in a mean way, she thought, her heart contracting with fear. His eyes glinted into hers with such steely coldness that an involuntary chill skittered down to her toes.

143

Everything told her it would do no good to fight. Not against this man. Not this time. So much for the Mace.

She went slack and still, except for her ragged breathing. His fingers pressed against her face with a force that seemed easily capable of breaking her bones. But even through the pain radiating toward her scalp, she forced herself not to struggle, not wanting to give him any excuse to hurt her.

She saw the bastard smile.

"Good girl." The voice was cool, curt, and satisfied. He released his killer grip on her mouth but still held her pinned down on the bed.

The sheet had slipped, revealing one breast, but there wasn't a damned thing she could do about it. "Who the hell are you?" she managed to croak, feeling hideously vulnerable in her nakedness.

"Who do you think?"

Frustration railed through her, and Cat tried frantically to tug the sheet up, but he wouldn't let it budge. "What is this . . . twenty questions?" she gasped.

"No. An entirely different game. I thought you were searching for a Scrabble partner."

Dagger. Cat's eyes narrowed to furious green slits. "Jack Galt gave me your number, you fool. We're on the same side. Let me go *right now* or I'll report you to . . . to . . ."

"Exactly."

"The CIA." Cat bit out between clenched teeth.

Dagger tightened his grip on her.

"The FBI." She wriggled furiously.

To her horror, he swung a leg across her body and knelt astride her on the bed, and she felt the sheet slip even lower.

"The White House, you cretin!"

This time he put a hand to her throat, his elbow resting on her breast. "You don't know who the hell I answer to, Ms. Hansen, and I intend to keep it that way. Maybe you should quit while you're ahead."

Cat swallowed, trying to calm her thudding heart. She didn't know if she was more angry, more humiliated, or more scared. *This bastard is trying to scare me*, she suddenly realized. And with the knowledge, some of her fear drained away, leaving more space for the anger.

Whatever he has in mind, it isn't rape or murder. At least I don't think it is. Then what the hell does he think he's doing?

As she scowled into Dagger's hard-planed face, she suddenly sensed that this man had his own agenda — and whatever game he was playing, he would see it through.

"I've never played Scrabble in the nude before," she ventured, moistening her lips. "And I hate strip poker. Do you mind if I get dressed?"

Something flickered behind those cold eyes. Amusement perhaps? Approval? As suddenly as he had swooped down on her, he let her go. Cat yanked the sheets up to her chin the moment he hoisted himself from the bed. Warily, her eyes followed his tall form as he picked up her can of Mace, pocketed it, and then turned to flick on the bedside lamp.

"You've got two minutes. Get dressed."

Cat bristled. Who died and made him commandant of the world? But she was so grateful for the chance to cover herself, she swallowed back a retort and grabbed up her apricot cotton sweater from her duffel bag.

I despise him. I despise everything about him, she fumed, throwing on the sweater and tugging up her jeans. And although he stared out the window all the while, ostensibly giving her privacy, she was positive he knew every damn thing going on in the room.

Even if I had my gun here, I wouldn't have a chance to use it. If I tried to pull it on him now, he'd be on me in a flash. Her animosity deepened as she zipped her jeans and glared at his profile. She'd always hated ultrahandsome men. Their looks seemed to go hand in hand with an air of conceit and a shallow self-absorption. She'd observed it with wry amusement from behind the lens of her camera, wondering how certain movie stars and politicians might have turned out had Mother Nature been less generous with their physical attributes. Yet this man, this Dagger, was very different.

Oh, he was handsome all right, with his mop of dark hair, lean muscularity, and aura of cool menace. But he was a far cry from a pretty boy, his features more blunt than sculpted, more rough than slick. She sensed from the easy way he stood, feet planted apart, gazing out the window, that his looks didn't mean anything to him. In his black T-shirt and jeans, his hands thrust into his pockets, he was all dark, smooth energy and rangy strength. Yet despite the cool veneer, he seemed to radiate a restless heat, like a steel piston pulsing out the fiery heartbeat of the city below. A man of quickness, intelligence, and strength. A man to be reckoned with.

Jack Galt said he was the best. Through her outrage, Cat felt a lick of excitement. Dagger was *here.* He was going to help her. She didn't have to like him, she told herself, yanking at the laces of her espadrilles. She just had to take what he could give her — use him and his information and be done.

But as he turned back to stare at her from the window, the expression in those cobalt eyes sent uneasiness prickling through her. *Don't take him too lightly. Don't underestimate him. He won't like being used.*

"Do I call you Dagger, or *Mister* Dagger?"

"Don't call me anything. Don't call me, period. You've already called once too often."

"So that's what pissed you off." Cat squared her shoulders and glowered right back at him. "It's your own fault. You never got back to me. So how was I to know you got my message? Jack Galt didn't even know if you were in the country!"

"I am and I would have. But I don't like your

147

style, Ms. Hansen. And what's more, I don't like your playing junior detective. You don't know what the hell you're doing or the kind of people you're up against."

"I have a pretty good idea." Cat stuck out her chin, her hands splayed on her hips. "Try ORBA or Talon International. Or how about Ryan Industries, Christopher Hemmings and his Patriots of the Second Amendment, or Ivan Guenther's Desert Scorpions. Shall I go on?"

He reached her in two swift steps, frowning down at her, his face dark with anger. "Jack Galt talks too much."

"I never said he was the one who told me." Cat's eyes blazed defiance. "I'm quite resourceful — and fully capable of ferreting out information for myself."

"And fully capable of getting yourself killed — possibly your sister as well."

From outside came the wail of a siren. Cat felt a hot flush creep into her cheeks. "Don't bet on it, Dagger. I intend to be very careful."

He leaned closer, seizing her arm in an iron grip that made her gasp. "If you're so careful, then tell me how I was able to get into your room." Dangerous sparks flashed in his eyes. "It was a piece of cake. Child's play. If I'd wanted to kill you, you'd be dead."

She couldn't deny the truth of it. Her knees suddenly began to shake, and she felt a desperate urge to escape both that scorching gaze and the tightness of his grip. She licked her dry lips and spoke with a bravado she was far from feeling. "How *did* you get in here? I know I double-locked the door."

"Trade secret, Ms. Hansen. And last time I checked, you're not in the trade." He gave her a shake. "So get yourself back to Arizona, take care of your grandmother, and leave the jungle to the beasts."

Fresh outrage spurted through her. Cat wrenched free, loathing his arrogance. Who was he to tell her what to do? "You're starting to remind me of my ex-husband, Dagger, and believe me that's not a compliment. Listen, Jack Galt said you could help me — that's the only reason I called you. He said you owed him a favor."

"Did he?" One dark eyebrow cocked.

"Yes, he did. So do us both a favor — just tell me something I don't already know. Something, anything. And then I guarantee I'll never call you again. You'll go your way and I'll go mine."

This must be what it's like to bargain with the devil. She held her breath, waiting, trying to keep her desperation from showing in her eyes.

"And what the hell would you do with that one piece of information?"

"I'd . . ."

"Fuck it up for everyone else."

"Try me and see," she insisted. For a moment Dagger seemed to weigh her words, and then suddenly he grabbed her again.

"The last thing I need is a hysterical relative

149

running around half-cocked, mucking up the work of a score of seasoned professionals, not to mention a half dozen government agencies. I'd rather deal with a terrorist on a suicide mission than a loose cannon like you."

"You bastard! This is my sister we're talking about — my *sister!* Not some faceless, anonymous case number. I *have* to do something or I'll lose what's left of my mind!" Cat sucked in her breath, fighting for some semblance of self-control. The hotel room seemed to fade away, leaving only the two of them in a livid darkness, the anger palpable between them, flaring like red stoked coals. "I've already lost too many people who were dear to me, and I'm not going to lose Meg — even if I have to run a suicide mission myself to save her!"

Dagger stared at her, reading the determination blazing so vividly on her face. He'd underestimated her. He'd thought she'd have cracked by now, that she'd have backed down and agreed to run home, her tail tucked between her legs. And, God help him, they were some legs.

Thanks, Jack. You could have warned me.

She looked even younger and more vulnerable now than she had when he'd first surprised her in the dark. There was a passionate plea in her eyes that might have torn at his heart — if he'd still had a heart. He'd locked it up after he'd lost Susan and Amanda, and had vowed never to pull out the key.

So he steeled himself against that silent plea and let go of her. "Ms. Hansen." He scraped every bit of patience he could muster into the words. "I'm sorry about your sister. I know how helpless you must feel. But believe me, you've got everyone from the U.S. Army to the National Guard on your side — and a few others I'm not at liberty to tell you about. *Go home.* Trust me, and go home."

"Trust you?" Cat stared at him in disbelief. "You damned . . . arrogant . . . patronizing . . . son of a bitch." Her voice lowered to almost a whisper. "Why in the world should I trust you? You broke into my room, you scared me half to death, you practically crushed my jaw, you man-handled and threatened me, and now you want me to trust you to find my sister?" She shook her head with incredulity. "All I can say is if you're in charge of her rescue party, Meg would be better off finding her own way home!"

Before the last words were out of her mouth, Cat knew she had made a huge mistake. She took a step backward and her heart started to thud. She'd gone too far; she knew it by the glitter of his eyes and by the way his fingers flexed. Then he moved so swiftly that she didn't have time even to gasp before he forced her into the wing chair beside the white-curtained window.

Dagger leaned over her, his body blocking her from rising, his arms braced on either side of the chair, hemming her in. "We can do it the easy way, Ms. Hansen, or the hard way — as they say in the movies. The easy way, you leave Washington within the next half hour. Get yourself to the airport and take the next flight back to Phoenix. The hard way . . ."

"I'm breathless with dread," Cat bit out. But her knees were trembling so much, she was glad she was sitting down.

"The hard way," he continued silkily, "means the police barge in here in about twenty minutes. They'll find the stash of cocaine I've hidden in this room — complete with your fingerprints on it. Of course, I'll have supplied them with your name and a full description. . . . Let's see, that's about mid-twenties, five foot five, honey brown hair . . ." He pushed her back as she tried to jump up. ". . . pretty if you like the type, rather interesting green eyes, and a nonstop mouth. What's it going to be, Ms. Hansen? A quick flight home, or who knows how many nights pacing a D.C. jail cell before you can get it all straightened out?"

"You bastard."

Was he bluffing? There was no sign of it on his cool, unruffled face.

"I don't believe you," she countered, her nails digging into the upholstery. "How did you get my fingerprints?"

"Trade secret, Ms. Hansen."

"I hate you. You'll pay for this."

"It would be my pleasure to escort you to the airport."

"I'd rather hitch a ride with Charles Manson."

"Suit yourself." He straightened and studied

her, unsmiling. "If I were you, I'd start packing."

With that, he swung toward the door and proceeded to unlatch each of the three locks she'd so carefully bolted earlier that evening. Cat sat rigid in the chair, watching him, wishing with all her heart that she had never called upon someone named Dagger for help.

"It's been real," he tossed casually over his shoulder, and she caught the ghost of a thin smile before he reached into his pocket and pulled out the canister of Mace. He pitched it to her, and she instinctively reached out and caught it.

"Eighteen minutes and counting," said Dagger, and without another glance, he slipped into the hall and shut the door.

Cat slumped back in the chair, too stunned to try to rise. She realized that her nails were digging into the arms so hard she'd punctured the upholstery. *What am I going to do?*

So shaken and weary and frustrated that she wanted to scream, to throw something at the blasted door, Cat instead decided that she'd better get out of here. Quickly. On a jolt of panic she realized that Dagger probably had a dozen other spooks like him in the lobby, making sure she left.

She jumped up and began throwing things pell-mell into her duffel bag. Damn Dagger to hell. Instead of helping her, he was turning this into a nightmare.

Cocaine — somewhere in this room.

She wondered wildly if it were true, but there was no way she was going to stick around to find out.

Ten minutes later she was in a cab, heading toward Dulles.

"The adjoining room," she gasped aloud suddenly, as the cab wound its way along the cloverleaf. "He came in from the adjoining room."

The young, gum-smacking cab driver swiveled her shaved head. "Whad'ya say?"

"Nothing. Just talking to myself." Cat stared out at the dull glow of moonlight in the summer sky. Realizing how Dagger had gained entry to her room didn't make her feel any better. How could it? From the moment she'd phoned him, she'd been outsmarted, outmuscled, outfoxed.

She glanced behind her, peering at the flood of headlights shimmering behind the cab. There was no way to tell if she was being shadowed by Dagger or one of his slimy cohorts. She'd done some following of her own — she'd trailed and photographed and lost enough celebrities to have learned a trick or two about eluding a tail.

What am I thinking? How can I expect to flout the direct orders of a government agent and get away with it?

She couldn't. It was madness, as insane as trying to walk a tightrope in cowboy boots. She was out of her element, and she knew she should just give up and go home to wait with Gram — and brace herself for whatever the terrorists did next.

With the thought, a strange twinge of relief came over her. Yes, she would go home. It was the smart decision — the only decision, really. Dagger had left her no choice. If anyone was following her, let them. Let them watch her change her ticket at the ticket counter and board the damned plane. She'd had enough. She'd been scared out of her wits, threatened and terrorized by a man who was supposed to be on *her* side; she was shaken and exhausted, and all she wanted was to sleep in her own childhood bed and then wake up to Gram bringing her a cup of hot tea.

And then get the news that Meg was safe. That she was coming home.

Meg. Tears blurred her vision and all the headlights melted together like the afterburn of a flashbulb. In her mind's eye she saw again that hideous photo of Meg — bound, bruised, helpless.

Oh, God, I can't do this. I can't go home. Not while Meg is still out there somewhere being hurt and threatened. Not while there's any chance I can get to her.

She took slow, deep breaths. Against all reason, she knew what she was going to do.

Cat tipped the driver at the airport, glanced around briefly, and then headed straight for the American Airlines ticket counter.

She didn't buy a ticket. Instead, she made a show of asking questions and shuffling her return ticket, then inquired when the next flight departed for Phoenix and from which gate.

I'm not down for the count yet, Dagger. You may have nicked me, but I'm not about to bleed to death.

Clasping her original return ticket, dated two days later, she hurried through security and took a seat in the nearly empty lounge adjacent to Gate E7.

Only then did Cat allow her gaze to drift around the nearly empty airport, checking out the few other people listlessly awaiting this predawn flight: several businessmen gulping from Styrofoam cups of coffee and perusing newspapers; a college student with dreadlocks, lugging a guitar; a businesswoman already at work on a laptop computer; and two sleepy children holding their mother's hands. Feeling like Dr. Richard Kimball in *The Fugitive*, she studied them with what she hoped was a casual once-over. Which one was the spy who'd blow the whistle on her if she didn't board this plane?

Maybe Dagger had already moved on to his next victim, trusting that she was sufficiently intimidated and wouldn't risk antagonizing him further. She waited, pretending to search for a lipstick in her purse as the gate agent made the first-class boarding call. When he began to board the coach passengers, she checked her watch, stood up, and strode to the washroom. So far, so good, she thought as she pushed the bolt on the third stall. She leaned against the door, listening, but it appeared no one had followed her.

Okay, hotshot, what next? If you're going to match wits with James Bond, whatever you come up with next had better be good.

Unzipping her duffel, she pulled out a long, gauzy ivory skirt, strappy sandals, and a lace tunic. It took the agility of a contortionist to wriggle out of her espadrilles, jeans, and sweater in the cramped stall and change into the new outfit, but she managed it. She almost dropped one of her gold chains into the toilet but caught it just in time and then draped it, along with two others, around her neck.

She stood in front of the sinks and mirror, her hands shaking as she applied bright red lipstick and rimmed her eyes with a wide swath of navy eye shadow. As she smoothed her hair behind her ears, an idea flashed into her head. With one movement, she yanked out her floppy black slouch hat, the one with the huge pink silk flower that she'd bought in Soho, and shoved all of her hair beneath it.

Not bad, she thought, peering at her reflection. Not bad at all. She added her large dark sunglasses and studied herself from all angles in the mirror.

"Here goes nothing," she muttered under her breath as the bathroom door opened and several women straggled in. Now that the next flight of passengers had arrived and begun flocking to the washrooms, enabling her to blend in with the crowd, it was time to make her move.

She lingered at the mirror while two of the women finished washing their hands and touching up their lipstick, waiting to slip out between them, but just as she started for the door a woman she guessed to be a college student sauntered in swinging a large Bloomingdale's shopping bag.

Struck by another sudden inspiration, Cat stopped her as she made a beeline for the first stall.

"I'll pay you five dollars for that shopping bag."

The girl, whose washed-out face and straggly red hair looked as if she'd slept the entire night on the plane, stared at her blankly. She shifted her shoulders, adjusting the bulging khaki knapsack on her back. "You only want the bag? I keep the teddy bear, right?"

"Absolutely." Cat pulled a five-dollar bill from her wallet and held it out.

As a pregnant woman jostled around them and entered the first stall, the girl peered from the five-dollar bill to Cat and back again. "Make it ten and you've got a deal," she blurted, snatching the five from Cat's hand before Cat could change her mind.

First James Bond and now Goldfinger, Cat complained silently, riffling through her wallet. She thrust five singles into the girl's open palm and grabbed the shopping bag from her, yanking out the teddy bear and tossing it back.

"Don't spend it all in one place," she muttered as the girl turned toward an empty stall.

Cat stuffed her duffel into the shopping bag, then took a newspaper someone had discarded from the trash bin and layered it across the top, concealing the duffel. She nearly gasped aloud when she saw Meg's picture blazing up from the paper.

Don't worry, Meg, I'm not about to give up. Once I've outsmarted this Dagger bozo, I'm going right to the Department of Commerce to start my research. Hang in there, kiddo.

Cat took a deep breath and strolled out of the ladies' room in the wake of two older Indian women in saris, and without glancing left or right, strode through the quiet terminal toward the baggage claim. She sauntered past the empty carousels and veered off only at the last moment toward the exit and the bank of idling taxis.

"Holiday Inn, please."

"Which one?"

"Whichever is closest to the Capitol." And then she slumped against the backseat of the cab, sweat curling under her armpits, shocked that she'd actually pulled off this escape. She glanced out the window behind her. It didn't look as if she was being trailed. She hadn't noticed anyone following her from the baggage claim area either, but she couldn't be certain.

Think positive, she told herself as the cabbie roared from the curb. *You made it.*

Yet she couldn't relax. Every nerve ending quivered with a tension so compressed she had to force herself to take deep breaths. She remembered how Dagger had materialized in her room in the middle of the night, and half expected him to sit up in the front seat and place her under arrest. She couldn't stop the cold, involuntary shudders convulsing along her spine any more than she could stop from trying to help Meg, even if it meant defying the whole damned government.

The 747 had just reached its cruising altitude of thirty thousand feet when he reached for the phone.

"It's me. Everything status quo?"

"Running down a few new leads. Nothing that can't wait until you land. I'll fax you."

"And our friend? Is she safely out of town?"

The voice in Dagger's ear came back smooth and cheerful. "Sure is. Tailed her right up to the boarding gate."

"You saw her get on the plane?"

"Couldn't hang around that long. Something came up. Norm beeped me right before the boarding call. But last time I saw her she was sitting at the gate with her ticket in her hand, looking as docile as my spaniel."

Dagger's mouth tightened. He couldn't picture Cat Hansen acting docile or being anybody's pet — particularly not a pet dog. She was pure feline — from the green shimmer of her eyes to the unconsciously sensuous way she moved. She'd sprung up from that bed fighting like a tigress, and if he'd given her the chance to have scratched his eyes out or blasted him with her Mace, she'd have done it.

"So you don't really know that she boarded that plane."

"Well, I assume that's why she was sitting there with her duffel bag on her lap and her ticket in her hand."

"Don't bet on it." Dagger frowned and shoved the phone back into its cradle.

I did everything but put her in handcuffs, he thought wearily. *What that woman really needs is a straitjacket.* He accepted the coffee the steward brought and gulped it down, hot and black. *Well, if Cat Hansen gets in my way, she'd better have nine lives because she's going to need every last one of them.*

With the cool precision that had marked his career since he'd graduated from Annapolis, he turned his thoughts from Catriana Hansen and focused on her sister. Flipping open his worn black briefcase, he lifted out the most recent file and sighed. Pretty slim. Those two agents meeting his plane had better have some new leads to fatten it up.

He sensed he was running out of time. He had a hunch this thing was primed to escalate — and fast. And unless he was wrong, innocents were going to get hurt.

Cat scrunched her eyes closed, wincing — they felt like Brillo pads beneath her eyelids. She tried to block out the headache pounding across her temples as she shut the heavy book before her, sending dust motes flying through the Department of Commerce.

She was done. Finally. She had the names of

161

every member of the boards of directors for Ryan Industries and Talon International, and she had taken copious notes and photocopied numerous documents dealing with the Desert Scorpions and the Soldiers for the Second Amendment.

She hadn't slept more than four hours at the Holiday Inn before getting down here in time for the doors to open, but somehow she'd lost all track of time while she was working. Now it finally hit her that she hadn't eaten a thing since last night. But by the time Cat gathered up all of her research and staggered out into daylight, squinting into the hazy brightness of the late afternoon, she was too exhausted even to think about reading a menu.

"I'll sleep a few hours, order room service, check in with Gram again, and then catch a flight to San Francisco," she decided as she stepped into the hotel elevator. She'd made up her mind to start on the West Coast with Ryan Industries. They were one of the leading weapons mail order houses in the country. Even more interesting, she'd discovered that their CEO, Keith Sanderson, was on ORBA's board of directors, serving on the same lobbying committee as Charles Latham.

They could be in on this together, Cat thought blearily as she jammed the plastic card into her hotel door lock. *Maybe by tomorrow I'll know a lot more.*

She flung her research files on the bed, flopped down beside them, and sipped from the can of warm Coke she'd substituted for breakfast. For some reason Dagger's cool, dark image flashed into her mind.

You certainly have your work cut out for you, Dagger. And so do I.

That's when Gram called and told her about the body.

14

It was two in the morning San Francisco time when Cat checked into the Ritz-Carlton. She leaned against the counter as she filled out the registration card, feeling almost too weary to stand. As she followed the bellman along the flower-carpeted hall leading to her room, she tried not to think about the last time she'd been here.

It had been her honeymoon. It seemed like a lifetime ago.

She and Paul had spent a week in San Francisco and then another week meandering along the coast through Carmel and Santa Barbara. That was the summer before she'd started her first real photography job at *Colorado Colors*, the regional travel magazine put out by the state chamber of commerce — the summer before Paul snagged his first big client.

As the bellman pushed open the door to her room, Cat flashed on Paul scooping her off her feet and carrying her across the threshold of their deluxe pastel honeymoon suite. He'd deposited her on the king-size bed with a Groucho Marx leer while their bellman had chuckled and lingered beside the gold-foiled bottle of champagne in its ice bucket, waiting for his tip. That was the only spontaneous moment of their entire honeymoon, she reflected now as she dumped her duffel bag onto the gleaming oval table beside the window. Paul had planned out every single minute, from the time he wanted room service to deliver their morning croissants and coffee to the route they would take to the Golden Gate Bridge and which restaurant they'd try on Fisherman's Wharf.

Cat had longed to wander and look, to soak in the sights and moods of the city, but as always in those days, she'd done it Paul's way, even suppressing her disappointment when he'd insisted on squeezing in a business meeting and two dinners with potential clients.

Now she stared at herself, reflected against the darkness looming beyond her window, remembering how she'd tried to convince herself that Paul's ambition was a good thing. He was the most energetic, diligent, and promising architect at Rodgers and Dillingham, the one everyone expected to bound straight to the top. In graduate school he had resolved to design an award-winning building by the time he was thirty — and he had. That same year, the year his magnificent office high-rise had risen like a blazing bronze jewel to tower above the aquamarine bay, their marriage had collapsed in a heap of dusty rubble.

Shoulders slumping, she turned from the window. It still hurt. No matter how much she told herself she was better off without him, better off on her own than chained to a corporate lifestyle with a corporate son of a bitch who devoted more energy sucking up to the boss than he did to remembering he had a wife, it still hurt to have failed at something so important to her. And the hurt had become nearly unbearable when Paul had abandoned her for another woman — abandoned her while she was most vulnerable. After losing their baby.

Don't let him or this city get to you, she told herself as she sank down on the bed, her back to the magnificent moonlit skyline. *And don't start thinking about Vince either,* she scolded herself, kicking off her shoes. *So what if you've struck out twice in the love department? Let it go. You can't afford to get sidetracked while Meg's life is on the line.*

Poor Gram. She'd endured six hours of gut-wrenching terror when the Coast Guard pulled that body from Miami waters. Buried in the Department of Commerce, Cat had been unaware of the daylong newsbreaks and bulletins speculating that it might be Meg. She had heard from Gram in one breath that the dead body had turned out to be a poor runaway who'd been missing for nearly three months. They'd both felt unspeakable sorrow for the young woman, but it was coupled with a staggering, numbing relief for themselves. So far, based on all they knew, Meg was still alive.

But those madmen were still out there, their demands unmet.

Madmen. Quickly, Cat jumped up to look for an adjoining room door. There was none. She flopped back on the bed, smiling smugly. *Besides, Dagger thinks I'm safely back in Arizona, scared out of my silly little mind.*

She gave a small, bitter laugh, thinking how she'd outwitted him, but even as she did, her cheeks ached, a reminder of those hard fingers digging into her flesh.

Cat could only hope that he wasn't on his way to check out Ryan Industries, too. Dagger Do-Right was the last person she wanted to run into.

"Strategy, think strategy," she told herself, but it was hard to think at all when she was so exhausted that her brain felt like a mass of soap bubbles all popping at once.

The shrill ring of the telephone made her jump. She stared at it in stark terror for a panicky moment before she remembered that yes, someone *did* know she'd come here. She'd phoned her boss, Simon, from Dulles, and had asked him to call her if he could dig up anything on Keith Sanderson or Ryan Industries.

"Cat, good news, bad news," Simon boomed at her. "Good news is that you're all set. Tomorrow morning, ten o'clock. I've got you an interview with Sanderson himself — he thinks he's doing an interview on the increase in weapons mail-order sales to women. Your name, by the way, is Andrea Boyce — you're one of our senior editors. Wing it."

"That's my specialty. A wing and a prayer," Cat cracked. "Simon, you're a gem. Now hit me with the bad news."

"Sanderson's been out of the country for the past two months, on a buying trip to the Orient and thereabouts. I'd say he's probably not your man."

She frowned, worrying her teeth along her lower lip. "The trip could be a convenient alibi. He could have masterminded this from anywhere."

"So what are you planning to do?" She heard Simon quietly munching and could picture him peering over the top of his horn-rimmed glasses into a package of Gummi Bears, searching out the green ones.

"I'll get as much as I can from Sanderson, and then I'll punt."

"Just be careful. Don't take any chances with these guys. Get what you need, and get the hell out of there."

"You got it, boss. Anything else?"

"Take good notes. Maybe we'll really run this little feature somewhere — give Andrea Boyce her first byline."

Cat was smiling as she hung up the phone, enjoying the tinge of excitement needling along her spine. *Take that, Dagger. I've got my own sources, thank you very much. To hell with you and your superspy operation. Andrea Boyce can do her own digging with a press pass and a pencil.*

All she needed was a good night's sleep and she'd be ready to take on Ryan Industries. She clicked on the TV, then burrowed under the blankets and propped three pillows behind her head. But as she tried to draw up a list of interview questions, her yawns became more frequent and the images flickering across the television screen lulled her to sleep. At some point, the pencil and pad of paper slid to the floor while Cat slept on, depleted beyond anything she'd ever felt before, lost in a dreamless sleep as thick as the cool gray smog gathering over the moonlit whitecaps of San Francisco Bay.

15

Ryan Industries' corporate headquarters was a steel jungle, a labyrinth of hard edges, polished granite, and snow-white marble. The only soft things in the vast, glittering executive suite were the dead ones — a huge bearskin rug mouthing a silent greeting in the reception area, and giant elk, caribou, and moose heads glaring down from the slate gray walls like disembodied deities.

"He'll see you now."

Cat set down Ryan's bulky mail-order catalog, its glossy pages bursting with glamorous color pictures of every variety of knife and gun, and followed the matronly middle-aged British secretary into Keith Sanderson's corner office, straining to catch the woman's clipped, softly spoken words.

"Would you care for a cup of tea, dear? We have Earl Grey or Lemon Lift. Forgive me, perhaps you'd fancy an espresso?"

Too nervous to think of drinking anything, Cat shook her head. Before her, a man seated in a cobalt leather chair swiveled away from the expansive window to face her.

"Miss Boyce, pleasure to meet you."

Cat pondered Keith Sanderson as she grasped his outstretched hand, wondering, even as she said hello, if this thirtyish, healthy-looking sun-tanned man in crisp white collarless shirt and olive slacks knew where her sister was being held and by whom. With his sun-lightened blond cowlick and California golden boy features, Keith Sanderson looked more like someone who'd surfed his way around the ten best beaches this side of Carmel than like a multimillion-dollar arms dealer.

After forcing herself to smile cordially through the briefest exchange of pleasantries, Cat flipped open the reporter's notebook she'd bought this morning and set a mini–cassette recorder on the huge granite desk, its surface uncluttered except for a set of keys, the de rigueur black Mont Blanc pen, and one short, neat stack of papers. She was impressed by the neatness of his office, the weapons catalogs chronologically bound atop the credenza, the sleek arrangement of Rolodex, fax machine, ten-line telephone, and paper shredder beside them.

"You don't mind if I tape the interview, do you? I find it helps me transcribe my notes and I'm less likely to quote you out of context or to get something wrong. . . ."

"By all means." Sanderson relaxed into his leather chair as if it were a chaise lounge and regarded Cat with a genial smile. "So what is it

171

you'd like to know?"

She began with the questions she'd prepared about the increasing number of mail-order purchases by women, jotting down statistics, sales figures, and explanations with a display of reportorial interest that would have done Lois Lane proud. All the time she was seething to know if behind that laid-back facade was a man devious enough to mastermind a terrorist plot and yet sit here parrying her questions with bland ease.

"Don't suppose Margaret Hansen is one of your subscribers," she tossed off with what she hoped was a casual smile, carefully watching his reaction.

"Not by a long shot." Sanderson flashed a grin, then leaned forward, schooling his face into an appropriately sober mask of concern, a look Cat found incongruous with his fly-away cowlick.

"It goes without saying we're appalled by what's happened, although we feel she's terribly misguided. But, hey, this is America and she's entitled to her opinion. Personally, I liked it better when Miss America wore high heels in the swimsuit competition and Bert Parks did his corny little bit at the end. But this is the nineties, right? And the world's a different place. Nowadays Miss America has to tout a platform, and so we have this chick who goes around shooting off her mouth about things she doesn't really understand — and a lot of people are influenced by that. What with her stature and media exposure and all."

Cat felt her fingers curling viselike around her pencil. "So you're not shedding any tears over her kidnapping? At some level, you feel she got what was coming to her?"

"Hey, now." Sanderson held up a large manicured hand. "Don't start putting words in my mouth, Ms. Boyce. We certainly don't advocate violence. And no one affiliated with Ryan Industries wishes Meg Hansen any harm. But I will say that it's unfortunate our Miss America never bothered to learn the truth about weapons ownership in this country and the importance of upholding our Second Amendment. If Americans can't defend themselves, we may as well chuck the whole Constitution."

His eyes were bright, his broad face flushed. Cat saw that he believed deeply in what he was saying. Was it deeply enough to have acted upon it?

Before she could respond, the intercom buzzed.

"Sorry to interrupt," the secretary's voice interjected briskly, "but Mr. Preston's secretary is calling from Palm Beach to inquire whether you're going to make it down to the party."

Preston. Cat straightened in her chair, her antennae up. She'd written that name half a dozen times at the Department of Commerce. Kent Preston — CEO, Talon International.

She strained to remember; without her notes, the names and companies on her suspect list blurred together in her memory. But she seemed to recall that Talon International owned numerous munitions factories in South America and was a major U.S. firearms importer. Unlike Ryan Industries, they didn't appear to have any connection with ORBA.

"Damn, I thought I got back to him before I went away." Sanderson frowned.

"Well, I reminded you numerous times," the secretary chided, sounding, Cat thought, like the long-suffering mother of an adolescent.

"The party's this Saturday, isn't it?" He began riffling through the small stack of correspondence on his desk. From the center of the pile he extracted two glossy black cards emblazoned with thin gold script. "You're right. The invitation and response card are still here." Sanderson sighed. "Tell Corey I'm sorry; my sister's wedding is this weekend."

Sanderson dropped the invitation into the wastebasket and turned his attention back to Cat, a slight squint tightening his features as he refocused on their conversation.

"Oh, yes, Miss America. I can't say I agree with the tactics of these kidnappers, but I have no argument with what they're trying to achieve."

"I couldn't help overhearing what you said to your secretary." Cat slanted him what she hoped was a beguiling smile. "Is Corey Preston one of the Talon International Prestons?"

"You *have* done your homework, Ms. Boyce." He nodded approvingly. He picked up his Mont

Blanc pen and jabbed the cap in her direction. "Corey's on Talon's board. You definitely want to talk to Talon before you write up your story. They produce some pretty nifty ladies' specials — some of our biggest sellers come from their factory in Caracas."

"Thanks. I will get in touch with them. Who's their CEO?"

"Kent Preston and his son James took over when Corey's father died last year. Corey was pretty steamed — his daddy had been grooming him for the top spot since prep school."

"What happened?"

"Well . . ." Sanderson shifted in his chair, his expression suddenly wary. "Corey had some trouble in college. I don't know the whole story, but Corey's father changed his will to favor his brother and . . . well, Corey's still on the board of directors."

"I'd like his number." Cat tried to sound matter-of-fact. Although she had Talon International's business addresses and phone and fax numbers zippered securely in her purse along with those of every other suspect on her list, she'd love to get hold of the home address and phone number no doubt printed on that fancy invitation in the wastebasket.

Sanderson checked his Rolodex and scrawled a number across his business card. "There you go. Anything else I can help you with?" He glanced at his watch and made a face. "I've got a lunch meeting in ten minutes, so I'm going to have to cut this short, sorry to say. . . ."

"It's quite all right. I think I have everything I need." Cat stood and shook his hand. *Almost everything,* she thought. *Those keys would be nice . . . and the invitation.*

There had to be a way. She watched him rise and walk to the door, holding it open as she stuffed her tape recorder back inside her purse.

"Actually, I do have one or two more questions," she improvised. "If you're leaving now we could wind this up in the elevator."

"Sure, no problem. Mrs. Sedgewick," he called, "I'll be back by two."

He picked up his briefcase and sauntered out beside Cat, leaving the ring of keys lying right smack in the middle of the desk.

In the lobby Cat headed straight for the bank of telephones. She waited with a receiver to her ear, watching from the corner of her eye until he ambled past the archway of potted plants that fell in tiers from hollows carved into the walls. When he was safely outside in the afternoon sunshine, she slipped back into the elevator and rode up to the fourteenth floor.

"How stupid of me!" she exclaimed to Mrs. Sedgewick. "I've left my pen behind — at least I think I did. . . . Would you mind if I just went in and grabbed it? I won't be a minute."

The secretary rose at once. "I'll get it for you, dear. What does it look like?"

"It's a gold Waterman pen — my brother gave it to me for my twenty-first birthday. . . ." Cat chatted on, trailing her into the office like a friendly puppy.

"I must have set it down on the desk when I was putting my tape recorder away. . . ."

"Oh dear." Mrs. Sedgewick paused before the desk. "Mr. Sanderson forgot to take that file along after I spent half the morning preparing it for him. It's a good thing that young man's head is sewn on tight," she tsked. "Hmmm, I don't see your pen, dear."

"Maybe it rolled under the desk, or into the wastebasket." Cat began rummaging through the small trash container.

The secretary knelt on the carpet. "Nothing I can see under his desk." That long-suffering mother tone was growing more pronounced. Quick as a wink, Cat stuffed the invitation into her purse and then palmed the ring of keys.

Mrs. Sedgewick struggled to her feet as the phone rang. "Now what?" she muttered under her breath, turning to snatch up the receiver.

Cat slipped the key ring into her purse and waved her pen at the secretary on the way out.

There was nothing in the files.

Late that night, Cat sat at Mrs. Sedgewick's desk and stared at the screen, skimming down the endless list of directories, calling up any file that even remotely suggested what she was looking for. Then, there it was — ORBA — hidden away in a "Regulations" batch file. And the damn thing wasn't even locked!

177

With a flick of the keys it was there on the screen. Miles of correspondence, contact names, and addresses, memos detailing lobbying strategies, pages of statistics, newspaper and magazine articles scanned into the computer, and letters and check numbers that hinted strongly at highly placed payoffs. She absorbed as much as she could, searching for some mention of Meg, of the plot to overturn the gun laws. But she came across nothing, and she turned her attention to Sanderson's Rolodex, desk drawers, and credenza, trying keys on the set she had swiped until she found the right ones.

She memorized the order and location of each file, each piece of paper she touched, then carefully replaced everything exactly as she had found it.

Maybe Ryan Industries wasn't involved after all. If they were, no clues were readily apparent in this swift search of the offices.

Cat wondered if she could slip out of the building as easily as she'd managed to get in. She had waited outside the front doors, out of sight of the security guard, until a man carrying a laptop computer breezed out. She snagged the heavy glass door before it could swing shut and she was in, strolling quickly toward the sign marked EXIT at the opposite end of the lobby from the security guard.

Security guard? The muscular young blond in the crisp gray uniform hadn't looked up from her magazine once. Cat probably could have used the elevator, walked right by her, but she didn't feel like taking any chances. Her flowing adrenaline fueled her with enough energy to hurry up the fourteen double flights of stairs. Then it had been a relatively easy matter to find the right key and let herself into the inner sanctum of Ryan Industries.

She'd made a thorough search of every office in the suite, but so far her sleuthing had gotten her no more than a little exercise and a headache. Nothing she had found here tied Ryan to the plot against Meg.

Maybe it was time to turn her attention to Talon International. *Maybe I'll just crash Corey Preston's little party. I've worked enough celebrity soirees to know that with a little ingenuity and determination, any Tom, Dick, or Mary can get lost in the crowd and rub elbows with the rich and seedy.*

It stood to reason that the Preston kid might have invited other people from the gun industry besides Sanderson, and if she could manage to flit around undetected she might overhear something useful.

She closed Sanderson's desk drawer and locked it, then paused in the doorway, thinking hard. She'd checked everything . . . except the paper shredder. She hurried toward it, her heartbeat quickening as she saw the stack of papers waiting beside it in the wire basket. Bingo.

Her eyes tore over the papers, most of them rubber-stamped CONFIDENTIAL in bright red ink. Sales figures, in-house memos, and the like.

Suddenly Cat's attention sharpened on the paper in her hands. The letterhead was Talon International's and the signature was Corey Preston's.

". . . and regarding those C-82s that were outlawed in the Farrell Bill — well, you might want to save a few pages of catalog space for these babies. The battle was lost, but the war's not over. They'll be back on the market. We're manufacturing them like crazy and will be able to ship the minute the tide turns — and it will, Keith, soon. Mark my words. America's going to wake up — wake up big-time — BIG-TIME."

A chill crept over Cat. America's going to wake up . . . Wake up America? Isn't that what the terrorists were calling their little campaign? Could this be what she was looking for?

And Corey Preston had written it.

Cat had no time to ponder the implications, for outside in the hall she heard a door close, the scraping of buckets, and the voices of the cleaning crew as they made their way down the hall.

Great.

She replaced the rest of the papers in the wire basket, then folded the Preston letter into her purse. She had to get out of here before anyone spotted her.

She passed Mrs. Sedgewick's desk and the poor polar bear rug sprawled on the floor, flicked off the lights, and eased the door just wide enough to see out. The hallway was empty save for the rolling trash bin and vacuum cleaner two doorways down.

She was almost at the stairwell exit when she realized she was still clutching Sanderson's keys. *Good one, Mata Hari.* Cat darted back to the door, fumbling to find the right key, her fingers shaking in time to the tremors in her knees. *Got it.* She flew back into Sanderson's office, bumping into the chair as she moved through the darkness, and dropped the keys where she'd first found them that afternoon.

Her hand was on the lobby doorknob when she heard someone jingling a ring of keys directly on the opposite side of the door.

Oh God, they're coming in. Panic swooped through her. There was no place to hide, no time. . . . In a second they'd be in, the lights on, and she'd be standing here like a deer caught in head-lights — one more poor dumb animal. And by the time Ryan Industries was done with her they would have her head mounted right alongside the moose.

"Hey, Rodríguez. Get that vacuum back here! How many times do I have to tell you that file room gets sweeped up, too? Whatsa matter? You got a hot date with that security guard downstairs or somethin'? Man, she wouldn't even tell you her name." The man laughed.

"Yeah, well, I read it on her badge, asshole. Allison. Allison Czechowich."

"Czechowich! You wanna check somethin' out, check out your damn work, before the boss fires your lazy ass."

Cat exhaled as she heard a string of muffled

curses and the blessed sound of retreating footsteps.

Go. Go!

She flew along the hall and down the staircase,
taking the steps two at a time, stopping only to
catch her breath briefly on the fifth floor. Her
lungs felt as if they were going to burst out of her
chest, but she forced herself to keep going.

Somehow, she managed to collect herself before stepping out of the main floor stairwell into
the lobby. She still had to get past the security
guard.

Cautiously, she cracked the door open and ventured out, trying to look as if she belonged there,
as if she had every right to be leaving this building
after ten-thirty at night. She started toward the
door. It was dark outside, and she couldn't wait
to melt into that lovely darkness.

She glanced over her shoulder just as the security guard looked up from her magazine.
Czechowich opened her mouth, but before she
could say anything, Cat gave a jaunty wave and
called out, "Night, Allison. Don't work too
hard."

Allison Czechowich hesitated for just a moment. It was all Cat needed. She sailed out the
door and turned quickly up the street, breathing
in the sea-tanged sweetness of the night air.

Exhilaration pumped through her. Dagger
couldn't have done better himself, she thought,
as she flagged down a taxi and headed back to
the hotel.

In her purse she had an intriguing letter from Corey Preston and an invitation to a party.
She'd need a new dress.

16

Though she had been sent on assignment to celebrities' mansions from Beverly Hills to Majorca, Cat had never seen anything like the Prestons' Palm Beach estate. Mizner's architecture was in a class by itself. Cat sucked in her breath as she wove through the drunken crowd around the swimming pool. The place was posh beyond belief and it was huge — someone had mentioned twenty-five bedrooms. She was sure that tonight all of them were occupied.

The average age of Mr. Corey Preston's guests appeared to be mid-twenties, with a sprinkling of exuberant nineteen-year-olds hell-bent on proving how wild and hip they could be. She spotted the drummer for a rock band she'd once photographed when they were still a warm-up act — he was swimming in the buff with two nubile blonds, twins endowed with enough for quadruplets.

On the upper balcony, where the Mauling Lions were blasting out their latest Grammy-winning number, colored strobe lights flashed, revealing between pulses the gyrations of two couples and a single naked male who were too stoned even to notice the giggling brunette shimmying down the overhanging palm tree with the moves of an erotic dancer.

Everywhere Cat looked there were young, beautiful, laughing, shouting people, most of them drunk or stoned. Those clothed wore all manner of attire from Birkenstocks and cutoffs to tiny little cocktail dresses or classic Armani slacks paired with linen jackets. As a tuxedo-clad waiter handed her a beer, she wondered which one of these frenzied lunatics was her host.

The air hung humid and heavy with a cloud of marijuana smoke overlaid with the scent of gardenias from the glazed pottery tubs staggered along the perimeter of the pool and terrace. A bemused waitstaff snaked through the crowd, passing silver trays of marinated octopus, timbales of Thai-spiced mushrooms, and sushi. Flutes filled with golden champagne were everywhere, more abundant than the fairy lights strung from the fronds of every palm tree on the property.

"Excuse me," Cat kept murmuring as she fought to negotiate her way across the crowded patio. It was difficult to maneuver amid the bobbing, swaying bodies of the young and glittering. They almost appeared to be worshiping the moon, Cat reflected as she reached the French doors — wild, entranced pagans dancing out some erotic summer ritual.

"Watch it, babe. If you want to dance, just ask me."

Cat found herself suddenly caught against the warm, muscular chest of a very tall sandy-haired young man with laughing eyes and a cleft chin. Her eyes locked on the enormous tattoo emblazoned across his left pectoral — a greenish serpent coiled around a smoking pistol.

"I'm Rick," he told her as they began to dance, there in the vast sunken room where a dozen or more people were dancing and still others were sprawled on the ivory damask sofa or one of the sling-back chairs, guzzling beer and watching the forty-foot-high wide-screen TV suspended from the ceiling. "Didn't catch your name, babe."

"Didn't tell you."

He grinned. "I'm listening."

Cat slinked her hands down her body, skimming them along the clingy red dress that had pushed her nearly maxxed-out Visa card to the limit. Now she had his full attention.

"I'm Lou. Lou Alcott."

She said it half joking, and waited. No flicker of recognition passed his limpid eyes. He nodded, placing his hands on her shoulders. "Friend of Corey's?"

"Uh-huh. You?"

"Yeah, we go way back. Got our MBAs together and then took off on a little six-month safari through the Congo. Wiped out every four-legged creature that crossed our path — man, it was awesome."

He laughed. No, snickered, Cat decided, trying to keep the distaste from showing in her face. She flung back her hair, grinned at him, and gushed, "Oooh, hunting. I've always thought going on a safari sounded so . . . rugged."

"You don't know the half of it. Hey, want to see a few of the trophies we brought back?"

She followed him down a cool hallway tiled in gleaming black-and-white marble squares, up a dazzling checkerboard staircase, and through a maze of rooms and corridors until they reached what seemed to be an L-shaped wing of the house. "Ever been up here before?"

"Not lately."

"Well, this is Corey's wing — kind of a playhouse. He remodeled it after his old man died. There's the master bedroom suite, the Jacuzzi-sauna room, his game room, and here," he said, throwing open a heavy pickled-oak door, "is the trophy room."

Cat blinked as she stepped into an eerily lovely recreation of a jungle. It wasn't a room, exactly, it was a pavilion — an enormous diorama overflowing with plants and vines and a waterfall that trickled noisily down a jutting rock wall. She breathed in warm air, thick with humidity, that smelled pungently of moss and damp earth. The sounds of birds twittering and insects droning filled her ears.

"This is incredible," she breathed, and meant it.

Rick led her forward and she gasped as she

caught sight of the massive Asian elephant — stuffed — beyond the bank of foliage.

"Got that one myself." Rick draped an arm around her shoulders. "Had a hell of a time smuggling that sucker back here, but Corey and I have our ways."

Cat's heart thrummed faster. So Corey Preston wasn't above poaching — or smuggling. It must have cost him a fortune in payoffs to do it. Goose bumps prickled her bare arms as she spotted a black panther crouched on a rock above them. It looked poised and ready to spring at the lifelike gazelle posed sipping water from a miniature water hole surrounded by sand.

This room made the reception area of Ryan Industries look as innocuous as a pet shop. Corey Preston must have brought half of Africa home with him.

"Pretty cool, huh?" Rick snaked an arm around her waist, pulling Cat close enough so that she felt the tension in his sinewy limbs and smelled the tang of pool chlorine on his skin. "There's a group of us that tries to get to Africa at least once a year. But when Corey can't get to the Congo, he brings the Congo to him."

Rick's hands were starting to roam up her body. Cat decided she'd better put an end to this particular safari before she turned into a different kind of trophy.

"This is great, Rick. It's fantastic. But I'd really like a drink." Deftly, she tried to wriggle out of his hold, but he tightened his grip.

"Not so fast, babe. We just got here."

"I'm deathly allergic to ferns. I swell up with hives and start to itch. . . ."

"Baby, you make me itch." His breath was warm on her eyelids, and then his mouth clamped onto hers as he swung her against the wall. Filled with repugnance, Cat was about to give him an elbow in the ribs when suddenly the lights went out.

Blackness clamped down, a suffocating impenetrable blackness that amplified the eerie jungle sounds around them. Rick let her go, and through the murky darkness, Cat could hear him swearing and punching buttons that must have been concealed in the rock-covered wall beside them. Night sounds swelled, and a canopy of stars bloomed across the ceiling.

A cold voice spoke beside them.

"You're a dead man, Rick."

Cat blinked in the sudden brightness that flooded the trophy room. She gazed in shock at the handsome young man staring back at them through the sight of an AK-47 assault rifle. His full lips were pursed in concentration, his fingers steady on the gun.

"Fuck off, Corey!" Rick slammed his hand against the rock above Cat's head. "Your timing sucks, man!"

"Looks like I caught you with your pants down, Ace. Ready for the terms of surrender?"

"Yeah, sure. What is it this time?"

"I'm feeling generous." Corey motioned toward Cat with the barrel of the gun. "I'll let you off with a simple introduction to your friend."

Cat felt the fine hairs at her nape tingle as he lowered the rifle, smiling coldly.

So this asshole is Corey Preston, deposed heir of Talon International.

He was handsome in a dark, sneering way, and sleekly dressed in a V-necked beige shirt and matching linen slacks that looked striking with his deep tan and midnight hair. There was something leonine about his face, especially his deep-set golden eyes. But as compelling as he was, he gave her the creeps. She flicked her gaze past him, first to the tall platinum-haired girl in the black lace bikini, starkly, haughtily beautiful, all angular cheekbones and legs — and then to the man in the shadows beside her.

Cat's knees nearly buckled as she met Dagger's cobalt gaze.

What in hell was he doing here?

"Unh, what did you say your name was again, babe? Lou, that's it, right? Lou . . . Lou Alcon . . . No, I got it, Alcott. Corey Preston, say hello to Lou Alcott. But wait, I thought you two knew each other."

"I don't believe I've had the pleasure," Corey said slowly, his eyes narrowing on her. "Lou Alcott. Our own Little Woman. No shit."

She wished the foliage would engulf her. She dared not look at Dagger, or at the blond who was all over him. "I was kidding with Rick when I said that," she began. "Actually, my last name is . . ." She hesitated for only a fraction of a second, as from the corner of her eyes she caught the fluttering fronds of a palm tree just beyond Dagger's shoulder. ". . . Palmer. Louisa Palmer." Cat grinned and tossed her head. "Great party, Corey. But turnabout's fair play. Who are your friends?"

His eyes never left her face. "This is Bethany and her friend Nick. But you'll have to remind me where we've met. I can't seem to place you."

Cat swallowed, her brain racing, but before she could speak, Dagger interrupted. "Louisa and I met in Cannes last winter." He stepped in as smoothly as a hawk dive-bombing its prey. "You were there, too, Bethany."

"Cannes was the pits last winter. Who remembers? This year I'm going to Portofino. You should come, too." Bethany stroked her fingers through Dagger's hair, not even glancing Cat's way.

"It was at Felix's premiere, wasn't it?" Dagger continued, raising an eyebrow at Cat.

"Why, yes," she began, shivering at the steel in his eyes. "I remember now —" But Corey cut her off, wheeling angrily toward Dagger.

"Fuck off, man. I asked her where *we* met."

"Corey, you honestly don't remember?" Cat pretended to pout. "Why don't you think about it while Rick and I go for a swim?"

He snagged a finger through her spaghetti strap. "Pretty fancy bathing suit," he taunted, flicking his gaze down the slinky red dress.

"Silly." She laughed, trying to keep from trembling as she removed his hand. "I left my stuff in the cabana. Come on, join us; it might refresh your memory." Then she tucked her arm through Rick's and began tugging him playfully along with her.

"What's the rush?" Like lightning, Corey extended the gun muzzle to block their way. "The pool's not going anywhere, and we were just getting reacquainted."

My God, he's scary as hell, Cat thought, her flesh chilling. It was as if beneath that handsomely chiseled surface there was no emotion, no heart. Was he merely a spoiled rich kid who'd been foisted off on nannies, boarding schools, and prep schools — given everything money could buy except love or affection? Or was there something else lacking . . . a basic connection with humanity, a moral soul?

He's capable of this plot against Meg, Cat decided as she met his unwavering stare and tried to decide how to counter it. He'd have the means, the money, the manpower.

And the motive. According to her research, his family stood to lose millions from gun control legislation that curtailed growth of the gun industry.

"Chill, Preston. The lady wants to go for a swim." It was Dagger who pushed the gun muzzle aside.

It was just the opening Rick needed. "We're outta here, man."

"Enjoy your swim, Louisa," Dagger drawled as they walked past him. "Watch out for sharks."

She could feel his eyes on her, as sharp as blue granite. She had a feeling the sharks would show her more mercy than Dagger would if he got within ten feet of her, alone.

Next thing I know I'll have a cop on each arm, escorting me out of here. How the hell am I going to help Meg from a Palm Beach jail cell?

She suddenly realized that Rick was leading her right to the edge of the pool. It gleamed in the night like an aquamarine jewel cushioned against black velvet. Ahead of them, a fully clothed couple danced right into the glinting water. Laughter roared up from the gyrating throng as the back splash walloped the pool deck, drenching them.

"I'll just be a minute," Cat murmured, deciding it was past time to ditch Rick. "Let me hunt up my suit. . . ."

"No way, babe." Rick shook his head and grinned at her, and before she could pull her hand out of his, he was jumping over the edge, tugging her along. For one mad, disbelieving moment she was sailing through the air.

The next moment she was underwater.

Gasping, Cat broke the surface. *There goes $350 worth of red silk and Lycra down the drain. Not to mention my makeup, my hair and my dignity.* She vowed that if Rick came anywhere near her she would blacken both his eyes.

But Rick was nowhere to be seen. By now there were thirty to forty people in the pool, bobbing and screaming and dunking each other. In disgust, Cat paddled to the nearest pink-tiled wall, cursing as she felt one high-heeled shoe float away. She was about to hoist herself over the edge when she found herself staring at a pair of beige Gucci loafers. Her glance traveled slowly upward, past the cuffs of a man's cream-colored trousers, past a golden belt buckle and a loose white shirt.

Dagger stretched out a hand.

Talk about leaping from a squall directly into the eye of the hurricane, she thought, hesitating just a fraction of a second before she closed her fingers around his outstretched hand and allowed herself to be hoisted onto the deck.

His voice, like the rest of him, was dry. "I believe this dance is mine."

17

The *Elena* surged through the choppy black waters, fighting the turbulent trade winds with the ease of a scythe slicing fields of hay. As the fifty-footer skirted the Yucatán Peninsula, bright moonlight silhouetted the tropical jungles that swept across the dark, distant horizon.

Late tomorrow we reach the island, J.D. thought as he paced the gleaming deck. One tiny anonymous island, a speck on the map — hidden in plain view in the midst of more than two hundred other tiny islands flung like buckshot across the western Caribbean. J.D. mentally reviewed his game plan. They'd wait until two or three in the morning, then duck in under cover of darkness and drop anchor in the hidden little cove that wound along the north coast.

The hardest work was done. Now it was a waiting game. The way J.D. saw it, their main objective at this point was to hold their prisoner tight, keep their heads down, and make contact with the Roadrunner.

Piece of cake.

He looked out at Ty, Frank, and Bramson, lounging on the open deck. If it weren't for the guns they wore or what he knew about them, they could be any group of men returning from a casual day of deep-sea fishing. But he knew better. These three were part of a handpicked cadre of top mercenaries operating in the Western Hemisphere, and fishing was not on their agenda.

While he and his team were entrusted with secreting the hostage away from the mainland, J.D. knew that other teams were already in place across the continent, awaiting subsequent phases of the operation. One phone call from Preston and the deployment of those sectors would begin.

Moonlight dappled the pockmarks on his face as he called the meeting to order. "I've just received a fax from the Director — he's issued his latest demands to Washington. Needless to say, the shit is about to hit the fan."

"Not our problem." Bramson, always the cool Norwegian, leaned back in his deck chair and lit a cigarette, the tip glowing red-hot like a tiny ruby in the semidarkness. "We just sit out here, far from the storm, and enjoy the ocean air."

"And keep Early Bird snug in her nest," J.D. snapped.

Frank turned, smirking, from the brass-fitted handrail. "I volunteer for the all-night shift."

J.D. slammed down his tumbler of white wine so forcefully that the liquid sloshed across the fiberglass table beside him. "The girl remains off-limits, Frank. Period. The Director is ada-

mant — no one touches her. Leave one finger-
print on our precious cargo and the Director will
arrange for a permanent vacation to the morgue.
Got it?"

"Yeah, we got it, all right. You don't need to
fucking draw us a picture," Frank snapped, agi-
tating the ice cubes in his glass of Chivas.

J.D.'s penetrating gaze shifted to Ty, who
shrugged his massive shoulders. "No problemo."

Bramson flicked the ash from his cigarette over-
board and yawned, stretching his bare arms overhead toward the starlit sky. "I never mix business
and pleasure. Two questions, though. Who the
hell is this Director and when do we get our hands
on those Cuban cigars?"

"In answer to your first question, the Director
remains anonymous. You've known that from the
start. As to the cigars, the Roadrunner should
have them waiting on the island, along with at
least another couple weeks' worth of provisions."

"The Roadrunner!" Frank snorted derisively
and downed the last of his Scotch. "That's about
all he's good for these days — grocery shopping."

Taut silence followed this remark. The only
sound was the slapping of waves against the
yacht's hull. J.D. stared across the white lami-
nated table, fixing Frank with eyes as sharp as
bayonet tips, but he said nothing.

"Seems I remember him saving your butt more
than once in Nicaragua, my friend," Bramson
finally drawled.

"That was the old Roadrunner. Before he lost

his nerve. He's become nothing but a pansy-ass."

J.D. controlled his temper with an effort. "It can be dangerous, Frank, to underestimate certain men. I suggest you remember that."

Frank Aldo had rubbed him the wrong way from day one of this job, but since Preston had handpicked the team, J.D. wasn't in a position to argue.

He had no quarrel with Bramson and Mather. They were seasoned professionals who left their personal quirks behind and knew how to work as a team. But Frank was like a molten volcano, constantly churning beneath the surface. He always wanted the last word, was always ready to argue or complain, even if it was only under his breath.

"Well, if you want the Roadrunner to be your little errand boy, so be it." Frank tilted the Chivas bottle, splashing amber liquid over the ice cubes melting in his glass. "So long as he doesn't screw up."

"*You* don't screw up!" J.D. jabbed his polished fingernail in Frank's face. "Let me worry about the Roadrunner."

Meg noticed the gold cigarette lighter right after she'd pushed away the empty dinner tray. How long had it been lying there on the floor, right next to the built-in chest of drawers? It must have fallen out of one of their pockets.

Fight fire with fire.

She didn't know whether she'd need it as a tool

or as a weapon. She only knew it might be all she had.

I have to get it before someone else sees it lying there.

But how?

There has to be a way. Come on, dammit. It's only ten measly inches from the foot of the bed.

Meg slumped against the headboard and squinted at the lighter in frustration. Even when she strained forward as far as the manacle would allow, it was still out of reach. She needed something. . . . Her eyes darted around the barren cabin. Not a damn thing.

What would Gram do? She was in plenty of tight spots.

Meg had always thought of her grandmother as someone who could handle anything with aplomb. Meg had struggled to live up to her high standard. Even when she'd found out she wouldn't make the Olympics and had gone into a tailspin, she'd pulled herself up, thinking of Gram, wanting to emulate the optimistic dignity with which she lived her life.

So what would Gram do? she asked herself again, her nails chafing against the mattress.

She'd tell me to calm down and think this through. Be resourceful. Open your eyes and really see.

What do I have here? She took a dubious inventory. There was nothing — some clothes, a pillow, the bedspread.

The bedspread.

She wriggled to one side. Tugging the orange

cotton coverlet from beneath her, she yanked the ends free of the mattress, her breath coming in short, hopeful gasps.

Careful . . . toss it too hard and you'll lose it . . . or push the lighter farther away. Take your time. Do it right. Her palms sweated with the realization that she wouldn't get a second chance.

The bedspread landed with a soft thump, enveloping the lighter in an orange cloud. Holding her breath, Meg reeled in her catch, heartened by the soft scraping of metal against the wood floor.

Footsteps thudded. Downstairs? Outside her door? Meg froze. Needles of despair pricked along her spine. *Oh God, if they come in now . . .*

But as she held her breath the footsteps moved past and then faded away. She heard a door close softly somewhere and relief drenched her. Wiping sweat from her upper lip, she felt as she had in her training days after swimming laps for hours, tiring to the point of exhaustion, then feeling her second wind kick in. Tugging at the bedspread once more, she worked feverishly, concentrating with her brows knit together until her little prize seemed within reach.

But for all her efforts the chain still stopped too short. Meg's throat was raw. Her eyes burned with unshed tears. She batted at the lighter with her foot, trying to curl her toes around the cool metal, but with a sudden rock of the boat, the lighter slid away. Gritting her teeth, Meg stretched out her leg as far as she could, straining against the chain until her wrist and fingers burned.

Gotcha.

She held her breath and dragged the lighter toward her with her toes. Perspiration dripped in her eyes, stinging, as she sprawled flat on the bed, groping blindly along the floor with her free hand. Just as she was ready to scream in frustration, she felt cool metal against her overheated flesh.

But as she scooped it into her palm, the door to the cabin opened. J.D. stepped in.

"What the hell are you up to?"

18

"I can't breathe!" Meg cried, shaking her head wildly from side to side. "You've got to let me out of here. Please, for a little while."

Meg did her best to look crazed and frantic. It wasn't exactly difficult under the circumstances.

"I'm choking to death," she gasped as J.D. regarded her in speculative silence. "I need . . . fresh air. Please take me out of this room."

He scanned the blanket mounded on the floor, the sheets twisting off the mattress, and her flushed, perspiration-soaked face. His fingers tapped the key ring on his belt. "Guess a few minutes on deck won't kill anybody."

As he glanced down to unhook the key ring, Meg slipped the lighter into her jogging suit's jacket pocket.

"Fifteen minutes," J.D. said curtly, clicking her free from the manacle. He seized her arm and pulled her off the bed. "Behave yourself."

"Gin!" Frank gloated, flipping his cards face up on the table. "Again. That makes five hands in a row. Guess some of us are just born win-ners."

"Stuff it, pal." Bramson tossed down his cards in disgust and scooped up a handful of salted peanuts. Frank never could keep a poker face. And there was nothing that pissed Bramson off more than an obnoxious winner.

Seeing his sour expression, Frank snickered. "Your deal, Bramson, unless you can't take los-ing."

The dark night air smelled of rain. A storm was brewing. The brisk breeze that whipped their hair as they began another hand hinted at it, even as choppy water slapped against the hull, sending the played cards skittering across the small table.

Digging out another handful of nuts, Bramson paused to study Frank over his cards. "What the hell is with you tonight? That shit-eating grin is getting on my nerves."

"Let's just say I know something you don't." A harsh chuckle escaped Frank's throat as he discarded the seven of diamonds. "And you know what, Bramson, baby? Since I'm feeling generous tonight, I might just let you in on this bit of privileged information."

"What information?" Ty flipped his jacket hood over his head and dragged his deck chair out of the shadows near the railing to join them around the softly lit table.

Now that he had their full attention, Frank widened his grin. "How'd you like to know the identity of our mysterious Director?"

"Like you'd have a clue," Bramson scoffed, drawing a card. "You heard J.D. Sounds to me it's such a deep dark secret he might not even know."

"Wanna bet?"

"Man, you're so full of shit your eyes are brown." Ty's short laugh echoed across the deck as he unwrapped a stick of spearmint gum and folded it into his mouth. "Who gives a shit who hired us as long as we get our pay and our Cuban cigars?"

"I do." Frank's chin jutted forward as Bramson called gin. "I'm sick of J.D.'s lousy attitude — he struts around here like some kind of Mafia capo."

"So?" Bramson's blue eyes were fixed intently on Frank's face. "You got something to say, say it."

"Well, I did happen to read a certain fax that came in. . . ."

"And the Director is . . . ," Ty prompted, tapping out a drumroll on the arm of his chair.

Smiling smugly, Frank glanced from one to the other as the yacht pitched slightly aft in the wake of a swell. "The joker bankrolling this charming international incident is some guy by the name of Corey Preston. Ring a bell?"

"Aldo, shut the fuck up!"

All three men started as J.D.'s voice cut through the salt-tanged night like a machete.

"Holy shit." Bramson nearly choked as he saw

the girl huddled beside J.D. at the top of the gangway.

She'd heard. That much was obvious from the expression on her face — and on J.D.'s. That idiot braggart Frank. Now they'd have to waste her.

Frank swallowed convulsively. "J.D. . . . I . . ."

"Didn't you hear me? Shut the fuck up. You've said more than enough already. I ought to cut your flapping tongue out."

All four men were staring at Meg, one thought humming between them.

Meg's knees buckled. She would have crumpled to the deck like a rag doll but for J.D.'s grasp. "Ty, get over here," he barked, his face mottled with fury in the pale artifical light. "Hang on to her."

Then J.D. was in Frank's face, his low-voiced, furious tirade so intense that Bramson, beside them, was showered with spittle.

Meg sagged against the railing, gripping it with both hands as Ty held her by the elbow. *They have to kill me now. Now that I know.*

Her dazed eyes strained to see in the cloud-laden moonlight, frantically searching out the horizon. To her right, she could discern a faint outline. Land?

She squinted, staring harder, her pulse racing. There were shadows — and lights. Was it only moonlight flickering off the water, or could it be an island?

There was no time to think, to weigh the odds.

She might never get another chance. In one smooth movement, she whipped the lighter from her pocket and snapped it into flame as she lunged around, setting Ty's shirt on fire.

For one awful moment, she watched the shock ignite across his face, heard his bellow, smelled the stench of butane and burning flesh, and then she was scrambling up over the rail, jumping feet first down, down, down toward the inky, swirling water below.

Don't get sucked under the boat. Head to the right. To the right.

Gasping, she broke the surface and tried to orient herself in the icy water. Gunshots zinged through the dark all around her, and from what seemed a great distance she heard shouts, curses — and then a splash.

Terror clamped hold of her, tight and jagged. *Oh, God, they're coming after me.*

Sucking her lungs full of air, she plunged deep underwater.

There was only one thing to do. The thing she had been born to do, trained to do.

She swam.

19

Her numb hands pummelled through water. She felt as if she'd been swimming all night. As fatigue dragged at every limb and her lungs worked like a bellows, sucking in air, blowing out air, Meg had only one thought: *Keep going.*

In relentless cadence, her arms and legs clipped like pincers. Up, over, splash, pull. Kick, kick. *Kick.*

And still the horizon floated like a distant mirage.

Through her exhaustion, Meg pushed on, focusing on the indistinct shape of land. How far was it?

Too far, a tiny betraying voice whimpered inside her.

She'd never felt so alone. So cold, so exhausted, so hopeless.

Something brushed against her leg. *Oh, God. Sharks? Jellyfish?* Heart pounding, she closed her eyes and swam on, half-expecting that at any moment giant jaws or stingers would slice through her legs.

The moon had vanished behind encroaching storm clouds, and darkness crushed her with its totality. Not even a star broke the dense curtain of blackness.

If only it wasn't so dark, she sobbed, each gasping breath searing her lungs. Suddenly, somewhere to her left, lightning speared the water.

And Meg grew cold with a new fear.

She forced herself to swim faster, arms and legs flailing. But with each stroke the waves grew stronger, pushing her back.

I'm not going to make it. It's too far. I'm too tired. It's hopeless. Exhaustion gave way to despair.

Thunder cannonballed through the sky as raindrops pelted her shoulders. And from somewhere behind her, her name sailed on the wind as the voices of her captors echoed in the eerie stillness. They were still searching, the boat slicing like a shark fin through the choppy water.

It's no use. No use. I'm going to drown.

Meg's toes stubbed against sharp rock, sending pain reverberating up her calves. Then she was half-standing, half-stumbling over the jagged shoreline, throwing herself forward toward the boulder-strewn beach, embracing the rocks with sobs and gasps and open arms, scraping her elbows and knees as she plodded up and over. She collapsed in the brush and vomited sea water until she was dizzy with the effort of dry heaves.

Land. Cold, hard, beautiful land.

But she wasn't safe yet.

With the wind plastering her torn, sodden jogging suit against her shivering skin, Meg glanced out at the sea, where whitecaps were starting to crest. In the distance, the yacht's lights flickered ominously like dozens of miniature searchlights sweeping across the water.

Meg staggered to her feet, frantically scanning the pitch-black terrain before her. She could have used that little gold lighter right about now, but she sure wasn't going back for it.

Fighting the pain screaming in her knotted calf muscles, she clambered wobbily over the rocks and slid down an embankment until she reached damp, mossy earth.

Ahead of her stood a small shack and a parked Jeep.

The Eagles' "Take It Easy" warbled from an old tape player rigged above the peeling wooden bar in Ernie's Cantina. Jake's sandals slapped against the dirt floor in time to the music as he splashed more bourbon into his half-empty glass.

"Pump up the volume," he bellowed as thunder drowned out the lyrics.

"It don't go up no more, man," Ernestine called, popping open a beer can and taking a hefty guzzle.

There were only five people in the tiny, dimly lit hut, still decorated with last year's Christmas lights, and not one of them was in any condition to drive home.

Staring into his glass, Jake groused, "When in

hell are you going to replace that piece of shit and get a jukebox?"

Sam, the squat, coffee-skinned lobster fisherman perched at the end of the bar, rolled his dark eyes. "Go home, Jake. Your temper is as nasty as the weather."

"Go to hell. I'll leave when I'm good and ready."

Big Veda, Ernie's tiny Jamaican cook, who also doubled as the island's postmaster, set down the dented enamel stockpot he was scraping out and stomped over to Jake's little table.

"Listen to Sam, Jake. Go on home." When Jake ignored him and picked up the bourbon again, Veda plucked the bottle from his hand. "The storm, my friend, it is coming in fast."

As if on cue, the lights flickered. Jake groaned. "I'm sleeping right here."

"No, you don't. Go sleep it off in your own bed." Ernie lumbered over and began wiping the sticky tabletop with a blackened rag, nudging Jake with her hip. "You're too drunk tonight to be any good in mine."

Big Veda and Sam hooted. Jake swatted her ample fanny.

"Wanna bet, baby?" He grinned from beneath his straw Panama hat and downed his remaining bourbon in a single guzzle. "There ain't a woman in two continents who's ever kicked me out of her bed yet."

"Well, I'm kicking you out of here," Ernestine announced firmly, giving his wide shoulder a shake. "Do us both a favor, honey, and go home." Though stern, her tone held a note of fondness. "I'm closing up this dump before the rain hits and my roof starts leaking. Come on, it's almost two in the morning and I wanna go to bed."

Jake stumbled up, knocking over the chair. He swore under his breath as he bent to right it. He hadn't been this blasted in months, and he felt like hell. Somewhere in the back of his mind he knew the morning would be worse and he dreaded it, dreaded the thunder already pounding through his skull.

Rain sheeted into the cantina as he opened the door and staggered out into the wild night. In the glare of silver lightning that strobed across the sky, a sodden figure suddenly swayed toward him.

"Holy shit." Jake stared as the figure collapsed against the rickety wall of the hut. "What the hell snake pit did you crawl out of?"

"They're . . . after . . . me." A woman's gasp, hoarse and desperate.

He blinked through the rain, wondering if he was hallucinating, or if there was really before him a woman sinking to her knees, with seaweed trailing from her streaming hair.

"Go on inside." He waved, an expansive gesture. "They're getting ready to close up, but I'm sure old Ernie will pour you a tall one."

"No, please." She lunged to her feet and threw herself at him, clinging to his arm. Jake saw that she was about five foot seven, slender, and scared out of her mind. Violent tremors shook her. Even in the darkness he could see her lips were blue, and her breath was coming in shallow, rapid hiccups. "They can't . . . find me. They'll kill . . . me. You have to . . . help me."

"You've got the wrong guy, lady. I'm not in the hero business." He tried to step aside, his mind blurred, confused. He wasn't quite taking in what she was saying, but she sure looked spooked. And she wouldn't give up that death grip on his arm.

"Don't you understand?" Her voice rose as the wind lashed his hat nearly off his head. "They're going to kill me!"

Jake grabbed his hat and squinted at her. *Just what I need. A damsel in distress. Probably a loony toon. But where in hell did she come from?*

Tourist boats didn't stop in Montigne. The island was too small, too off the beaten track. There were only sixty-six residents here, and he knew them all. Yet this was no apparition. It was a real live terrified female, about 115 pounds of soaking-wet babe with pleading eyes the color of a summer sea and long muddy fingers that clutched at him with ferocious desperation.

"Get in," he grumbled, jerking his thumb toward the Jeep parked crookedly on the gravel drive. "Lie down in the backseat and don't poke your head up no matter what."

Jake was drunk, but he wasn't so drunk that he didn't scan the road in both directions as he bounced full throttle past the swaying mangroves.

Rain slashed at the windshield, and he could hear the woman's teeth chattering in the backseat.

What the hell have I gotten into now? he thought, twisting the wheel hard as he roared past Friar's Cove. *I need this like a case of dengue fever.*

The effects of the bourbon were already dissipating, his reflexes had kicked into high gear, and he felt tautly alert as he checked the rearview mirror for headlights.

Zilch. Maybe the babe is hallucinating, another one of those strung-out druggies whose plane crashed in Monkey Valley while trying to score a cool quickie million.

Dodging ruts already filled with water on the gravel road, he accelerated onto the nearly hidden, overgrown lane leading to his shack. "It's not the Waldorf, but it's high and dry and it's private," he said, throwing open the Jeep's door.

The woman huddled in back lifted her head, surveying the wood shack on stilts. "They'll be looking for me soon," she whispered.

Jake helped her up the broken cement walkway, slipping an arm around her waist as they climbed the rickety stairs. When he'd settled her inside on the well-worn plaid sofa bed, he handed her a blanket and stood back for a minute, studying her.

Hell, she needs more than a blanket. Her purple-and-aqua jogging suit was torn, soaked, and plastered to her skin. The hiccups had ceased, but her teeth still chattered like castanets, and her hair, strewn with seaweed and grass, hung like

Medusa's snakes around a face that was dirty and bruised and extraordinarily beautiful. She'd obviously been through hell, but under what circumstances and at whose hands?

"You don't understand," she repeated, rocking back and forth on the sofa. "They're coming after me. You have to call the police."

"Hold on, baby doll. I'll have to call the morgue if we don't get you into some dry clothes." He strode to the cardboard box beside the Formica dinette table against the wall and riffled through it, pulling out a rumpled gray terrycloth sweatshirt. "You can change in the bathroom — right over there. Meantime, I'll put up some coffee."

He took four steps into the adjoining kitchenette and set an aluminum pot on the gas stove. "Jake's special java coming right up," he called as she limped toward the bathroom. "Strong black island coffee with a shot of Jack Daniel's will bring you back to the land of the living in no time."

Why the hell am I playing nursemaid to some drenched chick who's in God knows what kind of trouble? Since when am I Sir Galahad?

He had a bad feeling in his gut. Almost as bad as the pounding in his head. A sudden crack of thunder and a simultaneous gust of wind set the wooden house shaking on its stilts. As the lights flickered, Jake dug in the cupboard for candles and matches. He decided he'd better heat up some of the conch chowder he'd cooked for dinner tonight. She looked like she could use a good hot meal.

When he returned to the main room with two mugs of coffee, she had changed into the sweat-shirt and was lying on the sofa with the blanket tucked around her legs.

"I left my wet clothes in the bathtub. Sorry, I didn't know where to put them."

"Don't sweat it. If it ever stops raining, I'll hang them outside to dry." He saw her flinch as the wind picked up, whistling through the boards and rattling the windows. Once again, the lights flick-ered, temporarily blotting out the few dingy fur-nishings of the low-ceilinged shack.

"Whoa, Betsy," Jake muttered, casting a wary eye at the old-fashioned green swag lamp swaying wildly over the dinette table. "The last time these babies went out, we didn't have power on the island for a week."

The woman, holding the coffee cup in both hands, peered anxiously toward the window. "Please, now will you call the police?" Her voice hitched with urgency. "Before the power goes out and we can't get in touch with them. . . ."

"Baby doll, I hate to break it to you, but this island's got nothing but a post office, a bar, and a lean-to general store. The nearest police station is two islands away — half an hour by boat and five minutes in my chopper — when it's working, that is. And right now it's about as dependable as these lights."

Huddled beneath the blanket, Meg felt her

thigh muscles tremble, from both terror and the aftereffects of her arduous swim. She gazed up at the brawny man seated in the deck chair across from her — Jake, he'd said his name was — her eyes filled with fright.

You're going to get him killed, too. He looks pretty big, pretty tough, but how could he be a match for all those paid thugs?

He'd been tipsy when she'd first stumbled into him, but he looked sober now, his hazel eyes light and clear beneath the twin slashes of his sandy brows, his mouth no longer slack but firm and decisive-looking within a broad, handsome face that was rough with several days' stubble. For some crazy reason, even as weak, sick with fear, and shaken as she was, a tiny voice inside her sighed, "Way to go, Miss America. You must look like hell. You finally meet an attractive man and you resemble a rodent who just crawled out from a sewer."

And then she knew she was halfway to lunacy. Why in God's heaven was she thinking about him being attractive when she probably wouldn't even live long enough to find out his last name?

"I don't know what to do." She gulped down the last drops of the coffee, each hot sip burning along her throat. "I just don't know how to get away. . . ."

"You're not going anywhere until this storm is over, and take my word for it, neither is whoever's on your tail. So why don't you just sit back, try to relax, and tell me what's going on here. For starters, what's your name?"

Still clenching the cup, she met his quizzical gaze. "Meg Hansen." She swallowed hard. "I know you won't believe this, but I'm Miss America."

His expression never changed. "Right," he drawled, leaning back in a canvas deck chair that looked too small for his brawny frame. "And I'm Donald Trump. Welcome to Mar-a-Lago."

She stared at him blankly. *I know I don't look like a beauty queen right now, but he's eyeing me like I'm an escapee from Bellevue.* "Listen to me," she said slowly. "My name is Margaret Elizabeth Hansen. I was drugged and kidnapped in Atlanta, and I've been held captive on a yacht for days. I had to swim who knows how far to get away from them, and I need you to believe me. They're already after me, and if they find me here, we'll probably both be killed." His expression hadn't changed. Meg licked her lips. "Don't tell me you haven't read about my disappearance in the newspaper."

"Part of the reason I'm holed up out here, lady, is that I don't want to be bothered with newspapers, television, and junk mail by fax. I pick up a newspaper once a month — at most. And I like it that way." He leaned forward, his elbows on his knees. His eyes looked pure green in the murky lamp light. "So why don't you just take a deep breath and run all that by me again."

Meg did, recounting as coherently as she could everything that had transpired since she'd found

Burnsie slumped and bleeding on the hotel's bathroom floor. The story tumbled out, all of it, up until the moment when she jumped over the side of the yacht.

He stood up, paced back and forth before the sofa, and paused to glare at her. "You're telling me that you swam here from a yacht — with the seas kicking up like they are?"

"You're looking at a former contender for the Olympic swim team," Meg said quietly, scooping her tangled hair behind her ears. "Another life-time ago."

"Let me get this straight. First you're Miss America. Now you're a female Mark Spitz. Who's been held captive on a yacht. . . ." Suddenly he stopped short, wheeled toward her and stared at her as if she had just sprouted donkey ears. "Shit."

"Then you believe me?"

"The soup's burning."

He disappeared into the kitchen and Meg noticed that on the table, alongside the typewriter and a red folder containing a thick stack of papers, was a cordless phone. On shaky legs she hobbled over and snatched it up.

"No use," Jake said from the doorway, fragrant steam curling from the mug of soup he held. "The battery's dead. Planned to get a replacement on my next trip to the big island, right after I got the damn chopper in running order."

Meg gritted her teeth. "So you're telling me we're completely cut off from the rest of civilization in this godforsaken place?"

"Until the storm's over, yep. And until I get the chopper —"

"— in running order," she finished for him, slamming down the phone. "I know. I know."

His hands dwarfed the glazed mug of piping hot conch stew he held out to her. "House specialty. You won't taste any better, if I do say so myself."

Meg hadn't realize how hungry she was. She ate ravenously, finally polishing off a third helping of the thick red chowder, redolent with salt pork, tomatoes, bay leaf, and garlic. The chunks of conch were spicy sweet with a hint of barbeque sauce and she eagerly scraped her spoon around the last drops of thick gravy.

"That was heavenly." She sighed. "You won't believe what they've been passing off as food."

"Well, every condemned soul deserves a last good meal."

Her eyes narrowed at him. "Have you ever considered a stint on David Letterman?"

"Never watched the guy." Jake took the empty mug from her and set it on the table. "Why don't you try to get some shut-eye? They won't be able to mount much of a search until the storm is over. Even then, they'll probably assume you've drowned and make only a cursory look-see. So I recommend you sleep and let me worry about the next move."

It was too tempting to resist. He looked so utterly competent, so completely certain that there was no more danger tonight. And she was so tired, so bone-weary spent, that all she could do was yawn as he eased her off the couch.

The sofa pulled out to a bed. He settled her in it with a pillow and a blanket that smelled faintly of leather and coconut. There was no need to turn out the lights, because as she tucked the blanket up around her shoulders, they flickered out and never came back on.

"C'est la vie." Jake spoke beside her in the darkness, sounding remarkably cheerful for a man who had a desperate fugitive taking up his only bed. This Jake was a cool character. An intriguing character. What in the world was he doing, living like a hermit out here in the middle of the Caribbean?

"Jake." Sitting up, she peered at him as a blaze of lightning illuminated his face, catching him with a frown hardening his features. "What's your last name?"

"Selden."

"Thank you, Jake Selden," she whispered. "Thank you for saving my life."

The trees thrashed as if they were being uprooted by the wind, which howled through the island. Jake waited for the thunderclap to end before he answered. "Don't thank me yet."

But as Meg succumbed to the weariness overtaking her, she felt unexpectedly calm, unexpectedly safe. He was a recluse, a stranger. She didn't even know if he believed her.

But he was willing to help, and he was all she had.

"I want you to shoot her on sight. Do you hear me? No exceptions. No excuses. She knows my name. I want her dead."

In the hospital corridor on the neighboring island of Tescole, J.D. grimaced into the phone. Corey Preston was beyond fury and J.D. couldn't blame him. J.D. was rigid with rage himself. In the twenty years of his mercenary career, maneuvering through famine, war, and plague, he'd never failed an employer, not once. And he wasn't about to let a slip of a girl put a black mark on his reputation now.

"We'll get her. You can be certain of it." His voice was clipped, smooth, professional, belying his own venomous anger. Though this morning a steady rain still pattered against the tiny island hospital's tin roof, Mother Nature's wrath had quieted to a grumpy displeasure. "Last night the storm prevented us from doing a thorough search, but there are only two islands she could have reached — this one and Montigne. If she made it at all."

"Assume she did. Assume she's out there. You find that bitch today!" Corey Preston shouted in his ear.

"You have my word. She's past tense." J.D. waited as a squat nurse brushed past him into Ty's fan-cooled room, carrying a replacement bag for his IV. "That little bitch did a good job barbequeing Mather. It'll be a pleasure to take her out. The team's on it even as we speak."

"It'll be your weenie roasted on a spit if she gets away," Preston snapped in his ear. The next thing J.D. heard was the slam of the receiver.

"Son of a bitch," J.D. muttered savagely, and then he blocked everything from his mind except the girl.

20

Meg awakened to the smell of fresh coffee and the drum of rain. Even before she opened her eyes, she felt the ache of every muscle in her body. She struggled up on one elbow, remembering immediately where she was. She'd made it through the night. Yet, as she saw the gray rain sheeting down the window pane, fear stabbed through her. The storm was nearly over, and so was her reprieve.

"Jake?" she called tentatively, throwing back the blanket and wincing as she eased her legs to the floor.

"Jake!"

She jumped as he stuck his head out the bathroom door behind her, his face lathered white with shaving cream and his broad shoulders bare.

"I just wanted to know where you were," she said feebly, suddenly realizing that under his sweatshirt she wore nothing but her panties. "I smell coffee. Is the power back on?"

"Gas stove. Comes in handy here in Montigne. I'll be out in a minute."

Meg couldn't wait for her turn in the shower. She shivered all over as she stepped beneath the tepid spray of water and let it wash away the grime of her midnight swim and her crawl through the island's rocks and underbrush. Now that it was daylight, she expected that at any moment, J.D., Frank, and the others would trample down the doors like rabid bears. And Ty . . . what had happened to him? How badly had he been burned? If he ever got his hands on her, after what she'd done . . .

She didn't want to think about what he would do.

"What's wrong?" Jake asked, as she emerged from the bathroom tucking his blue T-shirt into the khaki shorts he'd left hanging for her behind the bathroom door. She'd followed his advice and pulled his belt through the loops, knotting the leather at her waist to prevent the shorts from falling off her hips. She'd combed her damp hair with his hairbrush, and now, in the pale light of morning, her fresh-scrubbed face had a hint of color in it.

"I don't see how I can escape them. These men are professionals. And if the island's as small as you say, there aren't that many places to look."

"Chances are when the weather cleared this morning they took the guy you torched over to the hospital in Tescole. It's the only island for miles around with any decent medical facilities. My hunch is that a couple of them stayed behind to start searching."

224

Meg glanced uneasily toward the window.

"Relax, baby doll. That's the bad news. The good news is that no one saw you in Ernie's place last night except me. And I live in a pretty isolated section of the island. They're not going to find this place so fast. So I think you have a few minutes for breakfast."

For the first time, she noticed the table. He had cleared away the typewriter, the thick red folder, and the dead phone. In their place was a tempting array of food: sliced mangoes, chunks of fresh coconut and bananas, and an open box of Fruit Loops surrounded by chipped, mismatched dishes and bowls and a plastic jug of milk.

There was fresh coffee waiting in two mugs, and eggs sizzled in a frying pan on a potbellied stove that looked to be a pre–World War I relic.

As Jake slid two over-easy eggs onto her plate, she noticed for the first time the faded but still angry-looking burn scars marring his wide bronzed arms. She wondered what horrible accident could have caused them and winced at the thought of the pain he must have endured.

Jake looked very different this morning from the drunken, disheveled man she had first encountered outside that bar. He was clean-shaven and smelled enticingly of lime aftershave. His sandy hair was neatly brushed, the thick ends curling at the base of his neck. The olive tank top and black Bermuda shorts he wore emphasized his superb, deep-muscled physique. As Meg slipped into a chair and reached for a wedge of coconut, she tried not to stare at his broad chest or at the hard, sensuous line of his mouth.

"Is there any way off the island?" she asked, stirring milk into her coffee. "Aside from that disabled chopper of yours."

"There's a puddle jumper that comes through once a week — but it won't be back for days. Look, Margaret . . ."

"Meg."

"Meg, there's no golden chariot parked outside to whisk you out of here. You're going to have to lie low for a few days — and trust me."

"Jake, believe me, you're not the one I don't trust. I'm grateful to you . . . more grateful than you'll ever know. But . . ." She swallowed and passed a weary hand over her eyes. "Just my being here is putting you in danger. You have no idea what these men are like. They're killers, paid killers."

He set down his spoon and cocked an eyebrow at her. "Do you see me shaking in my boots?"

"You're wearing sandals." Spearing a slice of mango, she studied him over it. Now that he'd mentioned it, he didn't appear the least bit like a man who'd just been told that killers might at any moment arrive uninvited for breakfast. He looked relaxed, calm, and intent on his Fruit Loops.

"There's more coffee in the pot — help yourself," he told her as he sliced a banana into his cereal.

Meg shook her head in exasperation. "Are you deaf, naive — or too stupid to understand?" She leaned forward, emphasizing each word as if she were trying to communicate with an alien. "These men mean business. They know that *I* know who hired them to kidnap me. They won't stop until they find me and shut me up for good."

Jake's eyes turned the color of an icy green sea. "Then we'd better make sure they don't find you." He spoke matter-of-factly, as if they were discussing what brand of laundry detergent to buy at the grocery store. With one motion, he rose and scooped the cereal bowls toward the sink and then tossed her a ragged dish towel. "Come on, Miss America. I'll wash, you dry. And then we'll make plans."

She'd never met anyone like him. Last night outside the bar he'd seemed like an ill-tempered carousing jock, too thick-witted to be of much help. Later, he'd taken charge with surprising alacrity. And today she saw a man who appeared unfazed by the crazy dimensions of her tale and unafraid of the danger trailing her like the lit fuse of a firecracker. *Who are you, Jake Selden, and what are you doing here in the middle of nowhere?*

There were no signs of anyone else inhabiting the shack with him, none of the little touches that would suggest a woman's presence. Yet he didn't look like a man who would be long without one. Virility radiated from him, gleaming from his eyes, pulsating off his body like sexual radar.

What a time to be thinking about sexual attraction. Yet Meg was overly conscious of his knuckles brushing her hand as he handed her each rinsed plate. *You've been a virgin for twenty-three years, and only now that you're staring death in the face do you finally meet a man who turns you on like no one ever has before.*

You're nuts. Plain and simple, that's the only answer.

The story of my life — never having time for a boyfriend, just study, study, study and swim, swim, swim. And now that I've swum straight to Jake Selden, I don't have time for him either.

Life made no sense. But it sure beats death, Meg reminded herself, sliding the last of the plates into the cupboard and tossing the towel over a wooden chair to air dry. Though she'd cheated the grim reaper so far, she could feel his sickle swishing in her ear.

"Jake, I have to ask you a question." She watched his quick, sure movements as he put the flatware back into the drawer. "Why aren't you frightened by everything I've told you?"

He closed the drawer and turned toward her. One hand reached up to cup her chin. "Because you're scared enough for both of us."

"Fair enough," she whispered, her face flaming at the electricity of his touch. "But don't say I didn't warn you."

Jake's gaze locked with those vivid aquamarine eyes. Eyes that stared at him with trust and wonder and shadows of things past. She was something else. She'd obviously been through hell, but she'd fought back with everything she had. Looking at her, he saw courage, brains, and beauty.

Even in this dismal light, with little sleep, no makeup, and bruises still puffing on her cheek, she was gorgeous. Long lacy lashes, naturally pink full lips, smooth fair skin — and a sleek lanky body that made the simple shorts and shirt he'd given her look like something out of a Victoria's Secret catalog.

You've really landed in the middle of it this time, Selden, he told himself, swallowing back the urge to pull her close and taste those voluptuous lips.

Instead, he dropped his hand and turned away. "Think I'll head out back and see what I can do about that chopper. I've got a replacement part on order, but it seems to me I ought to be able to get her in the air without it. You stay inside, and don't so much as peek out the window." He reached into a small drawer beside the stove and pulled out a small black pistol. He set it on the countertop. "If you hear anything funny, kneel down on the floor under that window and get ready to use this."

Meg stared at the gun in disbelief, then burst into laughter. "Jake, you don't understand. I hate guns. That's the reason I'm in this mess. My entire Miss America platform has been an antigun campaign."

"This seems like a good time to rethink that position."

She shook her head. "My sister is the crack shot in the family. Cat would know exactly what to do with that thing."

"Sounds like a smart lady."

"That depends on your point of view. I happen to think it's smarter to get guns — and criminals — off the streets. Our parents had a gun in their drugstore the night some punks broke in and held them up," she said quietly, "but they never had a chance to use it. They were shot and killed in cold blood."

There was a tightness in his jaw that might have been compassion. "How old were you?"

"I was six, and Cat was nine." She closed her eyes for a moment. She'd spent the last year recounting the past in endless speeches and interviews, but this morning, with Jake Selden as her sole audience, the painful intensity of it rushed back with a vengeance. Meg turned abruptly and retreated to the sofa, swallowing back the lump in her throat. She picked up the blanket and began folding it into neat even squares, acutely aware of how intently he was watching her.

"From the moment it happened, it affected the two of us in completely different ways. I had nightmares for months on end, and she started sleeping with a baseball bat under her pillow. To this day, she carries Mace with her everywhere she goes." She threw him a rueful smile. "By the time we were teenagers, Cat took up target practice, and I set my sights on law school."

He lifted an eyebrow. "Harvard, no doubt."

"Nothing less." She tossed him the blanket and met his gaze steadily. "I want to fight my battles in the courtroom, prosecuting punks like the ones who killed my parents. I want to look them in the eye and send them away." Determination flashed in her face as she turned and without waiting for his help, folded the mattress back into the couch. "Maybe that will save other kids from what Cat and I went through — and maybe something I said this past year will help in the fight for tough gun laws."

Jake dumped the blanket on the table. He reached her in two strides and yanked her around to face him. "So you're telling me you wouldn't use that gun to save your skin if one of those bastards who's after you gets past me?"

She lifted her chin and her eyes narrowed. "You bet I would."

His lightning grin sparked a wildfire inside her. "Thatta girl." He ruffled her hair as if she were still six years old, and strode toward the door. "Stay put."

The shack felt empty without him. Meg mounded the cushions onto the sofa and went into the bathroom to see if her clothes had dried. Restless, she paced the wooden floor. She'd give anything if she could call Cat and Gram to tell them she was safe.

Safe? She wasn't safe yet, not really, though she felt a whole lot better having Jake Selden on her side.

He came in two hours later, drenched. During the course of the morning the rain had abated to a misting drizzle, which had plastered his sandy hair to his head and soaked his clothes until they

231

gripped the contours of his muscles like a second skin.

"No luck," he muttered, wiping his greasy hands and dripping face on the dish towel. "Yet."

"And no power, either."

He pushed the hair from his eyes. "At least your charming friends haven't shown up. Tell you what. I think I'll take a drive into town and see if anyone's been nosing around."

Meg clutched his arm. "*No.* Don't leave me here."

The frightened words spilled out before she could stop them. Humiliated by her own raw panic, she let go of him.

"It's only for a little while," Jake said gently.

Suddenly, before either of them realized it, he was holding her. "Don't worry, Meg. I swear I won't let them hurt you."

Meg laid her head against his chest, trembling as his arms tightened around her. It felt so good to be held. The solidity and warmth of him infused her with a sense of rock-hard comfort.

Buck up, she told herself, bracing for the moment he'd pull away. *Better that he scout out the enemy rather than stay here baby-sitting a sniveling coward.*

She lifted her head and met his assessing gaze with as much steadiness as she could muster.

"Will you be home for dinner, dear?" she deadpanned.

Again that swift grin flashed into his face and melted her insides. As quickly and naturally as rainwater streaming down the shingles, he dropped a quick, warm kiss on her mouth.

"Wouldn't miss it, baby doll."

21

The emergency room at Beth Israel Medical Center was jammed with walking wounded, but Jordan only had eyes for her daughter. Engulfed by stiff white sheets, Lori looked like a tiny crumpled doll as she lay on the narrow gurney.

"Mommy, it hurts."

Jordan leaned close. She murmured in Lori's ear as she smoothed the child's damp hair from her brow. "I know, baby, but the doctor's going to make it better. It will stop hurting very soon."

Lori screamed out as the nurse inserted the IV needle in the back of her tiny hand. "It's okay, baby; it will be over very soon." Jordan's chest ached for her. "You'll fall asleep for a little while, and when you wake up that bad tummy ache will be all gone." Then there would be the pain of the incision to deal with. One thing at a time, Jordan told herself, as she gripped Lori's free hand, waiting for the Demerol to kick in. Only twenty-four hours ago, Lori had been at the zoo with Mike. Now her appendix was about to burst.

Beyond the curtained alcove, there was the

234

hum of frenetic activity. The mingled smells of alcohol, antiseptic, and urine filled Jordan's nostrils, but she tried to shut out everything except Lori's wretched face.

"I want Daddy," Lori whimpered, peering frantically around at the green tile walls and the uniformed strangers bustling past her.

"He's coming, honey. I left him a message. . . ." The screech of metal hooks interrupted her as the curtains were dragged apart and a nurse with a clipboard marched through. An orderly, whose hair was enclosed in an elasticized blue cap, dogged her heels. Whistling, he grabbed the head of the gurney and smiled down at Lori while the nurse flipped through the papers on her clipboard.

"Ms. Davis?" she confirmed. Her smile was practiced, but there was a reassuring warmth in her light blue eyes. "And I gather this is our little patient, Lori?"

Jordan nodded, clutching Lori's hand.

"We're ready for her now. If you'd just sign this authorization at the X, we'll be all set. . . ."

"I want Daddy!" Lori screamed, and as Jordan scribbled frantically, from the corner of her eye she saw Mike striding toward them.

"How's my brave girl?" he asked so cheerfully and yet so tenderly that Jordan's throat closed up.

"Daddy, it hurts."

"They're taking her into surgery right now, Mike. It's her appendix."

Mike bent over the gurney and walked alongside, talking to Lori in a stream of steady, soothing words as the orderly pushed her down the hallway toward the set of green double doors. Jordan hurried along with them, promising Lori as she gave her one last kiss that when she woke up there would be a new coloring book and a big shiny balloon waiting for her.

The doors whooshed closed. Jordan and Mike stood alone in the bright corridor. They stared at each other.

"I got here as soon as I could."

"I know." Jordan's voice quavered as the aftermath of the mad rush to the hospital set in. At midnight, Lori had woken up screaming and Jordan had phoned first the pediatrician and then a cab, praying every second that Lori's appendix would hold out until they reached the hospital. Now her knees were suddenly rubbery and her eyes scratchy with tears she hadn't had time to shed.

"Come on, Jordan." Mike took her arm and led her down the gleaming corridor. "You look like you're going to collapse. Let's find some coffee while we wait."

They sat silently side by side in the surgical lounge, ignoring the quiet drone of the television, the tired whispers of the middle-aged Hispanic couple huddled near the window, and the restless pacing of a tall, gaunt, young black man who kept twisting the gold wedding band on his finger.

Mike had settled her in one of the upholstered

blue sling chairs and brought her coffee laced with just a smidgen of sugar, the way she liked it. It flowed warm and delicious down her throat, despite the cardboard taste of the vending machine's paper cup.

"Feeling better?"

"I'm fine, but I feel so stupid. I thought she just had the flu. I should have brought her to the doctor the minute she told me her stomach hurt."

"Jordan, give yourself a break. You're a great mother, and I'll take on anyone who says otherwise."

Jordan gave him a feeble smile.

As Mike took her hand, he frowned. "You're so tense." Gently, he began massaging her fingers, rubbing the tension from them. Jordan closed her eyes and leaned her head back, melting into the chair while the blinding anxiety ebbed away.

"You're a good man to have around in a crisis, Mike Bannister."

"I'm always here if you need me, Jordan."

The words tore into her heart. She wasn't sure she could believe them. On the day she'd signed the divorce papers, she'd never have thought she could count on Mike again. But during the last few weeks and again tonight, he seemed so different from the work-driven, frenetic, alcoholic cop he had become during his stint on the vice squad. Was it possible AA really had transformed him, one day at a time? He seemed so much calmer these days. More mellow than he'd been in a very long time.

Don't read too much into this, Jordan chastised herself, deliberately pulling her hand away. She sat up straighter and opened her eyes. Mike pulled back, too.

"It's my turn to get you some coffee." Jordan stood up, slinging her envelope bag over the shoulder of her red blazer. The heels of her black flats squeaked softly as she swung across the linoleum.

When she returned from the vending machine around the corner, the surgeon was with Mike, speaking in a low tone.

"Here's Lori's mother. Tell her the good news."

Lori was going to be fine, just fine, Dr. Curtis assured her, repetitively clicking the top of his ballpoint pen. Barring any complications, she could go home the next day, and when Jordan asked about her upcoming tap class, he guaranteed she'd be back to her old self in time to start.

"She's in recovery right now, Ms. Davis. Within the next half hour to forty-five minutes, she should wake up, and then we'll let you say hello to her."

When he was gone, Mike and Jordan stared at each other in mute relief.

"She's a tough kid." Mike's eyes crinkled. "She gets it from her mom."

"You better believe it." She took a deep breath, suddenly buoyant with relief. "Thanks, Mike. Thanks for being here."

"She's mine, too, Jordan," he said quietly, and she heard the edge underlining the calm words.

"Mike, I'm sorry." Jordan bit her lip. "I didn't mean . . ."

"No apologies necessary." Mike turned away and reclaimed his seat, picking up a copy of *Sports Illustrated* from the magazines scattered on the end table beside him.

Whatever peace they'd felt between them was broken now. Jordan sensed it, saw it in Mike's taut jaw. She hadn't meant to imply he wasn't a good father, but trying to explain would only make it worse. "I can't sit still any more," she told him stiffly. "I think I'll take a walk."

Mike found he couldn't sit still either. He read the same paragraph five times before he tossed the dog-eared magazine back onto the end table. Wearily, he rubbed his eyes with the heels of his hands.

As he opened his eyes and his vision came into focus, Mike spotted Jordan through the waiting room window. She was pacing the hall. Elegant, he mused. Jordan always managed to look elegant without any apparent effort at all. Even in the midst of an emergency in the wee hours of the morning, dressed in jeans and a simple blazer, Jordan appeared as polished as if she were lunching in midtown.

Something about the way she moved, the way she held her shoulders as she walked, spoke of old money, high class, a world he'd never known. But Jordan was the most down-to-earth person he'd ever met, and that was one of the things he'd always loved about her.

Love. Something twisted inside him. *Admit it, Bannister. You've never gotten over her. You never will.* As he shifted in his seat, stretching his legs before him, the shoulder holster dug into his rib cage, interrupting his thoughts just as his work had interrupted their marriage. *Don't blame the gun, pal, or the workload. It was you. You blew it. Big-time.*

The shrill pipping of his beeper had the Hispanic couple seated next to him glancing over. He squelched the sound, got to his feet, and strode to the pay phone.

Listening, he felt his stomach drop down to his kneecaps. He sprinted toward the elevator, nearly colliding with Jordan as she rounded the nurses' station, her arms hugged around herself. He wondered if he should tell her, but she looked so damned tired and she already had enough to deal with right here.

She'll find out soon enough.

"Mike! What's wrong? Where are you going?"

"Emergency. I'll call you later. Give Lori a kiss for me," he called over his shoulder as he charged between the slowly parting elevator doors. She saw him bang his fist against the number panel and saw the grim set of his mouth as the doors clamped shut.

A chill of fear curled tightly across her chest. She knew that look. Something had happened. But before she had time to wonder what it could

240

be, a nurse tapped her shoulder.

"Lori's awake now, Ms. Davis. Follow me."

At eight o'clock the next morning Lori asked why her Daddy wasn't there. Jordan, who'd spent the night on a cot in the small, semiprivate room, explained that the police department had needed Daddy to take care of an emergency.

"And where's my coloring book?" Lori pouted. "And my balloon?"

Jordan had forgotten all about them. "I'll just go down to the gift shop and get them, honey. I won't be a minute."

"Mommy, but I don't have my crayons."

"I bet I can find a brand-new box down there, too." Jordan smiled and kissed Lori's soft cheek. "Now, don't go anywhere until I get back." She winked.

As Jordan hurried down the hall, wondering if she should take time to dash into the cafeteria for orange juice and a bagel to bring back up to the room, she could see the waiting room crowded with a new group of worried faces. But instead of separate knots of people, everyone stood together, eyes riveted to the television set.

Oh my God. A sixth sense filled her with dread. She slipped into the lounge, edging to the front, noting the shocked, sickened faces around her with ever increasing apprehension. The television screen was filled with images of rubble and destruction.

"What's happened?" she asked the elderly black

man standing next to her.

He shook his head. "The Empire State Building. Didn't you hear? That damn fool 'Director'
did just what he said — he done blown a big hole
in it."

22

The next six hours were as tension-filled as any Jordan had ever known.

While she sat with Lori and tried to talk calmly and entertainingly to her, her mind kept darting north to Fifth and Thirty-fourth where Mike was probably at this very moment sifting through the rubble searching for secondary explosives.

She tried to blot his imminent danger from her mind, and she couldn't bear to think about Meg either. It seemed incomprehensible that she was a prisoner of men who would hold a woman hostage and blow up a building with no thought to how many people would be hurt. She had to focus on Lori, who was wearying of crayons and coloring books, and growing ever more fretful — complaining about her incision and the IV.

"Mommy, I want them to take this VV *out*."

"It's called an IV, darling, and they can't take it out just yet. But maybe this afternoon Dr. Curtis will say it's okay."

As Lori started to whimper, Jordan heard a light tap at the door. "Lori, look who's here," she exclaimed in relief as Mrs. Chalmers bustled in, her freckled arms filled with a giant Raggedy Ann doll who was sporting a bandage on one floppy leg.

"Well, now, Missy, you sure weren't kidding about that tummy ache. But before you know it, you'll be pumping so high on those park swings that I'll need my binoculars to see you."

Lori grinned and reached out her free arm for the doll.

"And you." Mrs. Chalmers frowned at Jordan. "You look like you belong in the bed next to her. Why don't you go on home for a shower and a long nap while I keep Lori company until you get back?"

"You're a lifesaver." Jordan squeezed Mrs. Chalmers's hand with sudden gratitude. As Lori began chattering to the Raggedy Ann doll, Jordan motioned Mrs. Chalmers toward the window.

"I haven't been able to catch up on what's going on. Have you heard the latest fatality figures?"

"Three dead right now and a few dozen injured, from what I heard before I came over. Thank the good Lord those idiots screwed up and the bomb didn't do as much damage as it could have. The police think it was supposed to go off during the daytime."

Jordan closed her eyes for a moment. "It's awful. I'd bet Mike's down there right now. He always seems to end up in the thick of everything."

Mrs. Chalmers gave her a shrewd look. "Listen, honey, that's one man who can take care of himself. I'm more worried about you. Go on home and get some sleep. Lori will be fine and dandy until you get back."

Jordan took a hot shower, slept for an hour, and fortified herself with a bowl of raisin bran before calling the office.

"The pageant received a new fax twenty minutes ago," Alana reported after first inquiring about Lori. "The Director's upping the ante. Next he's threatening to blow up a national monument unless Cavenaugh is released from prison. The rest of the fax is a rambling rehash of his previous demands about the pageant. And Meg." A moment of silence hung between them.

"If he touches one hair on her head . . ." Jordan's voice was tight. She blinked back tears, remembering how Meg had always loved to ride with her long hair loose, flying free. *Free.*

Please, God, let her be free.

"The FBI had better find this guy," Alana grumbled. "We've got a pageant to put on next week. And Hy Berinhard is more obnoxious than ever. Want to hear his latest suggestion?"

"No."

"For the interview segment, he wants each girl to explain how the world can best fight terrorism. And Miss West Virginia has dropped out — the runner-up is taking over her slot. Miss California and Miss Rhode Island are both skittish about continuing, so who knows where we'll be by next week?"

"Right now, I'm most concerned about where Meg will be," Jordan said. When she hung up the phone, her heart was so heavy she felt as if she'd swallowed back an ocean of tears.

She tossed her robe across the bed and threw on a lemon silk tee and a long black cotton jumper, with her most comfortable sandals. She had packed a small bag for herself and another for Lori bulging with toys, pajamas, a toothbrush, and the Fisher-Price cassette player. She was half-way out the door before she remembered she hadn't played her messages.

The sound of Alex's voice from the machine jarred her.

"It's ten A.M., Jordan. Alana just told me about Lori's appendix. Guess it blew about the same time as the Empire State Building."

His short chuckle jangled her nerves. Impatiently, she waited for him to continue. "I sent her a dozen long-stemmed roses — tell her she's supposed to share them with you. Right now I've got a major strategy meeting regarding our coverage of the Director's latest stunt. One way or the other, I'll catch up with you at the hospital later."

Strange, Jordan reflected as she reset the machine, *I haven't thought of Alex once since this emergency with Lori's appendix began.*

But she'd been thinking an awful lot about Mike.

Driving back to the hospital, she listened to the radio updates with a churning stomach. Fortunately, only a small corner of the Empire State Building had been damaged, but the bomb squad and rescue teams were searching the entire structure floor by floor.

She could picture Mike in the middle of all that chaos, cool and calm, his eyes narrowed beneath his hard hat, the centers darkened to cobalt with that keen alertness that intensified when he was working. A shudder passed through her as she envisioned him covered with grit and dust, sweeping the area for any other bombs while he methodically unearthed every shred of evidence.

If anyone had the tenacity to track down who'd done this, it was Mike.

As she pulled into a parking space two blocks from the hospital and cut the ignition, the irony of the situation hit her. Not only had the Director ensnared Meg in his machinations, he now had Mike caught up in them, too. He was like a giant spider, spinning his evil web in ever-widening circles.

She fought off a sense of suffocation, of being smothered in a sticky, unbreakable net. When she walked back into that hospital room, she had to appear cheerful and self-possessed, able to reassure her daughter that their world was normal and sane.

Normal and sane. What was that?

She only hoped Mike would handle the stress of the bomb squad better than he'd handled the pressure cooker of vice. Talk about jumping from the frying pan into the fire.

Good thing you don't have to worry about him anymore, she told herself as she hurried through the hospital lobby. Yet as she rode up to Pediatrics, she couldn't banish that image of Mike probing through that great scarred building, his life on the line every moment he stayed and sifted and searched.

The music pounding from the strip joint below reverberated through Russell Sima's ears as he paced the Oriental carpet that stretched from one end of his second-story office to the other. In his left hand was a solid brass lion's head paperweight. As he prowled, circling from the desk to the window and back again, he hefted the paperweight repeatedly into the air, letting it slap back into his palm with rhythmic precision. His two-hundred-dollar alligator shoes made a soft scraping sound every time he shifted direction, and the corded veins in his neck stood out bright blue against his sallow skin.

"How could this have happened, Leonard?" His voice was a low growl. "My reputation with Méndez is fucked. *Fucked.* Do you hear me?"

Standing with his head bowed beside the glassed-in bar, Leonard's shoulders sagged.

"Those idiots screwed up big-time, Mr. Sima. But even Méndez knows accidents happen. At least the bomb went off. . . ."

"Went off? It went off in the middle of the

damned night! It was supposed to go off at noon. *Noon!* And now I look like a total fuckup in front of the whole world. What's more, do you think Méndez is going to turn over the balance of our payment now? No way!"

"How do you propose we handle this, Mr. Sima? I mean, we can't kill the three screwups because they're already dead. The stupid bastards blew themselves up."

Sima whirled to glare at the other man, his fingers tightening on the paperweight. "And who the hell picked them for this job, Leonard? I want you to kill that fuckup."

"Uh, Mr. Sima. I feel an obligation to remind you that, uh, you picked them."

Sima hurled the paperweight into a wall of mirrors. Glass shattered into a thousand shards with a crash that drowned out the music. "I don't want to talk about this anymore, Leonard. I want some good news. Something that will improve my disposition. Give me an update on Mike Bannister's ex-wife and kid."

Leonard scratched the side of his nose. "The kid's in the hospital. Appendix, tonsils, I forget which. You want we should do the hit there?"

"Leonard," his boss chided. "Where's your sense of timing? It's much better to wait until the child goes home and Papa thinks his little duckling is safe."

"Whatever you say, Mr. Sima."

The music from downstairs grew even louder and raunchier, the bass pulsating through the floorboards like a monstrous, frenzied heart.

"Wait a day, maybe two. When the kid goes home, we'll throw a surprise party that fucking cop will never forget."

Jordan read to Lori from her Pocahontas storybook until her daughter's pale eyelids fluttered closed for the night.

"Tomorrow you can sleep in your own bed," she whispered, pressing a kiss to Lori's cheek.

The cheerless hospital room had been transformed by Alex's roses, balloons from Alana and an assortment of coloring books, dolls, and stuffed animals. But Jordan felt as if she'd been cooped up there for a week instead of a day, and as she laid the Pocahontas book on the nightstand, she gave in to the urge to prowl the halls for a while before retiring to her luxurious hospital cot for the night.

"Hey, gorgeous, can I buy you a drink?" Alex's voice behind her brought her up short. Jordan turned her head with a quick smile.

"It's only fair to warn you — I'm an expensive date. Vending machine decaf will set you back a whole dollar." Jordan laid her head against his shoulder as his arms went around her in a warm squeeze.

"Nothing's too good for my girl," Alex chuckled. "Lead the way."

Fifteen minutes later they were ensconced in the deserted lounge, with Alex regaling her with the day's war stories from his newsroom.

"Have you checked with your office this evening? CNN beat our tails today — on home turf yet. Any inside scoop you could give me from the FBI would put me eternally in your debt."

Jordan regarded him over her coffee cup. "Sometimes lately I'm not sure whether it's me you're interested in or my inside track on breaking news." She spoke lightly, but there was a keen glint in her eyes.

Alex took the cup from her hand and set it atop the pile of magazines strewn on the table. He brought her hand to his lips, palm up. Slowly, he kissed each fingertip, his lips warm on her skin. Then he drew her closer and kissed her mouth. "If we weren't in this hospital, Jordan, I'd show you what I'm really interested in."

"Let's see — three guesses," a familiar masculine voice drawled from the doorway. "And the first two don't count."

Jordan jumped. Mike's brawny frame seemed to fill the narrow lounge, but it was the sardonic expression on his weary, stubble-shadowed face that sent heat flooding into her cheeks.

"Didn't anyone ever teach you to knock?" she snapped.

"Lori's had a nightmare." He ignored Alex and fixed his gaze on Jordan. "They sent my team home for a couple hours' sleep so I swung by to see how she was doing. I got here a few minutes ago and found her sitting up crying for you."

"Oh my God. She was sound asleep when I left." Jordan bolted out the door without another word to either of them. The only sound in the lounge was the rapid squeak of her shoes fading along the corridor.

So this must be Alex Woods, the "Uncle" Alex whom Lori had complained about. Mike coolly studied the tall man unfolding himself from his chair. Fists clenched at his sides, he fought the urge to knock the bland corporate half-smile off the bastard's face.

The bastard extended his hand. "Alex Woods, Mike." Woods's grip was as self-assured as everything else about him. "I'm sure Jordan's mentioned me."

"Actually, no." Mike thrust his fists into the pockets of his dusty work trousers. For some reason he felt dirtier now than he had while crawling through that damaged building. He fixed the other man with a professionally neutral gaze. "But my daughter has."

Clancy's nicer than Uncle Alex, Daddy. I don't like him. When he's with Mommy, he tells me to go play in my room because they're busy with grown-up talk.

From the looks of it, they'd been busy with more than just talk. Mike knew it wasn't rational to resent this ultrasmooth son of a bitch — after all, he had Clancy in his life and in his bed — but he couldn't help it. Nothing he'd stumbled upon today had been rational. Nothing he'd seen in that rubble and certainly nothing about his relationship with Jordan.

They were divorced, finished, kaput. The only

tie that bound them together was Lori. And yet . . .

Good try, pal. You'd like to deck this guy and take Jordan home to bed. And make her forget she ever signed divorce papers.

"Your daughter's quite a chatterbox — I think she has more energy than any of the gophers I've got scrambling through my department. Sometimes I really feel for Jordan, having to work all day and then chase around after a kid all night. Guess this surgery ought to keep her sidelined for a few days, don't you think?"

You don't want to know what I think, buddy. Aloud, Mike said evenly, "I think visiting hours are over. I'll tell Jordan you said goodnight."

"Don't trouble yourself. I'd rather stick around and tell her myself." Alex plucked a cigarette from a gold monogrammed case. "Better not let Jordan catch me with this, though. She hates when I smoke. But you know, Mike, I've had a hell of a day."

Tell me about it, buddy. If this joker makes it out of here in one piece, it'll be a miracle. What the hell does Jordan see in him, anyway? Aside from the pretty-boy looks, the six-hundred-dollar suit, the spare change jangling in his pocket — which probably adds up to more than I take home in a week.

Instantly Mike knew that wasn't it. Jordan didn't care about money. She'd come from wealth and it held no glamour for her. She didn't need its trappings nor was she seduced by the status and accoutrements.

She must just have lousy taste in men.

He glanced up wryly as Jordan whisked back into the lounge and Woods jammed the unlit cigarette into his jacket pocket. God, she was beautiful. Even after the strain of an exhausting day like this, she glowed, her eyes as luminous as crystals.

"Lori's fast asleep — again." She sighed, tucking a strand of hair behind her ear. "And I'm turning in for the night, gentlemen." She glanced warily from one to the other.

At least they haven't killed each other yet. She had half expected to find a trail of blood leading down to the emergency room.

When Alex reached out and snaked an arm around her waist, pulling her to him with a possessiveness that was blatantly for Mike's benefit, she nearly flinched.

"Want me to tuck you in?" he offered in her ear.

Jordan saw the muscles along Mike's forearms stiffen.

"I think I can manage," she said quickly.

This was ridiculous. She felt the way she had when she was eight and Jimmy Miller and Willy Hudson III had fought like young Dobermans over who would sit next to her in the lunchroom, punching each other so wildly that they'd knocked over her carton of chocolate milk, spilling it across the floor. *One of us has to be a grown-up,* she thought. *It might as well be me.*

"I'll walk both of you to the elevator," she

announced, disengaging herself from Alex as she started for the door. A small, mean part of her wanted to revel in the satisfaction that Mike had seen her with Alex. After all, she'd almost literally stumbled into Clancy in his apartment.

And yet Jordan felt only a queer, sad pang. Mike looked so beat. He'd been working nearly twenty-four hours, he'd come here to see his daughter, and he'd found his ex-wife kissing another man. Not exactly an ideal ending to a lousy day.

Ex-wife. That's the operative word here, she reminded herself, suddenly wishing that both Alex and Mike would hurry up and go away. Yet as Mike stood before the elevator with his hands shoved inside his pockets, watching the numbers light in turn on the overhead dial, she suddenly touched his sleeve.

"Any luck today? Any clues?"

Mike glanced at her, his mouth tight. "We found part of the bomb. A few shreds of wire, some plastic. It's a start."

"I can't stop thinking about Meg. If only I hadn't suggested she enter the Miss Arizona pageant . . ."

"Jordan, stop it." Mike's hands shot out and gripped her shoulders. He gave her a short, firm shake. "You can't keep beating yourself up over this. It's not your fault."

"I've been telling her that," Alex chimed in almost peevishly.

Jordan and Mike glanced at him in surprise.

"She hasn't listened to me," Alex challenged. "So I really can't see why she'd listen to you."

She could have sworn she heard Mike growl. Then the elevator doors slid open and Jordan backed away in relief.

Men. An alien species put on this earth to mystify and confound the rest of us.

She held her breath, hoping Alex would have the tact not to kiss her goodnight. At this moment she found the thought of locking lips with him while Mike looked on about as appealing as eating porcupine quills. But Alex seemed determined to stake his claim. She was more annoyed than anything else when he doubled back and planted a dramatically possessive kiss on her before strolling into the elevator.

To her surprise, instead of looking furious, Mike's eyes suddenly glinted with suppressed laughter. "Sweet dreams, angel."

The doors closed before her tired brain could think up a witty retort.

She wanted to kill him.

She wanted to kill both of them.

With any luck, she reflected, trudging back up the hall, *maybe by the time the elevator reaches the lobby they'll have saved me the trouble.*

23

"Would you mind slowing down? Dammit, I can't walk like this."

Cat yanked her arm free of Dagger's grip. Scowling, she tugged off her single shoe, wishing she could pound its heel into his thick skull. Not that it would get her very far or do much to improve his mood. Before she even had time to catch her breath, he was dragging her down the driveway again.

He flung open the passenger door of a black Corvette convertible and gave her a push. "Get in, Mata Hari."

Almost before she'd had time to swing her stockinged feet inside, he slammed the door.

As Dagger peeled past the open gates of the estate, Cat began to shiver. For all the warmth of the night air, an arctic wind might have been blowing through her sopping hair and dress.

She was all too aware of how the dripping silk outlined her breasts. It was as if the damned material had shrunk three sizes, leaving virtually nothing to the imagination, and to her consternation the cold wind hardened her nipples into taut peaks that poked against the thin fabric.

"Watch the road, will you?" she bit out between chattering teeth as she saw him glance at her. She fought the urge to fold her arms across her chest to cover herself, refusing to give him the satisfaction of knowing just how much he had discomfited her.

"There's a jacket in the backseat if you're cold."

If I'm cold. "Yes, Einstein, I'm cold. Where is . . . oh, here."

Nice jacket, Cat grumbled silently, tucking the silky linen under her chin and letting the sleeves dangle across her shoulders. The rich, subtle scent of Drakkar enveloped her. Too bad Dagger didn't behave as nicely as he smelled.

"You'll want to take this south. I'm staying in Delray," she sniffed as they neared A1A.

In answer, Dagger turned onto A1A and headed north at seventy-five miles an hour.

Cat gripped the jacket tighter around her as the wind lashed her hair, whipping it against her face. For the first time, fear touched her, like a single sharp-edged claw raking down her neck.

Where was he taking her?

He can't murder you, he's a government agent. But he sure as hell could leave you stranded in the middle of nowhere as retribution for invading his precious turf.

She snuck a sideways glance at him as he floored the Corvette, and shivered involuntarily at the hard set of his profile illuminated by the console lights. Remembering his strength, and the ruthlessness she'd seen in his eyes, her stomach knotted.

He warned you.

She had no idea what the man beside her was capable of. As they zoomed around a dark Lexus, Cat barely had time to discern the young couple in the front seat, much less signal them for help. She watched the speedometer hit eighty.

Where was a cop when you needed one? The man drove with the same ice-cold confidence that marked his every move, maneuvering through traffic with the ease of a championship race-car driver. She dug down in the seat and closed her eyes, steeling herself to counter whatever Dagger had in mind.

"If this is a kidnapping, I think I should tell you that the FBI is already looking for one member of my family."

"Is that a note of worry I detect? I thought you were intrepid."

"Intrepid, not stupid," she muttered. Opening her eyes, she noticed that the highway still skimmed along high coastal bluffs. "Trust me, running into you was the last thing I expected tonight. Who the hell invited you to Palm Beach anyway?"

"Nice try, but I'm asking the questions, Ms. Hansen, and that one's at the top of my list. Answer away."

"If I tell you, will you take me back to Delray?"

"Not on your life."

He exited the freeway and swerved off on Celestial Way. Aside from two small apartment buildings, she could see only a small lake glimmering beneath the golden moon. Dagger parked in a small deserted lot between the buildings.

"Get out."

He came around the car as she opened the door, and pulled her to her feet so quickly the jacket slid onto the seat. "This way."

There was no one around. No use screaming or making a scene. Cat's heart skittered into her throat as he marched her across a small grassy area, past a clump of Australian pines, and down a beaten grass path that was swallowed up in darkness. She couldn't see where she was stepping, but little stones dug into her feet, and she had to bite back the urge to cry out. She'd be damned if she'd plead mercy from Dagger.

"Let me guess, Captain Hook. You've got a gangplank and a crocodile pit down here, and I'm the midnight snack."

"You can be breakfast, for all I care, if you don't start talking. I've got all night, but the crocodiles may not be as patient."

Her feet were suddenly cushioned in warm sand. A narrow beach stretched before them, glowing like a creamy satin ribbon in the darkness. The tang of salt water filled the air and the only sound was the faint cry of the seagulls on the bluffs.

"Very romantic," Cat said. "But if you wanted to be alone with me, you could have just said so."

"Do you think," Dagger asked softly as he pulled her past a barely discernible couple entwined on a blanket, "that you could be quiet for just two minutes?"

She deliberately raised her voice. "Then I couldn't answer all your questions, could I?"

He quickened his pace, scowling, pulling her along the beach. When he finally stopped, he spun her to face him. Cat saw his gaze flick down for a brief moment over the still-damp dress clinging to her breasts, then shift upward to her face. His jaw tightened.

"You have got to be the most argumentative woman I've ever met. Is it just me, or do you always have to get in the last word?"

"Careful, Dagger. You're starting to sound like my ex-husband again."

"You keep mentioning him. Still carrying a torch?"

There was no mistaking the spark of bitterness that flashed in her eyes and disappeared just as quickly, replaced by stony hauteur. "Just the opposite," she snapped. "But if you don't mind, I'd rather not discuss my personal life with you."

Cat turned abruptly and started back toward the car, her shoulders rigid. Dagger grabbed her wrist.

"Seems I hit a sore spot. Sorry."

She started to shake her head, but Dagger saw the hurt still in her eyes.

"Listen, I didn't mean anything by that remark. There's no need to look that way."

"It's the only way I know how to look."

His smile flickered and then disappeared so quickly Cat wondered if it was ever there at all. "It's not that I'm complaining," he offered.

"Well, I've got a complaint." Scowling, she jerked free of his hand. "I'm cold, I'm soaked to the bone, and I'm not in the mood for a moonlight stroll on the beach."

"But we have so much to discuss," he countered smoothly. "And the only bugs around here are the winged ones."

Goose bumps prickled her flesh. Bugs. She hadn't thought of that. *My God, what did I say to Gram from the phone in the motel?* She grabbed him by the lapels. "Do you think my motel room could be bugged?"

He shrugged. "I haven't stayed alive this long by taking chances. We need to talk and we don't need anyone else listening. So I'm prepared to stay out here until the sun comes up, if that's what it takes. Because I want answers from you and I'm not delivering you back to your motel until I get them."

The bastard meant it. Cat lifted her chin. "Fine. Ask away."

The sound of lapping waves crashed in her ears, but Dagger seemed oblivious. He watched her with cool intensity as she smoothed her tangled hair from her eyes.

"First of all, who invited you to Preston's party?" he asked.

"No one. I invited myself."

That got him. His eyebrows shot up.

"I think you'd better elaborate."

So she told him. She told him every detail of her escapade at Ryan Industries and what had brought her here to crash Corey Preston's slimy little soiree.

"You're a crazy woman," Dagger rasped, shaking his head. "Sanderson could have caught you raiding his office."

"He didn't."

"You were damn lucky. You could be facing a breaking and entering charge right now."

"Dagger, I don't care. I'm prepared to do whatever it takes to bring my sister home. Obviously, you've never lost anyone you loved or you would understand. I have, Dagger, more than once, and I'll be damned if I'm going to sit by doing nothing and lose my sister, too!"

Something darkened in his eyes. Something cold and painful. Then it was gone, and Cat rushed on, too caught up in her own agony to ponder what ghosts she'd stirred. "The way I see it," she continued grimly, "my hunch about Preston must be a damned good one. Otherwise, you wouldn't have been here poking around his estate."

There was no reading his expression as he took her arm. "Let's walk. It's going to look suspicious if we just stand here without cozying up like those two over there."

Cat glanced back at the couple now rolling under the blanket. "They're hardly in a position to notice," she remarked drily. Still, as Dagger kicked off his shoes and started down the beach, she followed willingly, noting for the first time two other couples tucked away beneath the palm trees and realizing with a tiny flicker of excitement that she was in the midst of an undercover assignation with a bona fide government operative.

He was being more reasonable than she'd expected. He was actually listening to her. Suddenly hope that she might persuade him to tell her what he knew sparked within her.

But before she could speak, Dagger asked, "What makes you think you can find your sister when countless government agencies are still looking around the clock?"

"Because Meg means a hell of a lot more to me than she does to any government agency," she shot back. "And I want nothing more in this world than to see my sister alive again."

She was really something. Smart, tenacious, and motivated as hell. Not to mention drop-dead beautiful. And her instincts were good. Damn good, Dagger reflected, halting on the beach to stare at her. All on her own, she'd shown up at Preston's, no more than one step behind him.

But she was an innocent, a civilian. He raked a hand through his hair. "This is dangerous work, Cat. You're already in over your head."

"I think my head is well above water, thank you."

"You'd be best out of it."

"I'm in — for better or worse." Her eyes

leveled on his. "Which means that we can work together or we can work separately. Your choice, Dagger, but I'm not about to back down. Corey Preston's involved. I feel it down to my toes. If you hadn't dragged me out of that party tonight, I'd probably have even more to go on by now. And there's no way I'll consider leaving Palm Beach until I've proven his part in this, one way or another."

Studying the determined set of her shoulders, the stubborn tilt of her chin, he had to admit she'd handled herself well at Preston's tonight. She knew how to think fast on her feet. With a bit of direction . . .

Dagger made a quick decision. "Guess I'd rather be able to keep an eye on you than have to worry about cleaning up after you."

"I knew you'd see it my way. Now, I've been thinking . . ."

"Whoa. This isn't the old West, Cat, and I haven't hung a deputy's badge on you."

"But . . ."

"No buts." He gripped her by the shoulders, hard enough to command her attention. "The two of us can theorize, brainstorm, and talk this out every plausible way, but we've got to be clear about one thing. I'm calling the shots."

"So you're pulling rank on me?" She tilted her head challengingly. "Should I put up with this, I wonder?"

"You don't have a choice." Dagger's hand went to her chin, tipping it up so she was forced to meet his eyes. "If you want to work with me, I'll need your word that you'll follow orders. This is my last official job, and I'm not about to end my career burying an uncontrolled civilian who goes off half-cocked."

He was a damnably self-possessed man, Cat thought, studying the firm angle of his chin shadowed by palm trees swaying in the moonlight. And disconcertingly handsome. His dark hair, lightly ruffled in the wind, tumbled over his brow in a way that made her want to smooth it back. The scent of his cologne mingled pleasantly with the tang of the sea, and the touch of his fingers on her chin created a gentle heat that warmed and steadied her. And if she stared into those compelling eyes for one moment longer, she'd agree to anything he said.

Don't be fooled, a voice inside of her warned. He might seem like James Bond and the Rock of Gibraltar rolled into one, but he was only a man. Like Paul, like Vince. They were all alike. Demanding that a woman honor and obey — just like the old marriage vows. Well, Paul had let her down and so had Vince, so what made her think she could count on Dagger?

Nothing. But he was right — she had no choice. She had to trust him as far as the investigation was concerned. But with nothing else, she told herself, removing his hands and taking a step back.

"Your word, Cat," he persisted.

She kept her voice cool and impersonal. "Fine,

you've got my word. I'll follow your damned orders."

But as she started to turn away Dagger pulled her back, wondering even as he did so what the hell he was doing. Looking for any excuse to put his hands on her, he reflected unwillingly. She looked so gorgeous, wrapped in an elegant dignity undiminished by the wet film of ruined silk and the windblown tangle of her hair. But it was more than that pulling at him. Beneath all that aura of composure, he'd just glimpsed a haunted vulnerability that had shone like a beacon to her soul.

"What's wrong?" he demanded.

Cat shrugged, and he saw the barriers fly up. "I'm not in the habit of trusting too many people these days. No offense, but men in particular are at the bottom of the heap." She straightened her shoulders and pulled herself up to her full height, which meant the top of her head still only brushed his chin. "So now I have a dilemma. I've just given you my word, but I have no guarantee you're going to level with *me*. I won't be left in the dark. Or told only what you want me to know."

Men in particular are at the bottom of the heap. "You weren't just burned, you were scalded, weren't you?" There was a grim line around his mouth. "The ex-husband, I suppose?"

Anger flashed in her face. "I'm not here to discuss my personal life."

"Fair enough, but don't hold me responsible for it."

"I only hold you responsible for my sister's safe return."

"What about yours?" he asked.

"I can take care of myself."

She probably could, under ordinary circumstances. But these were not ordinary circumstances or ordinary people they were up against. Staring down at her determined face, tension twisted through his gut. And a strange protectiveness flared inside him. It had nothing to do with her being a civilian. It had everything to do with her.

"We'd better get back and get you into some dry clothes," he said curtly. "You look half frozen." Cat saw his eyes flick downward to her breasts. Her nipples felt as hard as seashells, and she knew the moonlight was outlining them against her damp dress.

"I could use that jacket of yours right now," she muttered, flushing. She folded her arms across her chest and stepped back, wondering if her lips were blue. Why was she staring at Dagger's mouth and thinking about her lips? Something was happening between them. She didn't know what. Staring warily into his eyes, she found her voice, its tone a shade less defiant. "Don't you think it's time you took me home?"

More than time, Dagger agreed silently, yet he didn't move. He stood there trying to shake off the urge to pull her against him and warm her with his body. "Let's go," he said, but instead he pulled her forward into his arms.

Her eyes were locked on his. "This isn't the way to the car," she began, but her voice trailed away to a whisper as she leaned into the warmth of him, her body shivering in the shelter of his arms.

Slowly he lowered his head toward hers. "Cat." Her name flowed out like the warm tide before he could stop it.

His soft breath brushed her lips a moment before his lips did. Cat scarcely knew what was happening before waves of heat crashed over her like breakers thundering against the shore. She closed her eyes as the kiss deepened and his arms slid around her waist. Her nipples were crushed against chest muscles more taut and powerful than she'd imagined. She melted against him, gasping as his teeth found her lower lip. And then she was kissing him back, her arms locked behind his neck, her whole body pressed against the iron-corded length of him.

Dagger pulled her tighter, his mouth hungrily tasting, his hands roaming with sure pleasure over her back and shoulders, dipping to press against her waist. With her mouth open against his lips, Cat murmured shakily, "If you're looking for a gun, I don't have one on me."

"Making sure is half the fun." Dagger backed her against a palm tree. She was breathing shallowly, inhaling the intoxicating musky scent of him, reveling in the nearness of this man who had just kissed her with a blinding tenderness she'd never known before. Was this bliss or was it just the proximity of the ocean, bathing them in some primeval tidal rhythm stronger than reason?

Dagger stared down into her widened eyes, noting how the glisten of passion had intensified their vibrance, how they met his with unwavering wonder. He felt as if all the air had been sucked from his lungs.

A sudden sharp trill of laughter down the beach startled them. Dagger tensed and pulled back as one of the couples bounded toward the water and plunged in, squealing. Dagger released Cat, his arms dropping to his sides.

"That wasn't very professional. Sorry."

She drew a ragged breath. "Do you conduct all of your interrogations like this?" she asked, trying for an offhand laugh.

"None of them," he told her, then frowned. "You *are* shivering."

Abruptly he took her arm and started back toward the path. "Let's get you into some dry clothes."

Dagger scowled as he stooped to retrieve his shoes. He knew if she didn't change into something less revealing, and fast, he wouldn't be responsible for what happened. And he had to be responsible. There was more at stake here than whatever was happening between the two of them.

"I'm staying at the Riviera Palms in Delray Beach," Cat said as he switched on the Corvette's engine and then helped her slip into his jacket.

"Better button it," he advised her dryly, "or I

can't promise to get us home in one piece."

What do you think you're doing? a voice inside her shrieked as he buckled his seat belt. *This is just some insane hypnotic spell cast by ocean and moonlight — or else Dagger is one smooth operator who's perfected the art of feeding lonely, insecure divorcees exactly what they want to hear.*

She was being a fool.

He put the car top up and snapped it in place. "That should make for a warmer ride back." He roared out of the parking lot and zipped onto the highway with such cool, single-minded efficiency that Cat was sure his mind couldn't be whirling anywhere near as much as her own was.

"You had other questions."

"They can wait."

He drove in silence, following the coastal bluffs that loomed into the sky like ghostly watchtowers. Cat stole a look at him, this dark, magnetic man whose mouth had felt so exquisitely hot on her own. Headlights from opposing traffic swept across his face, revealing the blunt, handsome features she found so enigmatic and yet so irresistible. She wished she could read his mind, wished she could understand what had happened back there on the beach. Hands clasped in her lap, she fought the flicker of nervous anticipation that tingled up her neck, fought the urge to let down her guard, the temptation to follow where her feelings might lead.

As the car zoomed along the highway, she wondered what else this night might hold in store.

24

Dagger drank his coffee black. Like Vince, Cat reflected from her side of the coffee shop booth as she stirred cream and double sugar into her own. *Odd, this is the first time I've thought about Vince since I went to Washington.*

And then the thought of him dissolved just as quickly as the dark coffee lightened to creamy gold because Dagger leaned forward and touched her hand.

"That's better. You're much warmer now. For a while there you felt like a Popsicle in my arms."

"Literally or figuratively?" Cat regarded him through sultry lowered lashes. The gold clip that secured her hair off her face glinted in the bright overhead lights.

"What do you think?"

She smiled and settled her shoulders back against the booth. It felt good to be in dry clothes. At the motel she'd changed into a flowing linen vest and matching drawstring pants the color of melon. The coffee felt good, too, going down hot and strong.

And being here with Dagger — that felt ridiculously good.

"Ridiculous" being the operative word. She'd be damned if she was going to make a fool of herself over a man again. Especially this man. And under these circumstances.

"Let me say two things," Dagger began once the waitress had refilled his cup and sauntered off to the kitchen. The twenty-four-hour coffee shop was deserted except for an old man eating a cinammon roll and poring over the newspaper two tables away. "One — I'm truly sorry about your sister. Despite what you might think, I'm doing everything possible to locate her and get her home safely. Two," he continued, his gaze fixed intently on her, "this is getting complicated."

"I noticed."

"And the situation is complicated enough without the two of us . . ."

"I agree."

"Cat." He grasped her hand across the table and squeezed it tightly within his own. His eyes darkened, turning nearly black. "This isn't the time for you and me to sort out what just happened at Juno Beach. Or to sort out anything of what we're feeling."

She nodded quickly, reaching for her purse. "This is the time to focus on Meg. We need a strategy for investigating Preston."

Right down to business, wasn't she? This was about finding her sister after all, but at the first mention of sorting out what had gone on between them, she'd gone into hiding, retreating behind the investigation rather than even acknowledging the spark that had flared between them.

When she tugged out the sheet of paper, Dagger took it with a questioning glance.

"I rescued this fax from Sanderson's paper shredder. Doesn't this sound like Preston knows something the rest of us don't?"

Dagger scanned the glossy paper. "It doesn't prove anything on its own, but the reference to America waking up sounds like it could be more than coincidence."

The waitress reappeared without invitation and splashed coffee from a fresh pot into both of their cups. Cat picked up her steaming cup. "So what's our next move?"

"Bed."

She choked midswallow. "I beg your pardon?"

Dagger held his watch in front of her face, tapping the dial. "It's half past three, Mata Hari. I think we should get some sleep and regroup in the morning."

"Wait a second. I shared information with you. When are you going to tell me what else *you* know?"

Before he could answer, the cellular phone in his pocket rang.

Cat knew it was about Meg before he even said a word.

"You're sure? Do we have ID on the clothing?" Dagger listened intently, his eyes avoiding hers.

Her stomach churned. Every nerve ending

turned to ice, as if she'd just been plunged into a frozen mountain river.

"Fax me a copy of the report. I'll be back at my hotel in twenty minutes and I'll call you from there."

Cat grabbed his sleeve with shaking hands as he dropped the phone back into his pocket. "Was that about Meg?"

He eyed the waitress, who was now circling the tables replacing ketchup bottles. Dagger spoke in a low tone. "A bomb went off at the Empire State Building around midnight. Minor damage — the Director has claimed responsibility. And Charles Latham has been arrested as a material witness in your sister's kidnapping."

The color drained from Cat's face. "It *is* ORBA," she whispered.

"The FBI turned up a cache of plastic explosives in a warehouse Latham owns in Detroit. And there's a paper trail — he withdrew two million dollars from various ORBA accounts a week before the kidnapping and another million after."

"You said something about clothes. . . ."

"Besides the explosives, they found a garbage bag in the Detroit warehouse." Dagger took a deep breath. "The clothes your sister was wearing at the time she was kidnapped were inside."

"Oh, my God." Cat was drowning in that river now. The frozen water had just closed over her head. "Can they . . . make him tell . . . where she is?"

"They're damn well going to try. Look, I've got to get back to my hotel."

"I'm going with you."

One look at her white, agonized face and he knew he couldn't say no.

He watched her jump from the booth, her hands shaking as she hitched her purse across her shoulder. He wished like hell he could reassure her. But false words of comfort would be worse than silence.

He held open the door to the coffee shop. Head bowed, Cat shot past him like a streak of quicksilver into the darkness.

25

A crack of sunlight pierced between the drapes and hit Cat smack in the eyes. Daylight. Groggily she forced her eyes open and pushed herself up on her elbows. *How long have I been sleeping?* she wondered, searching her memory for everything that had happened the night before.

The bedside clock showed 8:10. She must have dropped off sometime after four. The last thing she remembered was slipping off her shoes and checking in with Gram while Dagger pored over the ream of facsimile paper that spewed with urgent regularity from his small black fax machine.

Dagger. She bolted to a full sitting position, her gaze darting around the large, shadowed suite. Where was he?

If he left without me, I'll kill him. Her bare feet hit the plush camel carpet at the same moment she heard water running in the bathroom.

Sighing with relief, she padded over to the picture window and swept apart the drapes. Sunlight poured in, warming the expensive pickled oak armoire and the dusky blue damask sofa with slanting golden rays. She ran a hand through her hair, studying the indentation in the center of the pillow scrunched at the far end of the sofa. She felt a pang of guilt that she'd taken over Dagger's bed and left him to squeeze his tall frame between those rounded sofa arms. But before she had time to fret over his discomfort, the bathroom door opened and he stepped out, patches of shaving cream streaked on his face and neck.

He wore only navy boxer shorts and a towel around his neck. His slicked-back hair was still wet, glistening with water droplets. He was magnificent. All corded muscles and dark, sinewy sensuality. Cat's gaze was drawn to that broad, furred chest, to the bulging muscles in his arms — it was an effort not to follow the whorl of hair trailing down his flat abdomen to where it disappeared below the wide elastic waistband of the boxers.

Whoa, girl, take it easy. But it was hard not to drool when she remembered how it had felt to be crushed against that chest, held in those arms, kissed by that mouth. She'd made enough of a fool of herself where men were concerned. This man would be the biggest mistake of them all. Dagger — she didn't even know his real name. Or if he was married. Or if she could trust him farther than she could throw a telephone pole.

"Good morning," she muttered with a cross between a smile and a shrug. She made a show of hunting amid the papers on the table for the room service menu, her face averted. "Guess I conked out on you. Any word on Meg?"

"Nothing significant." His voice was neutral and controlled. "Latham's claiming he was set up."

Cat paused, glancing over at him, her eyes narrowed. "How convenient. You don't buy that, do you?"

He yanked at the towel and began blotting up the shaving cream residue, all the while noting how the sun glowed off her sleep-mussed hair. His insides tightened. Even with the pale lavender shadows under her eyes and her clothes rumpled from sleep, she looked achingly lovely and all too ready to lead the charge.

He considered how to answer her. "I'm not putting my money on anything yet. This whole thing doesn't feel quite right. Latham's too smart to keep a smoking gun in his own warehouse. I'm waiting to see if the explosives found in the warehouse match those found at the Empire State Building. We'll talk about it over breakfast. Room service should be on the way up."

Cat nodded. He sounded so businesslike. There was none of the tenderness she'd seen at Juno Beach last night. Which was just as well.

She matched his tone with a tight nonchalance, crossing to the luggage rack where she'd deposited the duffel bag they'd retrieved from her motel room last night.

"I can be ready in a flash. Don't you dare try to sneak out of here while I'm in the shower."

He paused, the towel in one hand. "A bargain is a bargain. Do I look like the type to sneak out on a lady?"

"Well, you sure as hell are the type to sneak in," she muttered, yanking out her toiletry case.

In the bathroom, she stared at the closed door. She sensed that during the night he must have made up his mind to extinguish whatever tiny spark had started to flicker between them.

So much the better, she told herself. As he'd said last night, this was getting complicated. And right now, she had to keep focused on what was important and keep everything else simple.

Twenty minutes later she sat opposite him at the breakfast table that room service had wheeled in. Though her skin was still damp from her shower, she felt human again, wearing a daisy yellow sundress that skimmed her ankles and her hair swept up in a ponytail. Dagger wolfed down five pancakes, two fried eggs, a bowl of Special K, and a banana before she'd finished half of a cherry muffin. Where did he put it? He probably worked it off killing people, she decided, pouring them each second cups of coffee.

"I have a million questions for you, but how about if I start with an easy one?" She eyed him over her coffee cup.

If he was wary of what was coming, he gave no sign of it. In his white T-shirt and jeans he might have been a stockbroker on vacation without a worry except for what time he teed off and if there would be any lounge chairs available poolside by the time he'd shot eighteen holes. He cocked a noncommital eyebrow at her. "Just one? Go for it."

"What kind of a name is Dagger? I mean, you weren't christened that, were you?"

"Only by my buddies at Annapolis."

"So what's your real name?"

He tossed her the last muffin — blueberry — and pushed back his chair. "That's two questions. You're out of luck."

Cat glared. Why did her heart have to beat so fast over a man who wouldn't even tell her his real name? Unsure if she was more angry with him or with herself, she tossed the muffin back at him. He caught it one-handed, peeled off the wrapper, and popped half into his mouth.

"Well, *Nick*," she grimaced, spitting out the name he'd used at the party the night before, "maybe you'd rather tell me what you know about Corey Preston. Could he have anything to do with Latham?"

"Not on the surface. Neither Preston nor Talon International has any ties to ORBA — Latham and Preston aren't members, they don't even turn up on the contributors' list. According to the information that came in last night, Preston could very well be in the clear."

"I don't believe it." Cat threw down her napkin. "I saw that man last night. I looked in his eyes. They were evil."

"That may be. It doesn't mean he kidnapped your sister."

How could she make him understand? Cat groped for words, a shiver running down her spine as she remembered Preston blocking her path with that gun, ice shining from his eyes.

"There might not be any proof — yet. But I'm telling you, he's involved. I feel it in every single one of my bones. That might sound ridiculous to someone who relies on data, surveillance, and high-tech hardware, but something inside me is shrieking that Corey Preston is in this up to his eyebrows."

To her surprise, Dagger accepted her words with a nod. "You may be right."

"You mean you agree with me?" She stood up, bracing her hands on the table.

"I've done a thorough background check on him. Preston is brilliant, but he's still a few beers short of a six-pack. For one thing, the guy's a paramilitary fanatic." Dagger frowned before continuing, and she sensed he was weighing his words. "I can't get into everything we have on him, but as you noticed last night, he's obsessed with guns. And with computers. It seems he got himself into a little trouble in college. A bit of computer hacking, some grade switching and some money changing hands on a rather large scale. His daddy greased the right palms to keep him from serving time, but it cost Corey big-time. It cost him Talon International. His father apparently decided he was unfit to take over as CEO and turned over the corporate reins to Corey's uncle and cousin. Word is, he's one angry kid."

"So we've got a partially loony gun fanatic with a major chip on his shoulder. He damn well could be out to prove something." Cat stalked to the window, staring out at the glorious panorama of surf and sand. Palm Beach sunshine splashed down through the palm trees, casting swaying feathery shadows across the oil-slicked sun worshippers already prostrate on the pool deck. The sky was a cloudless blue sweep. It was difficult to imagine that amid such dazzling natural splendor evil could flourish. The type of evil that could conceive of a plot as cunning and far-reaching as this one. Cat spun back to face Dagger.

"Why do I have the feeling there's something more, something you aren't telling me?"

"Last time I checked you didn't have security clearance."

"So you know enough to be suspicious of him. Really suspicious. Do you think he's the Director?"

"Let's just say I'm not satisfied that he isn't. But from the looks of things in Detroit, Latham and ORBA have zoomed up to the top of the list."

Cat worried her teeth along her lower lip. "Just because there's no definite link between Preston and Latham doesn't mean they aren't *both* involved. If he's as brilliant as you say, Corey could have masterminded the whole thing and let Latham take the tumble."

"That's pure speculation." He watched as she took a turn around the room, noting the way her hips swayed beneath the sundress. She could be a very distracting woman, and he couldn't afford distractions. "There's nothing linking Latham to Preston — not a phone record, airline ticket, bank transaction — nothing."

"Then we'll have to find something, won't we?" Cat tilted her head and regarded him with unwavering purpose. "Starting with my shoes. That's our ticket back into the estate. Coming?"

"You've got my full attention until the sun goes down."

"What happens when the sun goes down?"

"I have to catch a nine o'clock flight to Detroit. In the meantime, I wouldn't mind turning up something that nails Latham and Preston inside a double coffin."

Cat scooped up the car keys and her sunglasses. "Let's do it."

An hour later, she slid the Corvette alongside the curb a scant half block from the Preston estate. "What's our game plan?"

"Play it by ear. Make a big deal about having lost your shoes and keep your eyes open." He reached into the glove compartment and pulled out a Sony videotape. "A little something for our host," he explained.

"A video? Let me guess. *Bethany Does Palm Beach?*"

"Not quite. It's packaged like an ordinary videocassette, but this baby's got a little something extra."

Intrigued, Cat's eyes lifted to his. "A bug?"

"A miniature camera and microphone, in one neat little package. All we have to do is tuck it on the shelf alongside the others in his family room, and certain of my colleagues will get a bird's-eye view of everything that goes on within those four walls."

Cat's smile sparkled clear up to her eyes. "Is this legal?"

"One hundred percent approved and authorized."

In one movement she sprang from the car, pushing her sunglasses up on her head. "So what are we waiting for?"

The petite Cuban maid who answered the front door looked flushed and beleaguered, the plastic bucket on her arm crammed with Pledge, Windex, Ajax floor cleaner, and enough paper toweling to carpet the lawn. She informed them brusquely that Mr. Corey was out on the tennis court and that she was too busy to hunt down a pair of red shoes.

"*Ay Dios*. Everything I find — shoes, jewelry, pantee-hose, sunglasses, everything — I put already in a box in the family room." She sighed, stepping aside for them to enter. She used the edge of the white apron tied around her black starched uniform to mop at the sweat dripping down her nut-brown face. "If they no there, señorita, I do not know. Go, look. It's okay. Me, I no have time."

She turned and trudged with her bucket up the marble staircase, polishing the banister as she went. Dagger and Cat were left in the cool spaciousness of the black-and-white marble-tiled foyer.

"Alone at last," Dagger whispered. His tone was light, but there was a predatory glint in his eye as he moved with a quick, coiled gait toward the sunken family room.

Signs of the party were still very much in evidence. Though the waitstaff had cleared away the litter of glasses, plates, bottles, and napkins, the room still looked like a hurricane had blown through. Sofa pillows were strewn about, videotapes were heaped on the floor next to the fireplace, and popcorn and nacho chips were ground with cigarette ashes into the pale plush carpet. Near the potted rhododendron they spotted a carton filled with jumbled clothing, cellular phones, beepers, and assorted other articles the revelers had left behind.

"Keep an eye on the patio door while I slip this into place." Dagger bent to scoop up an armful of tapes. While Cat paced back and forth between the patio and the foyer doors, he worked quickly to reshelve all the tapes, sliding the new one among the two dozen others lined up beneath the CDs. Suddenly she spun around as voices boomed from the TV.

"Dagger, we don't have time to watch Jenny Jones this morning." She stared as he pressed a video tape into the VCR and clicked the play button. "What do you think you're doing? I want to get upstairs before . . ."

She broke off as Ted Koppel loomed onto the forty-foot screen. Meg's hostage picture was silhouetted behind him. "What the hell is this?" she asked faintly as the camera cut to a split screen shared by Attorney General Kendricks and Sheila Tomkins from the Miss America Pageant.

"A strange sort of collection," Dagger muttered, fast-forwarding. "There are three more besides this one. Each tape labeled 'Gunning for Miss America.' Isn't that the news slug CNN has given Meg's story?"

Shock rippled through her. She nodded. Why would Corey Preston have taped so much news footage of the kidnapping? As Dagger hit the play button again, they saw a CNN anchor reporting on the Director's demand for front page coverage in the *New York Times*. Quickly Dagger inserted another tape.

All four were filled with a montage of news broadcasts, special bulletins, interviews, and commentary about the Miss America kidnapping and the Wake Up America terror campaign.

"This proves he's involved," Cat cried, pressing her fingers to her cheeks. Her heart was pounding like Niagara Falls.

Dagger gripped her by the shoulders. "Don't jump to conclusions, Cat. This doesn't *prove* anything. He might just be focused on this case because it affects his family's business."

As his eyes drifted past her, they suddenly darkened to a steel blue intensity. "Speak of the devil." He turned and quickly ejected the tape. In a flash he reshelved it along with the other "Gunning for Miss America" tapes and scanned the shelf with a critical eye, satisfying himself that his little addition was undetectable. By the time he turned back toward Cat she was gone.

"Cat!" There was no answer, only his voice echoing through the family room and beyond to the black-and-white marble foyer. Where the hell was she? He just had time to hunker down and start digging through the box before Preston slid open the patio door.

"If you're looking for your date, Bethany's not there." Corey held a tennis racket easily in one hand. A faint sheen of sweat glistened on his sunbaked skin as he gave a slow grin, showing a flash of white teeth. "Hate to be the one to break it to you, buddy, but the last time I looked she and Rick were having a private party in the cabana."

The bedroom was a shambles. The maid obviously hadn't been here yet. Black-and-taupe striped sheets lay tangled on the floor, along with the clothes Corey Preston had worn the night before — and a woman's gold lamé string bikini. Several empty wine bottles littered the dresser, and the air was stale and thick with the sickly sweet smell of incense, marijuana, and all-night sex. Cat wrinkled her nose, noting the burned-down candles on the nightstand and the silver platter on the bed, with remnants of brie, cracker crumbs, and browned fruit.

She scanned the massive mirrored room, noting first the huge ancient-looking battle shield mounted over the fireplace and then the enormous glassed-in gun collection. Whistling under her breath, she stepped closer to get a better look at the hundreds of guns showcased in the trophy case. All sorts of guns: antique pearl-handled Colts, sleek black automatics, long-barreled gleaming assault weapons, polished wood-handled military pistols. He was a gun fanatic, all right. This had to be one of the most comprehensive collections in the world.

But she wasn't here to look for the obvious. There wasn't much time. Hastily she began pulling out drawers, rifling through them for God knew what, praying she'd recognize what she was looking for when she found it.

She found it inside the nightstand after pawing through loose change, assorted pens, some maps, and a small key on a red leather cord, which she assumed opened the gun case. It was a notation on a scratch pad, scribbled in pencil. An odd notation. A long series of numbers, separated by dashes. No words. No names.

Cat tore it off, folded it in quarters, and stuffed it inside her bra.

She'd better get back downstairs before Dagger had her throat.

26

Dagger didn't say a word during the entire drive back to his hotel. When they had arrived in his suite and he had closed the door on the vast peach carpeted hallway, he sank into a Louis XIV wing chair, raked his hands through his dark hair, and shook his head at her.

"That was a harebrained thing to do, Cat," he said with quiet fury. "Wandering around Preston's bedroom uninvited. You could have gotten both of us killed."

Airily she tossed her purse onto the bed and plopped down beside it, tucking her legs beneath her, as casual as a coed. Talk about impulsive. There was no doubt it was part of her charm; she had the guileless beauty of a gamine, with that cloud of pale hair and those wide, expressive eyes. And beneath that deceptively soft facade was a headstrong female gladiator with more courage than a fleet of fighter pilots. But she was too damn impulsive.

Preston already seemed suspicious of her. Well, maybe not suspicious, but he'd kept staring at her as if he were still trying to place where he'd seen her.

Dagger didn't like it. He didn't like it at all.

"I was only trying to help," she said, lifting her chin. "We talked our way out of it, didn't we?"

"Temporarily, but I'm not entirely convinced he bought it." Thinking back on Preston's reaction when Cat had come sailing down the stairs, announcing that her red shoes were nowhere to be found, Dagger sprang out of the chair and began to pace.

Preston had studied her, studied both of them, his lips curled in annoyance. He hadn't exactly panicked to see "Louisa" skimming along the upper floor of his house and down the stairs, but there had been a trace of sweat along his upper lip, perhaps from the tennis match or perhaps from tension. Dagger couldn't be sure.

"Mi casa es su casa," he'd said with a shrug and strolled to the bar in the family room, leaving them to follow him. They'd declined the drinks he offered, made small talk about the party, and asked permission to search the pool deck and patio for the missing shoes.

"Don't let me stop you," Corey had tossed off over his shoulder, but Dagger hadn't liked the way he was scrutinizing Cat.

The shoe hadn't turned up deckside, where a half dozen assorted sandals and loafers that had apparently been fished out by the pool man were lined up like forgotten orphans, drying out in the brilliant midmorning sun. They'd left soon after, but not before Preston had sauntered out poolside and invited them to join his coterie at Le Bar that evening.

"We'll try to make it," Dagger had agreed, making a show of slipping his arm around Cat's shoulders, hoping Preston would buy into the ruse that he and Cat had left the party together and stayed that way.

"So are we going to Le Bar tonight?" Cat asked now from the bed, as if she'd been reading his mind. "Showing up cheek to cheek would probably allay any lingering suspicions Corey might have about our newfound togetherness."

Dagger drew in his breath as she shifted position to curl languidly against the pillows, one arm folded behind her head. She looked like a sea nymph reclining upon the satin comforter, a lovely mermaid whose flowing honey hair glistened in the sunlight. Oh, she could get under a man's skin all right. Straight through to the bone, to the heart, to the soul.

To distract himself, he turned quickly and unlocked the minibar, drawing out a wine cooler and packets of cheese and crackers.

"I'm flying out to Detroit tonight, remember? And you're not to go anywhere near Preston and his crowd."

She eyed him warily as she leaned forward to accept the wine glass he offered her. "I hope this is a request, not an order?"

"Good try. It's an order. So let's do this the easy way — not the hard way."

"This is sounding vaguely familiar." Much as she tried, she couldn't suppress an impish grin. "You're not going to try that old planted cocaine routine again, are you?"

He grimaced. The last thing he needed was a woman like her, testing him at every turn. He drained the last of the wine cooler and decided against reaching into the minibar for another. "We planted the bug. Now it's time for my team to see what comes of the surveillance."

"Don't forget about this." As Cat spoke, she reached into her bra and tugged out a scrap of paper. She waggled it in the air.

A tingle of satisfaction flitted through her as Dagger's eyes narrowed on her. He reached for the paper.

"What have we here?"

"Something I swiped from a notepad in Preston's bedroom. I didn't see much else, but it was a very spooky room."

"Meaning?"

"For one thing, it reeked of drugs . . . and he had this weird ancient battle shield over the fireplace, and the most incredible gun collection you've ever seen. And mirrors on the ceiling. The whole thing felt very creepy." Cat shuddered, remembering the kinky vibes she'd picked up prowling through Corey's macho lair. "Do those numbers mean anything to you?"

"INMARSAT."

At her bewildered look, he explained, "International Marine Satellite. This looks like a shore-to-ship number." Crisply, he tucked it into his wallet. As Cat started to speak he held up a hand. "It may have nothing to do with your sister, but we'll run it down anyway. I'll pass it along to the FBI field office when I get to Detroit."

"I wish you didn't have to go." The words were out before she realized how wistful they sounded. To cover her embarrassment, Cat slid off the bed and walked past him to the marble sofa table where the maid had placed her duffel bag alongside a fresh arrangement of coral gerbera daisies.

"Guess you have things to do. I should let you do them."

He touched her shoulder before he even realized what he was doing. "You're not slipping away that easily. You haven't promised me yet that you won't meet Preston tonight."

"Haven't I?" Cat turned and smiled winsomely up at him. "Must've slipped my mind."

"I'm beginning to think nothing slips your mind. Cat, this is serious. If Preston is the Director, he's far more ruthless than you're bargaining on." His hand wound through her hair, twisting it around his fingers. There was no mistaking the deadly seriousness in his eyes. "I admire your determination to help your sister, and I think you're the gutsiest lady I know, but I don't want to see you become another casualty in the Director's little war."

Cat's heart was thrumming like harp strings, and the melody scared her to death. The delicious leather and spice of his cologne intoxicated her. She felt the hard tension of his muscles as his body brushed against hers, and as she looked into those searing cobalt eyes she felt as if she were being sucked into an undertow.

Fight it, she told herself. She took several small, calming breaths. *You're mistaking his professional concern for something else. Don't make a fool of yourself. It won't do you or Meg any good.*

"Don't worry about me," she said as briskly as she could. "I'm a big girl and I can take care of myself. I've been doing it for a long time."

"I do worry about you."

Strange. In all the time she and Vince were together, she couldn't ever remember him saying that he was worried about her. Even when she was traveling alone, even when she was under deadline and stressed out of her mind, even when she landed in bed for two weeks with the flu from hell. His main worry was that they wouldn't give each other enough space.

This is different. Dagger is different from anyone you've ever known.

And what she was feeling? Was that different, too?

Cat's fingers curled into her palms. She'd better get out of here while the getting was good. Before she said or did something she'd regret.

"I don't put much stock in promises, Dagger," she said slowly. "I've never met a man yet who liked to make them, or one who knew how to keep them."

Dagger's arm closed like an iron band around her waist. Her face was so sweetly serious, he ached inside just looking at her. There was pain, as subtle as fog, shrouded deep in her eyes. Someone had hurt her — badly. The ex-husband? He wanted to kill whoever it was. To strike with his own hands whoever had caused that flash of wounded bitterness.

"I keep my promises, Cat."

She stared into his eyes. "I'd really better go. You have to pack. . . ."

"How about a kiss for luck?" Dammit, what had made him ask that? Her impulsiveness must be contagious. Or maybe it was just being so near her, so worried about her.

"That might not be such a good idea." Yet she let him draw her back into the circle of his arms, her heart thundering in her ears.

"I know: We don't need the complications. We agreed. But what's the harm in one little kiss?" He was pulling her in tighter, his arms cradling her back.

What's the harm, she thought weakly, leaning in toward him, her lips parting. Just one kiss . . .

His mouth brushed hers with great gentleness, sending waves of heat rippling through her. Cat's arms crept up around his neck. Her lips trembled against his, prolonging the kiss. Oh God, what was she doing?

When Dagger dragged his head back, dark passion shone in his face. "Sometimes in life, we get less than we ask for, Cat — and sometimes we get more." Then his mouth crushed down upon hers and her hands were in his hair, pulling him closer as she strained her hips against him. The kiss exploded through both of them and they forgot everything: the sunlight that poured through the windows like molten gold, the soft laughter that rose from the hotel's outdoor swimming pool, the danger that waited on the other side of sunset.

Cat was on fire as Dagger's kisses seared across her cheeks, her eyelids, her throat. She pressed her hips tighter against him, and he swung her around, pressing her into the door. When his hand slipped beneath her vest, she gasped in his ear, and her teeth closed softly against the edge of the lobe.

This is madness. You hardly know him. He's nowhere near your type. A few days ago you were terrified of him, and now you want him to come inside you, to throw you down on that bed and nibble across every inch of your body. You've totally lost your mind.

What was left of her sanity spun away into a whirl of pleasure as he rubbed her nipple with his thumb. Cat's fingers tore at his shirt, pulling it free of his trousers. She ran her hands up his torso, reveling in the trail of crisp tufts that snaked from below his navel. Her fingertips found his nipples. She explored them, rubbing gently until they were tiny twin peaks.

As Dagger's mouth seared along the pulse at her throat, Cat closed her eyes and tilted her head back. "This is crazy," she moaned.

"Lunacy." Suddenly Dagger scooped her up and carried her to the bed. Staring into her eyes, he lowered her onto the bedspread. She pulled him down atop her, twining her legs around his.

"This is a hell of a good luck kiss," he murmured in her ear, and then he was undressing her, his fingers sure and quick, bringing gasps of intense joy and tingling pleasure as they stripped away her clothes and began a deliberate, tantalizing exploration.

"Don't stop, Dagger," she gasped, her lips hot against his chest. "Whatever happens . . . Oh, God, don't stop."

"Not a chance, sweetheart." With his mouth clamped to hers, he slid her panties down her thighs and caressed the warm moist triangle between her parted legs. She spread them further apart, straining her hips upward to meet his probing fingers.

"I wanted to do this on the beach last night, right there on the sand."

"So did I." Cat tore at his belt buckle, twisting at his clothes until somehow they were both naked, the bedspread on the floor, the fanning breeze from the air conditioner doing nothing to cool their burning skin.

Intense pleasure throbbed in her breasts as Dagger loved each one in turn. When she pushed him back against the pillows and flicked her tongue across his lips, he groaned and threw a leg across hers. "Isn't this better than driving back to your hotel?" he whispered. In answer, she stared hungrily down into the gleaming blueness of his eyes and stroked her hands across the corded muscles of his body. Then, with the slightest shift of her hips she began a rocking motion against the length of his penis, thrilling as she felt it glide into her.

He grinned, pulling her hips down against him, thrusting slowly upward until he was buried deep inside her.

"Ummm, this is definitely better than driving back to the hotel," Cat whispered.

"Are you sure you don't want to leave?" he teased, nibbling his teeth ever so gently across her lower lip. And then neither of them said anything as he rolled her over and made her forget every coherent thought that might have ever danced through her head.

He took her soaring higher than the clouds that floated past the window. Each thrust seemed to drive them deeper into each other's souls. Each kiss seemed to fuse them, soldering their bodies as if they were fine gold wires meshed and twisted into an unbreakable chain. The room spun away in a kaleidoscope of red heat and golden sunbeams as Dagger plunged into her again and again, and she clutched him to her, arching in a primitive rhythm. Cat scraped her fingers through his hair, down his back, across his buttocks, gathering him to her, urging him deeper, wanting him with an exhilaration so dizzying that it hurt. Together, they rushed toward a pinnacle of shattering need and desperate release, climaxing in quick succession with a carnal force that left them gasping and replete.

"One little kiss, huh?" Cat murmured when she could speak again. "Can't say there was anything little about that — any of it." She nestled against him, watching the fading rays of sunlight gild the fine hairs curling down his forearms.

His laughter rumbled through the room. "I'll take that as a compliment."

Cat pushed herself up on her elbows and with one finger smoothed the dark hair from his brow. It was so good to lie here with him like this, both of them naked, glistening with the sheen of their lovemaking, caressed by the sun. She felt as if she were still floating on a star and she never wanted to fall off.

"You still haven't told me your real name," she said softly, tracing his lips with her tongue.

"And you still haven't promised me you won't go to Le Bar tonight."

Cat nipped at his lower lip. "I'll trade you. You go first."

Dagger sat up, propping the pillows behind him. The feverish gleam that their lovemaking had sparked in his eyes faded, leaving them the cool blue of smoke. How could a man who looked so dangerous, so tough, so ready for anything be so gentle and giving a lover? Cat wondered, her heart tight with emotions she hadn't dared to feel for a very long time.

Dagger looked away toward the windows for a

long moment, and then back at her. "My name is Nick."

"Nick what?" Cat prodded, one slim brow lifting. She wondered at the flash of amusement that touched his face before he answered her.

"Nick Galt."

"Oh, my God." She shot up, her hands flying to her throat. "You're not . . . Jack's *son?*"

"In the flesh."

Cat's mind reeled as she tried to take in that she had just spent an hour and a half in bed with the son of her grandmother's oldest friend. "Why didn't you tell me?" she demanded. "No wonder Jack gave me your number."

"Remind me to thank him."

Giggling, Cat shook him by the shoulders. Then suddenly she froze. "Wait a minute. Seems to me I heard Jack's son was married and had a daughter. . . ." She broke off as she saw the pain wrench his face. And then she remembered.

"Oh, my God. Dagger . . . Nick. I'm sorry." The memories flooded back. She'd been in college when Gram had imparted to her the news that Jack's daughter-in-law and grandchild had been on that ill-fated Pan Am flight over Scotland, the one blown from the skies by a terrorist bomb. Tears sprang to Cat's eyes as she saw the awful grimness settle along his jaw, and a sorrow deeper than the grave etched itself into his eyes.

"It was a long time ago, Cat."

"It doesn't matter how long. You never get over

something like that," she whispered, reaching for his hand.

"You're right. It took years before I could even get on a plane without imagining I heard their screams. Years before I could sleep through the night without dreaming of personally killing the bastards who did it."

"And I accused you of not knowing how I felt," she whispered in horror. "I told you you'd never lost . . ." Her voice broke before she could finish the sentence.

"Shhh, Cat. It's all right." Dagger gathered her into his arms. With sure, steady gentleness, he stroked her hair. "You didn't know. You couldn't have known."

They lay there together for a long time, neither of them speaking. And then, as the sun dipped momentarily behind a bank of clouds, he told her what he hadn't talked of for years. "Susan and I were married right out of school. It was first love, that pure innocent kind that seems meant to last forever, and when Amanda was born we thought we'd snagged the pot of gold right off the end of the rainbow. But fairy tales don't last." His voice hardened. "And real love doesn't come twice in a lifetime. At least that's what I thought . . . until now."

Cat searched his eyes, wondering at the implications of what he'd just said. A shadow crossed her face. "I know what it feels like to lose a child. I lost my baby," she whispered.

"Tell me," he said very gently.

"My unborn baby. I had a late miscarriage. I thought I would die — I wished I could."

"And your husband?"

"He left me a month later. So much for happily ever after." Cat shrugged with a hard, rueful laugh.

Dagger seized her and pulled her to him, staring into her face with such intensity that she caught her breath. "Don't, Cat. Don't cover up the pain with me. I know it hurts like hell. What a bastard. . . ."

She pressed two fingers to his lips. "He's not worth it. Don't waste your breath."

"Let's not waste anything. We have only a few hours before I have to leave for Detroit."

They stared at each other, and this time when their lips met the heat was infused with a tenderness born of scorched hearts in search of healing. As Dagger held her and stroked her cheek, she felt as if years of heartache were being smoothed away. Cat spoke with her lips nibbling his chest.

"What did you mean when you told me this was your last job? What are you going to do? Retire to a villa on the Costa del Sol?"

"Nothing quite so picturesque. I've decided that thirteen years in this line of work is pushing my luck. So I'm quitting at a dozen. My Dad's been after me to join him in private consulting for the past two years." Dagger dropped a kiss onto her temple and slid his foot alongside her calf. "I think I could be of real use to him there.

And we've always talked about working together someday."

"So you'll be working out of Washington?"

"Most of the time. But I won't live in the city. Actually, after all these years of hotel hopping, I'm in love with the idea of fixing up the right old house in the country and waking up in the same bed every morning."

Cat could see him there, in a rough-hewn cedar bed in a high-ceilinged room, with four-pane windows thrown wide to reveal a vista of emerald forest and gentle hills. She laced her fingers through his. "Have you found the house yet?"

"Maybe I'm superstitious, but I decided not to look until I'd finished this last assignment. I promised myself it would be the first order of business after handing in my resignation."

A tiny smile curved her mouth. "Speaking of promises . . ."

"Go on."

"I know how you can get me to promise to stay away from Le Bar tonight." She laughed, throwing a leg across his.

"I thought we already made that bargain."

"And I suppose you're going to hold me to it?"

"You're damn right I am," he said, rolling on top of her. "I'm going to hold you to an awful lot."

"Promises, promises," she gasped as they tumbled together onto the floor.

Eight P.M. came too soon for Dagger. He

stared down at Cat, curled asleep in his bed, wanting to wake her for one last kiss but not having the heart to disturb her sleep. She looked like a beautiful lost waif, lying there with one arm flung across the pillow and her hair spilling across her cheek. He resisted the urge to touch it, to touch her.

Go, a voice inside of him commanded. *Now.*

Still he lingered, something twisting in his gut. Conscience perhaps? He'd lied to her, and for that she might never forgive him — assuming he lived long enough to tell her the truth.

But that wasn't important in the scheme of things. What mattered was his agenda — an agenda that didn't include her. That *couldn't* include her. She wasn't trained for what he was going to do next, and he didn't have time to argue the point with her.

Standing there watching her sleep was only a waste of time.

He strapped on his shoulder holster, where the Smith & Wesson .38 was snuggled like an old lover, tucked the small Ruger into the holster fastened to his calf, and slipped on his navy linen jacket.

He left the room without looking back.

27

Cat stared numbly at the phone, wishing Dagger hadn't already gone to Detroit. Finally, slowly, she replaced the receiver in its cradle.

Gram had just given her the latest on the bombing at the Empire State Building. Shaken, she could only pray that some small scrap of evidence left there by the Director's goons would somehow lead to Meg. As she sat cross-legged atop the tousled blankets of Dagger's bed, morning sunlight slanting across the carpet, she shook her head, finding it difficult to comprehend the scope of this web of terror encircling Meg.

Her mind reeled with possibilities, questions, and fears as she reached for the phone once again and punched in Jordan's direct line. When Alana told her that Jordan was at home because Lori was recuperating from an emergency appendectomy, she closed her eyes.

"What next?" Poor Jordan must be beside herself, with so much to deal with.

"Why don't you call her at home?" Alana suggested, sounding harried.

"I will — right this minute. But Alana, before you hang up, any tidbits floating around from the FBI?"

"No, only the boat rumor."

"Boat rumor?"

"Ask Jordan, Cat — I've gotta run — sorry, we're briefing the press in fifteen minutes. . . ."

Boat rumor. Alana's words jolted her more awake than a thermos of caffeine. It seemed an hour before Jordan's voice came on the line.

"How's my little pixie doing?" Cat asked.

"She's coming home later this afternoon — if her fever stays down." Jordan took a breath. "Cat, someday when we're old and gray and wrinkled, we'll sit in our rockers and compare battle scars from this war."

"Unless we're *off* our rockers by then," Cat muttered, and Jordan gave a wry laugh.

"Just when you think you can't take any more — whammo." She paused, but not before Cat heard the throb in her voice. "Guess who was sifting through the rubble last night ten minutes after the bomb went off?"

"Oh God. *Mike*. I forgot he transferred to the bomb squad from vice. My God, how are you holding up, Tex?"

"I'm putting my nervous breakdown on hold until after this is over." Instead of Jordan's usual calm, poised tones, her high-pitched voice rattled words out so fast Cat had to scramble to absorb them. "Tell me how your grandmother is surviving."

"It's taking a toll on her, but you know Gram. She won't admit to anything. Listen, Jordan, I need you to fill me in on this 'boat rumor' Alana tossed at me a minute ago." Cat fluffed the pillows behind her, swearing she could smell Dagger's cologne.

"You haven't heard? It's promising but pretty sketchy — it hit just about an hour ago. The FBI won't confirm anything yet, but Alex's news department and the *L.A. Times* are chasing down a story speculating that Meg may have been taken out of the country by boat. Seems a boater called the Atlanta police this morning, saying he recalled seeing a transient fifty-foot yacht docked in Savannah the night before Meg disappeared."

The words hit Cat like a bombshell. *A yacht.* She remembered Dagger's reaction when she'd handed him the scrap of paper from Preston's bedroom. *Looks like a shore-to-ship number. . . .*

That bastard Preston is in this up to his eyeballs.

"Go on," she urged, her fingers clenching around the phone.

"Something about it struck the boater as not quite right. Apparently some suspicious-looking crates were loaded on what was obviously a pleasure boat. I don't know all the details yet, but NBC is going with it tonight. Cat? Cat, are you still there?"

"Jordan, I've got to run. Give Lori my love and tell her Auntie Cat is going to send her a special present very soon."

Shaking, Cat hung up the phone. It all made

perfect sense. Meg being held on a yacht — the shore-to-ship number she'd found in Preston's bedroom — and all that taped news footage.

Every instinct screamed out that Preston was their man.

And somewhere in his house was the secret that would lead to where Meg was being held.

Cat tore through her purse for the number Jack Galt had given her — Dagger's number. Surely he would check his messages.

"Darling, this is your Scrabble partner. Something's come up. I've got to play solitaire today." Cat closed her eyes and rocked back on her heels. She'd give anything if Dagger could be here with her now. If they could do this together. Suddenly the words just poured out.

"Dagger, I'm sorry, but I can't wait. You know where to catch up with me. I hate to play without you, but this is one game I can't afford to lose."

In less than fifteen minutes she had showered and dressed, and was stepping into a cab at the hotel curb before she'd even formulated a plan to get back onto Preston's estate.

Golden sunshine dappled the manicured lawns and long formal gardens as Cat paid the cab driver and turned toward the gate.

She could hear laughter and shrieks floating from the pool area as she strolled up that long, curving drive, her stomach in knots.

"Well, well, if it isn't Louisa." From the lemon-yellow upholstered chaise where he lolled, Preston's words were lazy, but they held an edge that made Cat's skin prickle.

Rick and Bethany waved from the pool and kept right on playing volleyball as their host pushed himself up on one elbow and surveyed the newcomer.

He studied her, his bronzed face expressionless behind mirrored sunglasses. "You missed a great party at Le Bar last night. Where's Nick?"

"Don't know, don't care. He wouldn't take me to Le Bar last night — he was really a drag. I didn't want you to think I stood you up, and your phone number's unlisted, so I thought I'd drop by to apologize." She hoped she was coming across as breezy and nonchalant. Preston was scrutinizing her, but it was impossible to see his eyes behind the glasses. All she could see were two miniature reflections of herself dressed in a pink silk cropped top and palazzo pants.

"No problem, babe." He scooped back a thick coil of wet black hair that had tumbled over one eyebrow. "How about a drink? Name your pleasure."

My pleasure would be to see you behind bars for the rest of your life, she thought, but aloud she said, "A mimosa would perfectly hit the spot."

His well-oiled muscles rippled as he sprang off the chaise and padded barefoot to the patio bar. Cat eyed the black thong bathing suit with veiled contempt and occupied herself trading desultory conversation with Rick and Bethany while Corey Preston fixed her drink.

"I thought you two were going to play tennis this morning before the sun got too hot," Preston called to them. Cat settled back on a chaise next to his and accepted the drink with a smile she hoped looked inviting.

"Too hot," Bethany complained. "I'd rather swim."

"Rick had his heart set on tennis, didn't you, buddy?"

Cat pretended not to see the pointed glance he and Rick exchanged. *Smooth, Preston, very smooth. Did you graduate from the Jackie Mason school of subtlety?*

The chaise creaked under his weight as he settled back against the cushions. By the time he had clinked his glass to Cat's, Rick and Bethany had disappeared down the brick pathway leading to the tennis courts.

"Alone at last," she toasted him with a grin, and took a delicate sip of her drink, keeping her gaze locked meltingly on his.

"I haven't been able to figure you out." Preston reached over and ran his finger up and down her arm. It took all of Cat's willpower to keep the smile plastered on her face.

"So you've been thinking about me?"

"What do you think?" Preston suddenly sprang off the chair with the coiled grace of a young lion and reached for her hand. "Let's go inside. The sun *is* hot."

"Can I see the trophy room again?" Cat asked as she tugged her to her feet. Some of the mimosa sloshed onto the tile deck, narrowly missing her palazzos.

"Babe," Corey Preston said, flashing his even white teeth, "you can see whatever of mine you want."

They paused beside the artificial waterfall and the curving lily pond set within the deepest part of Preston's private jungle.

Preston ran his fingers along her spine and watched her face as his hand dipped lower.

"Want to play Tarzan and Jane?"

She swallowed down the bile rising in her throat and turned to him with what she hoped was an intrigued expression. "Depends on the rules of the game."

He gave her a slow, arrogant smile that made her want to run as fast as she could in the opposite direction. "You take off all your clothes and jump in — it's a hot tub, by the way — and then I take off my clothes and jump in after you."

She managed a fairly credible giggle. "I adore a man with a sexy imagination."

"You wouldn't believe the things I can imagine when I put my mind to it." The grin spread, touching the heavy-lidded eyes. He pulled her close, cupping her buttocks and squeezing with fingers as strong as pistons.

"I can't wait to find out. But first things first." She eased away from his groping hands and swirled the ice in her glass. "Tell me what rock the bar is hiding behind. I'm empty."

"Sorry, the bar's all the way downstairs." He took the empty glass from her and set it on a smooth fieldstone rock. "Come on, let's go skinny-dipping."

"Oh, please, just one more little drinkie. Don't be a drag like Nick."

Something dangerous sparked behind his eyes. Cat held her breath.

He scooped up the glass from the fieldstone. "I guess it's better to be wet and juicy than parched and dry. This won't take long — feel free to start without me."

Cat perched on the rock, trying to appear enchanted by the vista around her, watching him from beneath lowered lashes as he slipped through the vines and shrubbery. She counted to thirty after he disappeared beyond the stuffed elephant.

Make it snappy, she told herself, springing off the rock. *You probably have only five minutes, max.*

With the stealth of Diana the huntress, Cat slipped through Corey's jungle, retracing their steps back to the door. The upper hallway was deserted, but from the floor below she could hear the faint, soft slap of his bare feet on the marble tile. The click as she turned his bedroom door handle seemed to reverberate through the house as loudly as if she'd slammed a mallet against that battle shield enshrined above the fireplace.

She was in.

She ran toward the nightstand, her eyes skimming the blank pad of paper where she'd struck gold before. Nada.

Spinning around, she yanked open the armoire and began rummaging carefully through piles of soft cotton sweaters, boxed linen shirts, and silk boxer shorts in every color and pattern imaginable. Still nada.

Cat bit her lip as perspiration beaded at her temples. She probably had less than a minute and a half to get back to the jungle. But as she peered frantically around the bedroom, which was now made up as handsomely and immaculately as Corey Preston himself appeared to the casual observer, she had no idea what to do next.

Go back. He'll be on his way up by now. If you bump into him in the hall you'll just have to say you were looking for the little girls' room.

Go!

Still she stood there, unable to move. Something bothered her about this room. Something was different. Not quite right . . .

And then she spotted it. She didn't know if it was her photographer's eye for detail or some sixth sense that zeroed in on the shield. It was ever so slightly off center.

That big heavy ancient shield was shifted a good three inches to the right. Her heart pounding, Cat walked slowly forward and touched the gleaming metal. As she did, she noticed the faint discoloration on the wall — where the sun had faded the paint around it, Cat realized. *This sucker moves.*

There must be a safe behind it. Her hands were already groping at the sides of the shield. Pressing, pushing, maneuvering. Because inside that safe could be the information she needed. And if Dagger came back and knew exactly where to look, she'd have bet Gram's entire collection of kachina dolls he'd know exactly how to crack it.

Suddenly the shield rolled sideways beneath her hands, and before Cat could do more than gasp, the entire wall, fireplace and all, swung away from her.

Shock hit her like the slap of a forty-foot wave. *It's not a safe at all. It's a room. A goddamn secret room.*

And there on the desk was Meg's tiara.

His foot had just touched the bottom step when it hit him. It had been bothering him since the first moment he'd laid eyes on her at the party, when she was hanging on Rick's arm in the jungle room. He finally knew where he'd seen her before.

He doubled back to the family room and set the drinks on the coffee table beside the crystal bowl of cocaine. A moment later he was popping the taped CNN news footage into the VCR, fast-forwarding, pausing, fast-forwarding again.

And there she was. Plunging through a sea of reporters outside a small adobe house in Arizona, hurrying as if the devil were after her, looking straight ahead, making no eye contact with any of the reporters trying to shove a microphone in her face. She looked distraught and angry, as if she'd deck anyone who tried to slow her down.

Lying fucking bitch. He ripped the cardboard videotape box in half and threw the pieces on the floor. He swept an arm across the table, sending the glasses flying. There were close to four ounces of cocaine left in the crystal bowl and he snorted a line up each nostril while he tried to absorb the fact that he'd let the enemy infiltrate his ranks.

That slut upstairs was no Louisa Palmer.

She was Miss America's fucking sister — and right now she'd landed her conniving little ass in every bit as much trouble as the big-mouth herself.

I've got to get out of here, Cat thought, clutching Meg's tiara in trembling hands. *Screw the jungle room. I'll make for the stairs and pray I don't run into him.*

She checked her watch. The taxi would be back at the end of the drive in another ten minutes. If she made it that far, she'd head down the street and intercept it.

She was still shaking from head to toe. Her quick survey of the room had revealed not only the tiara, set like a trophy on a velvet cushion, but also Preston's eerie, all-encompassing obsession with war. Shelves full of books on military strategy, volumes of *Soldier of Fortune*, a Chinese battle painting, a bank of computers. This wasn't just a secret room. It was the center of operations for a war.

Turning, Cat darted for the door.

"Going so soon?"

She fell back, heart hammering, as Corey Preston's sculpted body blocked the partially opened door.

Cat's blood froze. She felt like a butterfly strangling in a steel net. A butterfly waiting to have its wings ripped off. As she stared into Preston's swarthy face, the terror slamming over her in unrelenting waves made breathing hurt and her knees go soft as pudding.

She yearned to rake the tiara across his face, then choke the breath from him. There was only one thing stopping her — she didn't stand a chance.

As he edged his shoulders through the opening and approached her, his face was flushed. His golden brown lion's eyes were intent upon their prey and held a strange, unnerving glitter. "I see you have not only a thirst but also an appetite for invading other people's privacy." He sneered, snatching the tiara from her hand. "Haven't you heard about the Fourth Amendment? Or are you and your sister determined to wipe out the entire Bill of Rights?"

"I'd like to wipe out scum like you," Cat cried.

His smile blew a hole through her heart. "You stupid bitch. The only ones who are going to get wiped out are you and your sister."

"Where is she?"

His smile deepened.

"You bastard! Tell me what you've done with her!"

Suddenly his free arm shot out, and he seized her wrist in a death grip so painful it buckled Cat's knees. Preston's breath rasped against her ear. "You'll never know."

28

I feel like Donna Reed. All that's missing is an apron, a strand of pearls, and high heels.

Meg shoved a lock of hair from her eyes as she stirred the chicken and vegetables fragrantly simmering in the cast-iron pan. Not a bad meal considering the hodgepodge of ingredients she'd scrounged up from Jake's larder and the coconut palm growing crookedly outside. She'd spent the first half of the afternoon with the gun in her hand, keeping watch out the window — and the second half cracking open and scraping out the coconut. To get it, she'd dashed outside, heart in her throat, and snatched it from the ground beneath the palm fronds. Then she'd raced back to the safety of the kitchen.

Once she'd given up on playing Rambo, she kept her sanity by puttering around in the kitchen — hammering open and gutting that coconut took up too much time and concentration to allow for panic attacks.

Now, as she inhaled the tantalizingly spicy scent of Thai chicken and green peppers, she felt a sense of orderliness and control. There'd been no time for cooking her own favorites this past year, barely enough time to eat the food they'd plopped in front of her at all those banquets and picnics — and she'd long suspected that the same little gnome of a chef traveled around in Burnsie's suitcase to whip up the same tasteless meals time and time again. Cooking this meal was the first normal thing she'd done since she'd won her title.

Normal?

Shaking her head as she whirled the long wooden spoon through the coconut sauce, she laughed at the "normalcy" of preparing a gourmet meal while lurking in a shack belonging to a tall, shaggy stranger — waiting at any moment to be surprised and killed by the thugs who'd kidnapped her. Or, she reflected wryly, waiting for the tall, shaggy stranger to return and join her for a civilized meal and light dinner conversation about who'd take the first watch tonight, who'd load the gun, and who'd bury the corpses.

Over the sizzle of the meat she heard an engine.

She dropped the spoon and ran for the gun, scooping it off the kitchen table so hastily that she knocked the shards of coconut shell onto the floor.

Please be Jake, oh please be Jake, she prayed as she ducked down low and ran toward the window.

It was Jake.

"Honey, I'm home," he sang out, slamming the screen door behind him. He sent the Panama hat sailing across the room to find its mark on the peg protruding from the wall.

"Took you long enough," Meg threw over her shoulder, setting the gun down beside his typewriter and hurrying back to the stove. "What were you doing while I slaved over a hot skillet all day — playing eighteen holes of golf?"

"Tried, but I couldn't get a foursome," Jake deadpanned. "What smells so good?"

She switched off the burner, used a towel to move the skillet to the table, and faced him over the rising steam. "It's a variation on my grandmother's Thai chicken recipe — you were missing a few ingredients so I had to improvise."

"A woman after my own heart. I'm big on improvisation."

"How about information?" Meg moistened her dry lips. "What did you . . . find out?"

She was something else. He'd half-expected to find her cowering beneath the kitchen table, curled up like a whipped kitten, and here she was, hiding her fear under a bravado that might have fooled him if not for the faintest quiver in her voice and the tense set of her shoulders.

She looked enchanting, as enticing as an island princess with her caramel-colored hair spilling in wild tangles down her back, that long, curvy body encased in his T-shirt and khakis, and the gleam of coppery polish on those pretty little toenails.

He pushed away the impure thoughts roaring through his brain and focused on giving her an answer that would allay her fears.

"There's nothing to worry about. Ernestine hasn't heard of anyone nosing around — and since her bar is the meeting place for everyone on the island, she knows about it every time someone blows their nose."

"Does she know I'm here?"

"You haven't sneezed yet, have you?"

Meg grinned in spite of herself and picked up her fork. "Well, at least they're not pounding down the door yet." She stared at him as he inhaled a forkful of chicken and peppers. "Did you see any sign of the yacht?"

"Zip. I cruised down by the docks and even checked the cove on the far side of the island. Who knows, baby doll, maybe they capsized during the storm and they're all shark food by now."

"Wouldn't that be lovely." Meg chewed with relish.

"Hold on." Jake pushed back his chair. "A great meal deserves a great wine. Don't go anywhere."

"Don't worry."

She peered up at him as he poured the 1992 Ferrari-Carano Chardonnay into a wineglass for her and then splashed some into a coffee mug for himself.

He lifted the mug in a toast. "Cheers."

He was the most unusual man she'd ever met. She didn't know a lot about wine, but she knew this was a special vintage. It had been served at the White House luncheon she'd attended last March. How did a strapping hermit who lived like a beach bum and kept a typewriter and a loaded Magnum in his living room come by a bottle of Ferrari-Carano, as well as some of the more subtle spices and ingredients she'd stumbled across in his larder?

"Let me guess. You're a five-star chef who cooked one bad meal for the Shah of Gendhir and was banished to this island for life. Or you're ghostwriting the new *Silver Palate Cookbook.*"

"You got the banished part right, but it's self-imposed." She heard the edge behind his words and saw the quick flash of irony in his eyes. She wanted to ask him to elaborate, but something about the set of his jaw told her that getting any more information out of him might prove harder than cracking that coconut.

Though she tried to concentrate on eating, her eyes kept returning to his face. He was handsome in a sensual rugged way that mesmerized her even as she tried to ignore it. He was intriguing, all right. In fact, she mused, taking another sip of wine, if someone were to tell her she'd have to hide out here on this island with Jake Selden for the rest of her days, it wouldn't exactly be torture.

Come off it, she scolded herself, setting her glass down with a clink. *The stress must be getting to you. You're having fantasies about He-Man here when you should be visualizing yourself sweating through your first year of law school. That's what will get you home in one piece.*

Home. Her gaze shot over to the telephone.

"Is the power still out?"

"Afraid so. And Ernie heard the phone lines

will be down for at least a few more days." He stood up and carried his plate to the sink. "Thanks, kid, that was one helluva meal. I'm usually not one to skip out on KP duty, but I think I'd do us both more good if I get back to tinkering with that damned helicopter while there's still some daylight left."

"The sooner you get the copter running, the sooner we can fly someplace where I can call home and notify the authorities." Meg bit her lip. "I'm worried sick about my grandmother and my sister. . . . They must be frantic. They've grown rather fond of me over the years," she muttered wryly.

"Can't imagine why." He studied the depths of her eyes and struggled with the protective feelings she seemed to elicit from him. *Down boy,* he told himself. *She's Miss America. She's gorgeous, smart, going places, and she's not for you. You're a nobody — a nobody with blood on your hands and secrets you can't even bear to think about. So hands off. Think about fixing that helicopter so you can get her out of danger and out of your miserable life. The sooner the better.*

He controlled the urge to brush a finger across those soft, parted lips, to see if they felt as velvety as they looked, and instead he flicked his thumb playfully along her cheek. Like an uncle, he thought, an affectionate old uncle.

"Wish me luck."

"Luck." Meg stared after him long after he sauntered out the back door.

He worked all through the glorious sunset, from the first streaks of pale lavender through the blazing pinks and mauves and golds, past the glowing purple that spread like spilled ink to obliterate the last glowing rays of light. Darkness came, and the insects began their incessant trill, filling the night with their invisible presence, making Meg wonder what else traveled, unseen, in the jungle beyond their window.

Strange, but the moment Jake came in the back door, she stopped pacing, stopped gnawing her lower lip (Cat's habit — how on earth had she picked it up?) and stopped imagining that she'd be shot at any moment. *Don't be an idiot,* she told herself. *He's not Superman. He can't save you from all the bad guys.* But she felt so much better when he was there. His presence was sturdy, solid, strangely calming. He seemed so sure of himself, so sure of how to handle this unfathomable situation. He made her feel as if they could handle anything that came up, even Frank, J.D., Ty, and Bramson.

And Corey Preston.

The name had been whirring through her brain all day. Who the hell was he? And better yet, Meg thought as she regarded Jake through the flickering light of a candle, how much longer until she could get to a phone and nail him?

"Promise me something," she greeted him as he grabbed a towel and wiped the grease from his fingers. "If anything happens to me, if I don't make it and you do, promise me you'll make sure

Corey Preston gets what's coming to him."

"You're going to make it, Meg."

"But just in case . . ."

Jake tossed the towel onto the counter and went to her. "You drive a helluva hard bargain. Sure you weren't a loan shark in a former life?" At her look he dropped his hands to her shoulders. "Okay, kid, I promise. Just in case."

"And something else." She lifted her chin toward him. "In case you haven't noticed, I'm not a kid."

"Oh, I noticed all right," he muttered under his breath.

"Could've fooled me."

Jake's hands lifted to twist in her hair. His voice was low with warning. "Don't tempt me, Margaret Elizabeth Hansen. I'm no good for you. The truth is, I'm no good for anyone. You'd probably be better off with the guys you got away from."

"How can you say that?" she cried, searching his face. "They're cold-blooded killers."

"And how much do you know about me?" he asked harshly.

"I know that you saved my life. I know you took me in, gave me food and shelter. I know you're trying to help me even though you're risking your own life to do it."

Somehow her hands were on his face, cupping it between her slim fingers, feeling the scratchiness of the beard stubble that had grown since this morning. She felt him tense, felt the hardness intensify through his body. A strange excitement quivered through her.

"You've got me all wrong. I told you last night I'm no hero. You've heard of feet of clay? Well, I can go you one better. Mine are mired in quicksand. Oh, hell," he groaned as Meg pressed closer, her eyes soft on his, refusing to believe what he was trying to tell her.

"I'll warn you one more time, baby doll. We're on the edge here."

"Then let's jump," she whispered, twining her arms around his neck. Meg heard herself saying the words, but she was beyond words. Almost beyond thought. His physical presence was like quicksand pulling her. She couldn't get away and she didn't want to. Sensual heat spread through her as she saw his hazel eyes darken in the glow of the candle, felt the pressure of his arms snaking around her waist. Then he was kissing her, his mouth hard and hungry, and she was sucked under.

She was being crushed against a rock-hard chest, her lips bruised by the possessiveness of his kiss. And she was lost, lost in a thick, swirling pleasure that closed over her, blocking out fear, rational thought, and inhibition. She gave a low moan as he loosened the T-shirt from her waistband. His hands felt like warm leather against her skin, rubbing, searching as if memorizing the path from her waist to her shoulders. When he shifted back and slid his thumb to her breast, Meg gasped and gently bit down upon his stubble-grazed chin.

"Last chance, baby doll," Jake breathed against

her lips. He shifted her against his thighs, fitting himself there. "If you want to call it quits, this is the time."

"Don't you dare stop now." Meg kissed him with a fervor she'd never known she possessed. Never, ever had she felt like this. Wanted this. Never had she been so alive, so filled with such intense need and pleasure that all she wanted was Jake, to breathe in the spicy scent of him, to scrape her hands along the powerful muscles rippling down his back, to take him inside of her and ease the pain she'd seen in his face when he warned her away.

Suddenly a sliver of reason pierced the veil of heat enveloping her. "Jake," she gasped raggedly, drawing her head back in alarm. "What if they . . . show up in the middle of all this?"

"Don't worry. I hung the DO NOT DISTURB sign on the back door."

"I'm . . . serious," she breathed as he pulled the T-shirt over her head.

"So am I," he said, nuzzling her breast. His tongue flicked over the nipple, hot and raw and scratchy. "Dead serious."

"Don't . . . use . . . the word . . . 'dead,' " she pleaded, closing her eyes and giving herself up to the sweet sensations eddying through her.

Jake's laughter tickled against her rib cage as he tugged her over to the desk and dug a condom out of the drawer before pulling her toward the made-up sofa bed. Meg was beyond thinking as he yanked her down on top of him. They fitted themselves across the narrow cushions, kissing open-mouthed. As the candle flickered across the bare wooden floor and the plaid arms of the sofa, they shed their clothes and embraced, naked. Jake touched the dreamcatcher necklace dangling at her throat.

"Don't you ever take this off?"

It took a moment for her to realize what he was talking about. "This? No, not unless it clashes with what I'm wear—"

"It doesn't." He kissed her throat and her bare shoulders, and then gingerly brushed his lips across each of the bruises healing on her face. The expression in his eyes was so tender, her heart turned over and then soared toward him.

Sensations flickered through her, as light and rhythmic as the play of the candle-thrown shadows, then building with each kiss, each touch, until she swore nothing would quench the ever increasing heat raging through her.

"I . . . have to warn you," Meg panted, as Jake tossed aside a back cushion to better straddle her. "I've never done this before."

"You mean you've never made love on a sofa?"

"I mean, I've . . . never made love."

He turned to stone right before her eyes, staring at her with such incredulity it would have been comical if not for the scorching heat blazing inside her. "You're joking, right?"

"There are some things you don't joke about." Meg pulled him down on her, wrapping her legs around his. "Somehow, the right man never seemed to come along."

Jake groaned and pushed himself up on his hands. Sweat broke out on his face. "Baby doll, you better think about this. What makes you so sure I'm the right man? This is crazy. You're imagining I'm someone I'm not."

"Don't tell me what I'm doing, Jake." She pulled him back toward her and kissed his mouth, her lips lingering with a sweet intensity that rocked both of them. "I know what I'm doing. I know what I want."

Jake kissed the hollow in her neck. "This is a special occasion. Maybe we should open up this sofa bed."

"Don't bother," she pleaded, half laughing. "Take me, Jake. Take me right now."

"Now? You mean before you change your mind?"

"I'll never change my mind."

He lowered his hips, settling his full weight against her, feeling her delicate hipbones beneath him.

His own doubt dissipated as he stared into a face so lovely and filled with passionate yearning that he couldn't deny either one of them any longer.

"I'll be as gentle as I can," he muttered, parting her thighs and trailing kisses across her shoulders as he rolled on the condom.

"I'm not afraid." Her entire body seemed to mold against his, arching, giving off heat and scent in palpable waves of desire. "I could never be afraid of you."

Her words, her trust, her vulnerability triggered a letting go inside him, a letting go of pain and guilt and self-recrimination that evaporated like smoke from the candle. This sweetly beautiful woman trusted him — when for so long he hadn't been able to trust himself.

"Hang on, baby doll, you're in for the free fall of your life." His words were light, but emotion swamped him, swamped both of them as they came together in a fit so perfect there was no room for doubts or questions. There was only wonder and joy and a long, thunderous release.

29

The noon sky gleamed a brilliant turquoise the next day as Meg awaited Jake's return from Ernie's Cantina. He was late, and by twelve-thirty she was trying to convince herself that he hadn't run into trouble, that J.D. and the others weren't hot on her trail, that they hadn't somehow discovered Jake was hiding her, and that he wasn't lying dead somewhere on the beach.

This is insane, she told herself, pacing from the kitchen to the window, past the typewriter, and back to the window again. *He's probably trying to locate that part he needs to get the copter in the air. He'll be back any minute.*

She kept trying the lamp. Still dead. All the food in Jake's refrigerator was rotting, and with the electric fan perched uselessly in the kitchen window, the air grew more and more stifling.

Jake had left after breakfast, assuring her that he wouldn't be long.

"Just going to check in with Ernestine and make sure your friends haven't been nosing around."

"They're no friends of mine."

"Mine either," he told her, pulling her to him across the table and planting a kiss on her mouth that carried with it an echo of the previous night's magic.

Remembering, Meg plopped down on the sofa, drew her knees up, and hugged her arms around them, grinning like a kitten with a bellyful of milk. Last night *had* been magic — sweet, dizzying — a jungle symphony of desperate need and wild sensation, of an emotional crescendo like the reverberations of timeless, universal harmonies.

She felt like the first woman who'd ever made love.

She felt that for the first time in her life she *was* in love.

Cat will never believe this. Or Jordan. Or Gram. I only hope I live long enough to see their faces when they meet Jake. If they meet Jake.

Why isn't he back yet? Meg fretted, staring at the battery-run clock on the kitchen shelf. She peered out the window, saw nothing but a line of swaying palm trees and a hummingbird flitting over a clump of scarlet bougainvillea, then moved restlessly to the telephone again. For the hundredth time she listened to dead air, forgetting about the battery. In frustration, she slammed down the phone, sending the papers in the red folder beside it skittering to the floor.

"Oh, hell." As she bent to pick them up, she began to focus on the words. Absorbed, she read several lines. My God, it was a story. A novel?

she mused, hurriedly putting the pages back in order. Her fingers clutched the manuscript excitedly as she carried it to the sofa and began to read.

It was fiction — not only fiction but science fiction. And it was good. Jake had an amazing imagination, she reflected, then giggled to herself. *You already knew that.*

She lost track of time as she became immersed in the world he'd created, a futuristic world where computer chips implanted in the human brain provided instantaneous language translations, where time travel was controlled by the government, and where a rogue cop had discovered a terrible conspiracy. . . .

She hadn't realized she'd been reading for more than an hour until she looked at the clock. Where on earth was Jake? Uneasy, she shifted the manuscript onto the sofa and then she saw, mixed in with the typewritten pages, what looked to be a receipt stapled to a scribbled note. It must have fallen off the table with the manuscript pages, Meg realized, but as she started to set it down on top of the manuscript, the note's precisely written signature jumped off the page.

J.D.

Everything in the room blurred except that scrap of paper. Her hands began to tremble as she started to read.

Roadrunner — the boat checks out great. Here's your first $5,000. You'll get the rest

when we get to Montigne. We'll need to re-
stock provisions at that point. (See list below.) Rendezvous: September 2, Ernie's,
afternoon.

The rest of the note was a laundry list of supplies and staples, followed by those two neatly
printed initials: J.D.

Meg shook her head over and over in disbelief.

It can't be. It's a mistake. This sounds like
. . . She couldn't even bring herself to think
what it sounded like. It sounded like Jake was
involved with J.D., involved with the boat, involved with . . . the kidnapping.

Her hands shook so violently she dropped the
note to the floor. She bent to retrieve it and nearly
toppled over as blood rushed to her head. She
felt as if she'd been gut-punched. Sick and dizzy,
she forced herself to focus on the stapled receipt.
The words ran together in a fuzzy blur.

. . . a month's rental . . . pleasure craft . . .
Elena . . . destination: Caribbean . . .

Was I on the Elena? *I never saw the name of the
boat. But what else could this be? My God, it's signed
"J.D."*

She whirled and stared at the sofa where they'd
made love last night. *J.D. hired Jake to rent the
boat, to get the supplies, to help with the kidnapping.
He's in it. He's part of them. He's in it, you idiot.*

No wonder he was so sure of himself. He was
one of them. A thug. A thug for hire. And she

ran straight into his arms, like a rabbit into the wolf's lair.

Her heart pounded like an anvil in her chest as she stared out the window. *He's probably bringing them all back here with him right this minute.*

For a moment she couldn't move, could only stare in numb, frozen terror. *Away. I have to get away.* She bolted into the kitchen and retrieved the gun from the counter. Where had she seen that thermos while she was making dinner? Gun in one hand, she banged through the cupboards until she found it and filled it with water, setting the gun down only to screw on the cap.

A blanket. A jacket. Meg ran toward the closet and searched desperately, digging out a dirt-stained canvas backpack from behind a gym bag and some fishing tackle. As she yanked it out, she knocked over a rifle that had been propped in the corner. It hit her shoulder and thudded to the floor.

Meg fled, clutching the backpack, trying to calm her racing brain. *Don't panic. Think.*

She darted through the shack, throwing provisions into the backpack like a madwoman — one of Jake's sweatshirts, some matches and candles from the kitchen drawer, the thermos, a box of Cheez-Its, and, as an afterthought, the paring knife she'd used to scrape out the coconut.

She slung the backpack over her shoulder and with the gun clutched in a hand slippery with sweat, she ran outside into the searing sunshine.

Here goes nothing. Meg Hansen — Jungle Girl.

All you have to do is elude a team of professional killers — without a compass, a map, or a clue as to where you're going or how to get there. Damn straight, she thought, gulping back the sobs that ached inside her throat.

She squinted up and down the dirt road outside Jake's shack. There was no one in sight for as far as she could see. She turned from the road and ran in the opposite direction, straight into the brush and dense tangle of vines. The insects dive-bombed her like buzzards as she plunged into the canopy of green. She never slowed down and she never looked back.

30

Jake's voice rumbled through the shack. "Meg, we have to . . ."

He broke off. Silence greeted him. A strange, prickling silence. He stopped dead in the doorway.

She wasn't here.

He knew it even before he saw the open bathroom door, the quiet yard, the kitchen drawers pulled out. Where the hell was she?

"Meg!" His voice was harsh with urgency as he sprinted through the shack calling her name. In the yard, he surveyed the disabled copter and scanned the surrounding coconut palms and bougainvillea.

"Meg!"

By the time he retraced his steps into the shack and noticed the receipt and J.D.'s note lying on the floor beside the sofa, sweat was soaking through his shirt front.

Damn it all to hell. Jake slammed his fist against the wall, splintering the wood. She'd found it. He'd forgotten all about that note, but now she knew. . . .

Where the hell had she gone?

Minutes later he was in the Jeep, swearing a blue streak, the M-16 lying across the front seat as he jolted over roads where there were no roads, mowing down passion flowers and young bamboo shoots in his path.

The island was relatively small. On foot, not knowing the jungle, she could only get so far. One way or the other, he'd hunt her down by nightfall.

"Where the hell did Jake go?"

Big Veda hoisted the bowling-ball-size package onto the bar and peered around the dank interior of Ernie's Cantina with a pained expression. "That helicopter part he's been bitching at me about just came in. I hauled it up here from the puddle jumper because I saw him head this way a while ago."

"You missed him. He sucked back a beer with those three not long ago and left." Ernie jerked her thumb toward the three men grouped around the table, then flipped over their burgers and sprinkled a handful of onion on the griddle. "Maybe he's coming back. Maybe not. Go ask them."

Wiping sweat from his face, the little Jamaican padded over to the table. "You guys know where Jake went?"

The man with the long, pock-scarred face and the ponytail looked him over with eyes like a water snake's. "He went home."

"You sure?" Big Veda stepped aside as Ernie slid plates of burgers and fried plantains before each of them. "Aw, shit, now I gotta deliver it out to the shack. He needs this part; he needs it bad. He told me yesterday to bring it as soon as it came."

The red-haired man grabbed Big Veda by the arm before he could walk away. "Are you saying you've got the part Jake needs to fix his copter? That it over there?"

Big Veda settled his round, protruding eyes on the stranger and wrenched his arm away. "Unless Reynolds Machinery is sending him a helluva big Christmas catalog, that's it all right. You goin' out to Jake's place by any chance, mon?"

"Matter of fact," the blond Schwarzenegger type said between mouthfuls of Ernie's famous burgers, "we are. Jake invited us for afternoon tea."

"Tea?" Big Veda chuckled. "Then you'll take it and save me a trip?"

The one with the ponytail walked over and lifted the box, then set it down on the fourth chair at their table. "No problem, my friend. Consider it done."

When Ernie and the Jamaican cook had gone back behind the bar, J.D. flashed a smile at Frank and Bramson.

"Things are looking up, gentlemen. This is our lucky day. Half an hour ago Jake said he couldn't get the copter in the air, and now, presto, problem solved."

"Hallelujah." Frank wiped mustard from his mouth. "Can't say as I thought I'd ever look forward to seeing the Roadrunner, but now we won't have to comb this bug-breeding swamp on foot anymore. With the copter we'll be able to spot the girl anywhere on the whole damn island."

"Don't forget." J.D. glanced swiftly over his shoulder to make certain Ernie and the Jamaican weren't paying attention to them. "The Director's orders are to shoot her on sight."

"Don't worry," Bramson said, pushing back his chair. "After what she pulled on Ty, it'll be a pleasure."

Frank nodded. "Ditto. That bitch put our asses in a royal sling. With any luck, she'll be buzzard fodder by nightfall."

J.D. stared hard at each of them. "Make sure she is."

31

Meg felt as if she'd been running for hours. Sweat streamed over every inch of her body, causing Jake's shirt and shorts to cling to her skin as if she'd just pulled herself once again out of the sea. But she kept going. The farther she got from Jake's shack, the safer she'd be.

Her bare feet were cut and bleeding. *Why didn't I think to take a pair of his socks?* she lamented as she raced beneath a canopy of interlocking trees, trying to shut out the pain slamming clear through to her calves. *I took as much as I could think of from him — but not nearly as much as he took from me.*

She couldn't bear to remember that. About what a complete idiot she had been. Trusting him. Giving herself to him. Loving him.

She'd thought he was her protector. He was her enemy, the most vile, betraying, dangerous enemy of all.

And you thought Cat had bad luck with men, she told herself as she tore aside a tangle of scarlet vines and plunged through them, tumbling unexpectedly down a sharp incline. Palm branches scratched her face, narrowly missing her eyes, but she stifled back a cry of pain and ran on.

Thank God it was cooler in here, deep down beneath the cover of green. She felt like an insect as she bumbled through a grove of lianas, past gorgeous wild orchids, and across wet spiny leaves that clung to her bare feet. A macaw swooped overhead, shrieking out so suddenly that her heart slammed against her rib cage. A sweet, heavy perfume enveloped her, so heady it might have dulled her senses and made her sleepy if not for the fear pushing her forward. Enormous butterflies swarmed past her and over the brilliant tubular flowers clinging to rocks and vines as she descended deeper and deeper into the mossy, humid darkness.

The dense jungle enclosure stunned her. It was complete, stifling, as thick and impenetrable as a jade cocoon, rife with the chirping, humming, buzzing, and whirring of innumerable seen and unseen creatures.

Every once in a while she stopped and listened, dreading the sound of pursuit. But there was none. She wiped her sleeve across her clammy forehead and went on. She didn't know what she would do if Jake came after her.

Oh, yes, Meg thought as she skirted over a fallen tree trunk, *I know what I'll do. I'll shoot him with his own gun. I won't think twice; I'll just pull the trigger.*

So much for Miss America's antigun stance. When push comes to shove, shoot.

If that's what it takes to stay alive.

Tears streamed from her eyes, flowing into the mask of sweat, as she plunged on. What would she find at the far edge of this massive emerald wilderness?

If she ever reached the end. If she ever came out of here alive.

Jake's Jeep was nowhere in sight as they piled out of Ernie's red Ford pickup truck, which they'd paid her ten bucks to borrow.

"Hey, Roadrunner," Frank bellowed as he stomped up the steps to the screen door.

Bramson lugged the package around to the back, where he could just make out the glinting metal of the copter, silver against the blue sky.

Frowning, J.D. followed Frank through the front door.

There was no one home.

The place looked like it had been ransacked. Or like someone had left in one hell of a hurry. J.D.'s eyes scoped the room with swift expertise, but it was Frank who found the aqua-and-purple nylon jogging suit hanging on the back of the bathroom door.

"Looks like our own little Goldilocks has been sleeping in someone's bed."

J.D. reached the back door in four quick strides. "Bramson, get the fuck to work on that copter! Frank and I are going bear hunting."

It was night.

Not a star, not a sliver of moonlight cracked the dense canopy high overhead. It was so dark Meg couldn't see anything as she sat huddled with her back snug against the wide buttress roots of an old fig tree, but she could hear it all. The cacophony of the jungle enveloped her — the shriek of the birds swooping through the trees, the slither of invisible creatures beneath leaves and brush, the dull roar of the insects inhabiting the atmosphere, the snap and rustle of a thousand branches. And from everywhere around her rose the dank, overpowering odors of moss and mud and greenery, of vegetation so thick and luxurious it could choke you to death like a lasso made of tangled, twisting vines.

Exhaustion pulled at her, but she couldn't allow herself to fall asleep. She was terrified of what might surprise her in the dark. She had to stay alert. To watch and listen for any approach, human or animal. In the morning, she'd run again.

Run where? She didn't know how she would get out of this jungle or where it would lead her, but maybe by the time she got out, the electric power would be restored to the island and she could find a phone, call for help, and somehow get back to civilization.

By now Jake and the others would know she was gone. They'd be after her like bloodhounds. She didn't even dare light her candle, lest the tiny light be a beacon leading them straight to her.

Them. Jake was one of them.

She concentrated on listening, trying to differentiate the sounds, to determine if any of them were men crashing — or creeping — through the brush in pursuit. Yet, remembering Jake's competence, the training and expertise she'd sensed in all of them, despair rose in her. *Who are you kidding?* she thought. *How will you manage to elude men who hunt for a living, who no doubt know the jungle better than you ever will?*

She stifled a sob, but the tears slid silently down her cheeks, blending with the sweat pouring down her face. The humidity was so high she felt like a sponge. Everything was damp — her clothes, her hair, her skin. A few more tears wouldn't make much difference. She wiped her cheeks with the back of her hand. Part of her screamed, *Don't cry over him, he's not worth it.* Another part mourned his loss.

Lies you fell for, his lies, hook, line, and sinker, she told herself wrathfully. If only she could have that night back, take back all that she had given to him with such naive trust — the love, the faith, the single-minded joy — while all that time he'd been using her, in the most vile way a man could use a woman.

I was as blind then as I am now in this damned darkness. But no more.

A sharp noise somewhere to her left — or was it her right? — had her on her feet in an instant, clutching the gun in hands that were slippery with sweat. Her heart slammed into her throat. She strained in vain to pierce the curtain of blackness.

Nothing. She could see nothing.

It was just a bat or something, she told herself, swatting at the incessant mosquitoes swarming about her head. Meg leaned shakily against the tree, trying to ignore the bites and scratches itching on every part of her body. The meager meal she'd forced down of Cheez-Its and tepid water from the thermos threatened to bubble up. If the mosquitoes didn't kill her, her own fear would. She had to get control of herself.

She slid back down to the ground, gulping deep breaths, concentrating on the fragrance of the wild orchids that seemed to grow everywhere in tumbling masses, talking herself down from the verge of panic. Her fingers trembled over the necklace at her throat, the dreamcatcher Chevayo had given her to calm her night fears when she was a child. The small turquoise bead at its center felt cool and comforting, its surface smoothed by a thousand such touches over many nights.

You've made it this far, Meg Hansen. You can make it until morning.

Suddenly she thought of Gram. As a teenager her grandmother had been trapped for four days in the French countryside, trying to quiet a delirious soldier who'd been wounded by sniper fire while running arms to the Resistance fighters deep in the forest. *Gram made it out and you will, too. That same strong blood flows through your veins. That same dogged will to survive will get you through.*

Suddenly something moved directly above her.

347

She heard a faint slither, a whisper along the tree branch, and with a start, peered desperately through the darkness above. Ever so faintly, it swam into view, a snake — twining down toward her by slow degrees, its reptilian eyes glowing ever so faintly like ancient chips of marcasite.

An involuntary scream rushed out as Meg hurled herself sideways. She scrambled to her feet, grabbed her duffel, and fled, stumbling through the darkness with nothing but the gun and her own blind terror.

The insect and animal sounds intensified around her to a banshee pitch that filled her eardrums with an unbearable din. She crashed into branches, stumbled over ferns, slapped twisting vines away from her face with a panic-stricken horror. It was like being trapped in a house of mirrors that didn't end. She lurched onward, driven by an unreasoning panic that snapped the last shreds of her self-control. She couldn't stop, couldn't stop, couldn't stop. . . .

A huge weight hit her, knocking her sideways to the ground. She fought to move, to scream, but was pinned by a crushing beast that held her fast in oozing leaves and mud.

"Don't move, baby doll," Jake's voice panted into her ear. At last she could discern his features above her — a grim monster in night-vision goggles. "It's over now. It's all over."

32

The first thing Mike noticed as he slid into a parking spot near Jordan's building was the double-parked green Escort.

It was idling in the street two buildings down from Jordan's, but even as he slammed the door of his unmarked vehicle, he saw the driver peer into the rearview mirror.

Mike kept walking — fast but not too fast. The station wagon zipped out into traffic before he'd passed Jordan's steps. He sprinted toward it, squinting against the sunset to catch the license plate number. The sequence was burned into his brain even as he yanked a pad of paper and a pencil from his pocket.

"Get back to me as soon as you run it down, Vergada," he barked into his car radio, and scooped Lori's present off the front seat.

When Jordan led him in beneath the archway of pink, blue, and yellow balloons strung above the door frame, Lori cried out from the sofa. "It's Daddy! Daddy, what did you bring me?"

"I think it's a pony." He forced a grin and

shook the rectangular box over her head.

Lori's giggle was his reward. She looked so much better that his heart lightened as he studied her in her ruffled flowered nightie, her hair brushed back from her scrubbed little face. There was color in her cheeks again, he noted, and her laughter was strong. Like Jordan's, he thought, his glance shifting to the woman with whom he'd made this beautiful child.

He thought back to another present, one he'd never delivered to her. The night of Lori's second birthday, the night he'd been so drunk he'd fallen asleep on a bar stool at four-thirty in the afternoon and missed the entire party, leaving the Cabbage Patch doll on the floor of O'Toole's. The night Jordan had finally reached her limit with him and told him she wanted him out.

"It's a Madeleine doll! I always wanted one!" Lori cried, and held out her arms for a hug.

Mike's chest was tight as he bent down and hugged her, inhaling the scent of Johnson's baby shampoo in her soft, silky dark hair.

He looked up in time to see Jordan slip into the kitchen. He recognized from the set of her shoulders that she wasn't just going in there for a cup of coffee.

"Tell you what, honey bunch." He gave Lori a quick kiss. "I'm going to see if Mommy has any lemonade in the fridge — want some?"

"I'd purfer to have ice cream."

"Ice cream it is. Coming right up."

She was already playing with the Madeleine doll as he left her.

Jordan's hands were planted on the windowsill between twin boxes of geraniums. She was staring out at the garbage Dumpster behind the courtyard. There were tears rolling down her cheeks.

"Jordan . . . she's going to be all right. It's *all* going to be all right."

"Of course it is." She dashed the tears away and swung toward him, a smile pasted on her face. But Mike wasn't fooled.

"Tell me what's wrong," he said.

"Nothing. And everything." She picked up the coffeepot and began filling it with water. "Let's just say this hasn't been the greatest month of my life. And now that the pageant is getting so close, I'm terrified."

"Of what?"

"Of what will happen during the pageant when the Director finds out that we aren't going along with his demands. What if he takes it out on Meg? He's carried through on everything else he's threatened."

Mike took the overflowing coffeepot from her, set it down, and turned off the water. "They're going to find the bastard — and Meg — before it comes to that." He grasped her shoulders and stared at her with total conviction. "You have to hold on to that belief. I know how much Meg and Cat mean to you, Jordan. And so do they."

Jordan felt the warmth of his fingers searing through her silk T-shirt. She could smell the faint cool tang of his aftershave. It would be so easy to lean up against Mike, to rest her head on his shoulder, to ease some of the turmoil bubbling inside her by sharing it with someone else.

But she couldn't. She mustn't.

"I'm sorry, Mike." Wearily Jordan gave her head a shake. "I guess all of this must be getting to me more than I thought. It's been an emotional few days, and seeing you and Lori together just now brought everything to the surface — Lori loves you so much."

"Not half as much as I love her."

And you, he thought, but he wouldn't let himself say the words. Wouldn't let himself bridge those eighteen inches separating them. Wouldn't dare put his arms around her because if he did, he would never let go.

Unless Jordan wanted him to let go, which was a very real possibility. Right now he'd rather face a live grenade than face the fact that their separation was forever.

The doorbell interrupted. "That'll be Mrs. Chalmers, or Lori's friend, Kevin, from across the street. He promised to bring over his new pet frog." Jordan rolled her eyes. "If it gets loose, promise you won't leave until we find it."

"I'll stay as long as you want. *Ribbit.*" Mike teased, as she hurried back into the living room and he rummaged through the freezer for Lori's ice cream.

This is a good little homecoming party, Jordan mused an hour later as she gazed around the merry group assembled at the dining room table. There was singing and napkin throwing and chocolate cake decorated with gum balls. There was cookie dough ice cream and popcorn and lemonade and a frog in a shoe box. *My parents would be appalled,* she thought, and grinned to herself as she took note of each happy face around her. *You have to celebrate the good times in life, especially when they come in the midst of disaster.*

She tried not to think about Meg. Or about that unnerving contest phone call and the strange green car that had followed her later that same day. *Think about the party you'll throw for Meg when she gets home. And about how by then Lori will be up and running around and driving you crazy again.*

A good kind of crazy, she thought, watching Mike carry Lori back to the sofa, her little arms around his neck. Kevin dashed after them, clutching the box under one skinny arm.

"Don't you dare drop that frog!" she admonished, shooting Mike and Mrs. Chalmers a sheepish glance.

During the next half hour, Jordan's gaze kept wandering back to Mike, sprawled on the living room rug with Lori and Kevin and the frog. *If Alex were here, he'd be on the phone in the bedroom the whole evening. And he wouldn't get anywhere near the kids or that frog to save his life.*

But she pushed these thoughts from her mind. Mike and Alex were two completely different people. It wasn't fair to compare them. Mike was Mike. There was no one in the world quite like him. At least the alcoholism hadn't destroyed his soul, his strength, his incredible sense of humor.

In fact, she acknowledged to herself, he seemed to have licked it before it permanently destroyed all the wonderful qualities that had made her fall in love with him in the first place. *But,* she told herself with a brisk mental shake, stepping over Mike and the shoe box as she carried the cake plates into the kitchen, *even though a part of me will always love him, that's not the same as being in love with him — that kind of love is in the past. We've both moved on. We're different people now. We're not those love-crazy kids who got married four months after we met and lived blissfully in that cockroach-infested walk-up. And we're not the angry couple who battled over booze and neglect and denial.*

Jordan had no recollection of rinsing the dishes and loading them all into the dishwasher. She was listening to Mike's booming laughter and Lori's happy chatter. And she could only imagine what had made Mrs. Chalmers cackle, "Oh, Detective Bannister, you'll be the death of me."

By the time Kevin's mother came to pick him up and Mrs. Chalmers said good-bye, Lori was already half asleep. So was Jordan.

She left Mike rinsing out the coffeepot in the kitchen while she got Lori tucked into bed.

"Mommy, my own bed feels so good. I didn't like that bed in the hospital — even if I could make it go up and down."

"I know exactly what you mean." Jordan smoothed the glossy curls back from Lori's face and settled the sheet lightly over her shoulders. "But now you're safe and snug in your own pretty room."

"And Daddy's here. I'm glad, aren't you?"

"Yes, honey. I'm glad."

"Mommy, can I get a frog?"

Just what I need, Jordan groaned inwardly. *Kermit in the bathtub.*

"Well, you know, Kevin already has a frog," Jordan answered carefully. "Wouldn't it be fun to have a different little pet — maybe a kitten or a parakeet?"

"I want a guinea pig, like we have at school." Lori struggled to sit up, eyes wide and glowing. "Can I, Mommy? A guinea pig just like Fred, but we'll call him . . . What will we call him, Mommy?"

"Let's wait and buy him first. And when we look at him, we can decide what name fits."

"Goodie. Can we go tomorrow?"

"Maybe. Or the day after. Right now, young lady, you have to go to sleep."

"Mommy, will you stay with me for just a little while?"

"For five minutes." Jordan yawned and patted the covers beside Lori. "Scoot over and I'll snuggle in right next to you."

Mike put the coffeepot away and went back into the living room, wondering what was keeping

Jordan. He was debating whether or not to tell her about getting the license plate of that Escort. He hated to scare her with the news that it was still lurking around. Automatically, he went to the front window and scanned the street in either direction. No sign of the car.

He called the station. "Vergada. Got a rundown on that Escort yet?" Mike jotted down the name and address Vergada read him. It didn't ring any bells. The guy it was registered to was clean except for a few unpaid parking tickets. "I think we oughta dig up those outstanding bench warrants and haul this Mario Minelli in. Call me when you get him."

He paced around the apartment. He turned on the television. Still Jordan didn't emerge from Lori's room. At last he went to the doorway and stuck his head in. Lori and Jordan were sound asleep, snuggled together in the single bed.

The sight of them filled him with a fistful of emotions. Pain, loss, love, a fierce need to protect. *Whoa, buddy, back off, don't let all that chocolate cake go to your head.*

"Jordan." He put a hand on her shoulder. "Jordan, I'm going to split."

She turned over and reached a hand up toward him in her sleep. He held it in his own, staring at the narrow, tapered fingers. Staring at the unadorned third finger where her wedding ring used to be.

Suddenly Lori squirmed onto her side and dug an elbow into Jordan's ribs.

"This bed's not big enough for both of you," he muttered under his breath, and easily lifted Jordan into his arms. As he carried her into her lilac-and-teal bedroom, his muscles tautened with awareness. He'd never been in here before. The room was scented from the pink garden roses nestled in the ivory vase on the dressing table. It was softly lit by a gilt swag lamp hung low over the night stand. And it was pure Jordan. Elegant, feminine, gently seductive. A room made for a woman, yet one where a man could be comfortable.

He lowered her onto the thick teal comforter and arranged the lilac-flowered pillows beneath her head. Without thinking, he abruptly leaned down and placed a kiss on her forehead.

"Sweet dreams, angel." The old endearment burned his lips as he gazed down at her.

"Don't go," Jordan murmured, her eyes still closed, and suddenly her hand fluttered upward and encircled his neck.

Instinctively Mike tensed. "Don't go?" He gave a low groan. This was sheer torture. Jordan was obviously talking in her sleep. She probably thought he was Alex Woods.

The thought grated. "Gotta go."

"No, Mike. Stay."

He stared at her, stunned. "I don't think you realize what you're saying, angel," he whispered, but as he tried to disengage himself, knowing she'd be embarrassed as hell if she woke up now, Jordan did wake up. She opened her eyes and looked at him with naked need.

"Mike, sit with me a while." *Almost the same words Lori used with me,* she thought, not even understanding why she spoke them.

Then Mike was beside her, lowering himself next to her on the bed, and it seemed the most natural thing in the world to turn into his arms and stroke her hands through his hair.

"Jordan, I'm only flesh and blood," he said hoarsely. His lips nuzzled her ear. "Don't torture me."

"You're the one torturing me, Mike," Jordan whispered back, and then suddenly she was fully awake, fully aware, fully aroused. They stared into each other's eyes, the electricity sparking around them, and Jordan's hands cupped his face.

"I've missed you. I've needed you."

Mike felt like a bungee jumper about to plummet off a cliff. But there was no one he'd rather leap with than this beautiful hazel-eyed woman who owned his very soul.

He could see the outline of her breasts, the nipples taut and hard against the delicate silk tee. He could feel the warmth and sweetness of her breath on his face. Jordan always smelled like flowers, a garden full of them, waiting to be picked.

"Jordan, I damn well hope you're sure about this," he said huskily as he gathered her in his arms and traced her lips with his tongue.

She answered him with her body, easing against

him with deliberate invitation, her curves nestling against his hardness, her fingers sliding like tongues of flames down his back and inside his shorts.

"Stop talking, Mike, and kiss me."

He pushed her back against the pillows and began by kissing her fingertips. One by one. Wide-eyed, flushed, Jordan watched.

His mouth worked its way up one slender arm, sliding kisses across her shoulder, sending shivers down her spine.

By the time he had burned a path to her lips, Jordan's senses were ablaze. And when his mouth claimed hers, she gave one shuddery gasp and surrendered to the urgency that swamped her, pulling Mike down on her and encircling him with her legs.

The rightness of it enveloped both of them. It was as if the time they had been apart had sweetened this moment beyond anything they'd known before. Jordan had forgotten this unique passion, how intense desire could be. She and Alex had become lovers a few months ago, but it was predictable, pleasurable adult sex. It bore no resemblance at all to what she and Mike did together, with each other, for each other in the dimly lit rose-scented bedroom.

The hours passed and they lay entwined, sheened by the sweat of their lovemaking, glowing like the last soft candlelight thrown by tapers burning down. How many nights had they lain like this, Jordan wondered, their bodies curled into one another? How many times had Mike kissed her hair and told her she was the most beautiful woman in the world?

As the first tangerine streaks of dawn glowed in the sky, Jordan realized it was the little things she'd missed most — the trusting intimacy, the rough texture of Mike's hand sliding so gently across her thigh, the scrape of his beard on her shoulder, the way he called her angel while he was deep inside her and they became one single soul soaring toward heaven.

If only they could stay here forever, staving off the dawn and the uncertainty of the day ahead of them, savoring the sweetness and the passion and the abundant, flowing love she felt in Mike's arms. If only they didn't have to deal with the real world, with AA, terrorists, Hy Berinhard, and strangers tailing her in a green Escort.

As if reading her mind, Mike's arm tightened around her. "I think you should know I spotted that green Escort last night. It was just down the block. I managed to get the license number, and when they pick the joker up, I'll get a chance to ask him some questions. And he'd better have the right answers."

Jordan sat up and pushed her bangs out of her eyes, staring at Mike with undisguised fear. "He was back? Last night? Why didn't you tell me?"

"I didn't want to spoil Lori's party — and besides, it's under control. Just keep your eyes open, and I should have a handle on this by the end of the day."

By the end of the day. Jordan couldn't imagine that far ahead. And at the moment she didn't want to.

"Do you have to leave right now?" she asked, sliding her hands up Mike's chest and leaning across him.

"Depends on what you've got in mind."

The slow, deep kiss she gave him was just for starters. "Breakfast in bed. Among other things."

"I think I can work up an appetite."

33

Mario Minelli hunched down in the chair in the dark-paneled interrogation room, trying to avoid making eye contact with the cop prowling around him like a cougar getting ready to pounce. *It must be 110 degrees in this fucking joint,* he thought, wiping sweat from his rabbity face.

"I told you," he said, the chair creaking as he shifted in his seat, "I don't know no Jordan Davis." He groped in the torn pocket of his jeans for a cigarette, but the cop ripped the Pall Mall out of his hand before it reached his lips.

"This is a smoke-free environment, pal," Bannister snapped.

"Gimme a fuckin' break." He slunk deeper in the wooden chair and stared longingly at the cigarette the cop held inches away.

"Level with me about what's really going down, or you're going to eat this cigarette. And that's just the appetizer. Now, who you working for, punk?"

"Nobody. I don't know what you're . . ." Mario's voice trailed off. The expression in the cop's eyes was scaring the shit out of him. And as the cop leaned down right in his face, Mario saw a vicious ferocity in the dark blue eyes that rivaled anything he'd seen on the streets. He glanced nervously toward the blocked door, where the other cop stood with tree trunk legs splayed, his eyes on the ceiling. One hand rested on the butt of his gun.

They're gonna beat the crap outta me, he thought, panic nearly gagging him. *I saw what they did to Rizzo, and he still can't walk straight, the poor son of a bitch.* A little voice inside of him screamed, *Tell him what he wants to know and get the hell out of here.*

"Just give me the name. The *name*, Mario, you piece of shit, and you're outta here."

"But I don't —"

"The fuck you don't. What the hell is this?"

Bannister flung a scrap of paper at him and leaned over him so close Bannister was breathing down his neck as Mario read it. Shit, it was the broad's description and address — in his own handwriting.

"Maybe I got a friend in that building," he squeaked, humiliated by the terror in his own voice. Sweat was pouring down his face, as if the cop had upended a barrel of water over his head.

"Maybe you're going to end up in the morgue," the cop growled in a voice so low and vicious that Minelli was reminded of the Doberman that had nearly bitten his ear off when he was twelve.

With hands like steel mitts, Bannister grabbed his shirt front and yanked him forward nose to nose. "Last chance, Minelli. Give me a name. One name and you walk straight out that door."

"Sima," he whispered so low that the cop at the door couldn't make it out. "Now can I go?"

Mike swung away from him, breathing hard. *Sima.*

Russell Sima hated his guts. He'd sworn a bloody revenge from the day Mike busted him, screaming it across the courtroom for the judge and everyone to hear the day of his sentencing. Mike closed his eyes for a split second, picturing the slick, meticulously turned out drug lord he'd busted in the warehouse district — what, maybe six years ago? Was the pompous weasel already sprung from his cage and planning to sink his rotten teeth into Jordan — and Lori?

Over my dead body.

"Sima's out?" he snapped, wheeling back toward the punk.

"Don't ask me. You said I could leave when I gave you a name." Minelli lurched out of his seat and edged toward the door. With each step, his eyes flitted back and forth between the two cops. But just as he reached for the doorknob, Bannister grabbed his arm.

"That's my wife and kid you've been tailing, slime bucket."

Terror bulged in his eyes. "I didn't know. I swear I didn't know."

"If Sima finds out you spilled his name, you're

as good as dead. So if you want me to keep this our little secret, you're going to do exactly as I say."

Minelli felt his knees knocking together. How the hell did he get himself into this? "Hey, man, you said I could go."

"So go. But you won't last longer than spit on a griddle if you don't cut a deal. What I'm offering is the best you'll get, Minelli. Better than you deserve. You keep me informed of what Sima has up his sleeve and no one will know that you squealed."

"But what if he finds out I'm your snitch?" Minelli whined, scratching nervously at his armpits.

"Then I guess you're dead. But if you don't cooperate with me, asshole, I'll tip Sima off myself and you'll be dead even sooner."

Minelli fought for breath. He felt like he was going to throw up. "Whatever you say," he mumbled, knowing his balls were in a wringer. His voice dropped even lower. "Can I go now?"

The moment he slunk out the door, Mike turned to Vergada.

"Put a tail on him."

Half an hour later, Mike scanned his computer printout. Sure enough, Sima's name was on it. The bastard had served all of five years and been sprung less than two weeks ago.

Before he could put in a call to Sima's probation officer to find out everything he could about the past five years of Sima's time inside the joint,

Clancy slammed down the phone at her desk and hurried toward him, dodging past the day's collection of drunks, punks, and hookers being processed through the crowded station house.

"The lab traced the explosives used on the Empire State Building. Get this, Mike. It looks like there could be an international connection to the bombing. The plastics are the same type used in the TWA blast three years ago."

"The one traced to Jorge Méndez?"

"You got it."

Méndez. The international terrorist linked to much of the large-scale destruction perpetrated over the last decade. Mike's stomach clenched the way it did when he sensed a case was about to break wide open.

Méndez exported his plastic explosives on a scale that some nations exported wheat. He'd been eluding authorities for nine years, slipping between Middle Eastern and South American capitals with the ease of a chameleon.

But once the three goons who'd died in the explosion were ID'd, maybe there would be a way to trace the connection all the way back to the top banana.

Mike was already out of his seat and shrugging into his jacket. "When's the FBI briefing?"

Clancy checked her watch. "Twenty minutes. Dooley's meeting us there."

Mike's thoughts raced ahead as Clancy slid into the driver's seat of their unmarked Chevy and slammed the door. Three stiffs, Méndez, the Director. The question was, how were they linked? And was there time to connect the dots before the next bomb went off?

"You're awfully quiet, Bannister." Clancy swerved around a garbage truck. "Are we still on for dinner tonight?"

"What?" It took a minute for her words to sink in. "Uh, dinner . . . to tell you the truth, I forgot. I promised Lori I'd come and have dinner with her."

He saw her knuckles blanch against the steering wheel and braced himself for what was coming next.

"And with Jordan?"

"Matter of fact, yes," Mike said, trying to keep his voice casual. He stared straight ahead at traffic, feeling like a miserable low-down heel. He had to level with Clancy. No matter how things turned out with Jordan, it wasn't fair to string Clancy along when he felt the way he did.

"I'm not sure this is the time to tell you this," he began, but Clancy interrupted him, braking so sharply at the stoplight that they both pitched forward against their seatbelts.

"Just spit it out, Bannister." Her tone was as businesslike as the police badge inside her breast pocket.

Mike exhaled. "Jordan and I are working toward patching things up. I'm not sure if we will or where it's all headed. . . ."

"Did you sleep with her?"

He adjusted the air conditioner vent, blasting

himself to cool the sweat that suddenly drenched him. "Does it matter?"

"To me it does." She threw him a quick, hard glance before racing through the intersection. "I don't know what you want from me, Bannister. Is it my blessing? I'm supposed to be happy that you want to dump me and go back to your ex-wife? I'm supposed to be happy that you want our relationship to go back to being strictly professional and pretend the last few months never happened?"

"Hey, Clance, you've got every right to let me have it. Don't hold back," Mike said gently, studying the tiny gold beads glinting at her earlobes. "I know I've been a jerk."

"A prize jerk," she snapped, and then drew in her breath. "No, dammit. You're not. Maybe that's what I'm so mad about," she muttered as the wooden arm swung upward and she accelerated into the parking garage. "You're the most decent guy I've ever met — you were honest with me all along." The car slid into a spot, and she switched off the ignition, turning to face him. She took off her sunglasses, and he could see the disappointment in her eyes. And the glitter of tears. But she kept her chin up.

"I can't say I didn't see it coming." Clancy sighed. "I saw how you and Jordan looked at each other the other night at your apartment."

Mike frowned, his shoulders hunching. "Jordan and I are complicated."

"But you love her, right? You never stopped?"

He met her gaze with eyes as clear and steady as a mountain lake.

"Never."

Clancy's feeble smile trembled. "Then, partner, what can I say? For whatever it's worth, I give you my blessing."

"It's worth a lot, Clance. A whole lot."

It was after two in the morning when Mike read the prison warden's report. He'd asked the warden to fax him a list of all Sima's cellmates over the years, people Mike might want to talk to, who might have heard Sima mouthing off about how he planned to retaliate against the cop who'd put him away.

Now he squinted at the fax in front of him and gave a low whistle as he circled the name of Sima's most recent cellmate.

Antonio Santomauro. Why was that name familiar? He quickly scanned the fax to see what had landed Santomauro in the joint.

It hit him like the blast from a Roman candle. Santomauro was doing life for his part in the TWA bombing masterminded by Méndez. He'd smuggled the plastic explosives into the country and hired the thugs who'd set them in place.

The man was a bomber.

Was it sheer coincidence? Or could there be some connection between the Empire State Building blast and Sima's old cellmate? And with Sima just released from prison, could he be dabbling in a new line, courtesy of his cellmate?

He wouldn't be the first prison inmate to learn a new trade in the joint, pick up some useful new connections that opened up a brand-new world of crime.

This could be pay dirt, Mike thought, pushing back his chair and pacing around his apartment, automatically skirting the pile of laundry on the living room floor and the bike in the hallway.

Now there were two questions pounding through his brain. Was Sima connected to the bombing? And what the hell did he want with Jordan?

34

As if this day isn't zooey enough, Jordan thought as she took her seat at the massive oval table in the conference room, *by the time I get home this afternoon, Mrs. Chalmers and Lori will be home with the guinea pig and I'll have a new four-legged family member to clean up after.*

She took a sip from her water glass as the pageant officials and sponsors filed into the room. With the pageant only four days away, the contestants were already in Atlantic City, participating in prepageant competitions and rehearsals under heavy security and media attention. And so far none of the movers and shakers in this room had had a stroke or a nervous breakdown.

From across the room Sheila Tomkins gave Jordan a wan smile, while Hy Berinhard pretended she didn't exist as he sauntered toward a seat near the head of the table. *Fine,* Jordan thought, slipping her stockinged feet free of her pumps. *Be that way.*

The meeting came to order with silence, forced optimism, and decorum. It ended an hour later amid raucous discord, dire predictions, and grim bravado. The pageant was going ahead as planned, and nobody knew what on earth might happen.

Jordan wandered back to her own office in a dazed panic, her ivory suit feeling as tight as a straitjacket. She had orders to leave for New Jersey tonight right after work. There would barely be time to kiss Lori or the guinea pig before she'd have to dash to catch her commuter flight.

The phone rang before Jordan could even lean back in her chair.

"Mike on line one," Alana announced.

Two weeks ago, Jordan knew, her heart wouldn't have lifted the way it did right now. Just hearing his name made the world seem a little more sane again.

"Jordan, I've got some leads on the guy who's been tailing you. Now listen to me because I don't have much time to talk. I want you and Lori to get on a plane tonight and fly somewhere, anywhere. Just get out of town until I can put this guy out of commission."

Terror surged through her. "Mike, is it someone who's after you? Who is it?"

"Angel, there's no time for details right now. You have to trust me. Get yourselves on a plane. . . ."

"Mike, I am going on a plane — I leave tonight for Atlantic City. But I can't take Lori with me. . . ."

She heard his sharp intake of breath. "Then I'll

come by tonight and drive her up to your folks. Tell Mrs. Chalmers to have her packed and ready at seven o'clock."

"Mike, you're really scaring me. You're in danger, too, aren't you?"

"Don't worry about me, Jordan. Just leave your itinerary with Mrs. Chalmers, and I'll pick it up when I get Lori. You alert your folks, and I'll call you tonight at your hotel after I've got Lori settled. Gotta go."

"Mike." Jordan's voice broke. How many times had she spoken these words to him over the years? How many times had her heart been filled with such pain and apprehension that she could scarcely breathe? "Mike, darling," she whispered, "be careful."

"That's my middle name."

The rest of the day flew by in a fog. Jordan's stomach hurt as she went from meeting to meeting, made phone calls, gathered reports and media kits, and snapped them into her attaché. When she called Mrs. Chalmers and told her to get Lori packed, the baby-sitter told her that Mike had already given her the details.

"Should we forget about getting the guinea pig?"

"No, go ahead. Lori can take it with her. Promise me you'll be careful."

Jordan didn't even remember driving home. Even the blare of horns and traffic couldn't penetrate the dark anxiety that devoured her.

She kept glancing over her shoulder as she parked the car and made her way toward the door, but there was no sign of the green Escort anywhere on the street. Jordan's chest was tight with fear and with the pressure to remember all of the dozen things she still had left to do.

She had only thirty minutes to pack, say good-bye to Lori, and explain to her that Daddy was taking her on a surprise sleepover at her grandparents' house. *Please, please, let Lori and Mrs. Chalmers be back from the pet store,* she prayed. Otherwise she'd have to say her good-byes in a note and leave her instructions taped to the mirror in the front hall before jumping into the cab for the airport.

Her pumps clattered down the stone steps as she went through her keys, isolating the one that fit the dead bolt.

She turned the tumbler and rushed inside, kicking the door closed behind her even as she realized Lori and Mrs. Chalmers weren't back yet. She tossed her attaché onto the foyer table and rushed toward her bedroom, mentally ticking off which suits and blouses to pack — and then she heard it. A creak.

What was that? Jordan froze, her heart leaping into her throat.

A slender, mustachioed man strolled out of her bedroom. The gun he held casually in his left hand was pointed straight at her. Behind him came two others, goons built like twin Hercules. They started toward her, coming fast, as Jordan screamed and tried to run.

The goon with a crew cut knocked her to the floor with the butt of his gun, sending an explosion of flashing red pain through her skull. Dizzy, on her knees, she tried to focus through pain-bleared eyes. She braced herself for the next blow, her scream turning to small, choking sobs.

"Welcome home, Jordan. I hope you don't mind that we let ourselves in. It's better not to disturb the neighbors while we wait, don't you agree?"

Wait? Waves of cold terror washed over her.

"You know who we're waiting for, don't you, Jordan? She's a lovely child. I carry her picture close to my heart."

"No," Jordan gasped, trying to stagger to her feet. "Lori's gone. . . . She's visiting relatives. . . ."

"Liar." The mustachioed man made a *tsk* sound with his tongue. Too late, from the corner of her eye, Jordan saw the second goon closing in.

A huge fist slammed into her jaw and she knew nothing more.

Mike grimaced as bitter grounds slid down his throat with the last mouthful of reheated coffee. He tossed out the Styrofoam cup that had been perched on his desk at the station house for the past two hours, and with it, the untouched salami sandwich, the meat curling at the edges. Angry, he glowered at the phone. *Ring, dammit.*

Why hadn't forensics called back yet with positive IDs on those three stiffs involved in the bombing?

A cool, light clamminess clung to his skin. Tension throbbed through his shoulder blades. Every muscle in his body cried out for action.

This was how he'd felt so many nights on vice, in the moment right before a crackhouse raid. It was always the waiting that had gotten to him. Zeroing in on a target, the pursuit, the chase, the outwitting — those were all the things that made his blood race with a controlled exhiliration, that got him higher than any booze.

But the waiting was torture. It was like the ascent of the roller coaster and that split second of hanging in space that seemed to stretch for an eternity before the plunge.

He desperately wanted a drink.

Hell, what did he expect? That was par for the course. To one extent or another, that urge would always be there. He'd just have to live with it.

Ignoring the tumult of ringing phones and barking voices around him, the parade of hand-cuffed thugs, thieves, and pimps, the gaudily made-up hookers who clacked by wearing little more than their Day-Glo platform shoes and drugstore perfume, Mike yanked open his desk drawer and pulled out the framed photo of Jordan and Lori. He swung open the brace on the back of the frame and set the photo squarely on the desk.

And jumped when the phone rang.

"Bannister." Hairs prickled on the back of his

neck as he scribbled. "Got it." He slammed down the phone and stared at the names. He recognized them — Sima's goons, all three of them.

Sima's in this bombing up to his fucking eyebrows.

Strapping on his shoulder holster with quick, sure movements, Mike knew this would be an all-nighter. He'd get Lori safely to Jordan's parents and then call for backup to meet him at the warehouse district, where they'd ask some questions. But before he'd gotten halfway to the station house door, his phone rang again. A cold premonition had him sprinting back.

"Bannister."

The voice on the other end was a terrified whisper. "It's going down right now, man."

"Who is this?"

"Who the fuck do you think it is?" The voice cracked. "It's your goddamned snitch. I ain't got much time, man. It's going down right now. Your old lady and the kid. *Right now.*"

The line went dead in Mike's ear.

35

The phone kept ringing. No one made a move to answer it.

For the third time in fifteen minutes, the answering machine whirred in response and for the third time, the caller hung up.

Jordan stared at the mustachioed man sitting less than a foot away from her on the sofa. He was calmly sipping her good Scotch while his two goons crumpled newspapers and scattered them across the carpet and along the hallway into the bedrooms.

The one with the crew cut unscrewed a five-gallon can of gasoline. The fumes filled her nostrils, intensifying the terror bursting in her chest.

"Idiot, not yet. Screw that lid back on and wait until all our little chickens are in the coop and ready for the barbeque."

Frantically Jordan flexed her hands, testing the coarse rope that bound her wrists and ankles. Pain seared up her arms with each movement. Her tongue pushed futilely against the silk scarf they'd used to gag her, flailing against the sour taste of her own blood. But Jordan ignored her discomfort as she strained to hear sounds of Mrs. Chalmers and Lori returning with the guinea pig.

How could she warn them? There had to be a way.

But there was no way.

The mustachioed man saluted her with his drink. "Here's to revenge, Jordan. I never believed the old saying that it was a dish best served cold. Now I'll find out. I've waited more than five years for this day."

Bastard, she thought. *I'd tear your eyes out if only my hands were free.* She wondered what time it was. Mike wouldn't be here until seven to get Lori. By then it would be too late. She fought against the tears that burned her eyelids. She wouldn't cry, not in front of these lowlifes.

She heard Mrs. Patel calling her cat for dinner, and from the street came the familiar screech of tires and blare of horns. All the normal sounds of dinnertime in the city. But none of this was normal. It was insane. Her heart beat so hard she felt light-headed as she wrestled with the knowledge that she was helpless.

"The woman and the kid. They're coming up the street," the goon with the crew-cut announced from the window, then ducked back behind the door.

No, God. Not Lori. Please help me find a way.

The mustachioed man smiled as he drained the last of his Scotch and picked up the gun beside him.

"Ah, *bella vita*. Life is good."

Mike swerved his unmarked car against the curb, hitting the brakes so hard the visors shook. He intercepted Mrs. Chalmers and Lori ten yards from the building.

"Daddy!"

"Hi, baby." Mike scooped Lori up and sprinted back up the street with her. "Mrs. Chalmers, follow me," he ordered over his shoulder. As the older woman caught up with them, fighting to catch her breath, Mike set Lori down on the pavement. "We've got a police emergency down the block," he told the wide-eyed woman. "Take Lori across the street to Kevin's and wait there until you hear directly from me. Officer Douglass will accompany you."

As he spoke, he motioned over a middle-aged plainclothes officer who'd just slid his paunchy frame out of a second unmarked car.

"Understand? *Wait there.*"

Mrs. Chalmers sucked in a breath. Her eyes locked with his, the pupils narrowing. "I understand," she said tersely, and grabbed Lori's hand.

Mike was already wheeling toward the SWAT team piling from half a dozen cars along the street. "Sánchez, you and Callahan see if you can access the back through any of the neighboring buildings. Keller and I'll take the front."

"Hold on, Bannister." Lieutenant Pachla grabbed his arm. "This isn't your operation. I'll decide what positions we'll take. And I want you covering that front door from the roof across the street. Got it?"

"Like hell." Mike shook free of Pachla's grasp and went eyeball to eyeball with him. "That's my wife's car over there — she's in that apartment and she's not answering the goddamn phone. I'm going in and I'll wipe the sidewalk with anyone who tries to stop me."

Pachla's hound-dog face betrayed no emotion, but he jerked his head toward the apartment. "Then get the hell moving, Bannister. What're you waiting for?"

"Your ordeal is almost over now, Jordan." The mustachioed man flicked imaginary dust from the cuff of his Italian-tailored trousers. "But your husband's has only just begun. A pity that a child must die, but that will be on Mike Bannister's conscience for the rest of his life, not mine." He rose and leveled his gun toward the entryway while his henchmen took up positions on either side of the door.

Jordan flailed frantically at her bonds, her cries muffled by the gag. Her heart nearly exploded as she waited wild-eyed for the rasp of the key in the lock.

What happened next was a fiery blur. The door crashed inward in a shower of splintered wood, and then Mike was there, crouched and firing. The first two shots hit the mustachioed man in the chest, spraying blood and human flesh across the coffee table.

381

Jordan rolled to the floor as the room resounded with men running, shouting, shooting. A huge weight fell on her, pinning her against the base of the sofa.

"Stay down, angel." Mike's fingers pried the gag from her lips. "I've got you."

She had no idea how much time passed before deathly silence replaced the gunshots. Mike sliced the ropes from her wrists and ankles and eased her to her feet.

Jordan's stomach heaved, and she swayed sideways as she glimpsed the carnage in her home. The stench of gunpowder and death ripped through her lungs.

"Easy, Jordan," Mike soothed, his voice calm as he swept her up and carried her toward the door. "Close your eyes and keep them that way. We're almost out."

In the street, she drew deep breaths and clung to him, her knees shaking.

"Lori . . ." she whispered through parched, bruised lips, and Mike's arms tightened around her.

"Lori's fine. She and Mrs. Chalmers are at Kevin's under police guard. I headed them off just in time."

Relief coursed through every pore until she was dizzy and light-headed. *Lori's fine. Lori's fine.*

"Mike," she managed, throwing trembling arms around his neck, drawing solace from the heat and strength of him. "He wanted revenge against you. . . . They were going to kill Lori and me to punish you. . . ."

"I know, angel. Sima. He's dead now. He can't hurt us anymore."

36

Meg struck out with the gun, swinging straight at Jake's head as he flipped her over, but he wrenched the weapon away from her.

"You bastard!" she screamed, bucking against his bulk. "Let me up. I hate you!"

His hand clamped across her mouth. "Be quiet — we have no idea who's out there."

She fought frantically, arms and knees thrashing, and when he took his hand from her mouth to bracelet her wrists, she spat at him.

"I know who's out there," she cried. "Your buddies. Your low-down, murdering, slimeball buddies. Are you going to kill me now, or wait until J.D. gets here? He's the boss, isn't he?"

"You've got it all backwards, baby doll." He wiped the spittle from his cheek with his shoulder. "Keep your voice down — and just maybe the two of us will live long enough for me to explain."

"There's nothing to explain!" Meg shrieked.

Jake cursed and tore off the night goggles. For an instant she quailed beneath the ferocious glitter of his eyes before he grabbed her, smothering her mouth with his.

She struggled helplessly, wildly. Tears squeezed from her eyes even as her body responded with a heat she didn't want to feel.

"I hate you," she sobbed, as he lifted his head.

"I love you." Jake was breathing hard, sweat filming his face. "Maybe I shouldn't have done that, but I'm so damned glad I found you before they did." Jake smoothed the tears from her cheek with his thumb, his touch unbearably gentle; still, he didn't let her up. "Meg, I didn't betray you. No matter how it looks. I used to work with J.D. A long time ago. It's a sad, rotten story and I'll tell it to you some other time, but right now all that's important is that you understand what happened.

"J.D. got in touch with me several months ago. He paid me to hire and outfit a yacht — to grease some palms at Customs on several of the islands and buy some supplies, no questions asked. When I found you the other night, I put together pretty quickly just what yacht you'd been held on. Before that, I had no idea what they were up to. But from the moment I looked into your eyes, baby doll, I've been on your side."

Confusion and hope swirled through her. She was ashamed of how much she wanted to believe him.

"How can I know you're telling the truth?"

"I'm hoping there's a spark of salvation left

inside me. Maybe you can see it. You may even have ignited it."

He eased off her. As Meg struggled to sit up, he watched her through bleak eyes.

"I'd never hurt you, Meg. If I'd wanted to kill you, you'd be dead by now." Suddenly he fished in the brush beside him and produced the Magnum. "Here." He pressed it into her hand. "If it makes you feel better, use it, but I think you'd be better off letting me help you get out of this jungle alive."

Meg stared from Jake to the gun, then set it down next to her knee. Behind her eyes, hope flickered. "But you went to see them," she croaked in a voice that was totally unlike her own.

"We'd set up this rendezvous weeks ago. J.D. owed me money. If I hadn't shown up, he'd have thought it strange, started wondering, and the next thing you know, he and the others would have been pounding on my door." Jake plucked a leaf from her hair. "They showed me your picture. Asked me to keep my eyes open. I made it clear I'd have known about any strangers turning up on this island, and suggested they try Tescole. Speaking of Tescole, you'll be happy to know you put Ty in the burn unit of their local hospital."

"Too bad I didn't put him in the morgue."

Jake laughed. "A woman after my own heart."

Meg's heart was hammering as she considered all he was telling her. Jake wasn't one of them. He hadn't betrayed her. Last night hadn't been a cruel deception. She crawled into his lap without even thinking and laid her head against his chest.

"I shouldn't have doubted you. I should have known you're not like them."

"I'm not exactly Sir Galahad, either, pure of heart and noble of deed. Up until a few years ago there's not much I wouldn't have done if the price was right."

"I don't want to hear about it."

"You have to hear about it." He turned her toward him, cupping her chin so she was forced to face him, knowing that before whatever was happening between them went any further, he owed her the truth.

Meg's hands gripped his shoulders. She searched his eyes, looking for a goodness Jake prayed was there. He said it quickly, the words burning to get out.

"I was a mercenary. A paid thug you would say. J.D. and I worked together for a few years after my stint in Special Forces. Frank, too. El Salvador. Colombia. Morocco. Kenya. You name it. We raised some bloody hell, did plenty I'm not proud of." He sighed. "I had a chip on my shoulder as big as a tank."

"Why, Jake?"

"I guess it all started when my older brother, Chris, ducked off to Canada during 'Nam. I grew up fighting every kid who called the Seldens yellow-bellied cowards. Always felt I had to prove them wrong. Over and over again. Making Special Forces did it for a while, but before long I had to prove myself again. So I hooked up with an even tougher crowd. And then . . ."

"What happened?"

He looked away from her, a muscle jumping in his jaw. Fingers as delicate as orchid blossoms drew him back.

"You can tell me, Jake. I won't turn away from you."

"We were working with a guerrilla group in a part of the world where hundreds are even now being massacred on a regular basis. The leader of the group ordered my team to take out the leader of a warring faction. We knew which village he'd taken refuge in. It should have been your standard search-and-destroy mission. In and out."

The ragged breath shook through his chest like the rattle of dried gourds. Jake closed his eyes against the images that had tortured him with nightmares for years. Flames shooting like fireballs into the midnight sky. The screams of the women — and the children. The stench of burning flesh.

"Some of the team got carried away. Your pal Frank was one of them. They set fire to a hut to try to scare a family into revealing where our target was hiding. Next thing I knew the whole village was burning, people screaming and running through the darkness like human torches. Mothers, children, toothless old men, scattering like blind mice . . ." His voice broke, his eyes glazed over as he saw and heard again the terror of that night. "I carried children to the riverbank until my legs gave out. I've never seen such a sight, and pray to God I never do again."

Jake's shoulders began to tremble, his face contorted with memories. He felt himself sinking. Sinking again into that black quagmire, swamped with shame, despair, and helpless rage.

Then he felt her arms slide around his neck, pulling him to her, enveloping him in a cleansing white mist of trust and love. The blackness receded, the flames died, the screams faded.

Meg's voice was like an angel's caress in the night. "You've tortured yourself enough, Jake. It wasn't your fault. Let it go. You have to let it go."

Maybe he could. Maybe someday. Maybe with her there was hope.

For a long time, it was as if they were the only two people in the world, lost under the rich jungle canopy, sheltered by a fragrant mossy darkness that enfolded them within a fragile bower of peace.

Morning filtered through the leaves in glints of shining topaz. Meg awoke in Jake's arms, cramped but content.

"Did you stay awake all night?" she asked.

"I've had a lot of practice sleeping with my eyes open. Hungry?"

"You angel! You brought food?"

"No one's ever accused me of being an angel before," he said, opening his knapsack as a monkey chittered across the treetops overhead.

"You've been my guardian angel from the moment I first saw you." Meg began peeling the banana he handed her, her stomach grumbling as she watched him pull out granola bars and a wedge of cheese. "Heaven only knows why you wanted to rescue a drowned rat. But I'm sure glad you did."

"I couldn't help myself. You were the most beautiful drowned rat I'd ever seen."

A twig snapped sharply in the brush to their left and Meg froze. Jake was on his feet in an instant, the Magnum drawn. Meg could hear the blood pounding in her ears as Jake edged toward the sound.

Seconds crawled by like a parade of ants along a mangrove, but all she heard was the cacophony of insects and the twitter of the birds. Finally Jake turned back and gave a curt nod.

"A lizard. Relax. There's no reason to think they're on our trail. But I still think this is one instance when it's good form to eat and run."

"Run where? Back to your place?"

"We're closer to the boatyard. I know a back trail that will take us there. If luck is with us, the puddle jumper will make it in today. And on the outside chance the power's back on, we can use old Clem Hawkins's phone."

They gobbled down the fruit, granola bars and cheese, then took turns guzzling from Meg's thermos, saving Jake's as a reserve. While Jake was packing away the night goggles, Meg glimpsed the red manuscript folder stuffed inside his knapsack. He zipped up the bag and checked the ammunition stored in the outer pouch. Watching his quick, practiced movements, she noted with a twinge faded burn scars lining Jake's forearms.

"After that night . . . that terrible night . . ." She swallowed. "Is that when you moved to Montigne?"

"The very next week. I packed in my soldiering days for the life of a hermit."

"And a writer."

He whipped his head toward her. Surprise deepened the furrow in his brow. "Don't I have any secrets from you?"

"None at all." She smiled, thoroughly pleased with herself. "I found the manuscript. I read it — I hope you don't mind. Jake, it's wonderful. You're very talented."

Jake hefted the knapsack over his shoulder. "You're a little bit prejudiced, baby doll. All I did was spin myself a good long yarn to pass the time. Mostly on nights when I woke up in a cold sweat and couldn't go back to sleep."

"Well, I think you ought to try to get it published."

"And I think we ought to get our asses in gear and get the hell out of here."

Jake led the way, inches ahead of her, trampling down tall grasses and using a machete to cut a passage through curtains of vines. It was cool in the heart of the jungle, easy to feel sheltered beneath the interlocking web of trees towering overhead. But despite Jake's assurances, Meg was afraid that J.D. and company might still be on her trail.

She was a marked woman. She knew the Director's name.

They'd been walking for nearly an hour when they heard the thunderous roar of helicopter blades tearing up the air.

"Hit the ground!" Jake yelled, and hauled her down alongside him. "Don't move."

Wind currents churned the hot, humid air into a minicyclone, furiously swirling the leaves and treetops around them.

"Goddammit, they've got my chopper. I know that purr. Those bastards. Picnic's over, baby doll. They're on to us."

Fear sliced through her as sharp and metallic as the helicopter blades carving the air above. The huge machine seemed to circle endlessly, alternately thrashing at the jungle and retreating, the drone ebbing and flowing as it searched. Meg clung to Jake's hand, her sweaty face pressed into the earth. She felt the brush of insect legs crawling across her lips but didn't dare risk the movement of flicking the creature off.

Then the chopper was gone, the drone dying into the distance. Jake closed his eyes in concentration. "Sounds like they're headed toward the boatyard. With any luck, we can take the chopper right out from under their noses."

"Maybe we should just head back to your place and try the phone."

"That chopper's our ticket out of here."

"But Jake, there are three of them."

"I've had worse odds. Don't worry, Meg." He hugged her quickly as he saw the fear pulsing at her throat. She clung to him, and his gut clenched. "Nothing's going to happen to you," he muttered under his breath. "Trust me."

"I do trust you. It's them I don't trust."

Grinning, Jake tipped her head back and kissed her. Her ardent response nearly knocked the wind out of him, and he drew her closer, his arms tightening protectively.

"When this wild vacation of yours is all over, the two of us are going out on the town. Any town you say. We'll put on our fancy duds and party until we can't party anymore."

The light laugh that broke from her smoothed the worry from her face. "I know just the party we can go to. My Gram's seventy-fifth birthday."

"Count on it. But are you sure the folks back home can handle this particular souvenir?"

"You're no souvenir." Meg's fingertip rubbed the smudge of dirt from his chin. "You're a keeper. My keeper."

"I'll remind you of that when we get back to civilization. Right now we'd better hightail it to that boatyard and steal back my chopper." He slung his knapsack back over his shoulder, grabbed her hand, and set off into the jungle.

"Nothing in the shed but a couple of busted kayaks and some fishing rods. They haven't been here — at least not yet." J.D.'s voice carried easily across the boatyard to Meg's hiding place, where she crouched, motionless, beneath an overhang of rock and vine.

"I say we split up." Frank chucked his cigarette into a wheelbarrow and straightened up from beside the chopper.

As J.D. took one last slow glance around the dilapidated boatyard, his eyes skimmed right across the overhang that concealed Meg. Her limbs trembled as she tried to remain perfectly still.

"Makes sense. Frank, you stay put here in case they make a run for the puddle jumper. Bramson, you take me back for the Jeep and then circle this fucking island one more time. Maybe you'll get a bead on them."

From her hiding place, Meg watched as J.D. pitched a stone into the water lapping at the lip of the pier.

"Sounds like a plan, boys," Bramson replied. "They've got to surface sometime."

"Yeah, well, I want to be the one to get my hands on the Roadrunner." The edge in Frank's voice left no doubt as to what he would do. Meg's throat was dry as she clutched Jake's gun. Her calf muscles screamed from crouching in the same position for so long.

"I thought you were more interested in the girl," Bramson taunted. His words were like fists punching into her gut.

She took a deep breath as J.D. cut them off with a furious slice of his hand. "Enough. The

Director has meat hooks with all our names on them, and you're quibbling about who gets to kill who." Fury whipped through his voice as he turned toward the red-haired man.

"Frank — go find yourself some cover on the other side of the house. We'll pick you up at twenty-two hundred hours. Bramson, let's get the hell out of here."

Suddenly a faint crashing noise echoed from the woods that trailed along the beach. All three men spun toward the sound. Meg saw the glint of three guns.

When J.D. spoke again, his voice was so low Meg could no longer discern the words. She saw Bramson take up a position beside the chopper while J.D. and Frank slipped separately into the woods along the beach.

Meg's heart lurched as she wondered how Jake would manage to elude both of them. Unconsciously her fingers sought the comfort of the dreamcatcher necklace at her throat.

It was gone.

A bolt of panic seared her. *Something terrible is going to happen.*

Where was Jake? Had he already been caught, killed? The tension built to a thundering ache in her chest. Each snap of a twig rang in her ears like the report of a gun. Each sound exploded through her head. The sunlight beat down relentlessly, cooking her to a crisp as she crouched there with the gun, waiting, listening, praying. Just as she was ready to weep from the fear and the heat and the relentless dive-bombing insects, she saw a flash of movement in the brush near the tail of the copter.

Jake inched toward Bramson with quick, silent stealth. Meg would never have believed that such a large man could move with such surprising fluidity, never making a sound as his boots stole across the dirt.

Bramson heard nothing until Jake was on him, and then it was too late. He spun around, a look of bewilderment seemingly frozen for all eternity in his ice-blue eyes as the butt of Jake's rifle slammed against his temple.

He went down with a sharp crack, but even as Meg stumbled from her hiding spot, hell-bent for the copter, gunshots rang out from the woods.

"Hit the ground!" Jake bellowed, throwing himself into the dirt, the knapsack falling beside him. Through the dust, J.D.'s pockmarked face showed itself for a split second, then disappeared again behind a rock. Jake's bullet shattered the rock cover an instant too late, and a string of bullets answered back.

Meg clawed at the earth, inching toward Jake and the helicopter with the determination of a drowning horse fighting toward shore. The shadow of an airborne man darkened the air above her just before his weight slammed the breath from her lungs.

With a grunt, Frank backhanded her, slamming her, cheek first, into the dirt. Red light danced across her eyelids. He wrenched the gun from her and tossed it aside, then sprang to his feet. As he kicked her in the ribs, Meg heard her own agonized moan echo amid the din of renewed gunfire.

37

Battling for air, for life, Meg fought the dizzying pain with a determined frenzy.

As Frank lifted his boot to kick her again, she tensed every muscle, bracing herself for the blow. But instead of pain raining down on her, his blood suddenly spattered onto her face and neck.

Jake. Jake shot him.

In that split instant, she saw Frank grab his left shoulder, then curse and go for his gun. He leveled it toward the helicopter — *toward Jake.*

No! The word screeched through her brain even as she jackknifed sideways toward the gun in the dirt, even as she swung back and fired into Frank's chest, pulling the trigger again and again.

She lay there, stunned, the gun still pointed at where he'd been standing, her arms and hands shaking so badly she couldn't lower them.

Jake yanked her up like a rag doll, but not before she caught a glimpse of Frank sprawled openmouthed in his own blood. She gulped back nausea as Jake dragged her at a dead run toward the chopper.

Then the boatyard, the men, the guns, the blood all blurred together in a surrealistic kaleidoscope. The images were shrinking, growing minute and distant.

I'm losing consciousness. I'm fainting, she thought, and then she realized she was airborne. The chopper swayed high above the boatyard and the pier. The water gleamed like a long silver mirror. Jake was beside her, his hands moving deftly over the controls.

Suddenly a bullet shattered the windshield. Glass glistened on her lap and across Jake's knapsack.

"Get down!" he yelled. He swerved the copter in a dizzying serpentine motion, dodging the bullets Bramson peppered at the huge metal bird.

Meg saw cloudless sky above her, as brilliant as the turquoise on her lost dreamcatcher. Then came Jake's voice, sounding as laid-back as if they were going for a Sunday drive.

"We're out of here, baby doll. Next stop, the American Embassy. Time for Miss America to trade in her battle fatigues for a tiara."

38

Meg's tiara twinkled like a falling star as it sailed through the air. Corey Preston chuckled as Cat instinctively caught it.

"Hang on to that little souvenir, baby. It's all you'll have left of your precious sister."

"Don't be so sure," she flashed back. "You're not as smart as you think."

Preston seized her wrist and twisted it until she winced. "I was smart enough to catch on to you, wasn't I? Smart enough to mastermind an operation that has half the world quaking and the other half searching for me — and for poor little Miss America."

Cat's eyes glistened with pain as his fingers burrowed into her flesh, but she refused to cry out. "You weren't smart enough to keep Daddy from giving the company away, though, were you?" she taunted.

He flinched as if she'd slapped him full across the face. His bronzed skin flushed a dull red. "You're going to pay for that, bitch. Leave my family out of this."

"A little sensitive, are we?"

His grip tightened cruelly. Cat gasped and sank to her knees as Preston leaned over her, grinning. She fought to think clearly through the pain. This bastard knew where Meg was. She had to get him to talk.

As his grip relaxed, she wrenched free, her breath coming in harsh, ragged puffs. "Fine, we don't have to talk about your family. Let's talk about mine. Just tell me if my sister is alive and all right."

"Your sister is where I want her. Swimming with the fishies."

Fish. Ocean. That number I found was *a shore-to-ship number — I'd bet my life it leads to Meg. Maybe Dagger's on her trail right now — but that won't help me.*

"And speaking of swimming," Preston jeered, "it's too bad no one's ever warned you about the dangers of swimming under the influence. You're about to have a nasty accident."

Cat clutched the tiara as she staggered to her feet. "That would be stupid, Preston. It would attract too much attention — unless you *want* the police poking around this place?"

"Let 'em poke. You've just stumbled into the only thing I have to hide, and I guarantee the police will never find this room." A sneer curled his sensuous predator's lips. "Come along, Catriana Hansen; you won't need a bathing suit. One bottle of hundred-proof rum down the gullet and you won't even feel your lungs bursting."

He had the strength of Zeus. Effortlessly he dragged her by the arm through his bedroom and into the hall. Cat fought him every inch of the way. As they passed a bronze planter brimming with flowers, she reeled into it, sending it crashing to the floor.

Preston rounded on her, his face a livid mask. "Bitch!"

In that instant, she flung the tiara at his eyes and thrust her knee straight into his groin with the full force of her rage.

It bought her a precious second of freedom.

As he crumpled into himself with a howl, Cat spun toward the bedroom. She rushed inside, slammed shut the door, and twisted the lock.

"Dolph, get the hell up here!" Preston bellowed from the hall.

Cat's eyes flew around the room. Her heart was racing so fast she could scarcely catch her breath as she darted to the locked gun cabinet and scanned the array of antique weapons inside, her hands splayed across the glass.

The key. The key she'd seen in the top drawer.

"Dolph!"

The drawer crashed to the floor as she yanked it out, spilling pens, coins, maps, and the key onto the carpet.

The sounds of Preston's fists and shoulder pounding on the door shot adrenaline from her brain to her toes. She tried not to listen to the commotion, tried not to think about what they'd do to her if they caught her now.

"Kick it in," she heard Corey command. A huge blow rocked the door in its frame.

It's only a matter of seconds now. Move.

Her hands were shaking so badly she could barely twist the key in the lock. She seized an antique pearl-handled beauty from the shelf and clicked the barrel open. It was loaded.

The door rumbled behind her like the gates of hell. *Exit stage right,* she thought, running for the window. There was a crash, and the door shattered inward just as Cat jumped onto the upper balcony. She raced across the pine planks toward the stairs, which two nights ago had been packed with people laughing, drinking, and dancing. Risking a glance over her shoulder, she saw Preston and a hulking blond monolith charging after her. That moment was all it took to lose her footing. She stumbled and fell the last five steps to the ground.

Pain ricocheted up her ankle, but there was no time to think about it, no time to spare for the blood on her calf. Cat flew toward the driveway. A gunshot screamed out, whizzing past her shoulder.

She dove into the gardens, taking cover behind the rambling bougainvillea hedge flanking the cabana. She raised her weapon.

Preston was coming toward her, alone. He held a .38 snub-nosed pistol in his right hand. *Where the hell is the giant?* she wondered, fighting down panic as she scoured the area in every direction.

"Come out, come out, wherever you are." Preston's taunting singsong chilled her blood. "Where are you, bitch? It's time for your swim."

Cat fired. The report vibrated clear through to her shoulder, sending the bullet high — a good six inches over Preston's thick black curls. Swearing to herself, Cat still had the satisfaction of seeing him hit the ground and scramble sideways toward cover. An instant later, even that satisfaction died as a hail of bullets tore up the flower bed around her.

She aimed again, blinking through the sweat that was pouring into her eyes. *Calm and steady this time, just like at the firing range. This little baby's not so different from your SIG Sauer. You can do it.*

She waited for some telltale movement, for a glimpse of him, the seconds ticking by like the devil's metronome. *Where the hell was he? And what had happened to Dolph?*

Suddenly Preston lunged out of the shrubbery, charging at her in a terrifying zigzag. Her eyes locked on that sinewy figure expertly coming toward her. Concentrating fiercely, she willed her mind and fingers to become one. Through the clamor thrumming in her ears, she squeezed the trigger.

Preston went down like a lead pillar. From behind her she heard a scrambling of feet, and she whipped around, her breath wheezing out in a tight rasp as she saw Dolph bearing down on her like a fullback, his gun at the ready. She took aim and squeezed the trigger again, bracing herself for the reverberations up her arm, for the bloody impact of metal against flesh.

But there was none.

The gun had jammed. Dolph grinned as he slowly lifted his Glock and pointed it at her head. Suddenly she was knocked to the ground, and through the blur of motion around her she saw Dagger firing from a crouched position beside her.

Dolph bellowed as he toppled backward, his head splitting open against the cement planters, his blood pouring like deep wine into the flower bed.

Then Dagger's hands were on her, lifting her, pushing the hair from her eyes. "Cat, are you all right?"

She gaped at him. "Where did you come from? I thought you were in Detroit. . . ."

"That's what I wanted you to think." He pulled her to him, needing to feel the beat of her heart against his. "I've been inside that house for hours, planting cameras in every goddamned inch of it and playing hide-and-seek with Preston while searching the place floor by floor."

Dagger pulled back and scowled into her eyes. "My team caught your act on video. I recommend you don't take it on the road."

Cat's fingers clung to his shoulders. "The boat . . . the shore-to-ship number — I tried to call you, to explain. . . ." Her voice trailed off. She laid her head against his chest while she waited for the shudders to subside.

"It's all right. Stay put, sweet, while I check out Preston."

He kissed her hair and eased away from her, becoming all business as he went to Preston and knelt to check for a pulse. From a distance, Cat heard the wail of sirens, and with the sound all the pumping adrenaline seemed to flow out of her.

Suddenly the grounds were swarming with people. She didn't know if they were FBI, CIA, police. And she didn't care.

She saw Dagger speaking to a man in a black suit, who handed him a cellular phone. She saw Dagger say something into the mouthpiece, listen briefly, and hand the phone back.

Then he returned and helped her to her feet.

"What's going on? Is Preston dead?" she asked. *If he is,* Cat despaired, *we might never find out where Meg is.*

"He's alive, but he's in pretty bad shape. The bullet went through his neck."

"Can he talk? Can we make him tell us where Meg is?"

"No need." Dagger's fingers gently brushed dirt from her cheek. "It seems the Hansen girls are a hard pair to kill. I just got the word — your sister's safe, Cat. She's en route to Miami even as we speak."

Cat closed her eyes. *Meg was safe. Safe.*

Relief and joy surged through her like a geyser of icy golden champagne.

"Want a lift to the airport?"

"Depends." She opened her eyes and smiled at him through the shimmer of happy tears, this man who'd saved her life, who'd risked a bullet for her. "Darling, how fast can you drive?"

39

Lori bounced on the bed, watching the lid of Jordan's carry-on bag flop each time her feet hit the mattress. Mike's air-conditioning was broken and it must have been ninety-five degrees in the little bedroom, but that didn't slow Lori down for an instant.

Jordan blew her bangs out of her eyes and perused the narrow closet where she'd crammed in as many jackets, skirts, and dresses as would fit.

"Take your blue dress, Mommy. I like the blue dress!"

"You have good taste, baby. That's exactly what I planned to wear to the pageant." Jordan smiled as she lifted out the blue silk cocktail dress and a taupe-and-black suit, and clicked them onto the rod in her garment bag. She knelt down on the closet floor and pushed aside Mike's sneakers, hunting through the clutter for her black silk pumps.

"I don't know why you have to go away again, Mommy." Lori stopped jumping and threw her a doleful glance. "You just came back."

"I'll only be gone three more days, pumpkin, and you'll be here having fun with Daddy."

"I get to pick out the new house with him." Lori's eyes sparkled with pride. "My bedroom has to have enough room for Snowball, and his cage, and his food, and his toys," she reminded Jordan for the tenth time.

"We'll make sure we have plenty of room. Room enough for our whole family," Jordan said, and felt a pang of happiness catch in her throat. *We're a family again. Mike, me, and Lori.*

It felt so right, she couldn't believe they'd ever been separated, but some part of her realized that the separation had been necessary. It had been the impetus behind Mike's straightening out his life, the impetus behind all of them discovering how important they all were to each other, how much they belonged together, and how much more they still had to share.

She'd often heard it said that if you survived the bad times you could emerge stronger — that a piece of metal forged in fire could be tempered into something finer, harder, more durable than before. They'd survived the fire, she and Mike, and it had strengthened them. Just the sound of his cheerful whistling down the hall as he tackled the pile of clean laundry waiting to be folded on his sofa was enough to buoy her heart.

She could even deal with the bomb squad. She and Mike would deal with it together, with the pressure, with the uncertainties.

If he can do it, so can I, Jordan reflected as she zipped the garment bag. *One day at a time.*

"Go ahead. Leave us to make all the big decisions." Mike sauntered in with an armful of clean underwear and started shoving it in various drawers. "But don't be surprised when we put a down payment on a tree house in Central Park. I've seen one that has this little monkey's name written all over it."

Lori's eyes rounded in delight. "Really, Daddy?"

Mike knelt down and tousled her hair. "No," he whispered and gave her a wink. "But don't tell Mommy I'm just fooling."

"If I had a tree house," Lori told him solemnly, "I'd have everything I want. I'd have my mommy and daddy back together, I'd have Snowball, I'd have my Wedding Barbie, and I'd have a tree house."

"We'll see what we can do." Mike stood up and hoisted the garment bag off the closet door. "What have you got in here? Five tons of shoes?"

"Just the bare necessities, darling." She kissed him sweetly on the lips. "Wait until I pack for our second honeymoon."

"I'll have to hire Schwarzenegger to carry the bags."

Lori skipped around them in a circle. "Can I carry Snowball down the aisle in my basket when I'm the flower girl?"

"No!" Jordan and Mike answered together.

"No fair."

Jordan's eyes closed dreamily as Mike put his arms around her and nibbled on her ear. "Hurry back. I'm already missing you."

With her arms nestled around his neck, she slid her fingers through the dark hair curling above his collar, memorizing the texture of it, the heat of his gaze on her, the contented smile tugging at his lips.

"Ick — mushy stuff," Lori grumbled. "But at least you're not kissing yucky Uncle Alex any more."

"Never again," Jordan vowed, her sparkling gaze locked on Mike's. "That's a promise."

"Mommy?"

"Yes?"

"I just thought of something else I want — besides a tree house."

"What's that, pumpkin?"

"A baby brother or sister."

Mike sucked in his breath. Jordan's smile was melting his kneecaps.

"That," he told his daughter, as his arms tightened around Jordan, "we can definitely arrange."

The scent of roses was everywhere in the hotel suite, a heady perfume mirroring the sweetness of the day.

It was three o'clock in the afternoon, the pageant only hours away, and Meg had called Burnsie in her Atlanta hospital bed, just as she had each day since returning to the States.

"You tell those doctors you have to be in Arizona next month come hell or high water," Meg told Burnsie. "Gram and I aren't accepting any excuses."

On the other end of the line, Alice Burns chuckled. "Do the stores out west keep cookie-dough macadamia nut ice cream in stock? Then you can bet your buns I'll be there."

"I heard her, everyone," Meg yelled across the parlor crowded with flowers, clothing, shoes, and champagne bottles in ice buckets. "You're all my witnesses! Burnsie said she's coming to Gram's party and we're going to hold her to it."

"Give her my love." Gram glanced up with a smile from the hotel ironing board where she was steaming Meg's beaded gown.

"And mine." Seated on the floor in front of the television, Cat was nearly finished polishing her toenails. "Tell her to get her butt in gear because we're going to take her riding into Zane Grey country and show her scenery like she's never seen before."

Meg repeated all the messages and was laughing when she finally set down the phone. "Burnsie swears that after what we've been through, she's prepared to handle anything the Wild West has to offer."

Meg sighed the moment the words were out of her mouth. She'd give a lot right now for Burnsie's confidence. She hoped she had enough energy and composure deep inside to handle the rest of the day.

She found herself pacing restlessly back and

forth across the plush pearl carpet of the Presidential Suite, which Hy Berinhard had insisted on providing for her and her family. There was madness to his methods, however — he'd begun pursuing Meg with sumptuous bouquets and a damned attractive endorsement contract for Hi-Way athletic shoes even before she'd wrapped up her government debriefing.

"Sign it," Jordan had finally advised her. And Gram had agreed. "The shoes are great and so's the money. It's bound to come in handy down the road."

And so she had signed. The first commercial would air tonight during the pageant — it featured Meg in jogging garb dashing along the bank of the Charles River while the Harvard rowing team plowed their oars through the water trying to catch up with her.

"Hi-Ways — they can outrun anyone." Meg had had to speak that line for forty-seven takes.

The commercial ended with a close-up of Meg's running feet, and the voice-over tag line: Catch me if you can.

Right now she wanted to run out of here and as far away as she could. But that wasn't possible. She had an interview in an hour with *Newsweek*; she had to be backstage at the pageant immediately after that. And before she relinquished her tiara, she had to do her walk — that famous final walk down the runway before an audience of more than thirty million people.

"Nerves?" Gram asked quietly, studying her

with the steam iron in hand.

Meg stopped pacing abruptly, realizing she'd been completely lost in thought. It took her a moment to process Gram's question. "A little."

"Is it the pageant?" Cat screwed the cap on the bottle of fuchsia polish and eyed her sister's carefully schooled face. "Or are you worried about Jake?"

"He said he'd be back for tonight, but it looks like he's fallen off the face of the earth."

"He did leave you a note," Cat offered, wiggling her toes.

Meg grimaced. *Some note.* "Got some business to clear up. Be back for P-Day." That was all. He hadn't even kissed her good-bye.

"He'll be here." Cat threw her a reassuring smile. "I saw the way he looked at you when we were in Miami. The man never let you out of his sight."

"Well, he's sure out of my sight now." Meg stomped over to the window, her lemon silk short set clinging to her narrow figure, a figure more slender than ever since her ordeal. She stared out the window, remembering the night of love in Jake's shack, the feel of his arms around her when they'd hidden together in the jungle, the way he'd fought for her and opened up to her, showing her the scars he bore inside and out. It had been real, their love — she'd been convinced of that. But now, not having heard from him for days on end, doubt was creeping in on her.

What was going on in Jake's head? Was this all

414

just a lark to him? Another misadventure? One more mistake he had to run from?

"I tried calling him on Montigne," she said softly, "but the operator said his number's been disconnected. And Ernie hasn't seen him. I don't know what else to do."

"Well, the first thing you'd better do is get ready for that interview or Jordan will have your head." Gram wrapped the cord around the cooling steam iron. "The other thing you need to do is summon up a little faith. If your Jake is half the man you've been telling us he is, then he's a man of his word." Gram draped the off-the-shoulder silver gown over a padded hanger, then went to Meg and gave her shoulders a squeeze. "He'll be back, Meg dear. I'd be willing to bet my kachina doll collection on it. Catriana sized him up, you know, during all those debriefings in Miami, and based on what she's told me, it doesn't sound as if there's a wishy-washy bone in that man's body."

"Cat sized him up?" Meg turned from the window.

"Gram . . ." Cat shot her grandmother a warning look. "Wasn't it you who taught us that loose lips sink ships?"

"I don't believe it!" Meg exclaimed. "You were spying on Jake? Nick Galt must be very pleased you're such a quick study."

Cat grinned, and tapped a finger to her toenails, testing to see if the polish had dried. "If you want to know the truth, Dagger won't give me the satisfaction of admitting that I'm actually pretty good at this undercover stuff. But Gram heard from Jack that Dagger thinks I'm a natural."

She peered up at Meg, her eyes growing serious. "I wasn't *spying* on Jake, honey. Just checking him out. You're the only sister I've got, and with everything you've been through, I wanted to be sure you weren't confusing love with infatuation and throwing yourself away on some cross between Mad Max and Rambo."

"And . . . ?" Meg prodded, her eyes narrowed.

"I like him," Cat said simply. "Dagger does, too. And when Jake gets back here, I'm positive he'll even get the Jeanne Hansen seal of approval."

A sharp knock on the door sent Meg running across the parlor. As Jordan rushed into the suite and the brief hope faded from Meg's eyes, Cat and Gram let out disappointed sighs.

Jordan cast an approving glance at the brilliant flowers crowding the room. "Gorgeous!" she breathed. "This place looks like heaven." She fished a handful of cashews from a bowl on the table. "Thirty minutes till showtime, Meg. John Petoskey is doing the interview — he'll be a piece of cake. What are you wearing?"

"The Mizrahi suit and my best smile."

"Perfect." Jordan smiled at Meg, then turned her dark eyes toward Cat, who was gingerly rising from the floor. Cat wore nothing but a peach teddy and an aster tucked behind her ear, her every movement careful to avoid smudging the fresh polish gleaming on her cushion-separated toes.

"I still can't quite believe it," Jordan murmured slowly, giving her head a tiny shake. "We're all here. Together. In one room and in one piece."

Gram linked her arm through Jordan's. "Your phone calls meant a great deal to me, young lady. I'll never forget what a good friend you've been through all of this."

"I say it's time for a toast," Meg put in. "The four of us haven't had a quiet moment together since the beginning of last year's pageant." She retrieved the bottle of Dom Perignon that Hy Berinhard had sent, lifting it from its ice bucket and turning her attention to the cork.

As they gathered around, she splashed the pale champagne into four tulip-shaped glasses.

"*L'chayim.* After what we've gone through these past few weeks, it seems we should toast life," Jordan proposed, lifting her glass.

"And survival," Cat put in, holding the frothy champagne high.

"And togetherness." Gram raised her glass, then clinked it gently against each of the others. "*À votre santé.*"

"And the future," Jordan added. Their glasses chimed with a satisfying tinkle. Silently, they sipped the bubbly golden liquid.

As the chilled champagne tingled past the lump in Cat's throat, she glanced from Meg to Jordan to Gram and felt an overwhelming happiness.

A few days ago she'd feared she'd never see her

sister alive again. And now here they both were, smelling the roses and toasting the future.

A few weeks ago she'd been stuck in a dead-end relationship with a man she thought she loved. Little had she known what was a heartbeat away with Dagger.

Thinking of Dagger, she realized she'd better hustle back to their suite down the hall and get dressed. They'd planned to have a quiet drink in the cocktail lounge before joining Gram and Jack for dinner.

Jack Galt had flown to Arizona after Meg's escape so that he could escort Gram to the pageant. From what Cat had seen, he appeared to be as much in love with Jeanne Hansen now as he'd been during the war.

And Gram lit up like a firecracker the minute Jack entered a room. It was sweet seeing them together. Almost as sweet as the knowledge that Dagger would be waking up beside her tomorrow morning when the pageant and all the hoopla were over.

"Okay, ladies. Battle stations." Jordan set down her glass with a clank and led Meg toward the huge mirrored dressing area. "Let's get a move on. Time to take the world by storm."

Dagger was not in the suite, but the spicy scent of his cologne lingered. She smiled when she saw the huge bouquet of tiger lilies, and with eager fingers she picked up the note he'd left lying beside it.

Dad and I are doing some catching up —
business and personal. I'll meet you in the
lounge at five. By the way, these overwrought
posies came for you. Is it pistols at dawn, my
love?

Dagger

She knew who'd sent the flowers even before
she'd snatched the folded white card from the
bouquet.

The picture wrapped early. I'm cutting another film in New York all through the fall.
Give me a call as soon as you get home. All
is forgiven.

Vince

For a moment, Cat stared at the back-slanted
scrawl. *To think I wasted even one moment of my
life on this arrogant loser,* she mused in wonder-
ment. *The jerk wouldn't know a good thing if it hit
him in the balls.* She tossed the note in the wastebasket and stuffed the flowers in after it.

Dagger was waiting.

So was the rest of her life.

"He's late," Cat thought, scanning the dimly
lit lounge teeming with the friends and relatives
of pageant hopefuls. The air was electric with the
buzz of excited chatter, the partygoers' mood as
dazzlingly festive as their clothing. From above
the bar, the evening news flickered across a giant

television screen, the sound all but drowned out by the susurration in the lounge.

She was about to slip into a chair with a view of the lobby when she spotted Dagger. He half-rose from his seat as she wove past the congestion of tables to the shadowy corner booth he'd chosen. Her breath caught in her throat. He looked as sleekly leonine as a dark panther. The black tuxedo fit him as if it had been expressly made for the rangy muscularity of his body.

"I see you've replaced that snappy little red number." Dagger's eyes devoured her as they scanned appreciatively up and down the gold lace minidress. "Lovely."

She gave a playful tug on his bow tie. "You don't look too shabby yourself."

As the waiter poured champagne into their glasses, Dagger took her hand. Heat seared up her arm, across her shoulders, and through her breasts.

"I've got a proposition for you."

"I'm all ears."

"No, you're not, my love, or I wouldn't be proposing this."

"Sounds intriguing." Under the table, Cat snaked a leg around his. "Go on."

"I think you're trying to break my concentration."

"Who, me?"

"No, the redhead over there in the silver."

Cat whipped around to look, and the next thing she knew Dagger pulled her against him in the booth, an arm hooked around her waist so tightly she could scarcely breathe. His cologne intoxicated her with the rich subtlety of spice and citrus.

"Don't be so gullible, Catriana." He grinned. "You're the only woman on the planet who could break my concentration. Now, do you want to hear my proposition, or not?"

"Proceed, Mr. Galt."

He released her and Cat eased back in the booth. She reached for her glass and took a sip, surveying him over the tickle of bubbles.

Something flip-flopped in her stomach as he pulled a velvet jewel box from his jacket pocket and snapped open the lid. Nestled against the cinnamon suede interior was a necklace. Not just any necklace but a fabulous creation of stunning teardrop diamonds strung across the suede like a rope of glittering stars.

Cat caught her breath, her gaze sweeping in shock from the diamonds to Dagger's face.

"It's . . . gorgeous."

"Yes, it is." He sounded pleased. "It's also paste."

"Paste? You're giving me a paste necklace?"

"It's not a gift, darling. It's a prop. You see, even though I'm now officially retired from government service, I've agreed to do a small favor next week in London, and I could use a partner. Interested?" Dagger watched the excitement spark in her eyes. "We'd be back in plenty of time for Jeanne's party," he added.

Cat was trying hard not to show how much she loved the idea. She wanted to sound as business-like as he did. "What exactly do you need me to do?" There. She was certain she sounded quite calm, quite professional, and not at all like a child being offered a trip to Disneyland.

"Wear these. Look beautiful. And accompany me to a party for the Duke of Carlsbad."

"Sounds too easy. There must be a catch."

"No catch. You'll simply excuse yourself and go to the powder room at the appointed time. There, Lady Dunmore will admire the necklace and ask to try it on. Of course you'll graciously comply. Then she'll give it back to you and you'll rejoin me in the ballroom."

"That's all?"

"All it takes to transfer a certain microchip."

The sparkle deepened in her eyes.

"Your cover has already been arranged. Simon's done some work for my employers in the past, and he was only too ready to cooperate."

"Simon?" Incredulity made her voice squeak.

Dagger grinned. "He's already booked a shoot for you with Princess Anne, so for all intents and purposes *I'm* accompanying *you* while you're on assignment for *Celebrity*."

"Well, *partner*." Cat lifted the necklace to her throat. "What do you think?"

"I think I like the way that sounds."

Cat's slim eyebrows arched over eyes sparkling like twin peridots. "The way what sounds?"

Dagger traced his finger over the necklace, resting it above the gentle pulse beating at her throat. "The partner part."

"It does have a nice ring to it," Cat mused.

"Speaking of rings . . ." Dagger stopped short as an image on the overhead television caught his eye. Cat followed his gaze and saw Charles Latham speaking before a bouquet of microphones.

"Next thing you know he'll be running for president," Dagger muttered.

Cat set down her champagne glass. "I've heard that ORBA's coffers have swollen like the Potomac," she added. Since being cleared of all involvement in the kidnapping, Latham had become an instant media celebrity, popping up everywhere on the news and talk show circuit — there was even rumor of a book deal in the offing. Once Dagger's colleagues had gained access to the computer in Preston's secret room, the frame-up had unraveled like a skein of moth-eaten yarn, bringing Latham massive sympathy and support from militia groups across the United States.

As for Preston, despite the fact that the bullet Cat had fired had severed his spinal cord and left him a paraplegic, no one but the lunatic fringe had an ounce of sympathy for him. There was enough evidence against Corey Preston to put him away for life on any one of a dozen federal charges.

As the television screen shifted to outside the hospital where Preston lay under federal guard, Cat felt a sense of grim satisfaction. *No matter what the courts decide, I've made him pay the price.*

She turned away from the screen and reached for more champagne. Suddenly her hand froze on the glass and she lifted a questioning gaze to Dagger's face. "I believe you were starting to say something about rings? . . ."

"Was I?"

"You tell me."

His attention was now focused fully on her. Smiling slightly, Dagger reached into his tuxedo pocket and produced another jewel box, this one much smaller, a ring box of blue velvet, which he flipped open adroitly.

The two-carat marquis diamond winked magnificently, even in the candlelight. It was a breathtakingly icy stone, perched royally on a sweeping tier of gold.

"This one isn't paste." There was no teasing in his eyes now, only an intense warmth as he held her gaze. "It's as genuine as my love for you, Cat. And my desire that you be my partner — for life."

For life. Forever. To share that country house with him, that big cedar bed. And a future filled with promise, laughter, and maybe even children someday.

And she knew he meant it. Paul had run out on her, Vince had deserted her at the start of this ordeal, but Dagger had thrown himself before a bullet for her.

Sometimes in life, Cat, you get more than you bargain for. . . .

She held out her left hand, her fingers trembling with excitement. Dagger slipped the ring onto the third finger.

"Is this a yes?" he prodded, his eyes alight.

"Yes, yes, and yes!"

"And London? You're up for a little adventure?"

"Yes."

"Can you say anything but yes?" Dagger laughed, drawing her hand seductively up to his mouth and brushing a tantalizing kiss across her palm.

Wearing a smile more brilliant than the ring flashing on her hand, Cat reached out and pulled him to her. "How does I love you sound? I love you with my whole heart. I'll love you till the day I die. I love you, I love you, I love you."

"Sounds pretty damned perfect to me," Dagger said, and kissed her with the single-minded pleasure of a man who's found a diamond in a world of paste.

40

As Meg scooped her hair into a ponytail high on her head and twisted open the lid of her cold-cream jar, she listened to the rising clamor of voices outside the door of her dressing room. Out there, flashbulbs were popping for the new Miss America. Now the interviews, the spotlight, the endless blur of hotel rooms, plane schedules, and interminable chicken dinners belonged to some-one else.

It was over.

As she tissued the cold cream from her face, she thought back to a year ago, to the first morn-ing of her reign, to that exhilarating predawn photo shoot on the beach when everything was fresh and new, when her hopes for the coming year were as pearly as the morning sky. Before the cloud of ORBA had darkened her horizon, before threats and danger had become as much a part of her daily regimen as her morning swim.

As she tugged on jeans, anklets, and a Harvard T-shirt and slipped into her brand-new pair of Hi-Way running shoes, Meg pondered the irony of having campaigned against the indiscriminate use of guns, of having worked toward responsible gun control, all the while never imagining she would be forced to use a gun herself to save her own life and Jake's. That in order to survive, she would actually set a man on fire or that Cat would paralyze Corey Preston for life.

She and Cat. Guns had touched their lives profoundly since they were children. Guns had robbed them of their parents. And guns had saved their lives.

She dropped the cascade of dangling rhinestone earrings into her silk jewel pouch and drew the satin cords closed, shutting out the glitter. She stared at the slim silver gown she'd worn tonight, running her fingers lightly over the fabric before she slipped it into a garment bag. Too bad life was never quite as clear-cut as the tiny crystal beads winking up at her from her dress.

But for Meg, one thing remained perfectly clear. Honest people must find the courage to stand up to criminals like the ones who'd killed her parents, to vermin as evil as Corey Preston and Frank Aldo and their ilk. As she'd told the *Newsweek* reporter earlier this evening, her determination to become a prosecutor had only been strengthened by the ordeal of the past weeks.

"Harvard, here I come," she muttered, and draped the garment bag over her arm.

She'd thought she'd feel immense relief when her year was finally over and she had her freedom back. Instead, she felt a hollowness that went so deep it was like an endless tunnel burrowing through her soul.

She had her life back, but she didn't have Jake.

He had vanished as surely as her dreamcatcher necklace. How could someone she loved so much, someone who was so much a part of her simply disappear?

After one final sweep of the dressing room, Meg stepped into the corridor. It was deserted now, except for the security guards and stagehands going about their business.

"Are you all set, Miss Hansen? Ms. Davis told your limousine driver to wait right outside this door. Here, let me help you with that bag."

"Thank you." Meg relinquished it to the security guard and looked up and down the hall. "I'm supposed to be meeting Ms. Davis and my family." Surprised that Gram and Cat and the others weren't clustered in the hall, Meg fought the forlorn pang that she was sure was a natural letdown from the excitement of the night. "Do you know if they're waiting outside?"

"Your grandmother asked me to tell you that they'd meet you back at the hotel suite. They went on ahead to order champagne — and a midnight supper, she said. Sounds like the night's just beginning."

"Oh yes, we'll have a wonderful time. We'll probably still be up when the sun makes its appearance." She forced a smile.

It was a familiar gesture. She was used to doing that, curving her lips up so that she appeared carefree and serene, even when inside she was plagued with jet lag, nervousness, and homesickness. How long would it take her to metamorphose back into a real person who could look sad when she was sad, who could scowl, be grumpy, and even cry in public if that's what she felt like doing?

Better keep that stiff upper lip, she warned herself, trudging down the hall with the security guard trailing behind her. *It's going to be a long night. You don't want any of the others feeling as sorry for you as you do for yourself. They're doing this for you — so don't let them down.*

The security guard escorted her out to the long white stretch limo and opened the door. As Meg slid into the backseat, the driver tipped a hand to his cap.

"Good evening," she murmured through the opening in the smoked glass partition.

He grunted something she couldn't make out, which was just as well, since she had no interest in making small talk.

She sank back against the buttery leather seat. She had no interest in the champagne nestled beside her either, and no use for the stereo or the telephone. She laid her head back, letting the cool mist of air-conditioning envelop her.

Silence. Privacy.

Thank God for this brief reprieve between the frenzy of the pageant and the tumultuous welcome her family would have in store for her when she reached the suite.

This must be how Cinderella felt after the ball, Meg decided, closing her eyes as the darkened streets slid by the tinted windows. The Lucite partition glided open with a soft hiss.

"We're outta here, baby doll."

Meg's eyes flew open. She shot up in the seat and gaped at the driver. Jumping across to the bank of seats between them, she leaned through the opening and snatched the cap off his head.

"Jake!" she screeched, and he threw her a grin over his shoulder.

"You were expecting maybe Newt Gingrich?"

She scrambled over the backrest and into the front seat, a tangle of arms and legs and Hi-Ways. "Jake!" she screeched again, throwing her arms around him even as he eased the limo to a halt.

"I told you I'd be here." He caught her in his arms as she threw herself against him.

"But you missed the pageant."

"I'll see the video. Come here, former Miss America."

The kiss he gave her was worth the wait. Meg felt as though she would explode with happiness when Jake devoured her mouth and slipped his hand under her T-shirt.

"I've been worried sick about you all week," she gasped, nibbling kisses along his mouth. "Where have you been?"

"On a mission. Deep in the jungle."

Meg pulled back, her heart plummeting. "I thought you gave all that up. . . ."

"This was a special mission. I was the only one

who could carry it out." He reached into his tuxedo jacket pocket and yanked out a paper bag. "Special delivery from the floor of the jungle to Margaret Elizabeth Hansen." He turned the bag upside down and shook the contents out over her palm.

Her dreamcatcher necklace tumbled out — leather, turquoise, and a single white feather.

"Where was it?" Meg clutched the necklace in both hands.

Jake took it from her and, squinting, fastened it around her throat. "Right where I jumped you that night when you tried to run away from me."

"Fool that I was," she murmured, throwing her arms around his neck and offering her lips for another kiss.

"Remember that." Jake's thumb circled her nipple beneath the T-shirt, sending exquisite pleasure rippling low in her pelvis.

As he nuzzled her hair, a solid contentment took hold of Jake. She felt right in his arms. More right than anything had felt to him in quite some time. "It took longer than I thought to find it," he said. "And longer than I thought to clean out my place and throw back one last cold one with Ernie."

"You're moving?"

"That's the game plan. I thought I'd check out married housing at Harvard. Always did have a yen to commune with the spirit of our forefathers."

Married housing at Harvard? Meg's arms tightened around his neck. There was a glint in his eyes that sent her heart soaring. "Go on," she instructed, deliberately keeping her voice as calm as his.

"Thing is, I need a quiet environment, a nice little apartment with a spot for my typewriter — yet close enough to New York so I can meet with my editor when I need to."

"Editor?"

"Didn't I tell you? A funny thing happened on my way back to Montigne. I sat next to a guy who happens to be editor in chief of Red Planet Press, and by the time they served the last round of rum and pretzels, he'd read the first ten chapters of my manuscript. He loved it as much as you did."

"Jake, are you telling me you sold your book?"

"It looks that way. He's talking about a six-book series based on my characters. . . . Whoa, baby doll, hold it, you'll wrinkle the tux."

The kiss she gave him then was from the deepest part of her soul, the part that had been a lonely traveler for so long. It was a lingering kiss, one that tasted of need and longing and hope. One that had been pent up inside her all the time he was gone, all the time she was wondering if she'd see him again.

As her fingers curled through his hair and his mouth answered hers, Meg felt that she was closing a door on one part of her life and opening another.

Suddenly she drew back her head and gave him a long, intent look. "Back up a minute. What's that you said about married housing?"

"Spoken like a true lawyer. You don't miss a thing, do you?"

"Just answer my question."

"Well, I didn't want you to feel bad about giving up your title, so I thought I'd offer you another one. Mrs. Jake Selden. Unless you'd prefer Margaret Elizabeth Hansen Selden, future attorney-at-law."

Jake grabbed her hands in both of his. She saw hope mixed with unwavering love in his eyes.

"Hell, I don't care what name you use," he said quietly, "I just want you to know that the other title was yours for a year, but, Meg, this one would be for life."

For life. Her hands trembled within his. She thought her heart would burst with all she wanted to say.

"A life sentence," she whispered. "With no possibility of parole?"

"None." The light of passing cars flickered across Jake's face, illuminating the intentness of his expression. She saw the naked need in his eyes even as he tried to speak lightly. "Take it or leave it. But I'm telling you, Meg, it's as good a plea bargain as you'll get."

"Jake, if being in love with you is a crime, then I guess I'm guilty as sin." She snuggled closer against him, her eyes shining into his. The kiss they shared was long and devouring. "And if this is the punishment, then lock me up and throw away the key."

Suddenly Meg slid off Jake's lap. "Wait a minute." She snaked halfway through the partition and reemerged from the backseat with the bottle of champagne and two glasses.

"Darling, how are you at popping corks? Suddenly I feel like celebrating."

"Baby doll," he said gently, kissing her as he took the bottle, "I'll pop your cork anytime you want."

The champagne tasted cold and fruity, bubbling over like the happiness Meg felt. Suddenly she remembered Gram and Cat back at the suite waiting for her. "Oh my God, they've probably put out an all-points bulletin for me by now. Jake, do you think you can handle my family tonight?"

"Bring 'em on. The more the merrier. We've got a helluva lot to celebrate." Jake plopped his driver's cap on top of her head. "And when everyone's gone, we'll continue the celebration — one on one. Think you can handle *that*, baby doll?"

"Try me," Meg purred, shooting him a come-hither look.

"Keep looking at me that way and I'll be forced to make a detour." Jake chuckled, corking the champagne.

Meg smiled as she settled back against the seat. What had she been thinking a short time ago — that she felt like Cinderella after the ball? It was past midnight, but her coach was anything but a pumpkin and her prince was right beside her, as real as the dreamcatcher necklace at her throat. She was going to have her happily ever after ending, after all.

She studied Jake as he shifted the car into gear. The contentment on his face filled her with happiness. A simple happiness that flowed through her, more magical than any fairy godmother's spell.

In an instant the limousine shot away, moving effortlessly into the fast flow of traffic. Then it streaked off like a brilliant white comet racing through the starry night.

The employees of G.K. Hall hope you have enjoyed this Large Print book. All our Large Print titles are designed for easy reading, and all our books are made to last. Other G.K. Hall books are available at your library, through selected bookstores, or directly from us.

For information about titles, please call:

(800) 223-2336

To share your comments, please write:

Publisher
G.K. Hall & Co.
P.O. Box 159
Thorndike, ME 04986